MIDDLEM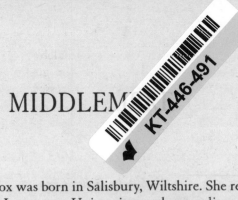

Judith Lennox was born in Salisbury, Wiltshire. She read English at Lancaster University and now lives in Cambridgeshire with her husband and three sons. She is the author of seven highly praised and top-selling novels: *The Secret Years, The Winter House, Some Old Lover's Ghost, Footprints on the Sand, The Shadow Child, The Dark-Eyed Girls* and *Written on Glass*.

JUDITH LENNOX

MIDDLEMERE

PAN BOOKS

First published 2003 by Macmillan

This edition published 2004 by Pan Books
an imprint of Pan Macmillan Ltd
Pan Macmillan, 20 New Wharf Road, London N1 9RR
Basingstoke and Oxford
Associated companies throughout the world
www.panmacmillan.com

ISBN 0 330 48001 4

1 3 5 7 9 8 6 4 2

A CIP catalogue record for this book is available from
the British Library.

Typeset by SetSystems Ltd, Saffron Walden, Essex
Printed and bound in Great Britain by
Mackays of Chatham plc, Chatham, Kent

This book is dedicated to Rosie Garwood,
with love and affection

My thanks to Anna Clements and Simon Tattersall for their invaluable help and advice. Many thanks also to my son, Dominic, for his assistance with the research for *Middlemere*.

PART ONE

The Men in the Forest

November 1942

Chapter One

It was when he took out the gun that she began to feel frightened.

From the moment she had woken that morning, the day had felt wrong. A verse from a song her father sometimes sang ran through her head. *The men in the forest, they once asked of me, How many wild strawberries grow in the salt sea?* Romy had always thought it a silly song. Strawberries did not grow in the sea, did they? Yet the strangeness of today made her think of the upside-down world of the song, where nothing was right, nothing was as it should be. *I answered them back with a tear in my eye, How many ships sail in the forest?* Yes, the day was topsy-turvy. But she hadn't been scared. Hadn't been frightened. Not until her father took out the gun.

The gun was kept in a tall cupboard on the upstairs landing. From her hiding place, Romy watched her father fit the key into the lock and open the door. His strong, callused fingers ran along the shotgun's twin barrels and then paused, as if betraying a momentary uncertainty. Then he cracked open the stock and slid in two cartridges.

Romy was hiding in the green cupboard at the far end of the landing. This cupboard was small and cramped, so she had to kneel, to fold herself up to fit. She could hear the voices calling from the garden, and by peering through the spyhole made by a missing knot of wood, she could see her father. When they couldn't find something, Mum always said: Look in the green cupboard. Things that were old and broken beyond repair found their way into the green cupboard: a single gaiter with all the buttons torn off, a teapot with a cracked spout and missing lid. As she knelt in the darkness, jigsaw pieces pressed into Romy's knees and feathers leaked from an old pillow, settling around her like soft grey snowflakes. Though she was wearing her coat and scarf, she felt cold. When her teeth began to chatter she was afraid that her father might hear. If he knew she was in the house, he would send her away with Mum and Jem. And she needed to stay here with him.

The men in the forest, they once asked of me ... Romy shivered. She had been woken that morning by the sound of her parents shouting. Her father's voice had been angry and defiant; her mother's shrill and tear-stained. Then everyone seemed to have forgotten not only breakfast but also school. There was no porridge, no bread. The stove had gone out. No one had fetched any water. Jem was half-dressed, in vest and shorts, one shoe on and one shoe off. Romy hurried him into his second shoe and tied the laces, then yanked his jersey so hard over his head that he yelled she was pulling his ears off.

The clock on the mantelpiece had told her that it was half-past eight. Past going to school time. Though she tried to feel pleased about the extra minutes at home, she found that she felt worried. Mum and Dad seemed to have forgotten about school. It was almost as though school didn't matter. Romy wondered what could have happened to make school, which Dad always said was the most important thing, not matter.

So she had stood in the kitchen, dressed in her outdoor clothes, her stomach rumbling with hunger, watching her mother cry and listening to her father shout, and then, when no one was looking, she had sneaked upstairs to the green cupboard. She liked the green cupboard. It was where she hid when she was feeling sad, or when she was in trouble and didn't want to be found. She'd hid in the cupboard after she had dunked Annie Paynter in the water trough; it cheered her up now to remember the dirty water streaming from Annie's yellow curls. And she hid in the cupboard when there were jobs to be done – peas to pick or coal to fetch. Mum always found her, though. Jem didn't like the cupboard because it was too small and dark and it made him think of ghosts.

After a while she heard her mother yell, 'Don't think I'm staying here to see you carted off to prison!' And Dad shouted back, 'Take the kids with you then! Can't have kids under my feet when they're trying to take Middlemere away from me!' And then, a few moments later, Mum said, 'Where's that dratted girl?' And Jem answered, 'Romy's gone to school.'

Then the door slammed and it was all nice and quiet for a while. Romy ate the apple she had filched from the basket on the dresser. She would stay in the cupboard all day, she decided. It was better than school anyway, especially on a Friday. The girls had to do needlework on a Friday, which Romy hated. She preferred doing sums to sewing aprons and knitting mittens. There was something clear and sharp and perfect about sums: you got the hang of the rules and then they were right every time. Whereas, no matter how hard she tried, the aprons and mittens seemed always to end up shapeless and tangled.

She was beginning to feel better, to believe that the world had come right again, when the noises started. The sudden battering and hammerings returned her with a jolt to the upside-downness of the early morning. Straining to hear, she made out locks being turned, bolts being shot home. Then there was a different noise, a loud grinding. She realized that her father was dragging the heavy farmhouse furniture across the kitchen floor. Opening the door a crack, she peered outside. She could hear in the distance the rumble of a car, coming down the track that led to Middlemere from the road. Then she heard her father's footsteps running upstairs. She pulled the cupboard door quickly shut.

The car came to a halt outside the house. Fists beat on the front door and voices called out, but Romy's father remained on the landing. Boots crunched on the frosty ground as the visitors walked round to the back of the house. Romy heard men's voices. Angry voices. It was then that her father took the gun out of the cupboard.

Romy didn't often feel frightened. She wasn't afraid of spiders, like Annie Paynter was, and she wasn't afraid of ghosts, like Jem. She hadn't even been afraid when the German plane had emptied its bomb-load over

Inkpen Hill and she had seen the bright gouts of fire along the ridge where Combe Gibbet stood.

She put her eye to the hole in the door. She saw that her father had tucked the gun under his arm and that he was opening the landing window. Bitter, freezing air fell into the house. Romy shivered again. Through the open window she could hear the voices clearly. Muffled by the cold and mist, they drifted up from the garden.

'Come on out, Mr Cole! No more nonsense, now!'

'Listen here, Sam, this won't do you no good, you know.'

'You won't take my house from me!' Her father was leaning out of the window, shouting down to the garden. 'You won't take Middlemere!'

'The committee has the right—'

The gun barrel struck the sill with a clatter of metal on wood. 'It has no right. No right at all! Get off my land, Mark Paynter!'

Mark Paynter was Annie Paynter's dad. He had visited Middlemere after the incident with Annie and the horse trough. Short and plump and full-faced, his pink scalp showing through his brown hair, Mr Paynter had then worn a suit and shiny shoes. Romy remembered how he had slipped and slid in the muddy yard, red-faced and awkward.

He didn't sound awkward now. He sounded bossy, Romy thought, like the big girls at school. As though he was enjoying telling her dad what to do.

Mr Paynter said, 'Don't be a fool, Cole.'

'Get off my land!' Romy's dad shouted.

'It's not your land any more,' said Mr Paynter. 'It

7

belongs to the County War Agricultural Executive Committee, so stop making trouble and do as you're told. You've been given every chance. We won't wait for you no longer.'

'Put that gun away, Sam!' called the other man. 'You'll only make things worse for yourself.'

Romy's father fired both barrels. The sharp crack of the explosions echoed against the hills and crows rose shrieking from the trees. Inside the green cupboard Romy whimpered and clamped her hands over her ears.

'I'm not going nowhere, Mark Paynter.' The used cartridges fell to the floor. 'And you'll get off my land if you know what's good for you. I'm giving you fair warning – next shot won't be for the trees. Don't want to spoil your smart clothes, do you? Now get out and don't come back!'

'I shall fetch the police! Don't think you'll get away with this! I shall—'

The window slammed shut, muffling the voices. Through ringing ears, Romy heard her father muttering to himself, and his fast, heavy breathing. He was leaning against the wall, his eyes closed. She wanted to run to him, to try to make it better somehow, but her legs were shaking and, besides, she knew that if she were to show herself, he would be angry with her. She wasn't supposed to be here; she was supposed to be at school. *Can't have kids under my feet. Can't have kids under my feet when they're taking Middlemere away from me.*

The silence persisted. The men had gone away, Romy told herself. She sat back in the cupboard, weak with relief. The men had gone away and Dad would put the gun back in the cupboard and everything would be all right again. No one could make them leave Middlemere. How could they? Middlemere was their home. Dad had stopped the men taking Middlemere away, and everything would be all right again and the world would stop being topsy-turvy.

Yet her father remained beside the window, holding the gun, the expression on his face a mixture of resolve and fear, and she did not yet sneak out of the cupboard and run to him and say: *Dad, I'm here, I stayed with you.* She remembered, a cold trickle of fear, that Annie Paynter's dad had said: *I'm going to get the police.* What if the police put her dad in prison? How would they manage? Who would look after the cows and the sheep?

Romy tried to reassure herself. Perhaps the police would help them. Perhaps the police would stop Mr Paynter coming back. She sat back on the heap of feathers, resting her head on her knees, closing her eyes, rocking gently to and fro, singing very quietly to herself. *The men in the forest, they once asked of me, How many wild strawberries grow in the salt sea?*

After a while, the silence began to seem more alarming than the shouting. The farm was rarely quiet during the day. Ma was always clattering about, cooking and cleaning and baking bread or making butter, or shouting to Jem and Romy to get ready for school or to come and help with chores. There were the ever-present sounds of the animals, the cows and the pig and the horse, and the dog, his paws clicking on the cobbles as he followed Romy's father across the yard. And the wind, soughing in the trees when the autumn gales got up or rustling through the corn when it stood ripe and ready to be harvested in late summer. And, over and above it all, her father's voice as he guided the carthorse across the field, or gave orders to the boy, or called greetings to Romy and Jem as they made their way along the short cut at the edge of the field to the farmhouse after school.

If she concentrated very hard, she could imagine that it was summer and that she and Jem were walking along the path. She could smell the sun-baked earth and the honeysuckle in the hedgerow. She felt happy and safe because she was coming home to Middlemere. Sunlight filtered through the tall beech trees and the meadow was golden with buttercups. The dark pool beneath the trees glittered. Jem was at her side and she was keeping an eye on him, just as she always did. She was Jem's big sister; she was eight and a half and he was only seven, so she had to keep an eye on him ... Cocooned in the darkness, Romy drifted off to sleep.

The sound of a car engine woke her with a jolt. She could not for a moment remember where she was. She had no idea how long she had slept. She stretched out her stiff limbs, listening. There were two cars this time. She knelt up, pressing an anxious eye to the spyhole. The small, pale circle of light showed her that her father was still standing beside the window, looking down at the garden. Romy shifted, cramped and uncomfortable in the cupboard. It made her think of church, kneeling on one of those little embroidered stools, all scrunched up between the pews. She wasn't used to going to church like all the other children were. She didn't know what to do; was convinced, as they all trooped in a long crocodile from school to parish church, that she would make a fool of herself.

Not that she was bothered if they laughed at her. She'd sort 'em out if they did. But Miss Pinner was fond of the cane and didn't mind using it on the girls as well as the boys. And then Romy's dad would hear of it and he'd come to the school to give Miss Pinner what for, and some of the girls, the girls whose dads were grocers and butchers, not farmers, girls like Annie Paynter, who wore pressed cotton dresses and had their hair in curls, would make fun of him. For the length of string that tied up his coat instead of a belt. For the way he spoke, the things he said.

A voice called out, so loud it made Romy jump. 'Mr Cole, this is the police.' There was a distorted, metallic quality to the voice that frightened Romy. She pictured it issuing from the throat of some great, lumbering, mechanical beast.

Her father flung open the window. 'Get off my land!'

'Come down here, Sam Cole, and let's talk peaceable.'

'Nothing to talk about. They're not taking my farm from me.'

'It's not your farm now,' Mark Paynter called up. 'It belongs to the County War—'

'Get off my land! And don't come back!'

'This is a police matter now,' boomed the metallic voice.

'They're trying to take my home away from me,' Sam Cole cried out. 'It's them you should be after! They're thieves! Trying to put a man out of work and his family onto the streets!'

'Don't give us no more trouble now, Sam. If you

behave yourself and come out peaceable like, then we might be able forget about the matter of discharging the offensive weapon.'

Through the spyhole, Romy saw her father take two cartridges from his pocket and slide them into the gun barrel.

'I'm not leaving my house.'

'Come down here now, Cole, and we can sort this out.'

There was a silence, then Sam Cole said, 'This is my home. This is my land.' His voice had altered, and the words seemed flat, tired, squeezed out through a dry throat. 'Middlemere's been farmed by my family for nigh on forty years. No one's going to take it from me. Not you, Mark Paynter, nor any bloody committee, nor any policeman, come to that. Don't think I won't use this gun. You'll take this house from me over my dead body.'

The way her father spoke made Romy remember the week that Maisie had died. *Think there's a God, do they?* Dad had said, as they had walked out of the churchyard after the funeral. *A God that makes little babies die like that.* And he had looked so tired, far more tired than he ever was after a long day's work in the fields, all the colour drained from his face, his large frame hunched, almost shrunken.

'Mr Cole—'

The gun clattered onto the sill once more. The metallic voice fell silent. In spite of the cold, Romy saw that there was sweat on her father's forehead. His hands, clutching the gun, trembled. The urge to run to him was almost irresistible. He wouldn't be cross, would he?

12

Not really cross. He was never so cross that he smacked her. Mum sometimes smacked her, but Dad never did. He'd roar at her, but she was used to that, wasn't she?

But if he knew she was here then he'd send her outside, send her to school, she knew that he would. There was a part of her that wished she were at school, bored and safe, doing her needlework. But how could she leave him all alone?

She paused, her hand on the cupboard door, irresolute. Then a sudden loud thump – a shocking, reverberating impact – seemed to make the house itself shake. Romy's fingers slid from the door and she pressed her clenched fists against her face as she tried not to cry. She heard her father curse, heard his hobnailed boots on the treads as he ran downstairs. She couldn't think what was making the terrible noise. She imagined great big wolves prowling around the house, their claws battering at the door, their red eyes glittering as they raised up their heads and howled.

The noise stopped. Her father came back upstairs. Flinging open the landing window, he yelled, 'You won't get rid of me that easy, Mark Paynter! I told you – over my dead body!'

Silence again. Romy scrubbed the tears from her face with her sleeve. She was cold and hungry and desperate for a pee. She tried to pray. That was what they did at school when something bad happened. They had prayed when Harry Fort had caught diphtheria and they had prayed when Lizzie Clark's brother's ship had been torpedoed by the Germans. Romy closed her eyes very tightly and pressed her palms together, and recited 'Our Father' and 'Now I lay me down to sleep' and a prayer they said at church, which Romy liked because it was all about sheep, and made her think of the high hills and her father's flock, cropping the scrubby grass.

She had got to, *We have followed too much the devices and desires of our own hearts*, when the noise began again. She could not tell where it was coming from. It seemed to surround her, loud and threatening: the wolves again, angry and vengeful, clawing at her home. Out in the corridor, her father glanced quickly from side to side as he strode along the landing. He was standing outside the cupboard in which Romy was hiding. If she had opened the door, she could have reached out her hand and touched him.

But he turned suddenly, heading for the attic stairs. The noise was coming from the roof. *I'll huff and I'll puff and I'll blow your house down.* Romy pictured the wolves moving the slates aside, sliding through the rafters to prowl around the attic, their slavering jaws showing their long, pointed teeth.

The shotgun fired again. A high-pitched scream echoed through the house.

Tears ran down her face and Romy shook with fear. Her dad had shot a man, had shot him dead, perhaps. Her dad was a murderer. She'd come across the word for the first time not long ago. Murderer. There was a scary, horrible sound to it. Though she closed her eyes, the awful word echoed over and over again. Murderer. She remembered the way the pig squealed when her father put the knife to its throat. She remembered the scent of pig's blood, warm and metallic. She knew what happened to murderers. One of the big girls at school had told her: *They hangs 'em on the gibbet. They hangs 'em till they're dead.*

Why hadn't she stopped him? Why hadn't she run after him and begged him to put away the gun? She crouched in a little ball in the corner of the cupboard, her small, wet fingers squeezed into fists. She heard the crash of breaking glass. She wanted Jem, she wanted Ma. She began to sing to herself once more, crooning like Ma used to croon to Maisie. *The men in the forest, they once asked of me . . .*

Outside in the garden, there was more shouting and the sound of running feet. Her father came back to the landing. Romy watched him through the spyhole. His breath came in great noisy gulps and his eyes were wet and teary. He ran his hand over his face. He was talking to himself, his voice low and tremulous. 'Take my home away from me, would you? Throw my family out into the streets? Not over my dead body. Not over my dead body.'

Downstairs the crashes and thumps became louder and louder. They were going to break the house down. *I'll huff and I'll puff and I'll—.* They were going to smash the windows and break down the walls until there was nothing left of Middlemere. And then they would take her dad away and they would hang him dead. 'Dad,' she cried out, but the word was lost in the noise. Now there were footsteps on the stairs, heavy, purposeful footsteps, as though an army was marching through Middlemere. Romy pressed her eye to the spyhole, but could not stop trembling, so that everything she saw was jerky and discontinuous.

Her dad was sobbing now. He was breaking open the gun, sliding out the spent cartridges and putting in two more. His fingers slipped and slid on the smooth metal. Romy flung open the cupboard door. 'Dad,' she cried again. Then he fired the gun.

The men in the forest, they once asked of me, How many wild strawberries grow in the salt sea?

Romy began to scream.

PART TWO

Map-reading

Spring–Summer 1953

Chapter Two

It was the spring of 1953 and Caleb Hesketh and Alec
Nash were in London, celebrating the end of their
national service. Earlier that evening they had ceremo-
nially burned their demob charts. The pieces of paper
had been divided into squares, each square representing
a day of national service, all triumphantly blacked in.
There had been seven hundred and thirty squares. Two
years of their lives.

Two years in which the old army adage of *Keep
your head down, keep your mouth shut* had been Caleb's
motto, too. It had served him as well during national
service as it had at school. And when he had had to
open his mouth he had adopted whichever voice suited
the circumstances – the rural drawl of his childhood for
the army, something smarter, classier, for school. It was
easier that way; it meant you didn't get picked on.

Not that he had been unhappy, either at school or in
the army. He was good at adapting, at fitting in. Two
years ago, arriving at training camp in windswept Catterick, he had known that he could take it. The army,
he had suspected, would be much like boarding school,
cold and uncomfortable, with rotten food and people
always telling you what to do. He could cope with that.
So could the working-class lads who had already put in

a couple of years on a building site or in a shipyard. It had been the grammar-school boys, the boys who had never left home before, who had wept into their pillows that first night.

Caleb's national service had been spent shuffling pieces of paper in a series of dreary camps. Tedium had been his enemy, not danger. There had been, he often thought, something rather farcical about his military career, especially when you compared it with his father's.

Caleb's father had been a carpenter. The Depression had hit Archie Hesketh badly, taking from him the small business he had built up in the West Country. Though he had left the village in which he had been born to search for work, nothing had lasted, and the family had struggled to make ends meet. Yet Caleb's memories of his early childhood were not of poverty and deprivation, but of laughter and companionship. His father had been a gentle, quiet man, who had never once raised his voice to his small son, who had been endlessly patient with him, pushing him on the swing in the park, teaching him to ride a bicycle and reading him bedtime stories.

On the outbreak of war in 1939 Archie Hesketh had joined up to serve in the British Expeditionary Force. In May 1940, pursued by enemy fire, he had fled the beaches of Dunkirk in an old paddle steamer. He had been posted to North Africa the following year and had died a hero's death at Tobruk in early 1942. Caleb had been nine years old when the telegram had arrived informing them of his father's death. He had felt a mixture of confusion and disbelief, and for a long time afterwards he had clung to the private conviction that a mistake had been made, that his father had been taken prisoner, perhaps, or was hiding in the desert. As for his mother, he still remembered how she had moved about the tiny cottage in which they had then lived, her expression lost, her hands moving aimlessly, as though her usual props – her optimism, her cigarettes and cups of tea, and the cheap, pretty fripperies with which she filled the house – had for the first time failed her.

His memories of his father had seemed to solidify with time, frozen into a series of snapshots and anecdotes. Not long after his father's death, Caleb had been sent away to boarding school, the beneficiary of a scholarship for the sons of men from his father's regiment. He had coasted through school, just as, more recently, he had coasted through national service. Leaving school, he had briefly considered enlisting as a regular soldier, but national service had soon put him off that. He had inherited neither Archie Hesketh's willing acceptance of authority nor his capacity for heroism. Realizing this, Caleb had felt slightly discomfited, slightly disappointed in himself.

Though he could have applied for a commission, could have escaped the noisy egalitarianism of the barracks for the supposedly more civilized constraints of the officers' mess, he had not done so, remaining resolutely in the ranks, mostly because he had doubted whether he could afford officers' mess bills, but also because it had been a relief to stop pretending for a couple of years. A relief to stop pretending that he was something he wasn't. As a scholarship boy at a minor public school, assuming the accent had been the easiest part. Not opening up himself to ridicule because of his lack of both money and background had been much harder work.

Now, at last, he had finished for ever with both school and army. Tonight he was celebrating the beginning of the rest of his life. The night seemed full of promise – of adventure, perhaps, or love. An escape from routine and tedium. A chance, after so long, to choose his own direction.

In a pub in Piccadilly Caleb and Alec ran into a chap who had been a few years ahead of them at school – Caleb remembered that his room had always smelt of burnt toast. They latched on to Burnt Toast's crowd, drifting through the cold, dark, rainy evening. Drinking beer with whisky chasers in a cramped little bar in Soho, they shouted over the music to a blonde and a brunette. The blonde was called Helen, the brunette Doris. Helen attached herself to Alec, Doris to Caleb. Caleb wondered whether it was always like that, whether people matched themselves, fair to fair, dark to dark.

Doris's hair was set in rigid waves. Her face was powdered to a pale, plastery matt, and her pneumatic bosom joggled against Caleb's chest as they danced. She was from Yarmouth, she said. Come down to London to seek her fortune (a giggle). 'And have you found it yet?' he asked, and she looked blank, slightly confused.

'I want to be a beautician,' she explained. 'I'm very good at nails.'

They bought chips and ate them walking through the streets. Doris ate all her chips and most of Helen's. Squeezed into a smoky pub, she drank the gin and oranges that Caleb bought her and told him that she was thinking of going blonde. 'Men always notice blondes,' she said matter-of-factly. 'They get first choice.' Caleb wondered whether to be offended and decided not to bother. When, out in the cold night air, Doris's face went green beneath the powder and she was sick into the gutter, Helen took her under her wing and led her off in search of a taxi back to their hostel.

Caleb and Alec found themselves in another bar, the sort of bar where you bought the hostesses enormously expensive drinks. Caleb smiled politely and shook his head when a girl approached him. He was running short of money. Even Alec, faced with an astronomical bill for a glass of champagne for a freckly redhead, looked slightly hunted. When no one was looking they ducked outside and wandered through a bombsite, perching on the remains of a wall, letting the drizzle cool their hot faces.

Triumphantly Alec flourished a scrap of paper. 'It's the address of a party.'

The party was in a tall, thin house in a street off the King's Road. The front door was ajar, and music and light spilled onto the pavement. Slipping inside, they found themselves in a long hallway with a black-and-white tiled floor. Guests were sitting on the stairs, one or two to each tread. Bottles and glasses glinted, and on the ceiling a chandelier swayed, catching the light.

Caleb roamed round the house, looking. He liked to look at things – at houses, people, gardens, the sea, whatever. This house was splendid in a shabby way. The furnishings were of dark, polished wood, the curtains worn velvets rather than the bright patterns that

Caleb's mother favoured. A careless elegance clung to the guests; their jewels were real, Caleb guessed, their dresses, even if decades old, from Paris or Rome.

He found a glass of something abandoned on a bookshelf and drank it as he explored. Oil paintings of stern, moustachioed gentlemen looked down at him from the corridors; he caught sight of his reflection in a gilt mirror and quickly ran a hand through his short, black hair. He wondered whether he should have worn evening dress. Almost every other man was in evening dress. Not that he possessed a dinner jacket. In fact, he had only one suit, the one he was wearing now, which he hadn't worn since he was eighteen and which was miles too small for him, and –

A voice said, 'Who are you?'

He spun round. She was slender and tall – only a couple of inches shorter than Caleb himself – and she had wavy chestnut hair. Her eyes, which were almond-shaped, were the same shade as her sapphire blue dress.

'Caleb Hesketh.' He held out his hand.

'Have we met before?' She frowned. 'I don't think so. I would have remembered.'

He said honestly, 'We may have come to the wrong party.'

She smiled. 'I think you've come to exactly the right party. I'm Pamela Page. This is my party.' She looked down at his glass. 'What are you drinking?'

'I've no idea. It tastes of turpentine.'

'I've some champagne. Much nicer than turpentine.'

He followed her into a room. 'There,' she said, 'on the sideboard. And turn the bottle not the cork. I don't want champagne all over the floor. Such a waste.'

He poured out two glasses. She smiled, her mouth turning up at the corners like a crescent moon. 'Lovely. My favourite drink. You do like champagne, don't you, Caleb?'

'I've never drunk it before.'

'You poor little thing.' She patted the sofa beside her. 'Come and tell me about your deprived childhood. No.' She frowned. 'Let me guess.'

Bubbles bounced on top of the champagne. Drinking, looking round the room, looking most of all at her, he felt a thrill of anticipation. His life had begun at last. He was on his way.

She said, 'You were born ... oh, somewhere in the sticks. You have an accent, darling, the teeniest bit. I'm good at accents. Then, let me see ... I expect you went to some frightful school, where you played rugby a great deal, and then...' Her long, thin fingers ruffled his hair. A shiver ran up his spine and he nearly choked on the champagne. 'Well, serving queen and country for the last couple of years, obviously. You look like a shorn lamb.' She sat back on the cushions. 'Am I right, darling?'

'Spot on,' he admitted.

'Now me.'

'You?'

'Yes,' she said patiently.

He stared at her. Close up, he realized that she was some years older than him, but you couldn't say that. So he said, inventing wildly, 'You're the daughter of a Scottish baronet. You were brought up in a draughty old castle in the Highlands. You escaped to London as soon as you could, to this house, which you inherited

25

from your maternal grandmother, who was the seventh daughter of a seventh daughter.' He paused, running out of steam.

'Completely wrong,' she said, but she was smiling. Her gaze drifted round the room. 'This was my husband's house, actually. He's dead. Dead almost ten years. Burnt to a crisp in his Spitfire.'

Her cool, light voice and the simple brutality of her choice of phrase shocked him. He mumbled, 'I'm sorry,' and she ruffled his hair again, and said, 'Don't be. It was a long time ago. Tell me, are you finished with the army?'

'I was demobbed this morning.'

'So what will you do now?'

'I don't know,' he admitted. 'I haven't made up my mind. I suppose I should be a teacher or a lawyer or something.'

'Sounds rather dull, darling.' She gave an ironic smile. 'And meanwhile . . . eat, drink and be merry?'

'Something like that.' He explained, 'I went straight from school to national service. I've never had to choose before.'

'How lovely to have everything all spread out before you. Your whole life, like a gigantic box of sweets.'

She put aside her glass and stood up. 'Shall I introduce you to some people, Caleb? That would be a start, wouldn't it?'

Caleb met Marcus, who made films, and Caroline, who modelled for Norman Hartnell, and Simone, who wrote for *Vogue*, and he danced to a scratchy gramophone, a bored-looking glacial blonde in his arms, and with a dozen others, crowded round a baby grand and bawled out the choruses to 'Jealousy' and 'Moonlight Serenade'. He also drank a great deal and ate dozens of canapés. Every now and then he caught a glimpse of a sapphire-blue dress, but, threading through the crowds in search of Pamela, he always seemed to lose her. As alcohol and exhaustion made his thoughts blur and slide, it seemed to him that she remained the only fixed point, a gleam of clear blue in an increasingly muddled sky.

He lost track of time; when he next looked at his watch it was half-past four in the morning. Alec had left the party hours ago. Bottles and glasses were abandoned on table tops and floors. Of the remaining guests, some had fallen asleep on sofas or stair treads. The house had a tired, mournful air; a girl sat on the landing, weeping, and in the kitchen a couple embraced, oblivious to passers-by.

Peering out of a window, Caleb caught sight of Pamela in the garden. Rain slid slowly down the pane, blurring her blue dress. Stumbling through French doors, slipping on the wet terrace and overturning a pot of browning geraniums, he did not at first realize that she was not alone.

When she looked up at him, her eyes were blank and cold. Her companion, who was thirtyish and handsome in an oily sort of way, drawled, 'Aren't you going to introduce us, Pam?'

'Of course. Eliot, this is—' She paused and her brow creased. 'Eliot, this is Christopher . . .' She shook her head impatiently. 'I mean, Colin—'

'Caleb,' supplied Caleb. 'Caleb Hesketh.'

27

'This is my fiancé, Eliot Favell.'

They shook hands. In the ensuing silence Caleb's manners, drilled into him by his mother and by school, rescued them all. 'I came to say thank you. For the party, I mean. It's been terrific.'

'So glad you enjoyed it.' A vague smile. 'Do keep in touch, won't you, darling?' She turned away.

He left the house. He was still rather drunk and images from the long night flickered through his head as he walked through the quiet streets: Doris's scarlet-lacquered fingernails resting on his arm as they danced; the freckled redhead in the Soho club. And Pamela, of course: beautiful, icy Pamela.

The sky began to lighten as Caleb came within sight of Victoria Station, the clouds parting at last so that a rosy glow painted the city's roofs and spires. Pausing, looking up, he felt a rush of elation.

In the entrance to the station he rubbed his tired eyes and yawned. He wondered what he should do.

It was time to go home, he realized. Time to go home to Middlemere.

The bus dropped Romy outside the Rising Sun and then she walked the rest of the way home. There were two pubs in Stratton and a shop and a church. Someone called out to her from the doorway of the second pub, offering to buy her a drink, but she smiled and shook her head and walked on. As she passed the churchyard, the two billy goats tethered on the verge looked up at her briefly and then went back to devouring a crumpled sheet of newspaper.

Romy lived in one of a small group of council houses a quarter of a mile from the church. The half-dozen pebble-dashed buildings were on top of a hill. Even in summer the wind seemed always to be blowing, making the washing jump and crack on the line, flattening the neat ranks of daffodils and tulips. Not that the Parrys' garden contained either daffodils or tulips; the front garden of 5 Hill View enclosed only a few struggling shrubs and an overgrown lawn littered with sodden cardboard boxes and battered children's toys.

Romy's mother was in the kitchen. Saucepans were rattling on the hob, filling the room with steam. Martha had a vegetable knife in her right hand and an infant balanced on her hip. The infant was screaming, his round, blotched face sticky with snot and tears.

Martha said, 'You're late.'

'The bus was full, Mum. I had to wait for the relief.'

'Here, take Gareth.' Martha handed Romy her half-brother. 'Don't know what's up with him. He's been like this all day. He must be going down with something again.'

Romy scrabbled in her bag. 'Pay day, Mum.' She gave her mother a ten-shilling note and two half-crowns.

Martha's tired face relaxed into a smile. 'You're a good girl, Romy.' She hid the money in an empty cocoa tin at the back of a cupboard. 'Change his nappy and put him in his cot. If Ronnie's up there, tell him to come down.' Martha lifted the lid of one of the saucepans and poked the knife into a potato. Then she said, 'Mrs Pike's boy was round for you. I sent him packing.'

'Liam?'

Martha nodded. 'Full of himself, that one. Needs taking down a peg.'

'Where's Jem?'

Martha drained the potatoes. 'He's not home yet.'

As Romy left the room, Martha said sharply, 'Don't make my mistake. Don't land yourself with a husband and kids at your age. You're better than that, Romy.'

After she had settled Gareth, Romy went to the bedroom she shared with her thirteen-year-old step-sister, Carol. Carol was peering into a mirror. There was a lipstick in her hand and an open powder compact on the bed beside her. Romy took a rapid indrawn breath.

'My things. You've been messing with my things.'

Carol's face was floury with powder. A smug smile played on her inaccurately crimsoned lips.

'Do I look pretty?'

'You look disgusting.' Romy lunged for the powder. Carol stepped sideways, scattering powder onto the bed – her bed, thought Romy furiously – *her* powder on *her* bed. Romy made another grab and Carol slipped, banging her head against the wall, and began to howl.

'I'll tell Dad what you done!' Carol ran out of the room. Romy knelt on the lino, scraping powder back into the compact. The powder was almost new and had cost one and six. From her secretarial job, Romy earned one pound eighteen shillings a week. Fifteen shillings to her mother and another ten on bus fare and stockings and lunch meant that she was only able to save thirteen shillings a week. At this rate, it would be years before she had saved up enough. Romy was careful with money, watching every penny.

Mind you, she wouldn't be working in a solicitors' office for one pound eighteen a week for ever. She paused, clutching the compact. She hungered for new sights and new experiences. Sometimes, seized by an undirected, unfocused anguish, she felt almost sick with longing. She wanted everything. She wanted nice clothes and to be able to afford new books and trips to the cinema. She wanted her mum not to be so tired. She wanted Jem to keep a job for more than a few months; she wanted him to stop disappearing for days at a time, and to keep out of the way of trouble-makers like the Dayton brothers.

She wanted a bedroom of her own so that she didn't have to share with the loathsome Carol. Most of all, she wanted to escape. She wanted to live in a city – Salisbury, perhaps, or even Southampton. Anywhere but boring old Stratton, with anyone but the horrible Parrys. Recently Romy had become increasingly afraid that no matter what she wanted, no matter how hard she tried, she'd find herself swallowed up, consumed and imprisoned by the dull sameness and cramped horizons of Stratton.

This time next year, she vowed, she'd have a better job and a place of her own. She would be nineteen then, almost twenty. Romy pictured herself sitting in an office, giving out orders and cashing cheques. She'd be wearing a smart skirt and jacket, and her make-up would be perfect, and her obstinately straight hair would somehow keep its curl.

She hid the compact under the mattress, next to her savings book. Opening the book, she looked at the balance and smiled. Thirty-seven pounds and six shillings.

Only two pounds fourteen shillings more and she would have forty pounds.

Everything comes to she who waits, Miss Evans, her teacher at the Grammar, used to say. *God works in mysterious ways*. Well, God hadn't quite managed to fulfil Miss Evans' ambition of a university place for Romy, and Romy hadn't had the heart to tell Miss Evans that even if her stepfather had let her stay on to sixth form, privately she thought that university was a monumental waste of time. You didn't get what Romy wanted by burying yourself among dreaming spires for three years. You got it by working hard. And you got it by not letting anything – or anyone – get in your way.

Jem didn't come home for tea. After Romy had finished the washing up, she went to look for him.

She tried the pubs first, peering into the smoky darkness of the bars of the George IV and the Rising Sun. There was no sign of Jem, but Mr Belbin, the grocer, called out, 'If you're lookin' for that brother o' yours, I saw 'im with Luke Dayton.' Romy's heart sank and she cycled off down the hill, methodically checking Jem's usual haunts: the dank, spidery air-raid shelter opposite the village school, the chalk pits that in this wet spring were full to the brim with coffee-coloured water.

The chalk pits were on the edge of woodland. Romy propped her bike against a tree and sat down on a fallen log, gazing out at the smooth brown water. She often came here; it was a good place for thinking, for working things out. You couldn't think at 5 Hill View because there were too many people. Not that 5 Hill View wasn't a great improvement on the succession of lodging houses and derelict cottages that had preceded it. Romy had worked out a long time ago that her mother had married Dennis Parry because of the house.

Dennis had been a widower with a small daughter; he had needed a housekeeper and a mother for Carol. Martha had needed a roof over her head for herself and her two children. Dennis Parry was a bricklayer, and if his employment was intermittent, at least between them Dennis, Martha and Romy earned enough to pay the rent. Even the subsequent arrival of Ronnie and Gareth had not seemed too high a price to pay for running water and an inside bathroom.

As for Dennis himself, Romy tried to ignore him, to pretend he wasn't there. When he yelled at her, she tried to picture him as a mouse, squeaking in the corner. When he hit her, she hid the bruises under long-sleeved blouses or thick stockings. Quick and nimble on her feet, she had learned to anticipate Dennis's short fuse and usually managed to avoid his blows. Jem hadn't the same knack. Jem's very presence, his appearance and tone of voice, seemed to ignite Dennis's resentment and anger. Dennis Parry reserved a special venom for his stepson. All the qualities that Romy loved best in Jem – his generosity, his good nature, his charm and spontaneity – seemed to provoke Dennis. All the qualities that made Romy fear for Jem – his lack of judgement, his impulsiveness and his sudden, short-lived anger – brought out the overbearing bully in Dennis.

She heard a car draw up at the roadside as she wheeled her bike back through the copse. Liam Pike was sitting at the wheel of the open-topped roadster. Romy had dated Liam in the interval between Liam's finishing school and beginning national service. Liam was tall and good-looking; several of Romy's friends had been in love with him. But there was something about Liam Pike that made Romy wary. There was still a suggestion of the spoilt, over-indulged little boy he had once been. And though Liam had gone to the Grammar like Romy, Romy's mother had once been Liam's mother's cleaning lady, which made Romy wonder whether Liam might look down on her.

Liam patted the steering wheel. 'A beauty, isn't she? Fancy a spin?'

Romy shook her head. 'I'm looking for Jem.'

'*Romy.*' Liam looked pained. 'It's been months. And I've only got ten days' leave.'

'Sorry.'

'Tomorrow, then?'

'I have to work mornings.' Yet her gaze slid back to the car, to the chrome wheels and leather seats. You could go anywhere in a car. You could get away in a car.

'Go on, Romy,' Liam coaxed.

She shrugged. 'All right. You can pick me up in Romsey after I finish work.'

Luke Dayton let Jem drive his car; Jem put his foot down, careening along the narrow track that led from the road to the Daytons' dark, dank little cottage. Jem liked to drive fast. Driving stopped you thinking. There was only the road and the car and the sound of the engine and the rattle of the wheels on the track.

At the Daytons' cottage they smoked and shared some beers with Luke's brothers. Then they played a couple of hands of poker, which cleaned Jem out of cash. Then one of the Daytons fetched his dad's shotgun and they walked through the thicket that surrounded the cottage, looking for rabbits.

But the report of the gun, mingling with shrieks of laughter, began to make Jem feel uneasy and after a while he broke away from the others and headed back to Stratton. In the course of the long walk the elation of alcohol and company faltered, and Jem hunched up his shoulders and hummed to himself, trying to escape the black thoughts that crowded in on him. He didn't like the dark, never had. Didn't like being alone in the dark.

It was two in the morning when he got home. He hadn't realized it was so late. He tried to be quiet as he let himself into the house, but Gareth's high chair was smack in the middle of the kitchen floor and, stumbling against it, flailing to keep his balance, he knocked a couple of plates off the table. Jem froze and held his breath. For a split second he thought it was going to be all right, that Dennis had slept through the noise, but then he heard the roar from upstairs and the sound of heavy footsteps. Then Dennis, in string vest and pyjama bottoms, was in the doorway yelling curses, and Jem was apologizing for waking him and for breaking the plates, and the phrases were stammering, tripping over themselves as he tried to placate his stepfather.

But he couldn't find the right words. He never

could. Wasn't clever enough. The first blow caught him on the side of the face; the next, on the top of his head, stunned him. Then his mother appeared, yelling at Dennis to stop, and Dennis smacked her so hard she slammed into the door jamb.

Anger replaced fear. A red mist seemed to envelop Jem and he went for Dennis, pummelling him with his fists, yelling at him, cursing him. He wanted to smash his ugly face. He wanted to kill him.

But Jem was seventeen and slight, and Dennis in his late thirties, thickset and muscular. Dennis seized a handful of Jem's hair and struck his head repeatedly against the wall. Jem saw stars and his legs began to turn to jelly. And at the first opportunity, when Dennis's grip slackened, Jem ducked out of his grasp and fled the house. Sick and dazed, he limped out of Hill View, out of Stratton. It had begun to rain and the chill droplets mingled with the blood and the tears that ran down his face.

In the morning shards of china from the broken crockery were scattered over the kitchen floor. Creeping downstairs in the middle of the night, Romy had seen Dennis, his fingers knotted in Jem's hair, hitting Jem's head against the wall. Martha had been screaming at him to stop; blood had been pouring from Martha's split lip. Martha had caught sight of Romy and had gestured to her, angrily ordering her to go back to her room.

Obeying her, Romy felt a familiar sense of shame. She couldn't stop Dennis hurting Jem or her mother. She knew from experience that, had she attempted to intervene, Dennis would only have hit her as well. Yet she hated herself for doing nothing. In bed she curled up into a small, tight ball and clamped the pillow over her head, her fingers in her ears in a futile attempt to block out the shouts and raised voices.

At work that morning her anxiety lingered. She wondered where Jem was and whether he was all right. She wondered how long it would take her to save up for somewhere of her own to live, somewhere where Jem would be safe from Dennis. It was an effort to concentrate on her work; she felt low and headachy. When, at mid-morning, one of Mr Gilfoyle's wealthy lady clients called at the solicitors' office, sweeping past the typing pool, trailing glamour and mystery in her wake, Romy found herself gazing after her, seized by a mixture of envy and longing. The client, who was called Mrs Plummer, had about her that indefinable air of the city, of cosmopolitan sophistication. She wore a fur coat and a black hat with a chic little veil. She had with her several carrier bags emblazoned with the names of Romsey's most exclusive shops. Gold bracelets clinked at her wrists, and the veil of her hat stippled her face with little, dark, dancing shadows. Her perfume lingered even after the door of Mr Gilfoyle's office had closed behind her – French, Lindy Saunders said, knowingly, ecstatically.

After a few minutes Mr Gilfoyle opened the door to his office and called out Romy's name. Armed with a pencil and her shorthand book, Romy perched on a stool in Mr Gilfoyle's office, taking down a letter. The letter was long and complicated, about rents and trust funds and tax. As she wrote, Romy studied Mrs Plummer covertly. She wondered what it would be like to be as rich as Mrs Plummer, as old as Mrs Plummer. She imagined Mrs Plummer's house to be enormous, full of gold candlesticks and oil paintings. The windows would be draped with long velvet curtains tied up by thick lengths of gold braid, and the cupboards would be crammed with fancy plates and glasses . . .

'Miss Cole?' Mr Gilfoyle's voice interrupted her daydream. 'Would you read the letter back, please?'

His sharp eyes rested on her as if he expected her to make a mistake, but her shorthand was, as always, perfect.

When they had finished, Mrs Plummer stood up. 'You'll send the completed documents to me to sign, Mr Gilfoyle?'

'I'll make sure you have them within the week.' Mr Gilfoyle shook Mrs Plummer's hand.

Romy offered to help Mrs Plummer with her bags. She carried them out through the offices and downstairs to the street. On the pavement Mrs Plummer said, 'How very kind of you, Miss Cole.' She smiled. 'What's your Christian name, dear?'

'Romy.'

'Romy . . . That's a pretty name. And unusual. You're good at your job, Romy. Do you enjoy working for Mr Gilfoyle?'

'I hate it,' said Romy. She felt herself go red, realizing that she had spoken out of turn. 'I mean—'

'Oh dear,' said Mrs Plummer. The corners of her mouth twitched. 'Why do you hate it?'

Embarrassed, Romy muttered, 'It's so boring.'

'What would you prefer to do?'

'I don't know.' Romy glanced once more at Mrs Plummer's lovely clothes and said curiously, 'What do you do, Mrs Plummer? Do you own a shop?'

'Certainly not. I own a nightclub and a hotel.'

Romy imagined dark, smoky rooms, full of elegant and impossibly sophisticated people. She sighed. 'So lucky.'

'Luck doesn't come into it.' Mrs Plummer's voice was sharp. 'You make your own luck in this life, never forget that. How old are you, Romy?'

'Eighteen. Nearly nineteen.'

'Then you've plenty of time.' Mrs Plummer opened her handbag and took out a small square of card. 'Here. Take this. And when you're next in London, look me up.'

Mrs Plummer's taxi drew up. Romy watched it move away from the kerb and disappear around a bend in the road. Propping her back against the wall, she stood for a moment, looking at the crowds of Saturday morning shoppers. She glanced at her watch. Almost midday. Only half an hour till Mr Gilfoyle shut up the office. She was to meet Liam Pike at one o'clock. She studied the card clutched in her hand. The name *Mirabel Plummer* was written in curly black writing above a London address. *Mirabel.* Romy closed her eyes and imagined different people, other worlds.

Driving north out of Romsey that afternoon, tall trees shimmering with tightly furled emerald leaves swooped out of the foreground and then fell far behind. Glimpsed intermittently between hedgerow and reeds, the river was a gleam of silver. As they neared Andover, Liam shouted over the noise of the car, 'We could get something to eat.'

Romy shook her head. She wanted to stay in the car. She wanted to keep travelling for ever.

'Are you cold?' asked Liam. He was steering one-handed, Romy's icy fingers enclosed in his free hand. 'I could put up the hood. Or there's a rug in the back.'

'I'm fine.'

She turned up her mackintosh collar around her neck, loving the feel of the wind in her hair. The road narrowed and rose. The farmland was dotted with thatched cottages and isolated hamlets. Every now and then thick, dark woodland encroached up to the road-side, shutting out the sunlight. Then the trees fell away as the car climbed up through the chalk hills.

Liam's palm slid from her hand to her thigh. Romy's gloomy mood returned with the expectation of the predictable tussle in the car. Liam would kiss her and then he would try to undo her blouse and she would push him away. Then he would sulk and she would have to cheer him up and eventually he would drive her home. She wasn't even sure that he particularly liked her. She suspected that he would have tried it on with any girl.

There was now a familiarity about the passing countryside. As if she had seen it in a dream, perhaps. She looked down at the map, but she had never been able to read maps, and the twisting lines and cobwebbed contour marks seemed to bear no relation to the fields and hills that surrounded her.

'Where are we?'

'That's Inkpen Hill,' said Liam. 'Hungerford's a few miles away.'

Inkpen. Romy's heart seemed to miss a beat. Again she scowled at the map, but it refused to give up its secrets and she threw it impatiently into the footwell.

And then the roads, hills and houses fell into place, as if someone had reassembled a jigsaw, and she knew where she was, knew it as if she had left it yesterday and not almost eleven years ago. She saw the high chalk ridge with its ancient pathway that followed the summit. The steep slope fell away, clouds scudding across the hillside and casting dark shadows on the grass and gorse. Now every turn of the corner, every rise and fall of hill and valley brought with it images from her childhood. A flint and brick school, its asphalt playground fenced with iron railings, stood at the edge of a village. A row of cottages, thatched with straw that had become darkened and unkempt, hunched beside the shop. A long time ago she had bought sherbet dabs from that shop. A long time ago she had known the sisters who had lived in those dilapidated cottages.

When she grabbed Liam's arm the car lurched across the road.

'Romy! You nearly landed me in the ditch!'

'Stop. Please. Just here.'

The car drew to a halt by the verge. Across the road a narrow lane led away up the hill. And over the brow of the hill . . .

She thought quickly. She had to be alone. She could not have borne not to be alone. She turned to Liam. 'I'm feeling a bit funny, Liam. Perhaps I need a drink or something.'

'We could look for a pub.'

'It's not opening time yet. There was a shop in that village we just drove through. Would you get me some lemonade?' She climbed out of the car.

He looked confused. 'Where are you going?'

'For a walk. I need a walk.'

'I'll come with you then.' Liam, too, got out of the car. His hand slid around Romy's waist and his fingers burrowed beneath the thin fabric of her blouse.

Her nerves were stretched to breaking point and it was all she could do not to push him roughly away. 'Liam. Not now.'

He looked annoyed. 'Romy—'

As she walked away, she called out, 'I'll meet you back here in ten minutes!'

A knot had formed beneath her ribs, making her breathless as she climbed the hill. When she and Jem were little, this was the route they had taken home from school. Then the narrow, puddle-pocked lane had seemed to go on for ever. Now it had shrunk, telescoped into a short, insignificant pathway.

As she walked along the track, she remembered it all so clearly. In autumn they had picked hazelnuts and blackberries and dusky blue-black sloes. Pinkish, oddly shaped spindle berries had shone in the hedgerow. Once they had seen a family of foxes, a flash of red-brown in the undergrowth. In the summer there had been poppies and scabious and ox-eye daisies, and in spring violets had peeped from beneath the hedges . . .

There were violets now; she paused to pick a bunch. Part of her wanted to turn round, to go back. Odd how a place could contain such warring emotions: such longing, such dread.

She walked on. There was the tree she had climbed for a dare: it had seemed a hundred feet high then, but now it was diminished, cut down to size, lopped and pollarded in the passing of time. And there was the stile where Jem had slipped, climbing over, and cut his knee. The stile led off the track into a beech wood, where the grey trunks of the trees seemed to be carved out of stone. Romy reached out her palm, touching the smooth, silvery bark. The dark, circular pond reflected the trees. They hadn't often played here, she and Jem: the confined air had seemed too close and airless, too filled with unease. Now long, snaking branches reached down to her. Brambles pulled at her hair and snagged at her stockings like sharp fingernails. The heels of her shoes sank into the soft ground and she saw the fat white fungi that swelled among the beechmast and dead leaves. She was holding her breath and her ribs were gripping her lungs like iron . . .

Then, with a gasp of relief, she was out in the open once more, standing at the top of the field. And there, in a shallow scoop of valley cut from the hillside, was Middlemere.

Some of the tension fell from her and, for what seemed the first time that day, she smiled. The flint and brick farmhouse faced away from the track, looking south down the valley. Hills rose up to either side of it, yet the view from the front of the house was unimpeded, the fields, woods and distant villages melding in the distance into a cobalt blue haze. As Romy walked down the hill, every footstep contained a memory. She was eight years old again and she was going home. She was walking back to safety, to contentment, to the place where she belonged. The sense of confinement and the longing to escape, which were always with her at Stratton, fell away. Here, in the great bowl of the valley, beneath the wide blue expanse of sky, she was able to breathe.

Yet as she neared the house, she saw that it had changed. The front door was painted crimson instead of the familiar, peeling green. The yard surrounding the house seemed smaller and was much tidier. Where were the barrels and buckets, the heaps of straw and sacking, the troughs and tools? Where were the animals, the pig in its sty, the hens clucking on the grass, the cat on the prowl, its emerald eyes skinned for the dash of a tiny brown mouse? And there were flowers, as well as vegetables, in the garden. Romy's mum had never had time for flowers. The yellow trumpets of daffodils nodded in the breeze. Romy stared at them. For one disconcerting, dizzying moment, she wondered whether she had made a mistake, whether she had followed the wrong path, had gone to the wrong house. Yet beside the front door she saw the sign, *Middlemere Farm*.

Walking round to the back of the house, she looked up to the landing window. Time shifted and for a fraction of a second she seemed to see the grey iron snout of a gun balanced on the sill. She shuddered and looked again. There was no gun, of course, only a fold of curtain flapping in the gap made by the open window. Romy pressed her fist against her teeth. When she drew her hand away, there was a bead of blood on her knuckles.

She gave the door a push. It swung open easily and she stepped inside the house. She stood for a moment, listening. Whose voice did she expect to hear? A stranger's voice protesting at her intrusion? Or those other voices, the ones that had whispered more and more loudly as she had walked along the track, making her way back to her childhood?

But the only voice she heard was her own, murmuring a greeting to the unknown usurpers of Middlemere. The only reply was the ticking of the clock and the creaking of an inner door disturbed by the sudden influx of air. The smell of the house jarred her. It was wrong. Middlemere should smell of baking and beeswax polish and, of course, the more pungent scents of the farmyard. The hallway itself was an equally disturbing mixture of familiarity and strangeness. The wooden floorboards had been covered with lino, and the walls, cream-coloured when the Coles had lived there, had been painted bright pink. Romy's fingertip traced the framed photographs that hung along one of the walls. The plump baby in a romper suit in the first snapshot was succeeded by a dark-haired child in patched dungarees, and then by a schoolboy in cap and piped blazer (the eyes were warier, she noticed, less trusting). The last photograph was of a young man in army uniform. Romy's fists clenched. She wanted to tear the pictures from the wall, to destroy these invasive images of a stranger.

A half-moon-shaped table stood against the opposite

wall. Letters were stacked on its surface. The letters, as yet unopened, were addressed to *Mrs E. Hesketh, Middlemere Farm*. Which was somehow particularly intolerable. The letters seemed to give official blessing to a stranger's appropriation of her home.

She went into the parlour. It was decorated in fresh yellows and greens, and the shelves and table tops were crammed with snapshots, ornaments and knick-knacks. Frilled curtains hung at the window and cushions were clustered on the sofas and chairs. Romy's gaze jerked from the china shepherdesses to the glass animals and the ornamental ashtrays. A voice inside her repeated, outraged: *My house. They have changed my house . . .*

Next door, in the kitchen, the heavy farmhouse furniture had been replaced by fitted cupboards and Formica. The old flagstones were covered with lino. From the centre of the ceiling there hung a light bulb encased in a frilly shade. Two taps protruded over the sink. When the Coles had lived at Middlemere the house had had neither running water nor electricity. They had fetched their water from the well and had boiled it in a big copper pan on the stove. The house had been illuminated by oil lamps, heated by coal fires.

Romy went back to the hallway. At the foot of the stairs she faltered, pressing her fingertips against her face, feeling the tears ache behind the bones.

Then a voice from behind her said, 'What do you want? What are you doing in my house?'

She spun round. She recognized him immediately: the dark young man of the photographs in the hall.

'Your house?' Her anger returned, tenfold. She could

hardly speak for fury. 'This is my house! Mine! You stole it! You stole my house and you killed my father!'

After she had gone, Caleb went outside and fetched a spade from the shed. Then he finished digging the trench that he had begun that morning, the blade of the spade cleaving into the earth. But the hard work failed to obliterate the shock of the girl's words, and after twenty minutes or so he paused, wiping the sweat from his forehead. Perhaps, he thought, she had escaped from a lunatic asylum. He imagined high, Victorian windows, and the girl rattling at the bars. Or, even better, she had been a ghost, a wraith from Middlemere's past . . .

No, she had been real enough. She had been wearing cheap, skimpy clothes, her tobacco-brown hair had been tangled, and her cinnamon-coloured eyes had snapped at him. Such hatred in those eyes. He wasn't used to people hating him. *This is my house*, she had said. *You stole it and you killed my father.*

Which was preposterous. He had been relieved when her friend had turned up, calling out to her from the top of the hill. She had turned tail and run, dashing out of the house and up the track as though pursued by demons. Caleb had had a quick look round the house to see whether she had taken anything. But his mother's housekeeping was still in the tea caddy in the kitchen, her jewellery in the box on her dressing table. And the china cherubs and pottery dogs on the mantelpieces were undisturbed. Which Caleb rather regretted: he

47

could hardly move without knocking the damn things over and wouldn't have minded a burglar thinning out the ranks.

The sound of a car made him glance out the window. Recognizing his mother's Austin Seven, he went outside to help with her cases. Betty Hesketh sold cosmetics door to door. The lipsticks and perfumes were stacked in two pink suitcases for Betty to display to her customers. Caleb kissed his mother on the cheek and lugged the cases into the hall.

Indoors, Betty unbuttoned her coat, unpinned her hat and fluffed up her blonde hair. 'Put the kettle on, lovie, I'm parched. That daft cow Glynis Prescott keeps changing her mind. First she wanted the Lily of the Valley, then the Jonquil, and now it's Lily of the Valley again. And the car's making a funny noise. It rattles when I go round a corner.'

'I'll have a look at it, Mum.'

Caleb made the tea. Betty delved into her handbag and brandished a paper bag. 'Fairy cakes. Mrs Watson gave them to me. Said the Miracle Face Cream's done her skin no end of good. You have them, lovie – they'd sit on my waistline. And Ted Morris gave me some nice lamb chops. Off the ration, of course.' Betty glanced at her son. 'You look like you could do with feeding up a bit.'

'Mum—'

'All skin and bone. I'll do you them both – you know I never cared for lamb. Too fatty.'

'Mum—'

'Put them in the larder, lovie, in the meat safe. Cakes in the cake tin.' Betty flicked open a compact and

peered in the mirror. 'Heavens above, I look a fright.'
She wielded a lipstick. 'Ted's calling for me at seven.'

'Ted?'

'The butcher, lovie, I told you.' Betty glanced at the
kitchen clock, dropped the lipstick and compact back
into her bag, drank the remainder of the tea, and flung
some potatoes into the sink.

'There was a girl here,' said Caleb.

Betty peeled busily. 'A girl?'

'In the house.'

'You know I don't mind if you bring your friends
home. Been stuck in the army for two years – you
deserve some fun.'

'I didn't know her,' he said, and when his mother
turned to look at him, he added hastily, 'I mean, I went
out for ten minutes and when I came back she was in
the house. Inside. Standing at the bottom of the stairs.'

'Perhaps she'd come for me. Come to order a
lipstick, something like that.'

He shook his head. 'I don't think so. She was angry.
She said – crazy things.' He fell silent. The odd little
episode seemed slightly unreal now, almost as if he had
imagined it.

But his mother said curiously, 'What sort of things?'

'That Middlemere wasn't our house.'

'Well, it isn't, lovie. You know that. It's Mr Daubeny's house.'

'Yes, but—' He almost wished he hadn't spoken.
Madwomen breezing in and out of your home . . . things
like that were best forgotten, weren't they?

Yet he could not quite shake off the memory of her
eyes, golden brown and full of hate. 'She said that

49

Middlemere was her house. And she said that we'd taken it from her and killed her father.' He shrugged, still perturbed by the memory. 'Crazy.'

Betty said, 'Did you get her name?'

He looked back at his mother, startled. Of course he remembered her name: it rang in his ears, yelled from the hilltop by her companion. 'Romy,' he said. 'She was called Romy.'

'Oh,' said Betty softly.

'Mum? What is it, Mum?'

'Nothing, lovie.' The potatoes fell into the saucepan with a splash. 'Boiled or mashed?'

After supper Caleb cycled to the village. Swanton St Michael's only pub was ancient and crooked, the haunt of gnarled old labourers and bored village youths. The farm labourers ignored him, and the village youths eyed him suspiciously, and the barmaid was twice his age and girth. He found himself remembering Pamela, with her sapphire blue eyes, her crescent-moon smile.

After a while, drinking on his own began to pall, so he cycled back to Middlemere. A butter-coloured moon emerged from its covering of cloud as he reached the house. Caleb recalled the Daubenys' gardener, Mr Fryer, telling him to plant at a waxing moon, so he raked over the ground he had dug that afternoon, scored lines into the earth with the hoe, and scattered seeds into the hollows. The moon cast a glazed stillness across the fields and hills surrounding Middlemere. He could have been the only person alive in the whole world.

He was banking down the stove for the night when his mother returned home. As she came into the kitchen, Betty said, 'She used to live here.'

He looked up. 'Who?'

'That girl. Romy Cole. I wasn't sure ... I thought there was a kiddie. I asked Ted.'

'She lived here? At Middlemere?'

'Before us. The Coles lived in the house before us.'

'But they – the Coles – moved away?'

Betty lit a cigarette. 'Had to,' she said.

'Why?'

'It was wartime, remember. The Coles were evicted because they weren't running the farm properly.' Betty exhaled smoke. 'He was a bit soft in the head, Mr Cole. Shot himself.'

Caleb stared at her. '*Shot* himself?'

'I didn't want you to know. When you were a kiddie, I mean. I thought you might be scared. Kids are always scared of ghosts.'

'Mr Cole shot himself *here*? In our house?'

Betty nodded. Then she said crisply, 'It was a long time ago, lovie. Eleven years. Best forgotten.'

It was late by the time Romy arrived home. The house was in darkness except for the front room, where her mother was sitting on the couch, a glass in one hand, smoking. The low light shadowed the swollen, purple bruise on the side of Martha's face.

Martha said, 'About bloody time. Your dinner's burnt to a crisp.'

'I'm not hungry.' Romy sat down beside her mother. 'Mum?' Tentatively she touched her mother's arm. 'You all right?'

'Course.' Martha pulled away.

'Your poor face—'

'I'm all *right*, I said.'

Martha's way of coping with life's difficulties was to refuse to acknowledge them. As though, if you avoided framing the knocks and slaps and insults with words, they might cease to exist. Sensing the fragility that lay beneath her mother's bravado, Romy had learned to collude with the pretence.

She changed the subject. 'Kids in bed?'

Martha nodded. 'Thank God. Where've you been? It's almost ten.'

'Middlemere,' said Romy bleakly. 'I went to Middlemere.'

Martha blinked. 'What'd you want to go there for?'

'I wanted to see it again, that's all.'

'More fool you, then.'

Romy thought of the photographs and the letters on the half-moon table and the footsteps in the hall. She remembered shouting at the intruder and felt for the first time a twinge of embarrassment. She said, 'There was someone else living there.'

'Course there was. Nice house like that. They'd want the rent, wouldn't they?'

'Someone called Hesketh. Mrs E. Hesketh.'

At first, Martha looked uninterested, and then she smiled and said bitterly, 'Betty Hesketh. My God, Betty Hesketh.'

'You know her?'

52

'Knew of her, more like.' Martha drew on her cigarette. 'Well, well. Betty Hesketh.' Her voice was contemptuous. 'She was always a cheap little tart.'

'What do you mean?'

Martha laughed. 'What do you think I mean? Took her knickers down to get a roof over her head, didn't she? Wouldn't be the first, nor the last. She was always fast, Betty Hesketh.'

Her eyes flickered to Romy. 'Oh, don't look like that. It's the way of the world, isn't it? If it hadn't been her, it would've been someone else.' Martha fell silent and then she muttered, 'Your father was a fool. It was his own fault. Didn't know when he was beaten.'

A grey worm of ash fell from Martha's cigarette to the carpet. Unsteadily Martha knelt down and began dabbing at it with a tea towel. Then she looked up suspiciously at Romy. 'You been with the Pike boy?'

'Just for a drive.' She changed the subject quickly. 'Where's Jem?'

Martha's face seemed to crumple. 'I don't know,' she said hopelessly. 'I think the silly little bugger's taken off again.' Martha made a tired gesture with the tea towel. 'He came back when me and Dennis was at the pub. Carol said he took a few things – clothes and that.' Her damaged features attempted a reassuring smile. 'He'll be back, don't you worry, love. Turn up like a bad penny.'

Romy went upstairs. Carol was asleep, humped up under the bedclothes. *Betty Hesketh always was a tart ... took her knickers down to get a roof over her head.* It wasn't hard to work that one out. Betty Hesketh – *Mrs E. Hesketh* – had gone to bed with someone so that she

53

could have Middlemere. Had gone to bed with someone so that she could have Romy's home.

Very quietly Romy slid off her shoes and jacket and lay on her bed. When she closed her eyes, she saw Middlemere again, curled in the hollow of the valley like a pearl in a giant's palm. She hadn't fully anticipated what emotions the house would bring back. It had been as though the building itself contained them; as though, in spite of the changes that the years had made, all that pain and loss still seeped from the stones.

She tried to think of something else. Parting from Liam, he had invited her to a party at his house the following Friday. What, she wondered, should she wear for a smart party at the Pikes'? Her clothes were practical and economical, hand-knitted jumpers and skirts suitable for the office. She imagined herself in tailored suits and furs like Mrs Plummer. *Mirabel* Plummer. Romy took the visiting card from her purse and, in the darkness, ran the pad of her thumb over the embossed lettering. *When you're next in London look me up* ... Romy had been to London only once, on a school trip to the British Museum. She had never stayed in a hotel, had never been to a nightclub. She had seen nightclubs in films, of course, dimly lit rooms where people dressed in enviably elegant clothes danced and drank and made bright, amusing conversation.

She must have dozed off, to be woken suddenly some time later by a shower of pebbles striking the windowpane. Opening the latch, she leaned out and saw Jem standing in the back garden.

'*Jem.* Where've you been?'

'I bought you a present!' He held out a large, pink, stuffed rabbit.

'Where'd you get that?'

'A bloke was selling them down the pub. And I got Mum some cigs.'

'Are you coming in?'

Jem shook his head. 'The old devil'll lay into me again.'

'Stay there then,' she called softly. 'I'm coming down.'

Romy put her coat back on and crept downstairs. As she opened the kitchen door, Jem hissed, 'Grab us some food, Romy, I'm starving,' so she took a packet of biscuits and a couple of apples from the kitchen cupboard.

Leaving the house, she led the way out of the garden and along the road to the parish church. There, in the graveyard, they sat in the shelter of the stout lichened headstone belonging to Maria Cartwright, spinster of this parish. The moonlight delineated Jem's profile: the dark brown eyes whose expression changed so easily from laughter to despair, the slightly snub nose and full mouth. Jem was seventeen now, his appearance an arresting mixture of the wild and the angelic. Every girl in Stratton was in love with Jem Cole, but to Romy he was still the little boy whose hand she had held as they had walked to school.

She said again, 'Where've you been?'

He made a vague gesture. 'Here and there.' His dark, curly hair was tangled and a chain of bruises ran up the side of his face. His clothes – too thin for a cold spring night – were creased and crumpled. 'I slept in Scutchers' barn last night,' he said. 'I don't mind. Hay's nice and cosy. And there's no one nagging you, laying into you.'

'But you'll come home, won't you, Jem?'

He shook his head. 'I've had enough. Can't take it no more. He hates me.'

Her heart sank. 'But *Jem* – where will you go?'

Jem ate the last of the custard creams and smiled confidently. 'I'm going to get my own place, Romy, that's what I'm going to do. Then you can come and stay with me. Sandra's getting a place in London. She told me you can get a room with a bed and a gas ring for a couple of quid a week.'

'What about your job?' Jem worked in a sawmill near Stockbridge.

'Miserable old bugger gave me my cards.'

'*Jem.*'

'It wasn't my fault, Romy. The foreman kept picking on me. Well, I couldn't just take it, could I?' Jem began to tear pieces of grass from the clumpy covering of Maria Cartwright's grave. 'It wasn't my fault.'

It never was. Always in trouble at school, Romy had hoped when Jem had left at fifteen that he would settle into a job. Lots of boys didn't like school, she had reasoned to herself; Jem wasn't much of a reader and his writing had never got beyond a laborious printing. He would be happier doing something practical, something with his hands.

Yet she had lost count of the jobs he had had since leaving school. He started each one with optimism and promises of good behaviour. But after a few weeks, something always went wrong. And it was never Jem's fault. The bus was late, which was why his timekeeping was poor. His colleagues ganged up on him. The foreman always gave him the rough tasks.

'Don't be cross with me, Romy,' said Jem, squeezing her hand. 'Please don't be cross. I didn't mean to. It just happened.'

His eyes were guileless, pleading with her. Her exasperation died, as it always did. Resting her head against his shoulder, she said, 'You'll never guess what I did today. I went back home. I went back to Middlemere.' She smiled. 'Do you remember when we pretended to be ghosts and Mum was mad because we made her sheets all dirty?'

'And when I dropped my boot down the well?'

'And the boats we made.'

'You told me that the log in the pond was a crocodile. I was scared.'

They fell silent, remembering. Then he said, 'I didn't like the job, Romy. The sawmill. I didn't like the noise.'

'Something else'll turn up,' she said comfortingly. 'Something better.'

'Course. Only—'

'What?'

'I've run out of cash.'

Her purse was in her pocket. She gave him a ten-shilling note. Standing up, he held out his hand to her.

'Come on.'

'Where are we going?'

'You'll see.'

They went inside the church. Jem opened the small

wooden door that led into the tower and Romy followed him up the narrow, winding stone steps. The bell ropes creaked in the breeze, and the high, hollow interior made the smallest sound echo.

'Look,' he said.

He was standing at an arrow-slit window. She followed his gaze. Lit by the moon, the woods and fields and houses were bathed in a magical glow. The road, a thin, silver ribbon, drew the eye far away, out of the stifling confines of Stratton towards new places and new sights. To somewhere different, Romy thought, somewhere better.

Chapter Three

The Daubenys' house, Swanton Lacy, was a few miles from the villages of Swanton St Michael and Swanton le Marsh. Caleb had always thought the house rather gloomy and ugly, and had never envied Mr and Mrs Daubeny their many rooms or their panelled walls. Swanton Lacy had once been famous for its garden, which predated the late Victorian house by more than a century. The garden's designer had made good use of the nearby river, coaxing it along channels and conduits, through dams and weirs, to create an artificial lake. Beyond, parkland dotted with venerable oaks and silver-trunked beeches soared upwards to the crest of the hill. Before the war, Caleb thought, it must have been glorious.

Yet, eight years after the war had ended, an air of neglect, even of violation, clung to Swanton Lacy. From early 1943 the grounds of the house had been used as a lorry depot. Though the Nissen huts had long since been demolished, their rectangular concrete bases, cracked and blistered with puddles, still showed through the thin covering of grass and weeds. Military vehicles had dug deep channels into smooth lawns, churning up ancient grassland, knocking down saplings and despoiling shrubberies and flower beds. Walls and bridges had been chipped and toppled, and wrought-iron gates and railings melted down for the war effort and never since replaced. The lake, and the swans floating on its glassy surface, seemed a last echo of the garden's lost perfection.

Caleb walked round to the back of the house and knocked on a door. A very fat woman wearing an apron opened it, glanced at him, sniffed and permitted him to walk through the kitchen. Mrs Daubeny's latest cook, Caleb assumed. As he made his way through the warren of passages that divided the servants' quarters from the rooms in which the family lived, he was surrounded by high ceilings and friezes of dark, polished wood, every surface knobbled and cross-hatched with ornamentation.

In the hall he encountered Mr Daubeny. Osborne Daubeny was a tall, powerfully set man in his mid-fifties. Caleb said a polite good morning and explained that he had come with the rent money. Mr Daubeny led the way to his study. The spacious room was made dark by the panelling on the walls and the small-paned, latticed windows. Grotesque carved figures sneered from the cornices; books and papers covered the desk. A map uncurled on a side table, its ragged corners held down with paperweights.

Caleb handed over his mother's five pounds and Mr Daubeny recorded the payment in the rent book. Caleb was about to make his escape when Mr Daubeny said, 'And have you completed your national service, Caleb?'

'Yes, Mr Daubeny.'

'What do you intend to do now?'

'I don't know, Mr Daubeny.'

'University?'

Caleb shook his head. 'I need to help Mum out. And anyway, it would mean being stuck away again . . . like the army . . . it wouldn't be *real*.'

'You didn't consider the army real?'

'I was just pushing paper about,' he explained. 'It wasn't like it was for my dad.'

'Of course. A soldier must always feel somewhat cheated in peacetime. But clerical experience is always useful.' Mr Daubeny frowned. 'If you mean to look for a job, I may be able to help you.'

Caleb said, surprised, 'Thank you, Mr Daubeny.'

'I'll let you know if I hear of something suitable. In the meantime, Fryer could do with some help in the garden. Go and speak to him and he'll find you work to tide you over.'

Mr Fryer was Mr Daubeny's gardener. Caleb had worked in Swanton Lacy's garden during many school holidays.

He said again, 'Thank you, Mr Daubeny.'

Mr Daubeny bent over the desk once more, pen in hand. Dismissed, thought Caleb.

Later it occurred to him that he had asked his question to even up the conversation a little, to shake off the sense of irritated subserviency that interviews with Mr Daubeny tended to produce in him. Much, much later, he thought how different his life might have been if he'd kept his mouth shut, made his exit, let the matter drop.

He said, 'Did you know the people who owned Middlemere before us, Mr Daubeny?'

Daubeny's pen paused only momentarily. 'The Coles? Of course. They were my tenants.'

61

'What were they like?'

'Cole was a difficult man.'

Mr Cole was a bit soft in the head, his mother had said the previous evening. An awkward customer, then, Romy Cole's father.

Caleb said, 'Someone told me that they were evicted from our house. And that Mr Cole killed himself because of that.'

Mr Daubeny's pen had reached the foot of the sheet of paper. He blotted it carefully and looked up. 'Why do you want to know about the Coles, Caleb?'

You stole my house and you killed my father. 'Because of the house, I suppose,' he said. 'Because it just seems – harsh. For a family to lose their home like that.'

'It was wartime.' Daubeny's explanation echoed Betty's.

'Yes, but—'

'In the early years of the war the food situation was critical. Hitler could have starved us out. There's no room for sentiment when your back's up against the wall. Middlemere was unproductive. And, as I said, Samuel Cole was a difficult man.' The smooth dome of Daubeny's forehead had creased. 'He was stubborn ... opinionated ... disrespectful ...'

Disrespectful. Caleb had to hide his sudden revulsion.

'Cole wouldn't take orders,' Daubeny went on. 'He always thought he knew best. He refused to comply with ploughing directives. Only planted what he wanted to plant. I think he saw himself as a cut above the rest. Well, that sort of thing's all very well in peacetime, but it won't do when there's a war on.'

'So you evicted him?'

Daubeny's eyes narrowed. He's going to chuck me out, thought Caleb. For being *disrespectful*.

But Mr Daubeny only said, 'It was all done according to the book.' Then he paused, and it seemed to Caleb that just the slightest hint of hesitancy, of questioning, flickered across the self-satisfied veneer.

'In the early Forties,' said Daubeny, 'we – the County War Agricultural Executive Committees – the War Ags, we called them – had to survey every farm in the county, to see how well each farmer was controlling pests and pernicious weeds, and whether he'd fulfilled ploughing and planting orders, that sort of thing. Mark Paynter was our district officer, if I remember rightly, so he carried out the survey.' Daubeny made a dismissive gesture. 'The results of the survey damned Cole. After that the whole business was pretty well out of my hands. It was Paynter's responsibility to carry out the eviction. Between you and me, he wasn't up to the job. He botched it.' There was a short silence, then Mr Daubeny said suddenly, 'Cole fired a shotgun, so Paynter called in the police. Things went awry and a policeman was wounded. And shortly afterwards Cole turned the gun on himself.'

Daubeny rose from the desk and went to stand at the window. 'You must understand,' he said, 'that Samuel Cole brought his misfortunes on himself. And you should remember, Caleb, that the Coles' misfortune was to your advantage. The cottage you and your mother were living in before Middlemere Farm fell vacant was in a derelict state. Beyond repair. The damp had got into the walls.' He said again, 'Why are you interested in the Coles?'

Caleb said, 'I met Mr Cole's daughter.'

Mr Daubeny's eyes were unfocused. 'The girl,' he said suddenly. 'She was in the house when the eviction took place. No one realized. So, you see, she saw her father die.'

From the flower beds behind the scullery, Evelyn Daubeny watched Caleb leave the house and walk to Mr Fryer's potting shed. She permitted herself the small, foolish fantasy that was her occasional habit and allowed herself fleetingly to imagine that he was her son. He wouldn't be called Caleb, of course, he'd be called Stephen. The first baby had been called Stephen. Caleb Hesketh must be barely a year younger than Stephen would have been, had he lived. 'Darling,' she would call to him, 'could you give me a hand with these flowers?' And he would smile and come to her and scoop up the daffodils and carry them into the house.

But he wasn't Stephen; he was Caleb, of course, that awful Hesketh woman's son, and after a second or two the fantasy evaporated, just as it always did, and Evelyn looked away, feeling slightly ashamed, and went back to placing daffodils in the trug. She had never much liked daffodils. They were so hopeless for flower arranging: you could never do anything with them, they just sat there, lacking any grace or subtlety. And Fryer favoured the garishly yellow sort. 'You want a nice bright daff, Mrs Daubeny,' he would say to her tactful requests for a delicate cream, or a small-headed narcissus. She had given up on the daffodils, though she had stood up to Fryer over the rose garden. Evelyn adored roses – the old-fashioned, rambling, scented kind – and had found the courage to put her foot down to Fryer's suggestion that he dig up the old roses and look for some nice colourful modern varieties to replace them.

She would do the flowers now, Evelyn decided, and then she would telephone Mummy and Celia. Mummy had really been quite down, poor thing, when they had spoken the previous week, and it was always best to give Celia a quick call to check that their lunch in town tomorrow was still convenient because Celia led such a busy life and difficulties occasionally cropped up at the last moment.

Evelyn arranged the flowers in the scullery and carried the vases through to the dining room. The dining room was in the centre of the house, an awkwardly shaped room with no outside windows. The walls were panelled up to the dado rail and painted a dark blood red above. There were never enough electric lights or candles and you tended to eat your food in a murky gloom. Though that was perhaps just as well, thought Evelyn grimly, as she placed the vases around the room, because the new cook, Mrs Vellacott, was proving rather a disaster. Quite apart from her sour character, she simply did not seem to be able to cook. It was odd, mused Evelyn, that someone should seek employment in a sphere in which she appeared to have no talent whatsoever. But then poor Mrs Vellacott was a widow who had lost her husband in the war, and her reduced circumstances had presumably forced her to look for whatever employment she could find. And it was hardly Mrs Vellacott's fault that she was – there was no other word for it – ugly, with her vast bulk and the wart above her eyelid that had made Osborne instantly nickname her the Witch of Endor. She should feel sympathetic towards Mrs Vellacott, Evelyn reminded herself. Not unnerved by her.

When she had married Osborne Daubeny in 1930, Evelyn had employed a cook, kitchenmaid, parlourmaid, gardener and gardener's boy. Swanton Lacy's staff had inexorably reduced throughout the Thirties until the war, with its increased opportunities for women, had left the Daubenys only old Fryer. During the war Evelyn herself had washed and cleaned and cooked. She had rather enjoyed cooking. Of course, there had been disasters due to her inexperience and clumsiness. Even nowadays Osborne still sometimes regaled dinner parties with the story of the exploding pudding. Guests roared with laughter at Osborne's tale of Evelyn's failure to realize the importance of leaving a channel for steam to escape the saucepan, and the suet pudding's consequent volcanic eruption from the steamer and adherence to the kitchen ceiling.

Since the end of the war, Evelyn must have engaged a dozen cooks, each of whom had been, for one reason or another, unsatisfactory. A woman came from the village three times a week to help with the heavy work, but really the only way Evelyn could manage was to skimp. Not that she was the only one. The last time they had visited the Middletons, who lived in Swanton le Marsh, they had dined in the kitchen. Beggars can't be choosers, Clare Middleton had announced as she had sat them round the old pine table, and we're all beggars now, aren't we? Evelyn had enjoyed the informality, but Osborne had been outraged, and had spent the entire journey home commenting on the Middletons' lapsed standards.

Now she ran an anxious finger along the dark, polished surfaces, checking for dust. Her fingertip came up grey, even though the room had been turned out two days previously. Swanton Lacy had always been a dusty house: when the sun shone, you could see the motes in the beams of light. Not that the sun ever reached this room. As Evelyn wiped a duster over the table top, she shivered: with cold, and with the vague feeling of dread that still, even after twenty-three years of marriage, preceded a dinner party.

Ridiculous, she muttered, giving herself a brisk shake. When you thought what other women had to put up with. When you thought of concentration camps and atom bombs and all the dreadful indiscriminate paraphernalia of warfare. When you thought, even, of what some of the village women had to endure. Shabby little houses and husbands who drank or were in and out of prison. And then there was that poor woman in Swanton St Michael who last summer had lost her child to polio . . .

At least she had a child, said the small, angry voice at the back of Evelyn's head, the voice that, as she became older, seemed to grow louder rather than softer. At least she was a mother. And wasn't it supposed to be better to have loved and lost?

'You don't know what you're talking about,' said Evelyn out loud. She gave a last, spiteful swipe with the duster and left the room.

*

Celia was late; waiting in Debenham & Freebody's restaurant, Evelyn checked her watch. Celia Buckingham was Evelyn's oldest friend; they had met at school. Catching sight of her friend in the entrance to the restaurant, Evelyn stood up and waved. Celia was wearing a crimson outfit which suited her dark colouring. Evelyn never wore red: it drained her.

'Darling.' Celia embraced her. 'Am I frightfully late?' She looked flustered. 'So sorry to keep you waiting.' She sat down, pulling off her gloves. 'Have you ordered?'

'Not yet.'

'It's all been a bit—' Celia broke off.

Evelyn looked closely at her. 'Are you all right?'

Celia delved in her handbag and drew out reading glasses and cigarettes. 'I'm fine. Perfectly fine.' Then her features seemed to crumple and she drew a long, shuddering breath and put her hands over her face.

Appalled, Evelyn whispered, 'Oh, *Cee*,' and patted Celia's shaking shoulders.

Celia muttered, 'Sorry. Sorry, Evie.' She sniffed loudly and bit her lip. Then she opened her red-rimmed eyes. 'So silly.'

'Not at all. Here.' Evelyn passed Celia a handkerchief.

Celia mopped her face and blew her nose. 'I must look a fright.' She took out her compact and peered, dabbing at her lipstick with a corner of the handkerchief.

Evelyn lit two cigarettes and handed one to Celia. She said gently, 'Is it Sarah?' Sarah was the youngest and most delicate of Celia's four children.

Celia shook her head. 'Sarah's very well. All the children are well.'

'Henry?'

'Henry's well, too.' Evelyn noticed Celia hesitate. Then she said quietly, 'It's me, actually.'

'You're ill?' Evelyn's mind ran quickly, anxiously, through all the ailments middle-aged women are prone to.

But Celia shook her head again. 'It's not that.' She looked away from Evelyn. 'I've been seeing someone.'

The waitress arrived to take their order. Staring blankly at the menu, Evelyn managed to order oxtail soup and plaice. When they were alone again, she repeated, 'Seeing someone?'

'He's called Gerald and I've known him for years and – well, it just *happened*.' In Celia's eyes there was now a mixture of shame and defiance, and something else that Evelyn took a moment or two to recognize: happiness.

'*Oh*,' said Evelyn. There was a silence. Then she said, 'Does Henry know?'

'No. Thank goodness. Though sometimes I think—'

'What?'

'That it might be better if he did. If he found out. Then it would all be out in the open.'

'Celia—'

'I suppose you think I'm rather awful.' There was an aggressive edge to Celia's voice.

'No.' Though she was aware of a slight distaste. 'No,' she repeated more firmly. 'You mustn't think that, Cee. It's just a bit of a shock.'

Celia gave a watery smile. 'It wasn't what you were expecting, was it? Rather a change from our usual chatter about children and servants and gardens.'

Evelyn felt a surge of anger at Celia's diminution of the staples of her life. She said, slightly too loudly, 'I know I can't contribute much when we talk about children, but I do try not to be *dull*.'

Celia looked startled. 'I'm sorry. I didn't mean—' She squeezed Evelyn's hand. 'Tactless of me. Forgive me, darling, please.'

Evelyn immediately felt ashamed of herself. Poor Celia was in this awful pickle and all she could do was to harp on about the same old griefs. And over the years Celia had been so kind, so sympathetic about the babies.

Celia was still talking. 'I do so look forward to our lunches. And I had to tell someone. I can't talk to anyone at home, of course, because they all know Henry and Gerald. But perhaps I'm assuming ... perhaps ...' She looked troubled.

Evelyn forced a smile. 'I'm a bit tired today, that's all. I don't mean to be touchy.' She looked at Celia. 'When you say you've been seeing Gerald, what do you mean, exactly?'

'I mean,' said Celia, 'that I am in love with him.' She smiled. 'If you met him, you'd understand. You'd adore him, Evie, I know you would. He's so kind. Such a good listener. He always tells me I look nice. Henry never does, you know.'

'Nor does Osborne.'

'No. Well, that's what you expect, isn't it, after all these years of marriage? But Gerald's such a dear. I'd love you to meet him. That awful time Sarah had croup and had to be rushed to hospital, it was Gerald who drove us. Henry was at the House, you see. Gerald waited at the hospital with me for hours. And when Gerald and Laura used to come to supper, he'd always open the door for me, and he'd carry the heavy things through to the kitchen – that was when our little chats started. Whereas Henry just *sits*.'

'Gerald's married, then?'

Celia looked miserable. 'Yes.' She stabbed at the ashtray with her cigarette. 'She's such a bitch.'

'*Cee.*'

'She is. So sharp. So unappreciative. I've felt sorry for Gerald for ages. I could see that he was unhappy. I always tried to cheer him up – just little things – I'd make sure he had the best malt whisky, and when *she* made remarks about him putting on weight – he's not overweight at all, Evie, he's just right – then I'd offer him the last portion of pudding. And he's such fun to talk to. Henry and I don't talk any more – I mean, not really *talk*, not properly. And then some things went wrong in the house – electrical things – and I had trouble with the car – and Henry was away, so I gave Gerald a ring.' Celia paused. Then she said quietly, 'And I realized – eventually I realized that I was in love with him.'

The waitress arrived with the soup. When she had gone, Evelyn asked, 'What will you do?'

'Do?' Celia's spoon paused, halfway to her mouth.

'Do you mean to leave Henry?'

'I don't know.' Celia tore her bread roll in half. 'I really don't know.'

'I mean ... *divorce* ...'

71

'Quite,' said Celia crisply. 'Rather a lot of my friends might never speak to me again. Mummy certainly wouldn't.' She frowned. 'I wouldn't care about that. But I do care about the children. How could I do that to the children? How could I put them through that?'

'Have you—' It was a delicate question and best, perhaps, left unasked, but she persisted. 'Have you and Gerald—'

'Oh yes,' said Celia proudly. Her eyes shone; her plain face looked beautiful, transformed by happiness. 'Oh yes, we are lovers.' She paused. Then she said quietly, 'I haven't loved Henry for ages. I was very young when we married – I don't think I knew what love was. But that doesn't mean that he deserves this. I may not love him, but he is a good provider and a good father.' Celia placed her spoon in the soup bowl. 'If I stay with Henry,' she said slowly, 'then I will long for Gerald for the rest of my life. If I leave Henry, then I'll hurt my children dreadfully. What should I do, Evie? What should I do?'

Travelling home on the train that evening, Evelyn had plenty to think about. That Celia was even considering divorce was a huge shock to her. There was something distasteful and sordid about the very word. You thought of private detectives and seedy hotels in Brighton. It was terrible to imagine Celia mixed up in that. Terrible to imagine what divorce would do to her reputation and her social standing. For her friend's sake, Evelyn hoped that Celia would see sense and hold back from the brink.

But mixed in with Evelyn's fears for Celia and her sympathy for her predicament were a few less respectable emotions. Over pudding, Celia had admitted that she and Gerald had been lovers for eight months. *Eight months*. During that time, they had lunched together on several occasions and Celia hadn't said a thing. Such a huge secret to keep from her best friend. Now, when Evelyn thought back, she remembered the small changes in Celia. The extra attention to clothes and hair and make-up. The renewed vivacity.

Though she tried to brush off her hurt and loneliness by berating herself for her selfishness, the feelings persisted. It seemed to Evelyn that she had foolishly underestimated the significance of the two and a half decades that had passed since she and Celia had left school. She had underestimated also the differences in their lives. They were neither of them the same people they had once been. Marriage had changed them, the war had changed them, children – or the lack of them in Evelyn's case – had changed them, leaving them without much in common. Their friendship was based on little more than sentiment and nostalgia. She had become of limited importance to Celia, occupying no more than a small niche in her life.

It took Evelyn longer to acknowledge that she also envied Celia, envied her transparent happiness and the intensity of her emotions. She had always tried hard to keep at bay any feelings of bitterness that Celia had managed with such ease to produce the perfect family of two sons and two daughters. Most of the time she had succeeded, knowing that these things are random, the luck of the draw. Now, sitting in the railway carriage, watching the countryside rush by, she was aware of a pang of jealousy. Doors were not closing for Celia; something new and exciting – if very troublesome – had entered her life. Celia not only had four children, she also had a lover. So many people to love, to be loved by.

As for herself ... Celia's words rang in her ears. *I haven't loved Henry for ages. I'm not sure that I ever did.* Did she love Osborne, wondered Evelyn. She had been nineteen when they had met and twenty when they married – had she loved him then? She had been flattered by his attention, certainly – Osborne Daubeny had been fourteen years older than her and his family far more venerable than her own – but had she loved him? She could not now remember. She had certainly never experienced the physical desire that now so transformed Celia. She went to bed with Osborne because it was her duty to do so and because she wanted children. But she had never particularly enjoyed it. She found it hard to see why anyone would.

Evelyn's parents had lived in India. When she was seven years old Evelyn and her mother had sailed to England. Six months later, Mrs Seymour had returned to India, leaving Evelyn to divide her childhood between boarding school and the home of an uncle and aunt in Suffolk. Years later, after a short Season in London, Evelyn had married Osborne Daubeny because, as young and naive as she had then been, she had known that he could give her the things she longed for: a home of her own, the security that money and background and breeding could provide, and, most of all, a family.

Yet the longed-for family had never materialized.

Her first pregnancy had miscarried at six months. The staff at the nursing home had not let her see her tiny, premature son: it was her fiercest regret that she had been far too ill to insist. At least then she would have had a memory. Another four miscarriages had followed, the last during the war. Four boys and a girl: in private, unvoiced ceremonies she had chosen names for each of her lost babies. Sometimes she dreamed of them, especially her first child, Stephen, whom she had carried longest in her unwelcoming womb.

In the eight years since the war had ended, Evelyn had become aware of a persistent sense of disappointment, of life not coming up to scratch. Doors had closed rather than opened. Her father had died, and there had been no more pregnancies. Their wartime difficulties with Swanton Lacy – the lack of servants, and the absence of money or materials to redecorate and refurbish – remained, worsening if anything. During the war, Osborne had been forced to sell land and property to pay the astronomical taxes demanded by the government; a few years ago, needing capital once more, another tenant farm and a string of cottages had gone the same way. The old stable block, badly damaged during the war, had not yet been rebuilt; as for the garden – so lovely when Evelyn had been a bride – it remained, in spite of their efforts, derelict.

And it seemed to her that recently her nerves had grown worse rather than better. She had plucked up the courage a few months ago to speak to Dr Lockhart, but he had merely said something vague about her time of life and had prescribed a rather unpleasant-tasting tonic, which had done nothing to alleviate her feelings of apprehension and gloom, or the flashes of anger that she sometimes struggled to contain.

As for Osborne . . . Evelyn stared out of the carriage window, trying to remember her days of courtship. He had been a handsome man, certainly, tall and well made, with those arresting dark, bluish-grey eyes. Osborne Daubeny's self-confidence and strength had, she recalled, made her feel protected and safe at a time in her life when she had often felt uncertain. Yet at some point over the years his unshakeable sense of his own infallibility had begun to grate. She had never once, she realized, succeeded in changing his mind. Indeed, he had fallen into the habit of telling her what she thought and what she felt, so that it seemed to her that even her opinions and tastes were not now her own, but her husband's.

Did she love Osborne? If someone irritated you, sometimes almost beyond endurance, could you still love them? 'Oh, for heaven's sake,' said Evelyn out loud, and the half-dozen businessmen in the carriage stared at her, and she had to hide her embarrassment by searching in her handbag for her powder compact. Of course she loved Osborne. She was his wife, wasn't she?

Yet she found herself thinking, as she had thought a thousand times before: if only she had been able to carry just one of the babies to term. Just one.

Romy borrowed a skirt from Lindy Saunders to wear for the party at Liam Pike's house. The skirt was black and close-fitting at the waist, flaring out from the hips to halfway down the calves. When Romy walked, the shiny cloth rustled and moved. She bought a pair of nylon stockings from a stall at Romsey market, and at a jumble sale in Stratton found a black, knitted top to go with the skirt. The top was a bit tight, but it would do. She spent an uncomfortable night with curlers in her hair and did her make-up carefully. When Liam Pike picked her up at eight o'clock, she noticed how his eyes widened when she opened the front door to him.

The Pikes lived two miles from Stratton in a large detached house surrounded by trees. As Liam drove through the front gates, Romy saw that dozens of cars were parked on the gravel drive. Indoors, Liam introduced her to his parents. Mrs Pike was wearing a calf-length royal blue satin frock and long matching gloves, and her hair was arranged in rigid curls. Though Mrs Pike smiled graciously at Romy, her eyes were measuring and disdainful. Romy was offered a cocktail from a tray; she seized it and gulped it down, hoping it would steady her nerves. After a few moments she realized that neither Liam nor his parents had touched their drinks, and that they were raising their glasses in a toast. 'To you, Mummy,' said Liam. 'Happy birthday.' The glasses clinked. Mrs Pike's disapproving glare intensified. Romy's face burned.

Mrs Pike asked Liam to fetch more ice. Romy was left on her own. No one spoke to her, and just the thought of butting into one of the self-assured little groups of guests made her stomach churn. Instead she wandered round the room. She noticed that she was the only woman wearing a skirt and jumper. All the other female guests wore long evening gowns and gloves that went up to their elbows.

But the *house*! Though she had expected to envy the house, it was awful – messy and untidy. No wonder her mother had given in her notice. You'd hardly know where to begin, cleaning this house. The sofas and chairs looked even older and shabbier than those at 5 Hill View. The wallpaper had faded and had begun in places to peel away from the plaster. The threadbare rugs were carelessly slung over bare boards, and on every surface there were heaps of books and magazines and newspapers.

She tried to work it out. The Pikes must be rich – they had cars and a fridge – so they must have *chosen* to live like this. Looking more closely, Romy saw that the Pikes' clutter was different from the clutter at 5 Hill View. The Pikes' magazines were bigger and glossier than the Parrys' – *Vogue* and *Vanity Fair* instead of *Picturegoer*. And the Pikes must have owned hundreds, perhaps thousands, of books. Most of the Pikes' books were hardbacked, the faded olive-green, ochre and crimson covers tooled with gold. The only books in the Parrys' house were Romy's, bought from jumble sales or second-hand bookshops, and Martha's romances, gulped down in much the same way as Martha gulped down a port and lemon, to blot out the present. And though the Pikes' furniture was, like the books, old, the dark, reddish wood felt pleasingly smooth and warm to touch, and the faded patterns of the damasks captured and held the eye.

It seemed to Romy that there were layers and layers of possessions in the Pikes' house, kept and treasured over the years, handed down from generation to generation. The Parrys' belongings were sparser, uglier and newer, bought to fill a need, their selection determined by price rather than by taste. The Parrys' things never lasted and would not be treasured; they broke or frayed within weeks or months of purchase. As for the guests – looking round, she saw a pearl necklace here, an embroidered stole there, a pair of silk pumps peeping out from beneath a long skirt. These women did not have to beg or borrow or to buy second-hand clothes: they looked in their wardrobes and they chose. Romy wondered whether that was what being rich really meant, being able to choose.

There was a lane off the Stratton road; driving Romy home at the end of the evening, Liam swung the car into the track and parked beneath the tall beech trees.

It annoyed her that he didn't even ask, he just *assumed*, leaning across the handbrake and taking her in his arms. She could smell the alcohol on his breath as he kissed her. His tongue coaxed open her lips and his hand stroked her breast. Her resentment retreated and she felt a stirring of pleasure and closed her eyes. Rain spat on the windscreen and the sharp wind tapped the branches against the car's soft top.

When he put his hand up her skirt, exploring the bare flesh above her stocking tops, her eyes flew open and she pushed him away. She wasn't going to get caught like that, not she, not Romy Cole. Angela Harris, who had been in the same class as Romy at school, had already got a couple of kids. Martha had been only nineteen when she had given birth to Romy. Romy meant to do something different, something better.

'*Romy*,' complained Liam.

'No. I don't want to.'

'Course you do. You know you like it.'

His fingers pushed insistently between her legs. She pulled away, tugging her skirt down. '*No.*'

He scowled. 'I wouldn't have thought,' he muttered, 'that one of the Parrys would be so bloody choosy.'

She stared at him. 'What did you say?'

He shrugged and gazed sulkily out of the car window.

Romy's heart was pounding. 'You think – you think that because of who I am – where I come from – I should be *easy*?' Her voice shook with fury.

She flung open the car door and climbed out. Before she stalked away, she hissed at him, 'And I'm not a Parry. He's not my father. I'm a Cole. I'm Romy *Cole*.'

She ran most of the way home, gathering up the taffeta skirt to keep it dry, her high heels slipping on the muddy ground. Liam had labelled her, categorized her, judged her. She was one of the Parrys from the council houses, the notorious, chaotic, slapdash Parrys. Because you couldn't get much lower down the scale than the Parrys, she should be thankful for whatever she could get. She should be honoured to lose her virginity to someone like Liam Pike. Parrys dusted and polished for Pikes – why should they not also attend to other, darker, needs?

When she reached Hill View, she found Dennis standing at the kitchen stove, a box of matches in his hands. The hob was scattered with fragments of broken match, evidence of Dennis's unsuccessful attempts to light the burner. The room smelt of gas.

'Let me,' she said impatiently. 'You'll blow the house up.'

She coaxed the damp matches to light and persuaded the cantakerous burner to issue just the right amount of gas. Dennis stood beside her, breathing heavily.

'There.' She put the kettle on the hob.

'Make us a cup of tea, Romy, love,' he whined.

As she reached up to get the tea caddy out of the cupboard, she said sharply, 'What is it? Why are you staring at me?'

'You look nice tonight, Romy. Very grown up.'

Dennis had paid her a compliment. In all the years she had lived beneath Dennis Parry's roof, she could not recall him ever saying anything nice to her. She supposed she should feel pleased, but instead she felt uneasy.

She glared at the kettle, willing it to boil. He said, 'You been out tonight?'

'A party.'

'Meet anyone special?'

'Not really.' Spooning tea from the caddy into the pot, her hand shook, trailing ashy leaves over the table top.

'You need to look after yourself,' said Dennis. 'Pretty girl like you.'

The kettle had not quite boiled, but she made the tea and went upstairs. In the bedroom Carol's inert presence was, for once, comforting. Hunched beneath the bedclothes, Romy tried to think of Middlemere, tried to think of the track with the spindle berries, tried to think of the wood and the pool and the house, as it used to be, before the Heskeths had taken it.

Tried to think of anything but the expression in

Dennis Parry's eyes as she had come into the kitchen, the wet taffeta skirt bunched up in her hand, the too-tight jumper clinging damply to her breasts.

Though Romy tried to reassure herself over the next few days, niggling doubts remained. She thought fleetingly of talking to her mother, but dismissed the idea. The last thing she wanted was to provoke another row between Martha and Dennis. And, besides, what could she say? *Dennis looked at me in a funny way.* He had neither touched her nor hurt her. Instead he had, for the first time she could remember, been nice to her.

She found herself wondering whether what had happened – if anything had happened, if she had not just imagined that something had happened – had been her own fault. After all, earlier that same evening, there had been Liam Pike, hadn't there? Liam, who had expected her to give herself to him. Doubts haunted her – was this skirt too short, that top too tight? Did the small ladder in her stockings or the scuffs on her shoes made her look sluttish, negligent? Might a carelessness in her dress suggest to onlookers that she would be equally careless in other matters? Now her hand hesitated, wielding her lipstick, unsure whether it was too bright a red. Now when men called out to her from the pub on her way home from work, or when they whistled at her from cars and building sites, she did not smile or wave back, but hurried on, her gaze fixed on the pavement.

A postcard arrived from Jem. On the front were half a dozen small photographs. Romy studied them:

the Tower of London, Tower Bridge, the Thames, its turquoise surface scattered with barges and pleasure craft. On the back, in Jem's childish hand, was a north London address. She wrote each day to Jem, but received no reply. If only they had a telephone. If only Jem was more of a writer.

The days passed. Dennis was just the same as he always was, oafish and loud. Romy reminded herself that he was, after all, her stepfather, and that he was old and married to her mother, and that, anyway, he had always disliked her. He could not possibly have looked at her in that way. She had made a mistake.

She began to relax a little, to let her guard fall. She was in the back garden one evening, taking down the washing from the line. She hadn't realized that Dennis was in the garden shed, and then the door opened and he was standing beside her, mumbling something about not being able to find his blue shirt. 'It's in the basket,' she snapped. 'I just took it off the line.' He didn't look in the basket, but stood there, as stupid and useless as always, so she delved among the shirts and pillowcases herself. And felt his hand stroke her bottom. No mistake this time, no possible misinterpretation. Just that lingering, treacherous touch. She didn't do anything, say anything, that was what humiliated her most of all afterwards; she just froze, unable to believe what was happening. Behind the bead curtain that covered the back door she could see her mother, moving round the kitchen. From upstairs she could hear the sound of Carol and Ronnie arguing.

And then her mother opened the back door and yelled that it was dinnertime, and Dennis walked away.

Walked back into the house, leaving Romy alone in the garden in the twilight as if nothing had happened, the shirts bunched up in her arms, a cold, frightened feeling in the pit of her stomach and the world upside down once more.

Caleb had started work at a removals firm called Broadbent's, on the outskirts of Newbury. He shared a cramped office with five other young men. The office had its pecking order. Loman was cock of the walk, and Pickering — shambling, bespectacled, socially inept Pickering — was at the bottom. Loman was tall, good-looking, muscular. He was also idle and incompetent, and a bully. Caleb recognized the type: every boarding-school dormitory, every army barracks, had its Loman. The strutting walk, the need to flaunt power, the pleasure in pinpointing and torturing the vulnerable — Caleb had seen them all before. Loman had a sidekick, Cottle. Cottle was Loman's fatter, plainer, less charismatic shadow; Cottle, if he had not been Loman's creature, might have been his victim.

Instead, Loman's vindictiveness found an obvious target in Pickering. Pickering lacked all the qualities that might have allowed him to defend himself against Loman. Confronted by Loman's practical jokes and aggression, Pickering's voice would rise and his gangling limbs would flail as he clumsily attempted to stuff spilt rubbish back into his wastepaper basket, or to mop up the ink that Loman had tipped over his desk. Caleb's attempts at conversation with Pickering were met with monosyllabic replies and a nervous, evasive glance.

Though he would not, like Loman, have tormented him, Caleb found that Pickering's failure to stand up for himself needled him, and the grating whine of his voice had the capacity to irritate.

The other two clerks, Goddard and McAulay, were pleasant enough. Like Caleb, they occupied the middle ground, neither Loman's cronies nor his victims. They neither colluded with Loman nor stood up to him. Caleb struck up an easy-going, intermittent friendship with Goddard. Goddard, sandy-haired and rabbity, said to Caleb over a pint after work one day, 'Loman's a jerk, but he can be quite an amusing jerk. And Pickering's a boring little bastard.' Which just about summed it up, Caleb thought. Given the choice, you'd have a more entertaining evening in the pub with Loman than with Pickering.

All six clerks were supervised by Mr Strickland. Mr Strickland's supervision was, in fact, minimal. 'Serving his time,' Goddard explained. 'Counting off the days till he gets his gold watch.' Strickland was due to retire the following year. None too soon, Caleb suspected: Strickland's infrequent visits to his clerks necessitated the climbing of a steep flight of stairs. 'Oh God,' Goddard whispered to Caleb one day, witnessing Strickland's greyish pallor and wheezing lungs, 'the poor blighter mustn't peg out on us here, or Loman'll sell his body to medical research.'

It took Caleb a while to work out what Goddard meant, but then, leaving the office one evening, he noticed the bulkiness of Loman's jacket pockets and guessed that they were stuffed with pens, pads of paper, rubber bands and paper clips, anything that Loman could flog on to his acquaintances or down the pub. Again, he knew the type, light-fingered out of habit as much as greed, indulging in petty theft to buck the system and to demonstrate his own invulnerability.

He realized that Loman had his finger in other, larger pies when, returning one afternoon from the building in which they garaged the lorries, he heard someone hiss his name. Looking round, he saw Loman skulking in the narrow passageway in which they stacked the rubbish. Half-hidden by sheets of cardboard and shattered orange boxes, Loman beckoned to him. Like the bloody Third Man, thought Caleb, as he crossed the forecourt. When he was within earshot, Loman muttered, 'You read books, don't you?'

Caleb had a sudden, improbable vision of himself and Loman discussing Sartre, or Proust, perhaps. Loman delved into the pocket of his raincoat and brought out a book. It was a copy of *Our Mutual Friend*, a very old copy with a crimson leather binding.

Caleb glanced at the Roman numerals written on the flysheet, then looked up at Loman. 'Where did you get this?'

'That's my business.'

Which told Caleb everything he wanted to know. He handed the book back to Loman. 'No thanks. You keep it. I've never much liked Dickens. Too gloomy.'

Part of Caleb's job was to assess the cost of a removal and to draw up and issue an estimate. Mr Strickland was supposed to be training him, but devolved most of the work to Goddard and McAulay. Caleb accompanied McAulay when he inspected the houses. Leaving the office, with its constant, stale, internecine warfare, he felt free. Sometimes he and McAulay drove out to the countryside, to the pleasant hinterland beyond Newbury. Measuring and making lists, listening to the dour, meticulous McAulay discuss times and costs with customers, Caleb's attention would wander. He would look up from his pad of paper to the gardens beyond. Some of the houses had acres of garden. A few were well tended, but many were unimaginative, a waste of such space, such views. On duller afternoons he would distract himself from his boredom by imagining what he would do with some splendid garden if it were his. In the margins of his notebook, he scribbled plans: allées and courtyards and secret vistas.

One evening Caleb and Pickering were the last to leave the office. Caleb thought that Pickering was looking more than usually hangdog. On impulse he said, 'I'm meeting Goddard in the Bull. Why don't you join us?'

Pickering shook his head. 'Can't.'

'Just a pint or two, Pickering. It's only the Bull, not an opium den.'

'I've work to do, Hesketh. Mr Wicksteed wants these figures before I go.'

Caleb shrugged on his jacket. 'If you made more of an effort – joined in a bit more – you might not have such a rotten time.'

Pickering glared at him. 'I'm not here to enjoy myself. I'm here to work.'

Pompous ass, thought Caleb, but he said, 'I mean – Loman. He might not pick on you so much if you weren't so – so bloody conscientious.'

Yet even as he spoke, he knew that was not true.

Loman bullied Pickering because Pickering was a short-sighted, shambling assemblage of nervous twitches. Loman bullied Pickering because Pickering had been to grammar school, whereas Loman had only made the secondary mod. And for a dozen other unspoken, shadowy reasons.

'Have it your own way, then,' said Caleb.

As he turned to go, he heard Pickering mumble, 'Anyway, I have to get home because of my mother.'

'Your mother?'

Pickering had taken off his glasses and was polishing them with a grubby handkerchief. 'I have to make her supper. She's not well, you see.'

'I'm sorry.' Caleb went back into the room. He took out a packet of Woodbines and offered them to Pickering.

Pickering sniffed and took one. He said suddenly, jerkily, 'Mum's in a wheelchair.'

'What's wrong with her?'

'She's got a wasting disease.'

'Your father—'

'Haven't got one.' Pickering drew on the cigarette, then glanced sharply at Caleb. 'You won't tell him, will you?'

'Loman? Of course not.'

'Only he'd take the mickey.'

'I won't say anything. Loman probably hasn't got a mother, anyway. Cooked up in a laboratory, like Frankenstein's monster.' It was a feeble joke, but it seemed to cheer Pickering up, for he smiled.

*

Romy began to have the nightmare again. She hadn't had the nightmare for years. She was trapped in the darkness and all she could see was the small circle of light. Shapes shifted, colours changed within the circle. The dream had a sharp terror all of its own, making her wake, gasping for air, struggling to cry out.

Carol muttered sleepily, 'Shut up, Romy,' and she had to resist the urge to climb into the other bed, to take warmth and comfort from her stepsister's inert body. Now when she thought of her savings book, hidden beneath the mattress, she no longer felt pride, but only anger at her own stupidity. In more than two years she had saved less than forty pounds. Earlier in the week she had looked in the window of an estate agent and had seen that the smallest house cost hundreds of pounds. A house like Middlemere might cost thousands. It would be years before she was rich enough to buy a house. How foolish of her, she thought savagely, to believe that she might be able to look after Jem and her mother. She couldn't even protect herself. Just as, years ago, she had not been able to protect her father.

She had always been wary of Dennis, but she had never before been afraid of him. Not really afraid. She found it hard to explain even to herself why, when Dennis had touched her, it had frightened her so much more than the years of shouting and blows. It was as though he had crossed an invisible line, and in doing so had reached some hidden, vulnerable part of her. Though she tried to reason with herself, her fear persisted. At night every creak of the floorboards, every sound in the darkness, became Dennis's footsteps creeping down the corridor towards her. She imagined the door opening. What would he say if she were to cry out? *I thought I heard a sound. I was just making sure everything was all right.* Or would he clamp his meaty hand over her mouth and make sure she couldn't cry out?

And she missed Jem. He had never been absent from home for so long before. Not that she would ever tell Jem about Dennis. Romy shivered, imagining Jem's reaction were she to do so. She wondered how Jem was, what he was doing, whether he had found a job. She hoped he was happy and well. The address given on the postcard had been 18d Kingsbury Road, which Romy thought sounded rather grand. She imagined a tall building looking out over parks and roads and rivers. She imagined living there with him and feeling safe and unafraid.

Once more she thought of telling her mother about Dennis. Yet she shrank from the consequences. Martha would shout at Dennis, and Dennis would hit Martha. And Dennis was bigger and stronger than Martha, so Martha would get hurt and it would be all Romy's fault. Or Martha would leave Dennis, and then where would they go? They'd have to take the kids with them – Martha would insist on that – and who would want to take them in? It would be like the other time, when they'd had to leave Middlemere. Romy had lost count of the dreary lodging houses in which they had lived in the hard years between her mother's marriages.

There was no one she could talk to, no one in whom she could confide. Lindy Saunders, her best friend at work, came from a large, happy family. Monsters like Dennis were outside Lindy's sphere of imagination.

Romy had none of the things that Lindy took for granted: the good-humoured hugs and kisses, the approval and love that were part of normal family life. Their absence seemed to Romy to indicate a failing in her.

She thought she had become used to having secrets – after all, she could never have told the girl who sat next to her at school or in the typing pool that her father had shot himself. Though she knew that some secrets gave you power, it seemed to her that those she kept only diminished her. They kept her apart from other people and they gnawed at her self-assurance. She had always tried to forget her past, shoving it to the back of her mind, enclosing it, perhaps, in the small dark cupboard of her nightmares. Now her secrets were beginning to seep out into her daily life, tarnishing it.

Sleeping badly, her exhaustion persisted throughout the day. At work her concentration slipped. She, who never made mistakes, forgot her shorthand and sent out misspelt letters. She dozed off over the typewriter one warm afternoon, and Miss Farley, who oversaw the typing pool, complained about her laziness, her lapsed standards. She forgot to send out an important letter and Mr Gilfoyle reprimanded her. Which added to her fears, making her afraid that she might lose her job, that she might sink further into poverty. Afraid that she might marry the first kind, uncomplicated man who asked her, just to get away from home. Then the babies would come and she would be trapped in Stratton for ever.

One evening she stayed late at work to catch up on unfinished tasks. Travelling home by bus, she had to force herself to stay awake and not fall asleep and miss her stop. When she got home, her mother was in the living room, peering into the mirror on the mantelpiece, putting on her lipstick. The kids were in bed, Martha explained; she was just going to pop over to Mrs Belbin's for an hour or so. Dennis had gone to the pub and wouldn't be back till late. Romy's supper was in the oven.

After her mother had gone out, Romy kicked off her shoes and curled up on the couch, still wearing her coat. The coal fire was lit, making the room pleasantly warm. Her eyelids felt heavy; she drifted off to sleep.

When she awoke, she knew that she was not alone. He must have made a sound and, besides, she could smell his tobacco and the acrid scent of the cement powder that always clung to his overalls. She opened her eyes.

Dennis was standing beside the couch; his shadow fell over her. When she tried to stand up, he said, 'Where're you going? Don't have to go, Romy.'

'I'm tired.' She knew by his unfocused eyes and clumsy movements that he was drunk. 'I'm going to bed.'

'It's only –' he frowned at the clock on the mantelpiece – 'only nine o'clock. What's a big girl like you going to bed at nine o'clock for?'

'I told you.' She tried to keep the fear out of her voice. 'I'm tired. And Mum'll be back soon.'

'Last time I saw her, she was in the pub with Pat Belbin. She won't be home for a while.' Dennis belched and scratched his belly. 'Aren't I company for you, Romy?'

'I have to get my supper—' She tried to stand up again, but he gripped her shoulder.

'I said, aren't I company enough for you, Romy?'

'Let me go!' she hissed. 'Leave me alone!'

He slapped her hard across the face. She fell back onto the couch. Dazed with shock, she could not stop the tears brimming in her eyes.

'That'll teach you.' There was pleasure and self-satisfaction in his voice. 'Always were a cheeky little bleeder, weren't you? Martha's been too soft with you. Well, you'll do what you're told now, or you'll feel the back of my hand again.'

'I just want to get my supper,' she pleaded. 'Please, Dennis.'

'That's better.' His stubby fingers, reddish with brick dust, kneaded her cheek, then her neck, yet he was looking at her as though he hated her. 'You speak to me nicely, Romy. Always been above yourself, haven't you? Always thought you were better than the rest of us.'

'I didn't mean to annoy you,' she whispered.

He continued to stare at her, dislike now supplemented by something else: greed and a kind of hunger. She tugged her skirt down over her knees and hunched her coat around her shoulders, trying to make herself shapeless, ugly.

'Better make it up to me, then,' he muttered. He crouched over her, bunching up her skirt and pawing at her thigh. His stubbly chin and wet mouth brushed against her face. She could smell his beery breath.

She brought the high heel of her shoe down his shin as hard as she could. In the seconds that he cried out and his grip relaxed, she ran out of the room and out of the house. She could hear him running after her, his heavy boots on the concrete path, bawling curses as she fled Hill View.

She ran past the yew trees, past the rectory. She had a stitch in her chest and her breath was coming in sobs. She thought she could still hear his footsteps, but when she looked back, the road was empty, and she realized that the pounding in her ears was the thudding beat of her own heart. As she reached the churchyard, the goats tethered by the wall looked up, opening their yellow eyes. Threading through the lychgate and between the gravestones, she did not stop until she had reached the sanctuary of the porch.

She waited for a long time, shivering in the darkness, staring out into the inky graveyard. She put up her fingers to her face, testing her bruised cheekbone. She did not at first sit down, but remained standing, hidden behind the entrance, her body tensed, ready to run again. After a while, she thought to search through her coat pockets. She had her purse, thank God, and a tube of Spangles. She ate one of the Spangles, her cold, clumsy fingers scrabbling at the wrapping paper, trying not to make a sound. He might be out there, hiding behind the wall or under the yew tree.

Eventually the church bells chimed ten o'clock, then quarter past, then the half-hour. Her shivering became less violent, the product of cold rather than fear, and she sank down onto the stone bench inside the porch. Outside, clouds hid the moon and stars. She remembered sitting in the graveyard with Jem. Maria Cartwright, spinster of this parish, had sheltered them. She had given

Jem a ten-shilling note; he had given her a pink rabbit.

Jem, she thought. She remembered the postcard, with its picture of Tower Bridge. She knew the address Jem had given by heart. She had always had a good memory. She scrubbed her eyes with her coat sleeve and ran her fingers through her tangled hair. Then, taking a deep breath, she left the porch.

It seemed to her that her feet crunched too loudly on the gravel path and that the anxious sound of her breathing could be heard for miles around. Every movement, every whisper of branch or beat of a bird's wing made her start. The lychgate creaked as she left the graveyard. As she half-ran along the verge, taking the road that led out of Stratton, grasses and brambles snagged her stockings and puddles splashed her legs. There were no streetlamps and several times she stumbled on the uneven ground. At last she heard the rumble of traffic and saw the lights of the main road ahead of her.

Stratton lay behind her, hidden by the curve of the hill. I shall never live here again, she promised herself. I shall have something different, something better.

Chapter Four

A man who sold vacuum cleaners gave Romy a lift as far as Basingstoke. Dropped in the town sometime after midnight, she slept for a while on a park bench and then, when the first rays of dawn had begun to show, she walked past curtained houses towards the London road. Milk carts clanked through the streets and paperboys cycled along the pavements, heavy bags balanced on the handlebars of their bicycles. Romy bought herself a cup of tea and a piece of toast in a small cafe crowded with factory workers – no more than that because she had only seven shillings and sixpence in her purse.

She stood on the verge beside the London road for more than an hour, her thumb outstretched, until a lorry driver picked her up. She shared her Spangles with him; he bought her a cup of tea and a bacon sandwich from a stall in a layby near Reading. He was a kind, fatherly man, who worried about her travelling to London on her own. She supposed that he had noticed that she had no luggage, noticed also the red stain on her face where Dennis had hit her. She tried to reassure him. Her brother lived in London; she was going to stay with him. The lorry driver had an *A-Z* in the cab; he looked up Kingsbury Road and wrote down directions for her on a scrap of paper. As he helped her out of the cab near an underground station, he pressed a ten-shilling note into her hand.

It was nine o'clock in the morning. She had only once travelled on the London Underground before, on the school trip, and then it had been in the company of thirty other girls. Now she stared at the map on the wall, but the coloured lines and dots made no sense to her. Standing in the foyer of the station, watching the passengers rush by, she struggled to quell her panic. Then she plucked up courage to ask the man at the ticket office for directions. Central line to Holborn, he said, not looking up from his booth, and then change to the Piccadilly for Finsbury Park. Gripping her ticket, she gave herself up to the hot, busy darkness, plunging on an escalator down towards the centre of the earth.

Men in pinstriped suits and bowler hats jostled her; everyone, she thought, dazed, seemed to be in such a hurry. In spite of the events of the previous night, in spite of her exhaustion and confusion, she began to feel excited. There was something heady about the noise and bustle; even the dusty smell of the Tube station seemed to promise adventure and opportunity.

She had to stand in the carriage, gripping the back of a seat, afraid each time the train jolted that she'd fall into another passenger's lap. She noticed how the besuited businessmen folded their newspapers up small to read them, not seeming to notice the crush. There were other girls on the train, girls much the same age as her, presumably bound for offices and shops. She studied their dresses and how they did their hair, just as she studied the map in the carriage with fierce and desperate concentration, afraid that she would miss her stop. Changing trains at Holborn, a warm wind blew through the dark tunnels; on the walls, posters exhorted her to visit sunny Broadstairs and buy Maclean's toothpaste.

Leaving the underground at Finsbury Park, the street smelt of exhaust fumes and wet pavement. It had begun to rain, a gentle drizzle that dampened her hair and sunk through the cheap fabric of her coat. She took from her pocket the directions that the lorry driver had written out for her. Cars hooted at her as she mistimed her dash across a busy road; she had to jump out of the way of a delivery boy's bicycle threading fast along the pavement. She looked up at the tall houses, so many of them, all crushed together.

Losing her way, she had to retrace her footsteps along Seven Sisters Road. She searched for street signs. Fonthill Road, Stroud Green Road, Woodstock Road. Mothers were pushing prams to the shops, and a very old lady shuffled slowly along the pavement, her gnarled little hands clutching half a dozen carrier bags. From an open window drifted the sound of a saxophone, exotic in the pale London air.

Romy turned a corner and there it was, Kingsbury Road. It wasn't quite as she had imagined it. It wasn't grand at all. The bomb site on one side of the road was grown over with weeds and saplings. Brown, papery stems of rosebay willowherb shivered among the ruins and the cratered earth glistened with puddles. The houses to the other side faced away from the sun, dampness trailing from the tall Georgian windows and marking the plaster like tear stains. In the front gardens blackened laurel bushes sprouted from a tangle of dust-bins and rusty pram wheels.

Romy climbed the steps of Number 18. Beside the front door was a row of labelled doorbells. The label for 18d read R. Hopkins. She wondered whether Jem had not got round to erasing the previous tenant's name or whether he was sharing the flat with a friend. She pressed the doorbell and waited, suddenly very relieved to think that she would soon see him again.

From inside, she heard footsteps. Bolts slipped, latches clicked. A blonde girl with curlers in her hair opened the door.

'Yes?'

'Is Jem in?' asked Romy.

'Jem?' repeated the girl.

'Jem Cole. He's my brother.'

'I don't know any Jem.' The girl made to shut the door, so Romy said quickly, 'He lives here. 18d Kingsbury Road.'

'I live in 18d.' The girl looked bored and irritated. 'Moved in a week ago.' She shrugged. 'Perhaps Jim—'

'Jem.'

'Jem, then. Perhaps he had the room before me.'

'But I need to find him—'

'Can't help you, love. You could have a word with Mrs Hennessy, if you like. She's the landlady.' She held open the front door and then headed off down a corridor; Romy followed her. Then the girl knocked on another door and shouted, 'Mrs Hennessy! Someone to see you!'

This door was opened by a small, hunched woman,

whose jet-black hair was swathed in a Paisley headscarf. Romy explained about Jem. 'He's gone,' said Mrs Hennessy, between puffs on a cigarette. 'Went more than a week ago.'

Romy's heart began to pound. '*Gone* . . . where?'

'Haven't a clue, duck.' Mrs Hennessy laughed. 'Didn't leave a forwarding address, did he? Did a midnight runner, the little blighter. If you find him, remind him that he owes me two weeks' rent.' The door slammed shut.

Back in the street, Romy began to walk in no particular direction. Her excitement had disappeared, replaced by fear. Jem had gone. Jem had left his lodgings without paying the rent. How, in this vast, populous city, would she find him? And if she could not find him what would she do?

She went back to the Tube station. Again she stared at the map, with its interweaving coloured lines. She saw that there was a station called Tower Hill. She remembered the pictures on the postcard: the bridge and the Tower of London. Perhaps the postcard was a clue; perhaps Jem was working near the Tower of London and he had bought the postcard after a day spent waiting on tables or washing glasses in a pub.

She took the train to Tower Hill. She could smell and hear the Thames before she saw it. The clouds had thinned and the water – which was not the blue of the postcard but greenish-brown – sparkled in the intermittent sunlight. Boats jostled on the river, sirens hooted and sailors called to each other in a flurry of different languages.

She must have walked miles that day. Back across

the bridge and around the Tower and up and down every one of the streets that branched off from it. Her optimism diminished as time passed. Though she enquired for Jem in countless pubs, shops and cafes, no one had heard of him. The sun went in and the rain returned, soaking through her thin mackintosh, chilling her. Her high-heeled shoes, bought for the office, pinched her feet, and her face hurt where Dennis had struck her. She had hardly slept for more than twenty-four hours.

In the late afternoon, weak with hunger and exhaustion, she went into a cafe and ordered egg and chips and tea. She devoured the lot, wiping up the egg yolk and chip fat with the last crust of bread. The cafe was warm and steamy from the kettles by the counter. She could have drifted off to sleep, but she forced herself to stay awake. She must think, she told herself, she must plan, but her tired brain darted around desperately, failing to come up with any solutions. She could not see how to find Jem: though her gaze was always fixed on the street outside, searching for him among the crowds who rushed along the pavement, he was never there. Now there was an ache in her heart, and a new fear. What if Jem's absences began to multiply, the days adding up to weeks, or months, or years? What if he went away and did not come back? What if, one day, he went so far away that she could not find him? In her mind's eye she saw him, buoyed up with the fragile, unfounded hope that was habitual to him.

She went to the lavatory at the back of the cafe and peered into the mirror. Her wet hair hung in dark rats' tails and her face was white apart from the red weal around her left eye. She had neither comb nor toothpaste nor lipstick. She pulled her hair over her face to hide the bruise and thought of her clothes in the wardrobe at Hill View and, worse, her savings book, hidden beneath the mattress, out of reach, unobtainable. She knew that she looked unkempt and desperate. Knew also that, looking as she did, no office would offer her employment, and no lodging house would give her a bed for the night on a promise of future payment.

People on their way home from work had begun to drop into the cafe for a cup of tea or something to eat. The small room was busy, every table occupied. She would not be able to spin out her stay much longer. Peering into her purse, she counted out her money. Eleven shillings and fourpence. Delving further, she caught sight of the white card tucked inside the fold of her purse meant for pound notes and drew it out. *Mrs Mirabel Plummer*, it said, in black, italic script. Underneath there was an address: *The Trelawney Hotel, 7 Parfitt Gardens, WC1*.

She got lost on the Tube, stumbling from one wrong line to another until eventually she backtracked and started again from scratch. Now she seemed incapable even of fear, her mood a mixture of exhaustion and a dogged determination. At Russell Square she asked directions to Parfitt Gardens of a newsboy, directions that she straight away forgot because she was so tired she seemed to have lost her capacity to remember things. Passers-by jostled her and she seemed to stand at the roadside for an age, waiting for a gap in the traffic.

At Parfitt Gardens the high facades of the elegant houses shut out the noise of the city. In the centre of the square were the gardens. Romy walked through tall trees and green, gloomy shrubs until she found a bench. Sitting down, closing her eyes, she breathed in the scent of roses, and let the song of a blackbird, perched high in a poplar tree, soothe her. It was as though she had been caught up in a storm and the wind had suddenly dropped.

She could have fallen asleep, curled up on the bench. It took a huge effort of will to get up and leave the garden and look for the Trelawney Hotel. Occupying much of one side of the square, it wasn't hard to find. Several townhouses had been joined together to make a larger building. Romy took a deep breath and crossed the road. When she showed Mrs Plummer's card to the doorman he peered at it suspiciously and said, 'I shall enquire whether Mrs Plummer is receiving visitors.' The door opened and closed, giving Romy a fleeting glimpse of the hotel's interior. She waited, shivering on the doorstep, feeding herself with a memory of bright lights and rich colours.

The doorman returned. She was shown into a reception hall with a black-and-white marble floor, crimson velvet curtains and glittering chandeliers. Guests in evening dress sat on the armchairs arranged around the perimeter of the room, or made their way down the wide, sweeping staircase. From an adjacent room she heard the music of a piano and the tinkle of glasses.

At the end of the corridor Romy was shown into a room. 'The young lady to see you, Mrs Plummer,' said the doorman.

Crimson and cream striped paper lined the walls of Mrs Plummer's sitting room, and there were more armchairs, more dark, heavy curtains. Mrs Plummer was wearing a dove-grey silk dress trimmed with black velvet. She peered over her half-moon spectacles at Romy and said, 'The solicitors' office. You are Mr Gilfoyle's secretary. And you have an unusual name, don't you? Romy. Yes, that's it. Romy.'

'Romy Cole. Yes, Mrs Plummer,' she said politely. 'I hope you don't mind me visiting you like this.'

'Not at all. Is this a social call, Romy?'

'Not exactly . . .' The words trailed away.

'Then tell me why you have come, dear.' Sharp dark eyes raked over Romy. 'Are you in some sort of difficulty?'

'I came to London to see my brother. But he's moved house and I don't know where he's gone.'

'I see.'

'And I don't have anywhere to stay. I don't know anyone else in London.'

Mrs Plummer frowned. Then she said, 'Sit down, Romy. Would you like some coffee? Or perhaps you'd prefer tea? I don't drink tea myself.'

'Coffee,' said Romy. And, remembering her manners, 'Please.'

Mrs Plummer picked up a telephone and ordered coffee. When it arrived, Mrs Plummer poured out two cups. The cup was made of a translucent china decorated with tiny blue flowers, and the coffee didn't taste at all like the Camp coffee they drank at Hill View.

'So you can't find your brother,' said Mrs Plummer slowly, 'and you have nowhere else to go . . . It seems to me that the best thing would be for you to go home.'

She muttered, 'I can't.'

'Why not?'

'I just can't, that's all.' She hadn't meant to sound rude, but it came out that way.

'Are you short of money?'

'Yes, but—'

'Then I shall lend you the money for the train fare. You can pay me back when you're able.'

Mrs Plummer went to her handbag and took out her purse. She selected two pound notes and held them out to Romy.

Romy shook her head. 'I can't go home. I really can't.' To her horror, tears welled at the corners of her eyes.

Mrs Plummer said sharply, 'Young girls often think the streets of London are paved with gold, but they're not. The city isn't an easy place for a girl to survive on her own. You'd be much better off at home with your family, believe me.' Then she paused, studying Romy more closely. 'Or is there something you're not telling me? Your face. What happened to your face?'

She could not speak. She did not know why she should feel ashamed of what Dennis had tried to do to her, but she did.

Mrs Plummer said briskly but kindly, 'You can tell me, dear. I've seen it all before. There's nothing I haven't seen. Did someone hit you? Yes? Who? Your boyfriend?'

She shook her head and mumbled, 'Haven't got a boyfriend.'

'Very wise. Men are nothing but trouble.'

Romy scrubbed her eyes with the back of her sleeve. Mrs Plummer passed her a handkerchief. 'Your family, then? Did someone in your family hurt you?'

She bit her lip hard. Mrs Plummer said softly, 'My father used to whip me. He thought that it was good for my soul. That was why I left home. There, I've never told anyone else that. How strange that I should tell you. But we could do with another chambermaid for the next week or two. One of the girls is off sick. Could you do that, Romy? Would you make beds and scrub floors in return for a roof over your head?'

Her head jerked up. She stared at Mrs Plummer. 'Oh *yes. Please.*'

'You'll be paid a pound a week. Meals and board all in. Temporary, of course,' added Mrs Plummer. 'Just until your brother turns up.'

That night she slept in a bedroom in the hotel's attic. The room was sparsely furnished but comfortable. There were two narrow iron beds, the second one belonging to Sally, the chambermaid who was off sick. The sloping window looked out onto surrounding roofs, which gleamed in the moonlight like an expanse of grey slate waves. Chimneys rose from the roofs like rocks piercing a stormy sea, and pigeons clustered on the chimney pots.

Standing at the window, Romy thought: I shall not think about Dennis again. I shall forget him. More memories to be enclosed in the cupboard at the back of her mind, where she put all bad things, and the door firmly shut. She was beginning a new life, in a new place, with a new job. The past would not touch her. She was Romy Cole and she was going to start again with something different, something better.

In the morning Evelyn woke with a buoyant optimism that gave her the courage to face Mrs Vellacott. After she had walked the dogs and breakfasted, she went to the kitchen. The room was cloudy with cigarette smoke and the sink and table were heaped with dirty dishes. Evelyn gave a little cough and Mrs Vellacott looked up from her newspaper.

'Have you remembered that we have guests tonight, Mrs Vellacott?'

Mrs Vellacott shuffled unwillingly to her feet. She was the most extraordinary shape, thought Evelyn. Her vast bulk protruded from her waist from all sides, as if she were wearing a crinoline.

'Yes, Mrs Daubeny.'

'There will be eight of us. I wanted to discuss the menu with you.' Evelyn gave an encouraging smile. 'The butcher has already delivered the beef, hasn't he, and the mushrooms for the soup will be sent over in the morning. And I think we shall have fruit flan and cream rather than apple fritters – a little less heavy, don't you agree?'

'Yes, Mrs Daubeny.'

Evelyn's gaze was drawn with unwilling fascination to the wart above Mrs Vellacott's eyelid. Looking away, she tried to frame her next question with tact.

'I wondered what cooking method you intend to use for the beef, Mrs Vellacott?' Mrs Vellacott looked uncomprehending, so Evelyn prompted helpfully, 'Do you follow *Mrs Beeton*, perhaps, or one of the French chefs . . .?'

'I just puts it in the oven, Mrs Daubeny.'

Which is why it tastes like shoe leather, thought Evelyn. She had brought *Mrs Beeton* with her; she placed the book on the table. 'I thought perhaps you might find this helpful.'

'Beef is beef. I don't hold with fancy cooking.'

Evelyn recognized scorn in Mrs Vellacott's voice. 'Nevertheless, I should like you to try it.' She glanced around the kitchen, at the unwashed saucepans and dirty floor, and said generously, 'Shall I ask Mrs Arnold to give you a hand this morning? You seem a bit swamped.'

Mrs Vellacott didn't even thank her, but just stood there, glaring at her, plainly longing for her to go. Which galled Evelyn because it made her feel as though Mrs Vellacott was doing her a favour instead of the other way round, which was just ridiculous.

So she found herself saying with uncharacteristic firmness, 'And I would prefer if you didn't smoke in the kitchen, Mrs Vellacott. It is unhygienic.'

As she walked away, Evelyn acknowledged that it was obvious – had been obvious for weeks – that Mrs Vellacott would have to go. She had put off the moment of dismissing her, dreading it. Which was so feeble of her. Osborne wouldn't have hesitated; neither would Celia. She could have asked Osborne to do the task for her, of course, but she shrank from that also. She was forty-two, for heaven's sake. Old enough to deal with her own servants.

Yet still young enough to have a child. Even Mrs Vellacott's barely disguised contempt had not been able to crush Evelyn's happiness. Her period was three days late: she hadn't been that late for ages. She had never been five days late without being pregnant. So only two days more and she would be almost certain. Plenty of women had babies late in life. A friend of Evelyn's called Brenda Lamb, who had come out in the same year, had had a daughter only six months ago. The wife of one of Osborne's tenant farmers had recently given birth to twins at the age of forty-four. Evelyn herself was her parents' only child, born when her mother was thirty-seven – five years earlier, admittedly, but that wasn't the point, was it? The point was that Mummy had had her late in life. Perhaps it ran in the family, having late babies. Perhaps this time – if it was a this time, and Evelyn's anxious fingers quickly touched wood – perhaps this time she would keep the baby, carry it to term.

Yet she knew that she must not allow herself to hope too much. Hope had been rewarded so many times only with disappointment that she was superstitiously afraid that the intensity of her longing might itself jeopardize any small beginnings of life in her womb. Yet, as she tidied and polished, she could not stop herself thinking: a baby, after all this time. A baby, after the despair of five miscarriages. She wouldn't care whether it was a boy or a girl. Wouldn't care whether it was dark like Osborne, or fair like her. Wouldn't care what she had to go through to give birth to a living child. If, at last, she were able to hold her son or daughter in her arms, she would forget her years of grief, her years of longing. Her feelings of frustration and her niggling sense of dread would disappear. Her life would have meaning and purpose.

That morning Evelyn vacuumed and dusted the drawing room and dining room, polished the silver and glassware, and counted the china. She saved the flowers, her favourite task, for after lunch, arranging sprays of flowering cherry and forsythia in the Japanese vases. Three couples were invited for the evening. Though she had known the Radcliffes and the Maxeys for many years, she had not previously met the Longvilles. She rarely met new people. Osborne did not see the need to extend their social circle; he was not, thought Evelyn, the kind of man who took to people.

By late afternoon Evelyn felt exhausted and her head ached, so she put on her coat and went outside. In the distance she could see Osborne standing beside the remains of the ruined bridge. The eighteenth-century arched bridge had once spanned the river as it entered the lake; photographs of a pre-war Swanton Lacy showed the exquisite fragility of the delicate stonework. In 1944 a drunken soldier had attempted to drive a jeep over the bridge and it had collapsed into the water. Time had not diminished Osborne's rage at that pointless act of vandalism.

After a brisk stride through the rose garden at the front of the house, Evelyn felt refreshed. She would check with Mrs Vellacott on the preparations for dinner, she decided, and then she would have her bath and get dressed.

She headed for the kitchen. There was a great hissing of steam and clanking of pans, and the hot-water geyser was making a frightful noise as usual, which was why, Evelyn supposed later, Mrs Vellacott did not hear her footsteps. The kitchen door was ajar, which allowed Evelyn, standing frozen in the passage-way, to witness the glee on Mrs Vellacott's face as she tapped the ash from her cigarette into the mushroom soup.

She didn't really look properly at the Longvilles until they were all sitting down at the table. Introduced to Hugo and Morwenna Longville over pre-dinner sherry, Evelyn was far too rattled and upset to form any opinion whatsoever of her guests. Half an hour later, picking at the first course (tinned grapefruit: too awful, but the thought of mushroom soup made her shudder) she was at last able to begin to form an impression.

Mrs Longville had the kind of looks Evelyn herself might have liked, given the choice: thin and graceful, with hooded green eyes and finely drawn features and dark hair that was just beginning to turn grey. Hugo Longville was both handsome and pleasant; he had kept the conversation going at the tricky start of the evening, when Osborne had been preoccupied with explaining his latest plans for the garden with Richard Maxey, and Evelyn herself had been too distracted to talk sensibly.

They had almost finished the first course when Osborne asked, 'Do you hunt, Longville?'

'Used to. Haven't ridden for a couple of years, though.'

'Good hunting country round here.'

'I think I'll stick to motor cars. More predictable.'

'Not the way you drive, Hugo,' teased Morwenna Longville.

Richard Maxey said, 'Bit of a road hog, eh?'

'I like to get the most out of a car,' said Hugo. 'I've never seen the point in pottering along at thirty miles an hour. Where's the fun in that?'

'Evelyn would disagree with you,' said Osborne. 'Evelyn likes to potter.'

Hugo Longville turned to Evelyn. She noticed that he had blue eyes, a proper blue, neither Osborne's dark, smoky grey nor the absence of colour that people so often called blue. She found herself explaining, 'The lanes around here are so narrow – so many twists and turns – and if one comes across a tractor—' Beneath that azure gaze, the phrases tripped and wilted.

'Evelyn will drive an extra mile to avoid a busy right turn,' said Osborne. 'She's never been at home behind a wheel.'

'I'm not much of a driver,' Evelyn admitted apologetically. She glanced around the table. 'Has everyone finished?'

She gathered up the bowls and carried the tray into the kitchen. There she leaned against the table, closing her eyes, and thought, hours to go, hours before she could curl up in bed and find solace in sleep.

She gave herself a little shake and opened the oven door. The potatoes were burnt, the spring greens yellow with overcooking. And there was the awful thought, that she really must keep at bay, that Mrs Vellacott might have done something to the other dishes: spat in the gravy or put mouse droppings in the fruit flan, perhaps.

112

Evelyn's stomach heaved and her head pounded. She searched through the dresser for aspirins and took three. Then Anne Radcliffe came into the kitchen, asking, 'Anything I can do, Evelyn?' so she made an effort to pull herself together.

By the time they had carried everything through and Osborne was carving the beef, the conversation had moved on to the subject of children. Josephine Maxey was describing the arrangements for her elder son's wedding.

'Paul's fiancée wants to have seven bridesmaids. I mean, *really*. I had two. I can't help feeling that there is something rather vulgar about seven. Only royalty need have seven.'

Evelyn asked, 'Do you have any children, Morwenna?'

'Two daughters.' Morwenna smiled.

'How old are they?'

'Jennifer is seventeen and Delphine is twelve.'

'Such lovely names . . . Are they family names?'

'Morwenna chooses the names,' said Hugo. 'Not my department.'

James Radcliffe said, 'Our three are utter horrors. I'm always so relieved when they go back to school.'

'Of course,' said Osborne with a smile, 'our brief experience of having children in the house was rather salutary.'

Evelyn felt a stab of annoyance. Osborne was going to tell the Longvilles about the evacuees. The Maxeys and the Radcliffes knew the story, it was one of Osborne's favourites.

She said, 'Any more potatoes, anyone?' but he was

not to be deflected. She heard the familiar phrases. *It was at the beginning of the war . . . The evacuees were all lined up in the village hall . . . had to pick 'em out . . . sorry specimens from the East End of London . . . most of them didn't look as if they knew what a bar of soap is for . . .* So familiar was his story to her that she could have told it word for word. Of course, if she had told it in her own words, it would have sounded rather different.

He was reaching the climax of his anecdote. 'Evelyn,' he said, 'chose the two ugliest and grubbiest little boys.'

'Should have picked a girl, like me, Evelyn,' said Josephine. 'Much less trouble. Gloria still sends me a Christmas card.'

Evelyn heard herself gabble, 'They looked so lost . . . they were showing off, behaving badly, but I knew that *underneath* . . . and no one else wanted them.' She found herself longing desperately for someone to understand.

'Evelyn thought she could smarten the pair of them up a bit,' said Osborne, and she thought, as she cut up her beef and vegetables and moved them aimlessly around the plate, that wasn't it, that wasn't it *at all*.

'They had head lice and scabies and every vile habit you can imagine. Ran back to London after a fortnight with a sackful of stuff from the house.' Osborne delivered the story's customary coup de grâce. 'I always say that Evelyn's tender heart cost me Swanton Lacy's Jacobean ladle.'

She couldn't seem to eat a thing. Nerves, she supposed. Though it tasted more like fury. She stared down at her plate, her fingers clenched.

'Anne's just the same,' said James Radcliffe. 'We still keep the children's nanny, even though Biddy's eleven now. She was Anne's nanny too, and she can't bear to let the old girl go, can you, darling?'

'Our servants are either cripples or criminals,' said Osborne. 'What was the last cook called, Evelyn?'

She murmured, 'Mrs Vellacott.'

'Looked like a witch. Had warts.'

'*Osborne*—'

'It's true, Josephine. I expected her to fly away on her broomstick at night.'

Anne Radcliffe gave a little giggle. 'It's so impossible to get good servants nowadays, isn't it?'

'It was obvious from the moment we engaged her that she wasn't the right type. Anyway, we had to get rid of her. At least she didn't turn us all into mice.'

'It wasn't funny,' said Evelyn. 'It wasn't funny at all. It was *awful*. She was mad.' Her voice shook. She realized that everyone was staring at her. She whispered, 'Excuse me,' and dashed out of the room, knowing that she was going to cry.

In the downstairs cloakroom she blew her nose and wiped her eyes. She had been trying all evening not to think about the unpleasant scene in the kitchen, but she could no longer put it out of her mind. Caught in flagrante, as it were, Mrs Vellacott hadn't even been ashamed. Quite the opposite: she had been insulting and offensive. Mrs Vellacott's incivility had rendered Evelyn speechless, so much so that though Evelyn had known herself to have been in the right, Mrs Vellacott had kept the upper hand. Now, as Evelyn took a deep breath and splashed cold water on her face, she wondered why she had submitted to Mrs Vellacott's mad diatribe, why she hadn't stood up for herself.

Neither had she stood up for herself when Osborne had told the Longvilles about the evacuees. Why had she not said, as she had longed to: *It wasn't like that. Those boys were just lost and lonely and confused, and they didn't know how to behave in a place like this. And at least, while they were here, the house was busy. And not so wretchedly quiet.*

Her hands slid from her face. She stared at her reflection in the mirror, at her pleasant but unremarkable features, surrounded by fair hair whose waves had wilted during her frantic rush in the kitchen. Her gaze fixed on the threads of grey that were beginning to show through the ash blonde and the tiny lines that feathered the corners of her eyes. Had she been afraid of Mrs Vellacott? she wondered. Had she been intimidated, cowed? Or was it herself that she was afraid of – afraid of the anger that boiled and bubbled just below the surface, an anger which, given an outlet, she might not be able to control?

There was a knock on the cloakroom door. Josephine Maxey called out, 'Are you all right, Evelyn?'

'I'm fine.' Evelyn unlocked the door. 'I'm just a bit tired. And it's the wrong time of the month.'

Which was true. The cramps had begun as she had fled the kitchen after dismissing Mrs Vellacott. Almost as though, Evelyn thought, Osborne had been right, and Mrs Vellacott was a witch and had cast the evil eye on her.

Chapter Five

There were thirty rooms in the Trelawney Hotel and Romy was responsible for ten of them. The other two chambermaids, Olive and Teresa, cleaned the remaining twenty rooms. Though Olive's hair was grey and her wiry body bent, she still, in her hours off, made up with lipstick and rouge and wore frilled blouses in shocking pink, her favourite colour, beneath a venerable sealskin coat. Teresa was much younger, only a few years older than Romy. She was Irish, a slight, pretty girl with light brown hair and green eyes, whose milkmaidish demeanour and devout Roman Catholicism were coupled with an occasionally foul tongue and an ear for scurrilous gossip.

Romy learned how to clean the rooms and make the beds. The sheets and pillowcases were so heavily starched that it was like making a bed with cardboard. Olive explained about hospital corners and Teresa showed Romy how to smooth the bedspreads so that not a crease rumpled their surface. When the beds were made, Romy wondered how the guests managed to squeeze themselves between the taut white sheets, and how they had the temerity to disturb the chill perfection of pillow and coverlet.

Each day the furniture had to be polished with

lavender-scented beeswax, the mirrors shined and the carpets vacuumed. Rugs and curtains had to be beaten, dirty crockery and plates removed to the kitchen, picture rails and skirting boards dusted and windows cleaned. And then there were the bathrooms: the vast white tubs to be scoured with Vim, the taps to be Brassoed, the marble floors to be scrubbed and the huge, fluffy white towels to be replaced.

She learned about the complex workings of the hotel. She discovered that the swift service and unobtrusive luxury which the guests enjoyed were achieved by endless hard work behind the scenes. She saw that Mrs Plummer ruled Trelawney's with a firm hand, and that even Mr Starling, the austere and dignified hotel manager, moved snappily when Mrs Plummer sent for him. One morning Mrs Plummer decided that she would check the bedrooms. Teresa looked pale and threatened to be sick. 'Just as long as it's not in one of my bathrooms,' said Olive tartly. But the inspection went smoothly enough, Mrs Plummer congratulating all three chambermaids on their efforts. When, each day, Mrs Plummer absented herself to her club for a few hours, the entire hotel seemed to breathe a collective sigh of relief.

Romy rose each morning at six and started work at seven. At eleven o'clock there was a fifteen-minute break for tea and a cigarette, and at half-past one they stopped for lunch. Huddled in a corner of a kitchen, they gossiped. Teresa told Romy and Olive about her admirers, who were legion. Olive described her ailments, which were equally various, and her four sons, who lived in the East End, and their wives and children.

Romy said little about her former life, deflecting questions by inventing a past so dull that neither Olive nor Teresa cared to enquire further.

She wrote to her mother, reassuring her of her safety and happiness, asking Martha to forward her clothes and her savings book. In a fit of generosity she scribbled at the foot of the letter, *P.S. Tell Carol she can have my face powder and my Yardley talc*. She worried about Jem. Where had he gone? Had he found a job? Had he somewhere to live, enough to eat?

During her afternoons off, while Olive knitted and dozed and Teresa conducted fitful flirtations from the back steps of the hotel basement, Romy explored London. At first, afraid of losing her way, she rarely ventured far beyond Parfitt Gardens, with its lush, green trees and lawn that seemed to keep cool and airy even on the hottest, dustiest day. But soon her curiosity overcame her and she headed out into surrounding Bloomsbury. She visited the British Museum, where she wandered among chill marble pharaohs and falcon-headed gods. She walked down Southampton Row and Kingsway to the river and along the Embankment to Blackfriars Bridge. She caught the Tube to Knightsbridge and explored Harrods, breathing in the scents in the perfume hall and the even more seductive aromas of wealth and luxury. Stratton had nothing like this. Even Romsey and Southampton had not compared to this. Brought up in the years of ration books and make-do-and-mend, she had not realized that it was possible to find so many beautiful things under one roof. She gazed at the satin gowns and crystal decanters, not daring to touch.

On sunny afternoons Olive and Teresa joined her in the gardens. It was Olive who told her about Mrs Plummer.

'Mr Trelawney gave Mrs P the hotel.' Olive's knitting needles clicked busily. 'He was a friend of hers.'

'He was her lover.'

'*Teresa*.' Olive looked disapproving.

'Well, he was so.' Teresa was lying on the lawn, her skirt tucked up to brown her outstretched legs. 'Everyone knows that.'

'When Mr Trelawney died,' said Olive, 'he left Mrs P the hotel. She had the nightclub already, of course.'

Teresa said virtuously, 'My Declan says no decent woman would be seen in one of them places. All kinds of things go on there. Naked women and all types of people.'

Olive frowned. 'Not in front of the girl.'

'Oh, Romy's a woman of the world, aren't you, Romy? Tell us about Mr Trelawney, Olive. Was he handsome?'

'Handsome is as handsome does,' said Olive dismissively. 'He adored Mrs P. She was a looker in her day, you know.'

'But did Mrs Plummer marry Mr Trelawney?' asked Romy.

Olive was counting stitches. 'Fifteen, sixteen ... He wanted her to, but she wouldn't. Begged her on bended knee.'

Teresa giggled. 'Did your husband beg you to marry him on bended knee, Olive?'

'Len? Not him.' Olive gave a coy smile. 'That's not to say no man has.'

'*Olive.*' Teresa sat up. 'Go on. Tell us.'

'It was a long time ago. A very long time ago. Before I was walking out with Len.'

'Did you turn him down?'

'He was a sailor,' said Olive crisply. 'You know what they're like – a girl in every port. My Len had a good job down the docks.'

Teresa said, 'Mr Fitzgerald's the only man Mrs Plummer's ever loved.'

'Who's Mr Fitzgerald?'

'He's a rascal,' said Olive. 'Johnnie Fitzgerald calls himself a businessman, but he's a rascal. She met him at the club – oh, years ago, in the war. When Johnnie's behaving himself, Mrs P's as sweet as anything. When he's up to his old tricks – well, you'd better watch out. Dust your picture frames and make sure the bedspreads don't have a single crease.'

'Last spring,' confided Teresa, 'Mr Fitzgerald turned up drunk as a lord and Mrs Plummer gave him his marching orders. They were throwing things at each other and Mr Fitzgerald called her all sorts of names. Names that a decent man would never use.'

'She took him back a month later.' Olive's knitting needles paused. 'Tail between his legs and begging her forgiveness. Money calls, remember.'

'Money?' asked Romy.

'Didn't you know? Mrs Plummer's going to leave Mr Fitzgerald the hotel. Which is why he'll keep her sweet.'

'I'd give in my notice if he came here, I'll tell you that for nothing,' said Teresa. 'I wouldn't put up with him lording it over me.'

'Hasn't got any family of her own, has she?' Olive clamped a needle under one arm. 'Never had any kiddies. Who else would she leave Trelawney's to? She's a few years left in her yet, mind. But she's led a life, hasn't she? Burnt the candle at both ends. Not that I blame her, might as well have some fun while you can.'

Teresa said dreamily, 'Mr Trelawney died of a broken heart, didn't he, Olive? Because Mrs Plummer wouldn't marry him.'

Olive snorted. 'He died of a seizure. Too much rich food. I've never met the man who's died of a broken heart. Most of them haven't got a heart to break.'

Caleb had been working at Broadbent's removal firm for three months. Bored by the routine, repetitive nature of his work and struggling to fit back into his childhood home, it was hard to remember the sense of freedom he had felt when, earlier in the year, he had been discharged from the army. In the clerks' office at Broadbent's, the atmosphere of bullying and intimidation persisted. While Loman and his sidekick, Cottle, continued to make Pickering's life a misery, Caleb, Goddard and McAulay kept their heads down, kept their mouths shut. Though Caleb tried to tell himself that it didn't matter, that Pickering wasn't his business, that he'd witnessed this sort of thing countless times before in those enclosed male strongholds of boarding school and barracks, something had begun to grate. He found himself wondering whether doing nothing made him complicitous, as much Loman's creature as Cottle was. At the end of each working day there was a sour taste in his mouth which only a few pints in the pub could erase. In his heart he knew that it wouldn't do, this job that Mr Daubeny had found for him, and that he was going to have to think of something else. If he could only work out what.

At the beginning of July Mr Strickland, the office manager, was taken ill. 'Ate a cheese and pickle sandwich in the canteen,' said McAulay gleefully, 'and turned blue in the face. Had to be carted off in an ambulance.' In Mr Strickland's absence a Mr Wicksteed was brought in from Broadbent's Hertfordshire branch to run the office. Within a day of Mr Wicksteed's arrival a cold wind was rushing through the stale air of the firm and there was the unnerving sound of the sweeping of a new broom. Invoices and estimates were checked, accounts audited. An uneasy quiet gripped the office and an unprecedented conscientiousness replaced the licence of the last few months.

In the pub after work Caleb was playing bar billiards with Goddard when Goddard said, 'Loman's looking a bit green about the gills.'

Caleb took aim. 'No more rubber bands and pen nibs, you mean?'

'Oh, I don't think he'll be too bothered about that.' Goddard played his shot, which went wide. '*Damn*.' He straightened. 'It's the other stuff, isn't it? Surely he's made you a little peace offering? Something to keep your mouth shut?'

Caleb remembered Loman, lurking among the cardboard boxes. *You read books, don't you?* He wondered whether Loman's gifts were judged to suit the recipient. A first edition for a bookworm, a fur stole or a silver bangle for a man who kept a mistress.

'He lifts the stuff from the lorries, then. Breakages—'

'And things get lost, don't they?' Goddard took a swig of beer. 'Some of the blokes who work on the vans must be on the take too. Someone claims they dropped a vase or whatever, and Loman smuggles it out and flogs it. The firm pays the customer compensation and Loman and his pals split the profit. Strickland was supposed to check the breakages, of course, but he didn't, did he? But this new chap's not going to be so generous.' Goddard grinned. 'I almost feel sorry for the poor bastard.'

A week after Mr Wicksteed's arrival three men from the loading bay were dismissed. The office was thick with rumour: the police were being called in ... Mr Strickland had been dragged from his hospital bed and forced to give evidence ... Yet life went on much as before. Loman continued to come into work and, after a few uneventful days, they began to relax again. Then one Monday morning, walking into the office, Caleb sensed the charged atmosphere. Only Cottle, Goddard and McAulay were at their desks; Pickering and Loman were absent. No one spoke; heads were bent over desks.

As he sat down, Caleb said, 'Someone's died, then?'

'Pickering's been sacked,' said Cottle.

'*Pickering?*' Caleb stared at him. 'Why?'

Goddard's pen swept fast across the paper. 'Because

of the breakages,' he muttered. 'It was Pickering's job to register the breakages.'

All eyes avoided Caleb. 'And Loman?' he asked.

'At the dentist, having a tooth pulled out.'

He was unable to speak to Goddard alone until the lunch hour. Cornering him on the landing, Caleb said, 'You're not going to let this happen, are you?'

'Let what happen?' Goddard's voice was studiedly light and unconcerned.

'Pickering, of course.'

Goddard shrugged. 'Not my business. Not yours either.' He ran downstairs.

Caleb followed him. 'We can't let Pickering take the blame for this. Everyone knows Loman stole that stuff.'

'Not Wicksteed.'

Caleb took a deep breath. 'Then someone needs to talk to Wicksteed.'

Goddard swung open the door and stepped out into the sunlit yard. 'Are you volunteering?' His pale-lashed eyes were hard. 'Because, if you do, remember that you'll be dropping us all in it. Not just Loman, not just Cottle. We're all implicated – Loman made sure of that. And you don't think he'll keep his mouth shut if the proverbial hits the fan, do you?' As they crossed the yard, Goddard shrugged. 'It was nothing much, after all. Just a bit of pilfering. Never anything big. The firm screws us with their lousy wages – we're only getting a bit back. Everyone does it, don't they? And the customers can afford it. You've seen some of those houses. Come on, what does it matter?'

'Pickering,' said Caleb obstinately. 'It matters because of him.'

'Pickering's an annoying little creep. So keep your mouth shut. Why shoot yourself in the foot for him?'

Caleb said, 'I wouldn't be shooting myself in the foot.'

Goddard's expression altered. 'Ah.'

'I take it you—'

'Course I did.' They had reached the gates. Goddard came to a halt. 'Loman gave me a carriage clock, if you want to know. I gave it to my nan and grandad for their golden wedding.' Goddard smiled. 'So you kept yourself pure, did you, Hesketh? Your hands are squeaky clean?' His lip curled. 'What a good little boy you are.'

He walked away. Caleb went back into the building. Passing Mr Wicksteed's office, he did not knock, did not enter, but just kept on walking. Goddard was right, he told himself. Pickering wasn't his business. *Keep your head down, keep your mouth shut.*

The following day Caleb spent the morning visiting houses to make estimates. He was relieved to escape from the office, where a hostile silence fell as soon as he walked into the room. Even the air seemed to have become stale and rancorous, hard to breathe. He checked the list of addresses he was to visit before heading to the garage to pick up the firm's van. The customers' names were Smith, Clarke, Lawson and Paynter. The last name stirred a memory. Driving out of Newbury, Caleb struggled to pinpoint it.

The first three visits were straightforward enough and he left Mr Paynter till last. Heading through winding country lanes frilled with yarrow and Queen Anne's lace, he looked out to where fields of golden corn, soon to be harvested, swept across the rolling hills. The high branches of the trees arched over the road and patches of sunlight glittered on the tarmac.

The Paynters' red-brick bungalow was on the outskirts of a village five miles from Hungerford. The For Sale sign protruded from a privet hedge. A wrought-iron gate guarded the bungalow's privacy. Caleb was parking the van when he remembered: *Paynter*. He paused, his hands resting on the steering wheel. Months ago, in a dark, panelled room at Swanton Lacy, Mr Daubeny had said: *It was Mark Paynter's responsibility to carry out the eviction. Cole fired a shotgun, so Paynter called in the police.* In spite of the warm weather Caleb felt a shiver run up his spine.

It wouldn't be the same Paynter, Caleb told himself. Paynters were probably ten a penny in this part of the world. Yet, checking the paperwork, he saw the initial: Mr M. Paynter.

He climbed out of the van and opened the gate. A young woman answered his ring of the doorbell. She introduced herself as Anita Paynter. 'My father will be home soon,' she explained. 'I have to go out soon to my shop. I run a florist's in Hungerford.'

Anita Paynter wore a pink cotton dress and her hair fell in smooth golden waves to her shoulders. Her face was carefully made up and a particularly cloying perfume clung to her as Caleb followed her through the house, making lists and measuring. He noticed that she wore an engagement ring on her left hand.

When he had finished she said, 'Would you like a drink? It's awfully hot.'

He followed her into the kitchen. As she prised ice

cubes out of a metal container, he said, 'Always a wrench, moving house, isn't it? Have you been here long?'

'Ten years.' She poured orange squash into a jug.

'Where did you live before?'

'Swanton St Michael. Do you know it?'

His heart gave a little jump. 'Very well. I live a couple of miles outside Swanton.'

'Really?' Her pretty face, with its pink lips and wings of black eyeliner, registered little interest.

He added, 'In a house called Middlemere.'

'Middlemere?' She handed him a glass. 'My dad was always going on about that place.'

His mouth suddenly dry, Caleb drank deeply. He heard her add conversationally, 'You know Romy Cole's dad shot himself there?'

He put the glass down. 'You knew the Coles?'

'Course I did.' She put the jug of squash in the fridge and flicked her hair into place. 'Dad ran the grocer's shop in Swanton. Romy Cole was in the same class as me at school.'

He said curiously, 'Were you friends?'

She pouted. 'We used to fight. Silly girls' stuff mostly. Hair-pulling and name-calling and that. She pushed me in the horse trough once. I had a new dress and it was ruined. My dad went mad.'

'Why did you leave Swanton?'

'Dad got ill; we came here then, and I started at St Faith's.'

'Ill?'

For the first time her bland features clouded. 'He

128

had a nervous breakdown. Because of what happened at Middlemere.'

'Because of Mr Cole shooting himself?'

She nodded. 'It wasn't his fault, but he felt bad.'

'Of course,' said Caleb encouragingly. 'Terrible thing to happen. But he's all right now?'

'Mostly. He still has bad nights. Mr Daubeny was ever so good to him, though.'

The hairs on the back of Caleb's neck stood up. But he said calmly, 'How do you mean?'

'About the shop and everything. When Dad was ill he had to close the shop and he couldn't pay the rent.'

'Mr Daubeny owned your father's shop?'

'Course.' She stared at Caleb. 'Owned most of Swanton, didn't he?'

He began, 'But why did Mr Daubeny—' but the sound of the front door opening interrupted him.

Anita Paynter hissed, 'That'll be Dad. You mustn't say anything about the Coles. It upsets him, see.'

That evening Caleb ended up in the pub in Swanton St Michael, with the gnarled labourers and surly youths and several drinks to accompany his brooding thoughts.

There was Pickering, of course, the fall guy, with his myopic, defenceless gaze and sick mother. Recently Caleb had found himself remembering a recruit at Catterick. Towler had been runtish and ungainly, intelligent enough to realize his own lack of aptitude and to be afraid of its consequences, too lacking in coordination or physical prowess to do anything about it. Because he was always out of step on the parade ground, because he constantly mislaid his bootlaces and his webbing and was incapable of reassembling his rifle, Towler had been the object of the sergeant major's loathing. Five weeks into basic training Towler had hanged himself. For a week – perhaps a fortnight – after Towler's death, a sense of shame had hung over the barracks. But it had gradually dispersed, diluted by self-justification and rumour. They had tried to help him, hadn't they? Someone remembered polishing his buttons for him. Someone else recalled buying him a pint to cheer him up. And there was the rumour (this always muttered, with narrowed, knowing eyes) that Towler had been a nancy boy.

And then there was Romy Cole. It was strange how she had lodged in his consciousness, like a hook in a fish's mouth, refusing to let go. He did not know her, his brief meeting with her had been both unpleasant and disturbing, but he could not seem to forget her. The sense of dislocation he had felt since leaving the army must have been felt by her also, he realized, when she had returned to the home of her childhood and found it occupied by strangers. Strangers who had altered what had once been familiar to her, putting their mark on the house, the land. Yet his own experience did not, he knew, compare with that of Romy Cole. Romy's father had died at Middlemere. She had witnessed his suicide. What feelings of displacement did that sort of tragedy leave in its wake? To Romy Cole the Heskeths were not merely strangers. They were usurpers.

You stole my house and you killed my father. Which was nonsense, of course. Pickering might be his responsibility; Romy Cole certainly was not. Yet it niggled, his conversation with Anita Paynter, and try as he might he could not put it out of his mind. He found himself comparing the two women: Anita, with her coiffured hair and smart dress; Romy, with her ragged fringe and cheap raincoat. Anita Paynter's summer sandals had picked carefully through the bungalow's carpeted rooms; Romy Cole's scuffed, unsuitable, high-heeled shoes had stumbled on the uneven ground as she had run away from Middlemere. Anita Paynter's careful maquillage had covered her face like a mask; anger, pain and hatred had been etched into Romy Cole's features as she had stood in Middlemere's hall and yelled at him.

He thought of the house, the Paynters' neat bunga-low, with its new furniture and fitted kitchen and refrigerator. He wondered what sort of house Romy Cole lived in. He remembered that Anita Paynter had said: *Dad got ill; we came here then, and I started at St Faith's*, and he wondered how, disabled by a nervous breakdown, Mr Paynter had been able to afford to buy such a house and school his daughter privately.

He bought another pint and sat down, acknowledg-ing at last the disquiet that rubbed like a pebble trapped in a shoe. Mr Daubeny had owned Paynter's shop in Swanton St Michael. Daubeny also owned Middlemere. Daubeny had sat on the County War Agricultural Executive Committee; Paynter had been one of the same committee's lesser functionaries. Mark Paynter might have carried out the survey that had led to the Coles' eviction, but on whose authority? Overseen by whose cold, controlling eye? According to Daubeny, Paynter had been both judge and jury to Samuel Cole. But what if the judge – what if the jury – had been *leaned on? Persuaded?*

Whether or not Daubeny had had a hand in the eviction of the Coles, one fact stood out. Paynter had been indebted to Daubeny. In much the same way Cottle, McAulay and Goddard were indebted to Loman. Which was why they did not speak out, why they let Pickering, the hapless dupe, sink into uncomprehending disgrace. It occurred to Caleb that perhaps complicity had bought Paynter, just as it now bought Cottle, McAulay and Goddard. Perhaps Paynter's nervous breakdown had been precipitated not only by the horror of Samuel Cole's suicide but by guilt.

Ridiculous, Caleb told himself. He was getting carried away, letting his imagination run away with him. If Mark Paynter had been acting at Daubeny's behest in evicting the Coles, then that implied a deliberate intent to harm the Coles on Daubeny's part. Why should Osborne Daubeny harbour such animosity towards one of his own tenant farmers?

But even if Daubeny had not engineered the Coles' eviction, neither had he protected them, as he surely could have. He had not shielded his tenant from the disgrace and poverty that must inevitably be the consequence of losing Middlemere. Why? Because, as Daubeny had told Caleb, the Coles had been inefficient farmers at a time of national crisis? Or had there been something more to it than that?

Caleb drained the dregs of his beer and ordered a whisky. He had known Mr Daubeny for as long as he could remember. Mr Daubeny had not been ungenerous to him: there had always been work for him in Swanton Lacy's garden in the school holidays and, in the lean years during and after the war, produce from the Daubenys' large kitchen garden had often found its way onto the Heskeths' table. Mr Fryer, the Daubenys' gardener, had taught Caleb a great deal; thanks to Mr Fryer's tutelage, Caleb had been able to establish a garden of his own at Middlemere.

Yet, in spite of Mr Daubeny's generosity towards him, he did not *like* Mr Daubeny. He had never liked him. It was not only the difference in their stations in life, not only Caleb's awareness that as the son of Mr Daubeny's tenant and the object of Mr Daubeny's occasional beneficence, he must not offend. Osborne Daubeny was too cold, too full of self-regard, too sure of his own invulnerability to attract affection. It seemed to Caleb that Mr Daubeny was quite capable of making the sort of judgement that had led to the Coles' downfall, quite capable of condemning a man for his overgrown hedges or the bogginess of his fields.

But if the reason for the Coles' eviction was as clear-cut as Daubeny had implied, then why had he helped Mark Paynter re-establish himself after his breakdown? If sentiment hadn't swayed Daubeny over the Coles, why might it have done so with the Paynters? *If* Mr Daubeny had helped Mark Paynter financially, Caleb reminded himself. He didn't know that; he was only assuming. Perhaps he was letting his imagination run away with itself again. Yet Anita Paynter had said, hadn't she, *Mr Daubeny was awfully good to us.*

Later that evening, walking somewhat unsteadily along the track that led from the road back to Middlemere,

Caleb had a sudden inspiration. He would find Romy Cole. Someone in the village would know where the family had gone, wouldn't they? He would find Romy Cole and ask her whether there had been any quarrel between her father and Daubeny. And if, as was probable, there hadn't been, then he could forget about the Coles, couldn't he? With a clear conscience he could forget the wretched girl and her mad accusations.

Climbing the stile, he slipped and fell into a nettle patch. As he stumbled to his feet and headed into the woodland, his thoughts turned to more pressing concerns. He would go and see Mr Wicksteed tomorrow morning, he decided. *Keep your head down, keep your mouth shut.* The old maxim had begun to seem tired and rather tarnished.

Sally, the chambermaid who had been off sick with appendicitis, returned to work at the end of August. Mrs Plummer called Romy to her office: Romy could help in the restaurant and cocktail bar on Fridays and Saturdays, she told her, and in the office with the paperwork during the week. Peering over her half-moon glasses, Mrs Plummer enquired, 'And has your brother turned up yet, dear?' Romy shook her head. Though she continued to sleep in the Trelawney's little attic bedroom, she felt, for the first time during her six weeks at the hotel, anxious and unsettled.

The days passed and there was still no sign of Jem. Mrs Plummer took to sending her on errands: to Harrods to buy stockings, to Oxford Street to choose a present for a waitress who was retiring, and to the chemist to collect a prescription. Romy enjoyed running the errands, enjoyed the sense of freedom she experienced, making her way around London by the quickest possible route.

One morning Mrs Plummer gave Romy an envelope. The name written on the envelope was Mr J. Fitzgerald. Romy remembered Teresa saying: *Mr Fitzgerald's the only man Mrs Plummer's ever loved.*

Mrs Plummer made it clear that Romy was to deliver the envelope to Mr Fitzgerald in person. 'You should try the Marrakesh, first,' she said. The Marrakesh was Mrs Plummer's club in Dean Street. 'If you can't find him there, the French pub perhaps ... or he may be dining in Wheeler's.' She gave a strained smile. 'Do what you can, my dear. If you can't find him, no matter, just bring the letter back to me.' Beneath her make-up Mrs Plummer looked pale and tired.

Dean Street branched off Oxford Street into Soho. Romy's explorations had previously brought her only to the fringes of Soho. Now, with the envelope clutched in her hand, she walked down Dean Street. She felt a flicker of excitement; it was as though she was stepping into a foreign land. As she dodged a heap of planks and scaffolding lying on the pavement, she heard from an upstairs room the sound of a piano playing 'My very good friend the milkman'. The workmen on the nearby bomb-site were roaring the chorus over the clatter and scrape of brick and cement.

A gaggle of sailors fell out of the adjacent pub, stumbling on the uneven pavement. As they staggered across the road, Romy paused, gazing into the window of a delicatessen. It was crammed with the most extraordinary things: red and black sausages coiled into the shape of a carthorse's halter, wheels of flat, soft cheese and tubs of tiny black and green fruit, glistening with oil, which she thought at first must be grapes but concluded could not be. And the smell . . . Romy closed her eyes, breathing in unfamiliar, glorious scents.

A sudden burst of shouting from the cafe at the corner of the street made her look up. A violent argument seemed to have broken out: half a dozen men surged up from the rose-coloured marble tables on the pavement, their arms gesticulating wildly as they yelled in a foreign language. All the men were dark and impossibly handsome, and they seemed to Romy to be very upset. Then the quarrel – if it had been a quarrel – was forgotten as suddenly as it had started, and they all embraced each other and sat down again.

The entrance to the Marrakesh was beside a greengrocer's shop. The blue door, with its faded paint and brass numerals, stood ajar. Stepping inside, Romy found herself at the foot of a narrow flight of stairs. The sounds – conversation, the chink of glasses and the occasional curse and howl of laughter – grew louder as she climbed the stairs. There was another door on the top landing. Through a small, diamond-shaped pane of glass, she could see into a crowded room. There seemed, she thought, to be some sort of a party going on. It was just after one o'clock in the afternoon: she hadn't thought it would be so busy.

She pushed the door open. The noise was deafening. Inside, she looked around. The walls were painted in shades of sand and terracotta, and brass lanterns inset with coloured glass swung from the high ceiling. Above the bar on the far side of the room was a sort of canopy, which she guessed was supposed to resemble a Bedouin tent. A sea of bodies divided Romy from the bar. She decided to ask the barman for Mr Fitzgerald. Gripping the envelope tightly, she said loudly, 'Excuse me,' and the man in front of her, who was wearing a grubby pea jacket, turned and said, 'Jake's buying everyone a drink. You'll have to wait your turn, duckie.' Then, to Romy's horror, he yelled, 'Jake! There's another one here! And she's wearing a uniform!'

It seemed to Romy that everyone in the room stared at her, in her black dress with white cuffs, which she wore to work in the hotel. There were catcalls and whistles.

'What'll you have?' someone shouted.

The man in the pea jacket said, 'Jake says what d'you want to drink?' and Romy shook her head.

'No thanks.'

'A Pernod,' he suggested. 'Or a gin and tonic.'

'I don't want—'

'We can't always have what we want, duckie. Jake's buying everyone a drink because he's sold a painting, haven't you, Jake? So you have to have a drink.'

There was another shout from the bar. 'Send her over here, Matty! Let's see whether she likes my painting!'

The crowds parted like the Red Sea, making a path for Romy to a man standing beside the bar. Jake was short and rather stout, and his longish, iron-grey, curly hair framed a battered, florid face. He was wearing paint-stained trousers and a corduroy jacket with patches on the elbows.

Romy explained, 'I'm looking for Mr Fitzgerald.'

'Johnnie? Haven't seen him.' Raising his voice, he yelled, 'Anyone here seen Johnnie?'

Someone said, 'I thought he was in France—' and someone else said, 'I thought he was in jail.'

Jake said to Romy, 'Have a look at my painting instead. It's much better to look at than Johnnie Fitzgerald.'

A canvas was stood upright against the bar. It was huge, more than six foot square. Bands of purple and turquoise paint were flecked with pink and white triangles and squares.

He said, 'Do you like it?'

Romy peered at it. 'I don't know what it's supposed to be.'

'Does that matter?'

'A picture should look like something.'

'Should it?'

'I can't see the point of it otherwise.'

'Ha!' said a bystander. 'That's you told, Jake!'

Jake didn't seem offended. 'It's a seascape,' he explained.

Romy thought of the steel-grey sea at Southampton docks, and the blue sea at Bournemouth beach. She said, 'The sea isn't purple.'

There was a roar of laughter. 'Come here,' said Jake. 'Clear out of the way, you rabble.' He took her elbow and led her to the far side of the room. 'Have another look.'

She looked at the painting again. 'I suppose it could be the sea,' she said doubtfully. She squinted. 'I suppose the white bits could be boats. And the pink squares could be houses.'

'It's called *Evening at Funchal*. Funchal is in Madeira. Have you been to Madeira?'

She shook her head. 'You should do,' he said. 'The colours . . . the bougainvillea, the plumbago . . .'

She didn't know what he was talking about. She said politely, 'I'm sure it's very nice.'

'It's all right, I'm an acquired taste. The *Tatler*'s critic said of my last exhibition that to walk into a room full of Jake Malephant's paintings was a shock to the nervous system. This is one of my gentler ones, which is why I've found a home for it.' He offered her his hand. 'There, now I've introduced myself. Who are you?'

'Romy Cole,' she said.

'Why are you wearing that extraordinary – though admittedly rather fetching – get-up?'

'I work at the Trelawney Hotel,' she explained.

He smiled. 'Of course. You're one of Mirabel's slaves.'

She was rather put out that he should call the formidable Mrs Plummer *Mirabel*. She said frostily, 'I have to deliver this letter. I have to get on.'

'You should let me paint you. With or without the uniform, it's up to you. You have an interesting face. One day you might be beautiful.'

She knew she had gone red. She said stubbornly, 'I have to find Mr Fitzgerald.'

'I always tell Mirabel she should fall in love with me and stop wasting her time with that scoundrel. Tell you what, I'll give you a hand.' He downed the remainder of his drink and began to push through the crowds towards the door.

'Mr Malephant, there's no need—'

'Jake, please. You have insulted my art, so we're friends now.' He glanced back at her. 'Soho's a maze, my dear, and I wouldn't like to think of you getting lost in it. Besides, some of the places Johnnie Fitzgerald frequents wouldn't let you through the door.'

They found Mr Fitzgerald in a pub in Old Compton Street. 'Three sheets to the wind,' muttered Jake Malephant, as he indicated to Romy the man seated in a corner of the room.

His dark head rested on the back of the banquette and he appeared to be sleeping. Empty glasses and packets of Player's were scattered around him. A cigarette, carelessly held between outstretched fingers, still burned. When she said his name, he opened his eyes, and she saw that they were dark, limpid pools. She saw too, as she looked for the first time into Johnnie Fitzgerald's ruined features, both beauty and cruelty. And she thought of her mother and Dennis, and of Mrs Plummer in her furs and veil, and thought how odd it was that such strong, practical women could tie themselves to such dangerous men.

Caleb went to see Mr Wicksteed. As he explained about Loman and the breakages, Mr Wicksteed's head remained bent over the desk and his pen continued to scrawl across the sheet of paper in front of him.

When Caleb finished, there was a short silence. Then Mr Wicksteed said, 'Mr Loman will not be with us any longer. There have been a number of infractions. This office has been mismanaged for years.'

'And Pickering?' asked Caleb.

'Mr Pickering was responsible for recording the breakages. What you have just told me makes no difference.'

Caleb stared at him, disbelieving. 'You're still sacking him?'

'Naturally.'

He felt winded. Mr Wicksteed glanced up at him. 'If that's all, then you may go, Mr Hesketh.'

Incredulity gave way to anger. 'It's not all. After everything I've told you – I've never heard anything so ridiculous and unjust—'

The temperature in the room seemed to drop by several degrees. Mr Wicksteed put down the pen at last and his eyes, coldly blue, focused on Caleb. 'When I want your comments, Mr Hesketh, then I shall ask for them.'

'For God's sake—'

'I said, you may go.'

Caleb went back to his desk. Throughout the remainder of the day, none of the other clerks spoke to him or acknowledged his presence. He was excluded, no longer part of the pack, cold-shouldered through both tea break and lunch hour. Sent to Coventry, he thought, savagely, and for what? For nothing.

He had found out through Mrs Pritchard, who ran the post office in Swanton St Michael, that the Cole family now lived in the village of Stratton, near Romsey. Mrs Pritchard exchanged Christmas cards with Mrs Cole, only Romy's mother wasn't Mrs Cole any more,

Mrs Pritchard had explained to Caleb, she was Mrs Parry. Martha Cole had remarried a few years after leaving Middlemere.

On Saturday morning Caleb set off for Romy Cole's house. Travelling, it seemed to him that he had been both inept and naive. He wondered whether this journey was a product of a similar naivety. He thought it quite likely that, if he found her, Romy Cole would slam the door in his face. Yet he persevered, stubbornly making his way south through Hampshire on a series of pottering branch lines and infrequent rural buses.

He reached Stratton at midday. An air of gloom and neglect seemed to hang over the small village, negating the bright summer weather. Even the churchyard was overgrown and mossy. There were half a dozen houses in Hill View. The Parrys' house, Number 5, was the scruffiest. The front gate hung aslant on its hinges and dandelion clocks dotted the front lawn. It didn't seem the sort of place, Caleb thought, that would long contain the fiery, furious Romy. As he approached the house, Caleb saw a small child, clad only in a short-sleeved jersey and nappy, totter unsteadily down the front path. The broken gate swung open more easily than the infant had expected; taken by surprise, he fell flat-faced onto the pavement. There was a substantial pause while he took breath, and then he opened his mouth in a red-faced, deafening howl.

Caleb picked him up and patted his back, and tried to distract him by showing him his wristwatch. With the infant in his arms, he wove through the broken tricycles and deflated rubber balls that lay scattered on the path, and knocked on the front door.

142

A young girl opened it. Caleb asked to speak to her mother and she dashed off into the recesses of the house. Caleb heard her bawl, 'Mum! There's a man and he's got Gareth!'

Gareth's howls had subsided to an intermittent whimpering and Caleb's wristwatch was wet with tears and dribble by the time a harassed-looking woman appeared. Caleb passed the infant to her and explained, 'He fell over. He's skinned his nose and knees, I'm afraid.'

Mrs Parry scolded both children and thanked Caleb. 'Naughty boy, Gareth – very good of you, I'm sure – shouldn't wander off like that – told you to keep an eye on him, Carol—'

Caleb explained, 'I came to see you because—'

'Yes?' Mrs Parry rocked the baby on her hip.

'I'm looking for Romy.'

Mrs Parry's tawny-brown eyes, which reminded Caleb sharply of her daughter's, glared at him suspiciously.

He said quickly, 'We met a few months ago—'

'Mum!' The girl, Carol, came back into the hall.

'Romy's living in London,' said Mrs Parry.

The baby was still howling; Carol pulled at Mrs Parry's apron. 'Mum, the potatoes have gone mushy!'

'Could you tell me her address?'

'I'm not sure . . . That's enough, Gareth—'

'Mum, the potatoes—'

'Oh, for pity's sake!' Mrs Parry's temper snapped. Flinging the baby across her shoulder, she gave the girl a clip round the ear and headed into the interior of the house. As she went out of view, she yelled back to

143

Caleb, 'Romy's working in a hotel. Somewhere in London – the Trelawney Hotel, it's called.'

On her Saturday afternoon off Romy wrote to her mother, mailing her a postal order for ten shillings. When she came back from the postbox, Max, the hotel doorman, said, 'Someone to see you, Romy. Says he's your brother.'

She looked across the square to the gardens. There sitting on a bench, his foot tapping restlessly on the grass, was Jem. There was a battered-looking dog of indeterminate breed curled up on the bench beside him.

She ran to him, flinging her arms around him. 'Jem! Where have you been?'

'Norfolk.' He grinned. 'Picking beans and peas. Last week I picked lavender. Smelt like a tart's bedroom.'

She thought he smelt of earth and tobacco, and the sourish scent of clothes that hadn't been washed recently enough. She stood back, looking at him. His dark curls were tangled, his skin burnt brown by the sun. He looked, she thought, like a gypsy.

'See,' he said, beaming at her, 'I got you a present.' He took out of his jacket pocket a paper bag.

It was full of lavender heads. Closing her eyes, she breathed in the scent. 'I tried to find you,' she said.

'I know. Mum said.'

'You've been home?'

'Just to get the rest of my things. I waited till the old bastard was out. Mum told me you'd gone to London.' Jem gazed across the road to the hotel. 'Fancy you working in a posh place like that, Romy.'

'I thought you'd never come back.'

'Daft bugger.' He touched her cheek fondly. 'I'll always come back. I told you before.'

'And now? Where are you staying now?'

Jem took out cigarette papers and a pouch of tobacco. 'A bloke I met at the farm in Norfolk's got a place in Battersea. We've been sleeping on his floor, me and Arthur.'

'Arthur?'

He stroked the dog's scarred nose. 'He just latched on to me. Poor old boy – some bastard hadn't been treating him too good, I reckon.'

'And work? Have you got a job, Jem?' As he licked down the paper and lit the cigarette, he shook his head.

'I bought a newspaper,' she said. 'I could help you find a job.'

'No need.' He took a brown envelope out of his pocket. 'Turned eighteen, haven't I? This was waiting for me when I got home.'

Inside the envelope were Jem's call-up papers. Romy imagined him in a khaki uniform, his hair shorn, confined with fifty other recruits in an icy barracks.

He said, 'You should come out with us tonight, Romy. Celebrate my last few days' freedom.'

'I've got to work this evening.'

'Monday then,' he said, and she nodded. Her heart felt near to bursting.

'It's so good to see you, Jem. How was Mum?'

'She's all right. She's working evenings in the Rising Sun. Not as posh as that place.' He nodded to the hotel and grinned. 'I bet they eat off gold plates in there.'

'White porcelain.' She remembered her recent conversation with Mrs Plummer. 'It's only for a while, Jem. They won't let me stay there.'

'Hey,' he said, putting his arm around her. 'Cheer up.'

'One day we'll have our own place, won't we? A home all of our own, without Dennis. When I've saved up enough money.'

He leaned forward on the bench, drawing on his cigarette. 'Somewhere nice, eh, Romy?'

She squeezed his hand. 'Come and see my room.'

He looked down at himself. 'I don't look right for a place like that, do I?' There were holes in the knees of his corduroy trousers, and the sleeves of his jacket were frayed.

'That doesn't matter.' Though it probably did; she would have to smuggle him up the back stairs.

But he shook his head. 'What time is it?'

'Almost five.'

'Got to go . . .' He dropped his cigarette end onto the grass and kissed her cheek. The dog slid off the bench to stand beside him, panting, staring expectantly up at him. 'I'll see you Monday,' he said. 'We'll have a night on the town.' He jingled the coins in his pocket. 'My treat.'

As she returned to the hotel, Romy saw that Mrs Plummer was standing on the steps, talking to the doorman. Mrs Plummer said, 'There's been a family reunion, I hear, Romy.'

'Jem's come back to London, Mrs Plummer.'

'I'm very pleased for you, dear. But I suppose this means you'll be leaving us.'

A car drew up in front of the hotel. Stepping into it,

146

Mrs Plummer said, 'Come and see me in my office tomorrow morning please, Romy. Eleven o'clock sharp.'

She went upstairs to her room to get ready for the evening shift in the bar. Sitting on the bed, she began to brush out her hair. Though the other bed was empty, Sally's nightdress, folded on the pillow, reminded her that the room was no longer wholly her own.

Soon, within a few days perhaps, she would have to leave the Trelawney Hotel. She had already outstayed her original invitation. Mrs Plummer had made it clear when she arrived that her position at the hotel was only temporary. Since Sally had returned, it had become obvious to Romy that there was no real job for her here, that her usefulness was fleeting, filling in for those who were on holiday or off sick.

She had bought an *Evening Standard*; now, she flicked through it, staring at the 'Jobs Vacant' columns. But her heart wasn't in it and after a while she put the newspaper aside. She rose and went to the window, looking out at the now familiar roofs and chimneys. The scent from the lavender that Jem had given her perfumed the room. Tomorrow morning, she thought miserably, she would go to Mrs Plummer's office, and Mrs Plummer would dismiss her. That had always been the arrangement. It had been kind of Mrs Plummer to let her work here as long as she had. Yet she dreaded leaving the Trelawney. She had grown used to it, attached to it. It had started to feel like a home, the staff a substitute for the family she had left behind. She would have to start somewhere new once more, this time with none of the sense of anticipation and excitement that had accompanied even that last fraught journey from Stratton to London.

She felt a sharp surge of resentment at the prospect of leaving another place she had come to love. It wasn't much to ask, was it, she thought bitterly, that she should have a home? It was as though the brutality and tragedy of that first expulsion from Middlemere had set a pattern, a pattern she was unable to break. The ordinary Eden of a home and a family, the Eden that most other people took for granted, was not to be hers. The original injustice seemed to have multiplied and it cast a long, dark shadow.

When she went downstairs, she looked across the foyer and saw him, the dark-haired man from Middlemere. She recognized him instantly from their one short, memorable meeting. Catching sight of her, he rose from his seat and crossed the foyer to her.

She felt a rush of anger. Why had he come here, this man whose family had taken from her her home, her childhood?

'Mr –' she remembered the name written on the letters on the table in Middlemere's hall – 'Mr Hesketh—'

'Caleb Hesketh.' He held out his hand to her, but she ignored it and beckoned him away from the reception desk to a quiet corner of the foyer.

'What are you doing here?'

'I wanted to ask you something.'

'How did you find me?' she hissed. 'Who told you I was here?'

'Someone in the village gave me your mother's

148

address. And she told me you were working here. I'm sorry to have troubled you. It's just – ' he frowned – 'that day you turned up at my house—'

'*My* house,' she said sharply.

He made a quick, placatory gesture. 'That day you turned up at Middlemere – that was the first time I'd heard about your family. I didn't know what had happened – to your father, I mean. But then I talked to a few people – to my mother and Mr Daubeny. Oh, and a girl called Anita Paynter, and—'

'Annie Paynter?' Momentarily she felt confused rather than angry. 'You talked to Annie Paynter? About me? Why?'

'Curiosity, to begin with, I suppose. And then – well, something didn't seem quite right.'

'I don't know what you're talking about,' she said coldly, 'or why you're bothering me.'

'Mr Daubeny said the eviction had been Paynter's responsibility, but it became obvious to me that Paynter had been in Mr Daubeny's pocket, so—'

She interrupted, 'Who's he? Who's Mr Daubeny?'

'Osborne Daubeny owns Middlemere. He's our landlord. Your family's landlord too, when you lived at Middlemere.'

Osborne Daubeny owns Middlemere. Wheels clicked and whirred, making patterns, joining strands. 'So he – Mr Daubeny –' she said slowly – 'decides who lives in the house?'

'Yes.'

She stared at Caleb Hesketh. 'He, Mr Daubeny, would have chosen who lived there after us?

'Yes, of course.'

149

'And he chose you?'

'Me and my mother.'

'What about your father?'

'He was killed in the war not long before we moved.'

In spite of herself, she found that she was curious. 'What's he like, this Mr Daubeny?'

'Rich. Upper crust. Thinks a lot of himself.'

'So you thought you'd find out why your Mr Daubeny took our house away from us? Don't you *know*?'

It was Caleb's turn to look confused. 'It was because of the war, wasn't it?'

'Maybe. But I don't think so,' she said scornfully. 'My father wasn't a bad farmer, no matter what anyone said. That was just an excuse, wasn't it?'

'An excuse for what?'

'So that he could give the house to his mistress.'

Caleb blinked. 'Sorry?'

'I worked it out months ago.' She couldn't help smiling at the expression on his face. She said, making it quite plain, 'Your Mr Daubeny threw us out of Middlemere because he wanted to give the house to his mistress. To your mother.'

In the high-ceilinged, marble-floored foyer, her words echoed. The shock in his eyes died and was replaced by something else; she found herself taking a step back from him. She heard him say, his voice low and angry, 'How dare you suggest a thing like that – how dare you suggest that my mother and Daubeny—'

'It's true. I know that it's true.' Yet something inside her seemed to falter.

'It's preposterous – and insulting—'

She said quickly, 'My mother told me.'

He had gone white. 'You're lying—'

'Am I?' Taking another step away from him, she flung over her shoulder, 'Ask your mother if you don't believe me. Go on, Caleb Hesketh. Ask your mother.'

She had been lying. Stumbling from the hotel to a pub then to the Tube, then to the bar on Paddington Station, and then falling onto the train, Caleb repeated to himself: she was lying.

The mere thought of his mother taking Osborne Daubeny as a lover revolted him. Romy Cole was a lying little bitch. No wonder Daubeny had thrown the Coles out of Middlemere, if the daughter was anything to go by. No wonder Daubeny had found any excuse to see the back of them if the father had shared Romy's penchant for hostility and insult.

The slow train stopped at every station from London to Hungerford. As the alcohol wore off, Caleb's anger began to fade, evaporating in the hot, stale air of the carriage, leaving in its wake wretchedness and desolation. He thought about his mother. Small – just over five foot – blonde and pretty, Betty Hesketh possessed a gusto and energy that belied her size. Living with her was like living with a whirlwind. Betty's housekeeping was enthusiastic but slapdash, which suited Caleb, who would have hated to live in dustless perfection. Her many enthusiasms – her snapshots and soft furnishings and whimsical china puppies and kittens – threatened to swamp the house.

Yet, in apparent contradiction to all those feminine

151

fripperies, a strong streak of independence and free-spiritedness ran through Betty Hesketh. She smoked and drank and drove a car and roared with laughter at off-colour jokes. Since Caleb's father had died she had worked for a living, in pubs and cafes and shops and, most recently, selling cosmetics from door to door. Because of that, though they had never been well off, they had not had to skimp along on a widow's pension.

It was Betty's oft-stated and much-cherished belief that you should enjoy yourself, that life should be fun. And they had had fun, Caleb and his mother. Though the war and the years of shortage following it had marked their lives, just as they had marked everyone's, he had had a happy childhood. After Archie Hesketh's death, Betty had not retreated into black-clad widowhood. She had still worn her pinks and her reds, had still painted her nails and curled her hair. There had been summers filled with picnics and trips to the seaside. There had been winters with Christmases when, if there had been even a sprinkling of snow, they had tobogganed down the hill on a tea tray.

An only child, Caleb had loved his mother with an intense, undivided passion. As he had grown older, his love had remained undiminished, though it had become mixed with a new guardedness. His mother's attendance at school functions had become for Caleb a confusing mixture of pride and embarrassment. Typical of his age group, he had longed to fit in, to be part of the pack, the same as everyone else. Yet Betty had always stood out, her laughter louder than that of the other mothers, her hats and lipstick brighter. And she had flirted. Withered old science teachers and fresh-faced young PE instructors had brightened at Betty Hesketh's arrival, twitching ill-fitting tweed jackets into place, running a comb through sparse grey hair. None of the other mothers had flirted, or if they had done so they had been subtler, more discreet.

As a schoolboy, he had taken for granted that his mother's flirtations were no more than that: flirtations. He had shared the common assumption of his peers that sex was only for the young. The idea that his mother might take things further was both disgusting and improbable, and not to be considered.

He knew differently now, of course. Almost twenty-one, it wasn't so easy to convince himself that his mother had spent more than a decade of widowhood confining herself to a flashing eye and a seductive smile. She had always had men friends. Throughout the years the butcher, the baker and the candlestick-maker had called at Middlemere to take Betty Hesketh to the pictures or for a drink. Some of the men friends had lasted for a week, some for years. The house was littered with their offerings – the bottles of scent, the boxes of chocolates, the potted chrysanthemums. Betty's ranks of admirers encompassed the plump and the thin, the well off and the poor, bachelors and widowed. And married men. Betty Hesketh's rules had always been her own, rather than those dictated by society.

That flaunting of the rules had furthered the isolation which Middlemere's geographical separation had imposed. The Heskeths had never fitted in; they had never become a part of the village. They had come from outside and they had remained outside. Sometimes, a small boy visiting the village shops with his mother, Caleb had seen censure on the faces of the other women, had caught fragments of whispered, viperous comments. He had not understood them then; he understood them now.

His boarding school education had meant that he had no real friends in the village; a solitary child, he had spent his school holidays working in Swanton Lacy's garden instead of playing with the local boys. *Swanton Lacy*, he thought, as he stared out of the darkened window of the carriage. Had Mr Daubeny given him work because Mr Daubeny had a soft spot for his mother? Had Mr Daubeny found him the job at Broadbent's because he had once been Betty Hesketh's lover?

Romy Cole's golden-brown eyes had glittered like a kestrel's as it hovered, pinpointing its prey. *Ask your mother*, she had said, *if you don't believe me. Go on, Caleb Hesketh. Ask your mother.*

Betty was out when Caleb arrived home. There was a bottle of gin under the sink; he poured himself a large measure.

He had been sitting in the kitchen for an hour when he heard the car draw up outside. He found himself getting up, going to the window to see who she was with, and then he drew back, hating himself.

The door opened and his mother called out, 'Hello, lovie!' She kissed him, and hung her coat on the peg. 'Nice evening?'

He shook his head. 'No, not really.'

She glanced at the empty gin bottle. 'That won't help, Caleb. You know that won't help.'

He said, 'How long have you known Mr Daubeny, Mum?'

She dropped the bottle in the bin. 'Years,' she said. 'Why?'

'Do you like him?'

She shrugged. 'Never really thought about it. What a funny question to ask.' She picked up the kettle. 'I'll make a cup of tea. Perk you up a bit.'

He could leave it alone, put it out of his mind, he told himself, forget what the wretched girl had told him. Yet he knew immediately that forgetting was impossible, and that Romy Cole's preposterous allegation would linger, seeping poison.

He said haltingly, 'Someone said something to me—'

'What, lovie?'

'It's so ridiculous—'

'Caleb.' She looked concerned. 'How much have you drunk? You shouldn't get yourself in such a state.'

'Someone told me –' he made himself look at her – 'that Mr Daubeny was your lover.'

He saw her become motionless, her back to him, as she held the kettle under the tap. He said quickly, 'I don't mean now – I mean ages ago, when we first moved here.'

She turned to face him. 'Caleb,' she said softly.

'It isn't true, is it, Mum?'

She was still clutching the kettle. There was in her eyes an expression he had rarely seen before. He could not bear to think that it was fear.

'Who told you this?'

'Romy Cole.'

She looked blank. 'Who?'

'That girl who lived here before us – the one who came to the house.'

'Yes. Of course.' She had put down the kettle and was scrabbling in her bag for her cigarettes. 'Romy Cole,' she said quietly. 'My God.'

'She told me that was why we got the house. Because you and Mr Daubeny . . . But she was lying, wasn't she, Mum?'

Betty didn't reply. Caleb's heart sped up, beating out the lengthening moments. He repeated, '*Mum*. She was lying, wasn't she? Tell me she was lying.'

Yet the silence persisted. His mother, who was never quiet for more than a few consecutive seconds, seemed lost for words. Caleb rose to his feet, knocking over the chair, which fell with a crack to the floor. As he stumbled outside, he heard his mother call out his name.

In the garden the night seemed to have intensified the scents of the stocks and the lilies. He took in a lungful of the perfumed air. Then he seized a chunk of flint and hurled it against the wall of the barn. It struck a stack of flowerpots, shattering the clay.

He heard the back door open and his mother's footsteps on the cobbles. 'Caleb,' she said 'listen to me, please. The only man I've ever loved was your father and that's the truth. God's honour. I'll never marry again because I'll never find another man as good as Archie.' The bounce had gone from her voice; she sounded shaken. 'But I won't live alone,' she went on. 'I won't live like a nun, it's not in my nature. I won't do that for anyone. Not even for you, Caleb.'

He swung round to face her. 'And Mr Daubeny?'

There were tears in her eyes. He said desperately, 'Tell me it's not true, Mum,' and she shook her head.

'I can't, son. I saw him a few times, you see. A few times, that's all. It was a long time ago.'

'God.' When, tentatively, she touched his shoulder, he jerked away from her. Staring at her, he gave a small laugh.

'I suppose it explains a lot of things, doesn't it? I mean, it's a big house for the two of us, isn't it? Rather *generous* of Mr Daubeny. Nice low rent, and so secluded – no nosy neighbours to see who's visiting. I can see that it would have suited Daubeny, if he'd had the hots for you, Mum—'

'Caleb—' Betty said sharply.

'I mean – you'd been on your own for a while, hadn't you? Must have been getting lonely. Must have been getting cold in bed at night—'

She took a step towards him. He thought she was going to strike him, but then she paused, shaking her head. 'Don't judge me,' she said softly. 'You have no right to judge me. You haven't lived as I've lived, you haven't had to make the choices I've had to make.'

'*Choices!*' he echoed. 'But that's the point, isn't it, Mum? You're not exactly *choosy*, are you?'

She flinched. He moved away from her and rested his forearms on the top of the fence, staring out across the inky valley. He heard her say, 'When you're young, you see everything so black and white. But it's not always like that. Most of the time everything's so grey you can't seem to see the right thing to do, so you just do what you think is best at the time. And sometimes you don't want to think at all.' She sounded sad. 'Sometimes you just want to forget, to lose yourself.'

'But *Daubeny*, of all people. How could you? So pompous – so self-righteous – no, worse than that –' his voice was thick with disgust – 'if he got rid of that family because of you. For God's sake, he practically owns the whole bloody village! Did he have to own you as well, Mum?' A new and more terrible possibility occurred to him. 'It wasn't like that, was it? He didn't – he didn't *force* you—'

'No. *No.*' She twisted her hands together. Then she said quite calmly, 'It was my choice. It's always my choice. A lot of the busybodies in the village can't cope with that, but it's always been my choice. I've always done what I wanted to, Caleb. For my own reasons and no one else's. And if I've made mistakes, then I've only myself to blame.'

Yet Romy Cole's words echoed. *Your Mr Daubeny threw us out because he wanted to give the house to his mistress.* He wondered, if that was the case, whether that made it better or worse. He said slowly, 'Was it because of the house? Was that why you went with him?'

She did not immediately reply. But eventually she said, 'That place we were living in before – you probably can't remember what it was like. An outside toilet. Damp in every room and holes in the roof. You had bronchitis every winter.'

His lip curled. 'So it was – a financial proposition? A business arrangement?'

'What if it was?' She sounded defiant. 'I saw a way of getting us a decent life. Was that so wrong? Was it? I did what I had to do. I'm not ashamed.'

Her next phrase hung in the air, unspoken. *I did it for you, Caleb.* She wrapped her arms around herself, and shivered. 'Evenings are always so chilly,' she muttered. 'I'll make us a cup of tea, shall I?'

His mother's solution for everything, he thought as she crossed the yard back to the house: for a bad day at work, for bereavement, for betrayal. Caleb stared out over the valley at the pattern of meadow and hedgerow. They had begun to cut the corn in the most distant fields; in the moonlight the shorn stubble gleamed like grey velvet. The tranquillity of the scene soothed him so that his anger ebbed a little, leaving him muddled and exhausted, all at sea.

Could he really demand that his mother, his pretty, gregarious mother, live the remainder of her life celibate? Would he have preferred her to have remarried? Would he have preferred her to have presented him with a stepfather, some intrusive stranger not of his choosing, who would have shared her bed, this house, their lives?

And if he found her taste in men appalling, then had he any right to criticize? He thought of his past girlfriends. A plump, snub-nosed farmer's daughter in the brief interval between leaving school and starting national service. A cook and a barmaid and a shop assistant when he was in the army. The shop assistant had had melting brown eyes and a laugh like a donkey's bray; the cook had been a pleasant, generous girl who had dumped him for a corporal after a couple of months. The barmaid – Jane? June? – had told him on their second date that she meant to be married before she turned twenty-one. She had described to him the

159

wedding dress she intended to make herself and had listed the numerous small cousins who would be her bridesmaids. Caleb had been immensely relieved when, a week later, he had been posted to another camp a hundred miles away.

And since leaving the army? He remembered the night he had celebrated his demob, the Soho bars and the Chelsea party. He had been elated, convinced that he stood on the verge of a life of adventure and freedom and love. And yet, almost six months later, here he was back in his childhood home, stuck in a dead-end job.

He went to the barn and began to pick up the broken pieces of flowerpot. His mind ran miserably through the events of the last few days. He knew that he was going to have to give in his notice at Broadbent's. The weeks and months stretched out before him, a featureless future coupled with a past that was not quite as he had believed it to be.

Leaning against the wall of the barn, gathering his breath, he saw his mother emerge from the house and place a cup on the step and then slip back indoors. After a while he drank the tea. And then he wandered around the garden, evicting slugs and snails, tying up loose fronds of rose and clematis, pulling out emerging shoots of dandelion and bindweed. He had drifted these last few months, but he wouldn't drift any more, he resolved. He'd work out what it was he wanted to do, and then he'd damn well do it.

Romy pressed her dress and took particular care with her hair when she went to see Mrs Plummer on Sunday morning. A lick of lipstick and a dusting of powder disguised the after-effects of a sleepless night.

The French windows in Mrs Plummer's office were wide open. Mrs Plummer was standing on the sunlit terrace. 'Such a lovely day,' she said, as Romy came into the room. 'Come and sit with me out here, dear.'

There was a small wrought-iron table and two chairs. A rambling rose clung to the wall. Nowhere will ever be so nice again, Romy thought. Nowhere will be like this.

Mrs Plummer said, 'Have you enjoyed working at the Trelawney, Romy?'

'Oh yes.'

'But now your brother has come back you intend to move in with him, don't you?'

She shook her head. 'Jem's got his call-up papers,' she explained. 'So he's off to the army for the next two years.'

Mrs Plummer frowned. 'If you're not going to live with your brother, what will you do?'

'I'm not sure yet.' She made an effort. 'I'll think of something, though.'

'Will you remain in London?'

'I'd like to. Perhaps I'll work in another hotel. I like hotels.'

'In that case . . . would you consider staying here?'

Romy's heart skipped a beat. 'At the Trelawney?'

'Yes. In a slightly different capacity from your present one.'

She said quickly, 'Anything. Cleaning . . . the kitchen . . . I'll do anything.'

'I've been thinking for some time that I need an

assistant. Some-one to help me with the day-to-day running of the hotel. Someone to type my letters for me, run my errands, take over the routine work. I've been keeping an eye on you, Romy, and I'm pleased with your work. You're a capable girl. Would you like to work for me?'

'*Me?*' She stared at Mrs Plummer.

'Yes, why not? I would expect you to travel with me sometimes. Would that be a problem?'

'*Travel* . . .' In a sudden and glorious reversal of fortune, the world was opening up for her.

'I've always been fond of Paris. And the south of France, of course, for my health. Well, Romy, what do you say?'

'Yes,' she whispered. 'Oh, *yes*.'

Romy sat on the bench in the gardens. She thought: I shall never be lonely or unhappy again. She had a place to belong to and a job to do. She had shaken off the past and had made a new beginning, a better beginning.

It seemed to her that autumn had just begun to touch the trees; against the blue of the sky the leaves were flushed with gold. She imagined the seasons passing, painted onto this small square of garden. The bare branches would be silvered by frost in winter and jewelled with emerald leaf buds in spring. And she would be here to see each passing day, each small alteration.

This time no one could take it away from her. It was hers, hers by hard work and good fortune and right.

She found that she now regretted her hastiness and hostility towards Caleb Hesketh. There were so many questions she should have asked him. She wondered why Caleb Hesketh had spoken to Annie Paynter, and what Annie had said to him. And she wondered what he was like, this Mr Daubeny – a cruel man, surely, to take a family's home and give it to his mistress.

Osborne Daubeny. It was strange, after so long, to know that name. To know the name of the man responsible for your father's death, and your family's exile, ruin and division. *Osborne Daubeny*. Romy said it out loud, tasting the syllables, and found that they were bitter, like the sloes she and Jem had once gathered as they had walked along the lane back to Middlemere.

The Bridge

PART THREE

The Bridge

1954–6

Chapter Six

Mirabel Plummer had always believed in luck. Not the unearned good fortune that some people seemed to expect from four-leaved clovers and black cats and suchlike, but the sort of luck that, as she had told Romy, you made yourself.

And she had always been lucky. She had learned very early in life to make sure that she was in place, her hands outstretched, waiting for the plums to fall. Sharp-witted and ambitious, she had quickly discovered how to recognize that moment when fortune turned a corner and led to new possibilities. She had never allowed the past to hold her back, had been ruthless with the present when it did not suit her, and had had the imagination and drive to know exactly what she wanted out of life. And she had never lacked courage: the courage to change everything, to risk everything.

She hadn't always been Mirabel Plummer, queen of the Trelawney Hotel. She had been born Ada Prowse, the third daughter of a Hampshire farm labourer who expressed his own fanatical brand of religion through self-denial and the physical chastisement of his daughters. When, at the age of fourteen, Ada left home to work as a kitchenmaid, her legs and back were black and blue with bruises.

The house in which she had worked had been the family seat of the Gilfoyles. Though she had escaped her father's stick, she soon encountered different challenges. In the cool darkness of the buttery a footman stole a kiss; rushing through corridors, her hands full of crockery, the younger son of the house stood in front of her, halting her. One of his hands reached for her breast, the other, with slow deliberation, moved aside folds of skirts and petticoats.

At first these incidents frightened her. She might complain to the housekeeper about the footman; to whom could she complain about Charlie Gilfoyle? But soon she began to see that she was not powerless, that her body was her weapon, her bargaining counter, that it could give her authority over those who were stronger, richer and better born than her. She had been blessed with clear skin, a wealth of chestnut hair, and a pair of bright blue eyes. An early developer, she could have been taken for a grown woman at the age of fifteen. She learned to flirt, to tease, to promise more than she ever intended to give. She exchanged kisses for favours and offered rather more for an ivory comb or a silver bracelet.

In 1914 war broke out. Six months later Ada left Hampshire for London, just walked out of the Gilfoyles' house one morning, her belongings, with her hoard of trinkets, tied up in a shawl, and the housekeeper yelling at her to come back and scrub the floors. She fell in love with London at first sight, something that only happened to her twice in her whole life. She soon found work driving a tram. She loved the job, loved the dusty, metallic smell of her cab, loved the excitement of steering the large, lumbering vehicle around busy city streets. In 1916, in a pub in Bethnal Green, she met a girl who had once been a chambermaid in the Gilfoyles' house. Charlie Gilfoyle had been killed on the Somme, the girl told her. Ada remembered Charlie, with his supercilious smile and his probing hands, and felt not a jot of pity.

In 1918 the war ended. She lost her job to a soldier returning from the Front and, in those hard years of unemployment and recession, struggled to find another. She could have gone back into domestic service, of course, but she had vowed never to do that. Instead she became a nightclub hostess in Mayfair. She had no illusions about the work, knew that all that distinguished her from the sad, painted creatures who walked the streets at night was her youth, her beauty. She worked hard, saved almost every penny she earned, and made clear to the clientele who frequented the nightclub that she expected presents of real value. No paste jewellery or rabbit stoles for her, thank you. She was choosy about whom she went with, but she never let sentiment stand in the way of good business sense. A part of her mourned her lost reputation: she put that part of her aside for now, to reclaim when times were better.

In the mid-Twenties, needing to recover from a botched abortion, she spent some of her savings on a cruise. At the crossing-the-line party she met Bill Plummer. He was dressed as Neptune, she as a mermaid. He was a big, clumsy man, who kept tripping over her tail. He was also, she quickly discovered, a rich widower.

They were married three weeks later, on the ship, within sight of Bill's home on a rubber plantation in

Malaya. The marriage lasted five years and it wasn't a bad life, she often thought, looking back, though she never got used to the heat, and some of Bill's tastes were rather ungentlemanly. But then, she had known for a long time that most of them were like that, best bibs and tuckers on the outside and like alley cats beneath.

When Bill was killed in a plane crash in 1929, she sailed back to England. She kept her married name, but changed her hairstyle and her Christian name. She had never like Ada; it had an old-fashioned, biblical ring to it. She chose Mirabel, a frivolous, pretty sort of name, which would suit the career she planned for herself. Three months after her return to England, she bought a nightclub in Soho with the money that Bill had left her. She got it for a good price, because, with the collapse of the stock markets, hard times had returned. She ran the place with an iron hand, and was careful to avoid trouble with the police and with other, less savoury, elements of society, who tended to muscle in when they saw the opportunity. She didn't allow gambling on the premises, and she didn't allow prostitutes to come into the bar. Though, knowing how easily she could have become one of their number, she sent out coffee and tea and a bite to eat most nights to those ladies who braved the rain and the cold on the streets outside.

She called the club the Marrakesh and had it done out like something out of the Arabian Nights. Nothing tasteless, mind, no houris or belly dancers. Just shades of sand and terracotta, and brass lanterns picked up in antique shops and street markets.

The club was a success. She made it her own, could

be seen most evenings sitting on a stool by the bar, drinking her favourite cocktail. Most of the men who came to the Marrakesh were in love with her, most of the women who accompanied them envied her. She could be a mother to her customers, or a sister, or a lover. She was a shoulder to cry on, a good sport, a spur to lost ambitions and forgotten dreams.

In 1933 she married again. Vernon Wright was twenty years older than Mirabel, and, she discovered within a few weeks of their wedding, uninterested in women. After she got over the initial shock, she didn't really mind. There were quite a few queers among the clientele of the Marrakesh, nice boys most of them. The marriage rattled along because both Mirabel and Vernon were after the same thing: respectability. Vernon, a successful businessman, needed a wife; she needed an entrée into a different sort of society than the Marrakesh had to offer. Under the respectable cover of a sexless marriage, they both pursued their own interests: Vernon and his sailor boys, Mirabel and her latest lover, Lewis Trelawney.

In 1940 Vernon died of pneumonia, after becoming lost in the fog when all the street signs were down because of the war, and Lewis died of the tuberculosis that had been eating at him for twenty years. Vernon left Mirabel rather a large sum of money and Lewis left her the Trelawney Hotel. Though the world was going to hell in a handcart, bombs raining down on London and all the talk of invasion, she felt, for the first time in her life, completely happy. She loved the hotel and knew that it was her passport to the respectability that she had for so long desired. She moved into a suite of rooms in the hotel. They were difficult years, of course, because of the war, but she had contacts through the club and knew in whose ear to whisper when she needed the rules bent.

Then she met Johnnie. Afterwards, she would always remember the first moment she had set eyes on Johnnie Fitzgerald. She was visiting the club, checking up on things, and Johnnie was sitting at the bar. He had looked up at her and she had fallen in love with him. It was as simple and as inexplicable as that. She, Mirabel Plummer, who had had the good sense to avoid love for the first forty-two years of her life, had fallen for him, hook, line and sinker.

And he had loved her too, hadn't he? She had been a prize, then, wealthy and independent, her figure as voluptuous as it had been at sixteen, and without a thread of grey in her hair. Their affair had been heady and ecstatic. Rather belatedly she had come to know sexual passion. She had learned what it was to hunger for a man, to long for his touch.

She had also learned, as time went on, the bitter taste of jealousy and the fear that she might lose him. Johnnie was wild, untameable. *You can't own me, Mirabel*, he had said to her during their first quarrel. And she couldn't. Whatever else she had managed to possess, she could never possess Johnnie. It would have been like trying to grasp a fast-running river or to still a storm.

She would have married him like a shot, had he ever asked her. He hadn't, though, and, as the years passed, their quarrels, which had at first been equalled by the passion of their reconciliations, became increasingly bitter and capable of wounding. There were grey hairs among the chestnut now, though she hid them with a tint, and since the change of life she had noticed a thickening of her waist, a slight sagging of her breasts. She hid her true age from Johnnie; now it frightened her to think that he might find out that she was almost ten years older than him. She learned to turn a blind eye to his more short-lived liaisons, but never learned to disguise the anger and grief that welled up in her when the flirtations threatened to become serious. She discovered that he was hopeless with money and baled him out time after time. She also discovered that in bed he could make her feel young again, young and infinitely desirable.

In 1953 her luck turned sour. She had stomach pains; when the doctors operated they discovered a growth. That was when she made her will; that was when, returning to her home village to see her sisters for the first time since she had left at the age of fourteen, she discovered that the Gilfoyles had lost their big house and that Eddie Gilfoyle, the only surviving son, had gone into the law to make a living.

She had been unable to resist the pleasure of asking Eddie Gilfoyle to draw up her will. Oh, the bliss of having one of that once-proud family fawning on her, satisfying her every whim! She had waited almost forty years for her revenge, and when it came it tasted sweet.

She thought her luck had changed once more for the better. She had begun to feel well again and she met Romy. Something in Romy reminded her of herself many years ago – the hunger in her eyes and her obvious impatience with the narrow milieu in which she found herself. And then, when Romy turned up at the

Trelawney, her face covered in bruises and with hardly a penny in her pocket, Mirabel Plummer, who was not at all a sentimental woman, found herself offering the girl a job. She hadn't regretted her impulse, or her subsequent decision to make Romy her secretary. Romy Cole was intelligent and ambitious, wasted as a chambermaid, and Mirabel had always hated waste.

They had their battles, of course, she and Romy. The girl had a temper, which she must learn to curb; she lacked polish, and had to be taught how to behave in polite society. Yet Mirabel found that, rather to her surprise, she enjoyed teaching her. She must be getting sentimental in her old age, she thought, with a wry smile. She had never had children of her own (there had been no pregnancies after that last, messy, abortion). Romy was the closest she'd ever get to having a daughter.

Looking at Romy, she often felt, along with affection, a pang of loss. Romy still had her future, her innocence, her optimism. Sometimes it seemed to Mirabel that she herself had sold most of these commodities rather a long time ago.

In the February of 1954 Romy travelled with Mrs Plummer to Nice. They stayed at the Hotel Splendide on the Boulevard Victor Hugo. Sometimes when Mrs Plummer had no other engagements they dined together, Mrs Plummer writing comments about the food and service in a tiny golden notebook, Romy always observant, always learning.

There was so much to learn. She had ironed out the

accent of her childhood, replacing it with something smarter, blander. She mustn't say *couch*, she must say *sofa*, mustn't say *living room*, must say *drawing room*. From the array of silver cutlery on the table she must choose the correct fork, the correct knife. She must wait for the garçon to draw back her chair before sitting down. She must hold her coffee cup elegantly and not clutch it in her fist. She must cut up her food into appropriately sized pieces, must always chew with her mouth closed and never talk with her mouth full. If she erred, if she reverted to her Hill View ways, Mrs Plummer was merciless. *A woman should sip her wine, Romy – to gulp it looks desperate.* Or: *If that's the way you intend to drink soup, my dear, then perhaps you should not do so in public.* The quietly spoken comments made Romy's cheeks burn, her heart pound. She never made the same mistake twice.

In the mornings Romy took dictation and typed letters; in the afternoons she was free to explore. Wrapped up against the weather in a pale blue wool coat that Mrs Plummer had given her – *It's very old, but it's Paquin, and I've never been able to bear to throw it away. And the hotel won't let you through the front door in that dreadful raincoat* – she wandered along the Promenade des Anglais. Waves crashed into the Baie des Anges and the fronds of the palm trees leapt like banners in the wind. She thought: *That sea is the Mediterranean Sea. I'm Romy Cole and I'm walking beside the Mediterranean Sea.* Which seemed to her a miracle.

After a fortnight they returned to England, slipping back into the pattern of life in the hotel, a pattern which was becoming familiar to Romy. January and February were the quietest months; then, throughout the spring and summer, the Trelawney became steadily busier. There were the hectic weeks of the Chelsea Flower Show and Wimbledon, weeks in which every room in the hotel was occupied and every table in the restaurant full, and women wearing floral dresses and chic little hats flitted through the lobby like brightly coloured butterflies. Then came August, and they could breathe again as the capital quietened and families left the city for the country or the seaside. Romy liked August, liked the exhausted heat that seemed to concentrate in the streets and squares, liked the languor that seemed to pervade London. During those dreamy, dusty weeks she flung open the windows of her bedsitting room and watched the pigeons peck and strut on the roof, or lay on the grass among the grimy laurels in Parfitt Gardens with Olive and Teresa, reading a book, exchanging desultory fragments of conversation.

In September, along with the autumn fogs it seemed, the guests returned to the hotel: businessmen working in the City, and bored, affluent, provincial housewives choosing their winter wardrobes. At the weekends couples came up to town to enjoy the treat of a night at the theatre, or a meal in a restaurant. Business built up until Christmas, when the porters put up a tree in the hotel lobby. The Christmas tree was huge: its feathery tip, topped with a star, almost touched the room's high ceiling. Mrs Plummer always decorated the tree herself with red candles in gold holders and painted wooden angels, bought in Austria before the war. The first time Romy saw the tree she was embarrassed by the tears that sprang to her eyes. She had to dart quickly back to her little cubbyhole of an office and blow her nose. Going home that night to her bedsit in Belsize Park, she thought it was because that was how Christmas trees were supposed to look. Though why that should make her cry she had no idea.

Her bedsit was her sanctuary, her citadel. Though it was inconveniently far from the hotel, and the morning's Tube journey involved a change of line, battling with pinstriped businessmen in the rush hour at King's Cross; though it was small and rather dark, she loved it. It was hers and hers alone, the first home that she had chosen by herself, that she had had all to herself. No one could spoil it or take it away from her. She had chosen it because it was on the top corner of the high building and had two windows, one of which looked across to Primrose Hill. There was a bed, which in the daytime she covered with a length of colourful material and half a dozen cushions, so that it looked like a sofa. The decor was rather gloomy, the walls were painted dark brown, the lino greyish: like living in a vicar's downstairs lavatory Jake said rather rudely, before donating sketches, exuberant cartoons of dancers and barmaids executed with a single confident arc of the wrist onto pieces of paper four-foot square, which Romy pinned to the walls.

Jake Malephant was her friend and mentor, her guide this past year and a half through Soho's unfamiliar and often confusing paths. At the beginning of their friendship, Jake had made a half-hearted attempt to seduce her, which she had rebuffed. He had accepted less easily her refusal to let him paint her. She couldn't have said precisely why she would have so disliked to be fixed on canvas by Jake or, indeed, any of the other raggle-taggle artists she encountered in Soho.

'It's very primitive of you, Romy,' said Jake irritably. 'I sometimes think you're afraid that I might steal your soul.' It wasn't quite that, of course. It was more that there were parts of her soul she did not want anyone to look at closely. To strip off all her clothes and give herself to Jake would have been easy compared to that.

Instead their relationship settled into an easy sort of friendship. They talked and drank together, cheered each other up when necessary, cooked each other supper every now and then. Jake was an inveterate gossip, hopelessly indiscreet, and needed an appreciative audience to share his secrets. He was protective without being overly so, undemanding and utterly unflappable. He was the first man Romy had known well who was not unpredictable or moody. Jem, Dennis, even her poor, long-dead father: each possessed a streak of wildness, capriciousness, even violence. There was something enormously restful about being with a man who did not seem constantly on the verge of losing his temper or plunging into the depths of despair.

If Jake remained a friend, there was a succession of other men who were more – or perhaps, she sometimes thought, less – than a friend. Some she dated once, none more than a half-dozen times. There was Julian, a photographer, and Martin, a diplomat's son, and Brian, a merchant sailor, and Lionel, an actor, and Marco, a romantic Italian waiter who gave her flowers – picked, she suspected, from other people's front gardens. All were fun in their own way and all, she discovered, began to pall quite quickly. One or two lost interest as soon as she refused to share their bed, another proposed to her on the third date and, when she demurred, looked elsewhere. One picked his teeth throughout an entire showing of *My Cousin Rachel*; another spent their dinner date describing his renovation of his old motor car. When she told Jake about her various hopeless admirers, he roared with laughter.

She didn't mind that nothing lasted: she didn't want love or heartbreak. She wanted fun and in Soho she found it. Soho was optimistic, exuberant, tolerant. Soho broke the rules of a greyish England marooned in the middle of the 1950s. With Jake, she ate oysters in Wheeler's, sitting at bare wooden tables laid with plates of brown bread and little bowls of olives and radishes. Jake bought her espresso coffee in the Cafe Torino; Romy bought him Fernet-Branca for his hangovers. When they forgot the time and talked into the early hours of the morning, they bought currant buns from Mrs Bill's coffee stall in the overgrown bomb site by St Anne's Church and ate them walking along the Embankment to Jake's house in Apollo Place.

On her afternoons off Romy danced with Jake in the Caves de France, to a trio playing old-fashioned dance tunes. Sometimes men danced with each other on the tiny dance floor, their eyes linked as if by a chain, their bodies touching. It shocked her at first, but then she began to realize that her shock was born of her upbringing in Hill View, like saying couch instead of sofa, or drinking her soup the wrong way. There were clubs Jake wouldn't take her to, of course: she argued a bit at first, then he told her the sorts of things that went on in them, and when she fell silent he said triumphantly, 'Ha! Knew you wouldn't approve. Once a working-class provincial, always a working-class provincial.'

For the first time in her life she felt carefree. It wasn't always like that, naturally. Working at the Trelawney, she was conscientious and ambitious. Gradually she gained experience from working in different parts of the hotel. It would be good for her, Mrs Plummer explained, to understand the operation of the entire hotel. When there were vacancies, through holidays or through sickness, Romy filled in. She spent a fortnight peeling vegetables and making salads for the sous-chef. She dealt with complaining guests at the reception desk and spent a week counting sheets and pillowcases with the head of housekeeping, a pleasant lady called Mrs Harper. She began to discover the almost military manoeuvres necessary for the smooth functioning of a banquet or wedding reception. She got to know the Trelawney's regular guests, their likes and dislikes, their idiosyncrasies and peculiarities. She knew which guest required the pens, paper and ink arranged in which particular way on the desk in his room, and which guest, in spite of her considerable wealth, always went home with the Trelawney's towels in her suitcase. She learned, often with immense difficulty, never to lose her temper, and always to be polite, however great the provocation. She had begun to realize what it was about the hotel that meant so much to her: the sense of order, that there was a time and a place for everything. The first nineteen years of her life had been punctuated by violence and disorder; she found that she craved tidiness, harmony and decorum.

She went back to Hill View twice a year, in January and August. At first she carried a penknife in her pocket. If Dennis had touched her she wouldn't have hesitated to use it. But Dennis seemed to have forgotten the incident that had prompted her to flee Hill View. How strange, she thought bitterly, that what had been so terrible for her could be unmemorable to him.

On her visits home she took her mother to Romsey for the day and bought her lunch in a restaurant. Martha was working five nights a week in the pub in Stratton; she had money of her own now, which she hid from Dennis. Dennis himself had work on a building site in Bristol, where they were rebuilding the city centre, which had been destroyed in the war. He stayed in Bristol during the week, only coming home at weekends. These days Martha looked a little less tired, a little less fragile. Coming home, Romy brought presents of nylon stockings and nail polish for Carol, toy cars and books for Ronnie and Gareth. She didn't know whether they read the books, but perhaps their mere proximity would rub off on her little half-brothers, sparking something in their unenquiring minds.

She worried about Jem. When he visited her, on leave from the army, she saw how he had changed. There was a bitterness about him, a loss of innocence that frightened her. She'd try to cheer him up through the few days that he stayed with her, and after a while she'd begin to catch glimpses of the old Jem, her familiar, bright, unpredictable, enchanting Jem. Then the day of his return to barracks would grow nearer, and he would become morose and cynical once more. He had spent the last six months caged in an army camp near Hamburg in Germany. His letters, brief and ill-spelt, leaked misery from every word. She wrote back to him, coaxing him, comforting him. *Only a few more months, Jem, that's all. Only a few more months and you'll be home.* Wherever, for Jem, home was.

And then, of course, there was that other fly in the ointment, Johnnie Fitzgerald. Johnnie was the pampered only son of a well-to-do carpet manufacturer who had died while Johnnie was still at school. When his doting mother had subsequently died in 1948, Johnnie had come into an inheritance of several thousand pounds, an inheritance which, rumour had it at the hotel, was fast being eaten up by his pastimes of gambling and drinking and his passion for fast cars. He owned a business importing rugs and artefacts from the Far East; hotel gossip reported that Mrs Plummer had sunk into it some of her own money. He had never married, but – hotel gossip again – was whispered to have a love child, tucked away in the north of England.

Sometimes Johnnie was attentive, charming and amusing, escorting Mrs Plummer to restaurants or to the races, or spending weekends with her at her cottage on the banks of the Thames near Henley. At other times there were quarrels and absences. Romy began to recognize a pattern. The quarrels would be intermittent at first. Then they would become more and more frequent, sharper and quicker to come to the boil. Typing letters one cold winter afternoon, Romy heard voices from the adjacent room. Johnnie's, petulant and sulky: 'I can't stand it when you try and keep tabs on me. I'm not a *child.*' And Mrs Plummer's, patiently reasonable: 'I'm not trying to keep tabs on you, darling.

It's just that when I don't hear from you for days, I start to worry. I couldn't bear it if anything were to happen to you.'

Then there would be one argument too many and either Johnnie would storm off, vowing never to return, or Mrs Plummer would throw him out. During the weeks of uneasy peace that followed his departure, he would drink and whore in Soho, while Mrs Plummer ran the hotel with her customary efficiency, her despair etched on her strained, white face, her temper volatile, liable to erupt. Eventually Johnnie would come back, his reappearance invariably preceded by some grand gesture – the delivery of a huge bouquet of hothouse orchids, perhaps, or a string quartet playing in the street beneath Mrs Plummer's bedroom at night. And the misery would fall from Mrs Plummer's eyes, and they'd be like young lovers again, always touching, laughing and murmuring to each other.

Romy couldn't see why Mrs Plummer – rich, elegant, businesslike Mrs Plummer – didn't give Johnnie his marching orders. If she had behaved as Johnnie did, she would have been out on her ear in an instant.

She said as much to Jake one evening. 'He's so horrible to her, Jake. But she always forgives him. I don't understand it.'

They were in Jake's studio. He was stretching canvases over frames. He looked up.

'That's because you're too young.'

She was insulted. 'I'm nearly twenty-one.'

'Exactly. Far too young. There's no need to look cross. You can't help being nearly twenty-one.'

'But he's so awful!'

'What about that brother of yours? Whatever he did, you'd forgive him, wouldn't you?'

'Jem's not like Johnnie.'

'Of course he isn't. Johnnie's a bastard, Jem isn't. But how many times have you had to bale him out? How many times have you slipped him a couple of quid to get him through to the end of the week? How many times has he turned up on your doorstep, needing help? Or not turned up when he said he would?'

She said crossly, 'That's different.'

'It's only different because you love Jem and you dislike Johnnie.'

'I can't think why anyone would love Johnnie.'

He raised an eyebrow. 'Can't you?'

'He's selfish . . . mean . . . conceited—'

'And when he wants to be, he's charming, amusing and good fun. And then, of course, there's sex. You have to assume that Johnnie Fitzgerald knows how to give a woman a good time.'

She said stubbornly, 'I can't see how that can make up for all the other things.'

'How many times have you been in love, Romy?'

'Well, there was Julian – and Lionel – and Marco—'

Jake made a dismissive gesture. 'You weren't in love with any of them. But Mirabel loves Johnnie. Adores him. God knows why, but she does. But then there's no rhyme or reason to love and there never will be.' He tapped nails into wood. 'Give them a while and they'll be like turtle doves again, billing and cooing. Which'll make your life easier, I dare say.'

In the early spring of 1955 Mrs Plummer and Romy

left England for Paris, where they stayed at the Hotel Crillon. Mrs Plummer was pale and quiet; in the afternoons Romy wandered alone through narrow streets and wide boulevards, overawed by the beauty of the city. A week after their arrival in Paris Mrs Plummer called Romy to her room. Opening the door, Romy saw that it was filled with roses. Huge bouquets of crimson roses filled vases on the dressing table, mantelpiece and desk. Their heady scent was overpowering and their petals unfolded to reveal dark, blood-red hearts.

Mrs Plummer was bright-eyed, elated. They would go back to England tomorrow, she said; Romy must book tickets for the boat train. But before they left Paris, she declared, they would visit a beauty salon.

In a room with pink walls and baroque gold mirrors, Romy had her nails painted pearl white and her shoulder-length hair cut short and swept back from her face. When she looked in the mirror, a different image stared back at her. Chic, urban, and with an air of self-possession that took even Romy herself by surprise.

Two days after her return from France, Romy was in a pub in Dean Street looking for Jake, when she collided with a young man holding a book in one hand and a glass in the other. Beer splashed onto his jersey. She apologized and searched fruitlessly for a handkerchief to mop with; he found an inch of table to put down the drink and the book and, leaning forward, wrung beer out of thick black wool onto the sea of cigarette ends that littered the floor.

'It doesn't matter,' he said. 'It needed a wash.'

He was tall and thin and he had curling fair hair and carefully drawn features and a glorious smile that lit up his eyes, which were a light, clear blue – the colour, Romy thought, of the aquamarines which Mrs Plummer sometimes wore. She noticed that his cords had worn through at the knees and that there were holes in the elbows of his black turtle-neck jumper.

People pushed between them, dividing them. Romy caught sight of Jake, sitting at a table with a dark-haired woman. He kissed Romy's cheek, then stood back from her. 'Glory be,' he said, staring. 'Where's the permanent wave and the pleated skirt?' She was wearing denim jeans and a blue and white striped jersey, both bought in Paris. 'You look like a street urchin,' he added approvingly. 'Positively Dickensian. The nails lend a rather tubercular touch. Very sexy.' He began to scribble on a beermat.

'No,' said Romy repressively and snatched up the beermat.

'Why not? Why won't you let me draw you?'

'Because you'll give me a green face and square eyes.'

'Spoilsport,' he said equably. 'How was Paris?'

'Wonderful.'

'Mirabel's trying to make a sophisticate of you. I always tell her it's a waste of time. You can't make a silk purse out of – ow.' He picked up the pencil stub she had thrown at him. 'See what I mean?'

Jake introduced Romy to the woman beside him. Camille was pale and beautiful and sulky looking; she was wearing a black satin dress and black shoes with ankle straps. She acknowledged Romy with a slight inclination of the head.

Someone tapped Romy's shoulder. Turning, she saw the fair-haired boy. 'Let me buy you a drink,' he offered.

'But *I* spilt beer over *you*.'

'But if you hadn't,' he explained earnestly, 'then I'd have spent all evening trying to think up an excuse to talk to you. So, really, it was just as well. Fate, perhaps. Destiny.'

They perched next to the window, the only remaining space in the bar, wedged between coats and ashtrays. Outside a fine drizzle sheened the streets, reflecting the headlamps of the cars. He introduced himself. His name was Tom Barnes. When he looked at her, he made no attempt to disguise the admiration in his eyes.

He told her that he was from Preston in Lancashire, and that, after he had finished national service, he had worked in his father's furniture shop. 'It was soul-destroying,' he said. 'The same routine every day and every moment of it unbelievably boring. As bad as the army. Anyway, I had to drive down to London to deliver some stuff and I met Magnus Quenby. Magnus is writing a novel, like me. But he's almost finished it and he's found a publisher. He's a genius, actually. He showed me round Soho. It was like *liberation*. Everyone did what they wanted and they didn't give a damn what other people thought. And there's something going on all the time, isn't there? Night and day. Not like Preston. Dead after six o'clock. It was as though everywhere was murky except for this little bit of London, which was the most marvellous colour. So I stayed. I didn't go home. I knew I'd just shrivel up and die if I stayed there. You've got to cut the umbilical cord sometime, haven't you?'

He had a soft North Country accent. She wondered whether he was ever homesick.

'I've got a bedsit in Kentish Town,' he explained. 'It's not much, but then I don't need much. You mustn't let possessions take over your life, must you? You mustn't want things. Possessions eat you up.'

She thought of all the things she longed for – clothes and foreign travel and a nice house with lovely furniture and carpets and a fridge – and she said honestly, 'I've never thought of it like that. I suppose I've always wanted things.'

'Freedom is the most important thing, isn't it?' His eyes were bright and intense.

She asked him about his novel. Leaning forward, he sighed and ran a hand through his untidy hair. 'Well, it's supposed to be a young man's voyage of discovery, but it's taken me six months and I've only written three chapters so far. My hero doesn't have a job and isn't married because he's breaking with convention, so most of the time he doesn't do anything at all, and it's very difficult to write about someone not doing anything. It's all right when he's talking to people. I like writing the dialogue, but I hate doing the descriptions. It always comes out like – oh, the worst sort of writing. Bourgeois and sentimental, too many sunsets and thunderstorms.'

'I like sunsets and thunderstorms. The more sunsets and thunderstorms the better.'

'I don't suppose you like parties?'

188

'Parties?'

'Magnus is giving a party tonight. Would you like to come?'

'Now?'

'Yes. Would you?'

She had the sense of teetering on the edge of something new, something exciting. 'Yes,' she said. 'Why not?'

They left the pub and headed for Camden. Magnus Quenby's flat took Romy's breath away. The table, mantelpiece, windowsill and floor were covered in books, papers and dirty crockery; over everything lay a cobweb of grey dust. It was impossible to tell what colour the sofa had once been. When she crossed the room the soles of her shoes clung stickily to the lino. Through an open doorway she glimpsed the kitchen, a nightmare of unwashed plates and grease-spattered Baby Belling.

A dozen people were squashed into the two small rooms. In the kitchen Tom introduced Romy to Magnus.

Magnus Quenby was tall and thin, with a mop of greasy straight dark hair that fell in a hank over his thick, black-rimmed spectacles. He wore grubby corduroy trousers and a frayed turtleneck jumper. There was a watchful, scornful expression in his eyes, as though he looked for, and often found, stupidity. He gave Romy a brief nod before turning back to the coffee he was brewing on the stove.

'Did you bring anything, Tom?'

'Couple of bottles of beer.'

'I thought I had some in, but . . .' Magnus gestured wearily to the tottering piles of crockery. 'Can't seem to find it.'

Tom offered to buy beer from the pub across the road. Magnus vaguely patted his pockets. 'I'm a bit short of cash.'

'I've got a few bob.'

'Pay you back as soon as my advance comes through.'

Tom darted away to the pub. Magnus began to run encrusted cups under the tap. Romy went back into the living room. A red-haired girl said to her, 'Gorgeous sweater. Where did you get it?'

'Paris.'

'*Paris.*' The girl's plump, pretty face creased. 'Lucky thing. I'd love to go to Paris.' She held out her hand. 'My name's Psyche. Well, it's really Penelope, but that's so boring, isn't it, so I chose Psyche instead. What do you think?'

'It's lovely. I'm Romy.'

'You're with Tom, aren't you?'

She supposed she was. There it was again, that bubble of excitement and optimism. Psyche said, 'I'm a dancer, you see, so I have to have a name that fits.'

'A ballet dancer?'

Psyche looked suddenly depressed. 'I trained to be a ballet dancer but I'm too tall and too fat. I dance in a club. I'm trying out for the Windmill next week. I do some modelling as well, at Camberwell Art School.'

Romy told Psyche about the hotel. Psyche said again, 'Lucky thing. So *glamorous.* I'm not brainy enough for anything like that. I can't spell for toffee. That's the only trouble with Psyche, I can never remember how to spell it.' She peered into the kitchen. 'I'd better help Magnus with the coffee.'

Tom came back from the pub, his arms full of beer bottles. Psyche handed round coffee; Romy, remembering the grimy cups, opted for beer. Magnus said, 'I've had the most bloody awful week,' and a small, blonde girl with gold hoop earrings patted the seat beside her.

'Squeeze in here, Magnus darling.'

'The *New Statesman* has turned down my piece on the Bomb. Hadn't the guts to print it.'

The blonde girl said comfortingly, 'Someone else'll snap it up.'

'Will they, Susie?' Magnus scowled. 'None of them are brave enough to publish the truth. Freedom of speech? Pah.'

Psyche said, 'When's your novel going to be published, Magnus?'

'Summer, maybe autumn.' He shrugged. 'Not that it'll do much, I daresay. The vast majority of the writing in this country is designed to appeal to Mr and Mrs Jones in their semi in suburbia. Anything different – anything original, like *Bitter Fruits* – is ignored.'

'Oh, come on,' a thin, bespectacled boy protested. 'It's not that bad.'

'Isn't it, Dave? The arts are moribund. Bloated. Think of Psyche's dancing.'

Psyche muttered, 'When I've lost a bit of weight—'

'He doesn't mean *that*, love.'

'A safety valve for middle-class, middle-brow businessmen. That's what those places are.' Magnus gestured widely; coffee splashed the sofa. 'It's all about not challenging, isn't it? You mustn't rock the boat. You mustn't attack the status quo. Most of all, you mustn't make people *think*.' His long arms flailed like windmills. '*Agatha Christie. Daphne du Maurier.* Those are the books that sell.'

Dave said, 'I didn't think you cared about sales.'

Magnus looked irritated. 'It's a question of being allowed a voice. And anyway, it's the principle. Art should *provoke*.'

'Do you think so? That's one of the functions of art, certainly. But only one.'

'The only one that matters.'

'What about comfort? Consolation?'

'For God's sake. Next you'll be saying escape.'

'Well, why not?'

'Because that's not what literature is for.'

'Isn't it? What about *Don Quixote*? And *Romeo and Juliet*? You don't think that in part they were written to provide an escape from what must have been a pretty grim existence?'

'I adored *Rebecca*.' Psyche sighed. 'So romantic.'

'Well, there's an example. We're supposed to admire the upper-crust hero in spite of the fact that he's a murderer—'

'You *have* read it, Magnus—'

The battle raged. Tom's arm crept round Romy's waist. Someone put a record on the gramophone; amid a wasteland of empty beer bottles and dog-eared paperbacks, couples danced. When Romy danced with Tom, he held her carefully, his hands hesitant on her body, his lips and breath fluttering around her ear like moths. At first his kisses were fleeting, full of doubt, the brush of skin against skin; then they lingered for just a second or two, as if to stay longer might cause her to break, to shatter. Though she had been up since seven in the morning, though it was past midnight and she should have been tired, she felt wide awake and alive, the blood rushing through her veins, her body registering every small pressure of his. When he whispered, 'Come back to my place,' she shook her head, an automatic response. If she had allowed herself to think a little longer, she might have given him a different answer.

A few days later, on her afternoon off, coming out the hotel she saw him, leaning against the railing that surrounded the gardens in the centre of the square. It was raining and the sky was a dark, angry grey. Drops of water uncoiled from the leaves of the trees and plastered his hair to his head, soaking his thin jacket. When she asked him how long he had been waiting, he said: *Not long. For ever.*

They went to the British Museum. She took him to her favourite rooms, the oriental and Egyptian galleries. He said, 'All the places I'd like to go to. All the things I've never seen. Geishas in kimonos. And mountains – proper ones, conical, with snow on top. And people eating with chopsticks. And pyramids, of course.'

They walked among glass cases containing tall Chinese vases and tiny Korean lacquer boxes and porcelain bowls painted with brightly coloured butterflies. She showed him the wall-painting of Queen Ahmes Nefertari, night-black and serene, standing among the acanthus flowers. An onyx cat gazed at them from a plinth;

schoolgirls in blazers and grey felt hats wove between the stone pharaohs and painted sarcophagi. When he took her hand and his thumb pressed against the hollow of her palm, the hairs on the back of her neck stood up. Walking back to the hotel, she felt exhilarated and carefree; she could have skipped round the puddles.

The next day a letter arrived at the hotel. There was a single sheet of paper inside; on it Tom had scribbled: *I can't stop thinking of you.* She had a sense of things moving too fast, sliding out of control. She wanted to hold back, to stand motionless on this delicious clifftop, where anything and everything seemed possible. Yet when he telephoned the hotel to arrange to meet her at the weekend, she found herself agreeing easily. There was a feeling of inevitability about it, as though whatever she did, whatever she said, she and Tom would jostle along together for a while. Fate, he had said. Destiny.

On Sunday they visited an old churchyard, where the stone angels' unworldly faces bore the marks of war and time. Mosses and ivies straggled over lichened gravestones, rain dripped from the cypresses, and the yews bore berries like coral beads. At night he took her to a dark, ramshackle pub on the banks of the Thames, where there was the smell of the river and of rotting wood, and the lap of water against the piers. When the door creaked, Romy looked up, half-expecting to see a wherryman in breeches and greatcoat or a gnarled sea captain with pegleg and parrot.

She saw Tom every Sunday. She got to know his friends: Magnus and Dave and Psyche and Susie, and the raggle-taggle mixture of students, would-be writers and artists who trailed around with them – hangers-on, Romy sometimes found herself thinking, at the court of Magnus Quenby. Magnus, with his cold glare and his biting intellect, controlled and orchestrated them, egging on the heated discussions that lasted into the early hours of the morning or until Romy crawled back to her bedsit and its blessed solitariness and silence, or until she fell asleep on the floor among the grubby cushions and cigarette ends and coffee cups, her head pillowed on Tom's knees, his hand stroking her hair. She had become a part of the crowd, accepted, her presence taken for granted. There was something immensely surprising and satisfying about that.

They hardly ever took the Tube, hardly ever hopped on a bus. They walked the length and breadth of London, hand in hand, talking, always talking. It took her a while to realize that Tom had no money, no money at all. That he walked because he couldn't afford to do otherwise. That compared to Tom Barnes, she was rich. Delivering newspapers in the early mornings and washing up in a coffee bar earned him just enough to keep him from starvation. The bleakness of his bedsit in Kentish Town shocked her as much as the squalor of Magnus's. There was a sofa, covered in brown shiny stuff, which folded down into a bed, and a table and a chair. On the table were a typewriter and paper, pencils, a spare ribbon and an ink rubber. Tom's clothes hung on a peg on the back of the door or were bundled into a carrier bag; books were scattered in little heaps around the room. There was a kettle and a saucepan beside the gas ring and a single-bar electric heater, which gave out a clogged warmth that smelt of burnt dust.

One bright May afternoon she lost her virginity on the shiny brown sofa. They were kissing and cuddling, and then her body, which needed his so badly, made the decision for her. Yet it wasn't quite how she had expected it to be. She had a cold and couldn't breathe when he embraced her. His anxious fingers fumbled with the French letter so that it leapt out of his hands, and she had to bite her lip, to choke down the nervous laughter that she knew would mortify him. The whole thing was over so much more quickly than she had imagined it would be, and was in some unaccountable way both so much less and so much more than she had anticipated. Then he was crying out loud and hugging her tightly and kissing her, and they were sliding from the sofa to land in a tangle of clothes and blankets on the icy lino. She watched him as he lay back with his eyes closed, aware of a mixture of feelings. Relief – virginity was, she knew, unfashionable among the denizens of Soho – and pride – she had moved on to another stage in her life, had moved another long step further away from the dragging narrowness of her Hill View upbringing. And fear, of course. What if the French letter hadn't worked? What if she were to become pregnant? How completely that would destroy all her hopes and ambitions.

And tenderness. Tom's long limbs were like white marble. She found herself afraid for him: the hopes and ideals that informed him did not seem to her sufficient armour against the world.

A few weeks later a guest was taken ill in the hotel. Romy was sent to find Mrs Plummer. She was about to knock on the door when she froze, her fist bunched. The sound of weeping made her teeth clench. 'Johnnie, I can't bear it when you talk to me like that. Johnnie, *don't*.' And then the door was flung open, and Johnnie Fitzgerald was standing in the entrance, his dark face enraged, shouting, 'You have to stop nagging me, Mirabel! You don't *own* me! You're not *married* to me! If you won't treat me properly, then there's plenty of women who will!'

Catching sight of Romy, he paused and bared his teeth in a grin. 'Perhaps you'd better give her a minute,' he said lazily. 'Tidy herself up, tuck herself in, if you know what I mean.'

He sauntered off down the corridor. Romy wanted to spit at him, but instead she cursed him beneath her breath, using words she would never have dared to use out loud in the Trelawney. Yet she did as he had suggested, waiting several minutes before she knocked softly on the door, making sure her expression did not register the shock of Mrs Plummer's tear-stained face and ravaged features.

'Hatpins,' said Venetia Seymour, peering vaguely at her dressing table. 'Can you see where I have put my hatpins, Evelyn?'

'Here, Mummy.' Evelyn took down a blue glass dish from the mantelpiece. 'Shall I?'

'Please, dear.' Venetia placed the cream straw hat on her head; Evelyn wielded the pearl-tipped pins. There was nothing to pin the hat *to*, she thought, as she tentatively slid pins into the straw. Her mother's once-luxuriant fair hair had thinned into a narrow white rope, which she wore in a bun on top of her head in the style of her Edwardian girlhood.

Venetia glanced out of the window. 'A veil, do you think, Evelyn?'

'No, Mummy. It's May. Just pleasantly warm.' And it's Bournemouth, she might have added, not India. Sea and sand and day trippers, not flies and heat and dust.

Venetia drew white gloves over fingers knotted with arthritis. 'There. I think we are ready.' In a creaking of stays and a sweep of old lace and Parma violets, she rose to her feet.

'Your shoes, Mummy.'

The straps of Venetia's white kid shoes were unbuttoned. Venetia glanced down and frowned. 'Oh yes. Of course. Evelyn dear, could you . . .?'

Kneeling, Evelyn fitted the buttons into the holes. As she stood up, she glanced surreptitiously at her watch. It was almost three o'clock. It had taken an entire half-hour to help her mother get ready to go out. And their stroll along the seafront – well, hardly a stroll, more a very slow promenade – must include tea and cakes at Bealesons, which, even though her mother hardly ate anything, always took an age. And at this tail end of the summer season, the roads out of Bournemouth might be busy.

In Bealesons, they nibbled cucumber sandwiches and drank Darjeeling tea. Conversation was sporadic, consisting largely of Venetia recounting news from her friends.

'Rose has just become engaged. She and her young man are to be married next summer.'

'Rose?'

'Dorothy's granddaughter.' Dorothy was an old schoolfriend of Venetia's.

'How is Dorothy?'

'Bearing up.' Venetia cut a tiny sandwich into minute quarters. 'The operation set her back, I'm afraid, but she hopes to leave the nursing home within the month. Sadie Jones is in the same nursing home, did I mention that?'

'At least they can keep each other company.'

'I'm afraid they are in rooms at opposite ends of the building. Legs in one wing, eyes in another, you see. Still, just knowing there's a familiar face must help . . . And Billy Cannadine passed away, did I tell you? Winifred will miss him terribly, of course, though the last months were a trial for both of them. More tea, Evelyn?'

'I'd better not. I'm going to have to head off soon.'

Venetia's thin hand retreated from the teapot. 'I mustn't hold you up, then.'

Evelyn was aware of a pang of guilt, the guilt that tended to pervade her visits to her mother. She explained, 'Kate's coming to stay.'

'Kate . . .' Venetia frowned. 'Celia's daughter?'

'She telephoned a few days ago. I have to meet her at the station.'

'How is the poor child? So unpleasant, divorce.' Venetia's gaze, no longer vague, rested on Evelyn. 'It was in the newspapers. Henry Buckingham is a Member of Parliament, after all.'

'Kate's fine,' said Evelyn, though she suspected that she wasn't at all. 'She's sixteen now. Not a child. I'm sure she understands.'

'Do you think so?' said Venetia coolly. 'I doubt that. And what will her mother's behaviour teach her? To put herself before everyone else. To put herself before her husband and her children.'

Evelyn felt obliged to defend Celia. 'Celia was very unhappy, Mummy. She didn't find it an easy decision to make.'

'*Unhappy?*' repeated Venetia. Her bird-boned shoulders rose and she looked down her long, thin nose at her daughter. 'What has *unhappiness* to do with it? One doesn't expect to be happy. Or one shouldn't. No one *required* Celia to marry and have four children. She chose to do so and she should stick it out. Not bale out at the first difficulty.'

A silence descended on the tea table. Then Venetia said, 'And you look tired, Evelyn. All this rushing about.'

Evelyn felt scolded rather than sympathized with. Venetia insisted on paying the bill and they left the restaurant. The sky had clouded over and the day trippers were gathering up buckets and spades and towels, making ready to leave the beach. Children shrieked, rushing along the pavement, and families, hurrying to railway and bus station, pushed carrycots full of babies and bags. Marooned in this stream of humanity, Venetia seemed impossibly frail, vulnerable to all these careless, careening strangers. Evelyn imagined them colliding into her and with a single blow reducing her mother to a heap of dust and splintered bones.

Venetia's house, which faced the sea, was far too large for one person. It had been bought for two, but

Evelyn's father had died only a few weeks after the purchase had been completed. As they entered the hallway, Venetia said, 'Now you must go, Evelyn. You must get home before it's dark.'

'Will you be all right, Mummy?'

'Of course I will. We've had a lovely day, haven't we?'

'I'm sorry I have to rush. Let me take your hat.' Evelyn extracted the pins, and laid her mother's hat carefully on the huge carved armoire that took up half the hallway.

Venetia said, 'If you could just help me with my shoes before you go ... I can't reach them myself, you see. This wretched arthritis. I don't usually do them up. But I know that they look rather untidy.'

Evelyn was horrified. She had an awful vision of her mother tripping over a dangling shoe strap and tumbling, in a heap of flowered crêpe de Chine and pre-war undergarments, to the foot of the stairs.

'So dangerous, Mummy. You might have a fall.'

'I'm very careful, Evelyn. I always take a firm hold of the banisters.'

'Can't Mrs Dawson ... ?'

'Mrs Dawson can only come in the mornings,' said Venetia. 'And there's no need. I manage perfectly well. Cynthia Paget has told me of a device that one can obtain to do one's shoes up. It looks like a crochet hook with a very long handle. There are advertisements in the *Telegraph*, apparently. I intend to send off for one.' Venetia extended her cheek to be pecked by Evelyn. 'Now, off you go. Drive safely and have a lovely time with Kate.'

Evelyn felt, as she always did when leaving Bourne-mouth, a mixture of guilt and relief. When, soon after the end of the war, her parents had moved back to England from India, Evelyn had looked forward to a new chapter in her life. She had never really known her parents. Throughout her childhood and adolescence and during the first decade and a half of her marriage they had lived thousands of miles apart. Letters and photo-graphs, however frequently sent, could not compensate for such distance. Evelyn had hoped that their return to England would mark the beginning of a closer relation-ship. But her father's death, so soon after they had bought the Bournemouth house, had been a blow, and somehow, nine years on, Evelyn still could not have described herself and her mother as close. She was never sure where the fault lay – in Venetia's independence and unwillingness to admit vulnerability, perhaps, or in her own timidity. Or their separation had simply been for too long and was unbridgeable.

And there was something so relentlessly depressing about her fortnightly visits to Bournemouth. Confined to the house by her arthritis, her mother had made few friends in the town. Evelyn could imagine all too well that her mother's intelligence and reserve, coupled with her unfamiliar background – all those years in India – might seem to many off-putting. Venetia had never been at ease with the telephone; she never chatted, but looked upon the phone as a vaguely threatening means of imparting essential information. Her social life seemed to be carried out now almost exclusively in the pages of letters – cream-coloured Basildon Bond from acquaintances in the British Isles and flimsy blue airmail from the few friends who had remained in India after independence. And now, of course, most of those friends – cherished for *decades*, many of them – were ailing, or dying. Gaps must yawn in her mother's life, gaps that Evelyn never felt capable of making up.

It often seemed to her rather ridiculous that she and her mother should live so far apart, each in a large, empty house. Yet when, after her father's death, Evelyn had suggested to her mother that she come to live at Swanton Lacy, Venetia had refused. She wanted to be beside the sea, Venetia had said firmly. That was what she had missed in India, the sea. Evelyn had suspected that Osborne, though he had never said so, had been relieved at her mother's refusal. It was hard to imagine her mother and Osborne sharing the same house: two proud, stubborn spirits contained beneath one roof.

Yet each dutiful visit pointed out to Evelyn her mother's gradual decline in health. Venetia was almost eighty now. Imagining the private battles that must accompany every getting up and going to bed, Evelyn's heart ached. Her mother needed live-in help, but the difficulties in finding the right person, let alone persuading Venetia to accept assistance, were enormous.

Driving away from the coast, heading north, the traffic thinned out. Always a nervous driver, Evelyn began to relax. Such a pleasure, she thought, to have Kate to visit. She began to plan treats and excursions.

At the end of the week Evelyn saw Kate onto the London train. They were making their farewells when she caught sight of Hugo Longville alighting from a train on the adjacent platform. Evelyn hugged Kate and made sure she had all her possessions before handing her into the carriage. She said firmly, 'You must come and stay with me whenever you wish, dear Kate. And I'm sure everything at home will work out for the best.'

Kate's face took on a sulky, miserable cast and she made an unconvinced noise. 'Here.' Evelyn pressed a five-pound note into her god-daughter's hand. 'Buy yourself something nice.'

The guard slammed the carriage door shut. The engine screeched and the train lurched out of the station. Kate leaned out of the window and waved, and Evelyn, with dreadful visions of decapitation, called out to her to sit down, and to remember to eat her sandwiches, and to give Evelyn's love to her mother and father. And then the train curled round the track and out of sight, and Evelyn's raised hand fluttered to her side and she felt suddenly forlorn.

Hugo Longville said, 'Pretty girl,' and Evelyn gave a little jump.

'My god-daughter. Mr Longville, how lovely to see you.' She held out her hand.

'How are you, Evelyn?'

'Fine,' she said, though her voice wobbled. 'Fine.'

He said, 'Hanky and tea. That'll sort you out. Here's the first – ' he handed her a handkerchief – 'and we can go to the station buffet, if you're not too fussy.'

The unexpected kindness made the tears flow faster, so that she had to blow her nose with Hugo Longville's clean white handkerchief. By the time she could speak, he had seated her in the cafe, and was collecting tea and buns from the counter.

He put down the tray on the table. 'I've had years of cheering Morwenna up after seeing the girls off to school. I know the drill.'

'You're very kind, Mr Longville.'

'Hugo, please.' He placed a cup in front of her. 'How old is your god-daughter?'

'Kate's sixteen. Seventeen in December.' She thought back over the last few days, which had been unexpectedly fraught. 'I hope she enjoyed herself. I had plenty of things planned and she didn't want to do any of them.'

'Difficult age, sixteen. Neither one thing nor the other. Jenny used to storm about. Lots of tears and slammed doors.'

'Kate isn't a very happy girl at the moment,' said Evelyn. 'Family troubles, I'm afraid.'

'I'm sorry to hear that.'

'I'd been looking forward to her visit for ages and then – well, she hardly spoke at first. She just seemed so cross. And then, one evening, it all came out. How unhappy she was. I felt so sorry for her.' She looked up at him. 'You just want them to be happy, don't you?'

'Morwenna always tells me it's just a stage. And she's usually right.'

'They change so quickly at this age, don't they?'

'Good Lord, yes. Delphine's still besotted with her pony, thank goodness, but Jenny thinks she's in love with some chap.' He looked rueful. 'She's only nineteen. Seems only yesterday she was playing with her dolls.'

'Do you like him?'

'He seems decent enough. If he's good to Jenny then

205

I'll put up with him. If he treats her badly, then – ' the blue eyes sparked – 'I'll kill him.'

She must have looked alarmed because he laughed and said, 'Don't worry. It won't come to that, I'm sure. And if your god-daughter's going through some sort of upheaval at home, that's probably why she's a bit moody. The girls found it frightfully upsetting when we left Clarewood.' He slid the plate over to her. 'Do have one, Evelyn. They're supposed to be currant buns, though the currants are rather thin on the ground.'

She took a bun and cut it in half and asked, 'Clarewood?'

'Our old place in Shropshire. We had to give it up after the war. Taxes and things, you know.'

'Osborne had to sell off land during the war. And then more land and several cottages a few years ago. Only that time it wasn't because of taxes,' she said, remembering. 'He had to pay a fine – he wanted to repair the stables, but he hadn't permission.'

'Hadn't got his building licence,' said Hugo. 'Caught me out on that one, too. Place was falling about my ears and I couldn't get the men or the materials to shore it up.'

'What did you do?'

'I knocked it down.'

She stared at him, uncomprehending. He went on, 'The whole caboodle. Had the house demolished. Every brick, every stone.'

'Hugo, how *awful*. I didn't realize – I'm so sorry—' She felt tactless, as though she had inadvertently mentioned a death.

But he said, 'Actually, I was relieved.'

'Relieved?'

'Enormously. Glad to see the back of the place.' He smiled at her. 'Really.'

She shook her head. 'No, that's not possible. I'm sorry – ' she flushed – 'I don't mean to contradict you, but—'

'Oh, I'm not saying it was an easy decision. We put it off for years, looking for a way to keep the house going. But I couldn't maintain it and no one wanted to buy it. And the National Trust didn't want to know – it was only a hundred years old and uninteresting architecturally, they said. And I couldn't make it into a motor museum, like Beaulieu, or open it to the public, like Longleat. Clarewood wasn't on that scale. It was just another nice little country house, and they're ten a penny these days.'

'Swanton Lacy is only sixty years old,' said Evelyn. 'The original house burned down at the end of the last century. It's not even a nice little country house.' When he began to speak, she interrupted him. 'It isn't, Hugo, I know it isn't, you don't have to pretend. It's the late Victorians at their worst, and quite hideous. Though Osborne loves it, of course. Now the *garden* – the garden is a different matter.' She smiled, remembering. 'The garden was beautiful.'

'Are you a gardener, Evelyn? I imagine that you are.'

'I love the garden. It's awful to see what's happened to it, of course. Though even in the war, when the soldiers were stationed at the house, all the busyness seemed purposeful, somehow. It made me feel that we were contributing, that we were a part of things.

Osborne hated it. The soldiers were so heedless, you see. But they were just very young. I wouldn't miss the house a bit if we had to leave it, but I would miss the garden.' She fell silent, surprised that she had admitted such a thing to a man she hardly knew. She gave a little laugh. 'Not that we have any intention of leaving. Things haven't got to that bad a pass.' She reddened again. 'Oh dear, I didn't mean – how tactless of me . . .'

'Morwenna and I have no regrets,' he said. 'Honestly. After we demolished Clarewood, we sold the land and we were able to buy a little place down here. I work in the City now, and Morwenna no longer has to contend with leaky drains and collapsing ceilings. We've made a new start. Best thing we ever did.' He frowned. 'The way I saw it, we had to move on. Or we'd become extinct, like the dinosaurs.'

At Swanton Lacy Evelyn found Osborne in his study. 'Kate's safely on the train,' she told him. 'And guess who I met at the station? Hugo Longville.'

A roll of paper was uncurling on top of Osborne's desk, its corners held down with weights. He did not look up as she came into the room, but stared, frowning, at the paper. 'I think I've established the original plan of the water garden,' he said. 'When they rebuilt the house, the architects laid new culverts to accommodate the new wing. The question is whether to stick with what we have now or whether I should go back to the original design. It's possible that the alterations were the cause of some of our difficulties. If I dig new water courses here and here – ' his finger traced a line across

208

the yellowing paper – 'it might stop the streams drying up in the summer and the lake flooding in winter.'

She said doubtfully, 'Won't it be awfully expensive? Wouldn't it be cheaper to repair what's there already?'

'It would be cheaper, but if we are going to restore the garden then it should be done properly.'

'Can we afford it?'

'It's been neglected long enough. It's ten years since those vandals took their leave of us, Evelyn. *Ten years.*'

When he removed the paperweights, the corners of the rolled paper snapped together. He went to the window. 'Look at it. People used to come from the other end of the country to see Swanton Lacy's garden. And now, just look.'

Going to the kitchen to start supper, Evelyn realized that Osborne had not asked her about Kate, and that she had not told him about Hugo Longville and his lost house. It seemed to her that their conversation had become limited to Osborne making unanswerable statements or barking out orders, while she herself murmured soothing responses while thinking about something else. She found it hard to remember when they had last had a proper conversation. Had they ever done so? Had they ever talked as she had talked that afternoon to Hugo? The question made her uncomfortable.

And Hugo's voice seemed to echo. *We had to move on*, he had said. *Or we'd become extinct, like the dinosaurs.*

Chapter Seven

One afternoon there was a knock on the door of the Trelawney's office. The receptionist came into the room.

'Yes, Jacqueline?'

'I'm sorry to disturb you, Mrs Plummer, but there's a young man to see Romy.'

Mrs Plummer said coldly, 'Then tell him to leave. Romy's busy.'

'I'm sorry, Mrs Plummer, but—'

'Really, Jacqueline.'

'– but I did suggest he came back later, and he refuses to go.' Jacqueline was red-faced. 'I think he's rather . . . rather unwell.'

'*Unwell?*' Mrs Plummer looked furious. 'Do you mean drunk, Jacqueline?'

Jacqueline nodded. Mrs Plummer's angry eyes fixed on Romy. 'You'd better go and see to it. No followers in the hotel: you know the rules. If you must make a habit of seeing that type of young man, then it shouldn't be in working hours.' With a sharp flick of her lighter, Mrs Plummer lit a cigarette. 'This is intolerable,' she snapped. 'Quite intolerable.'

Romy saw him as soon as she came out of the corridor into the lobby. Not Tom, of course, not her gentle Tom, who couldn't afford to drink too much, even if he had had the desire to do so. But Jem, slovenly and handsome in his khaki uniform, roaring drunk as he lounged against the reception desk, serenading one of the clerks.

She hauled him out of the hotel, pushed him into a taxi and gave the driver the address of her bedsit. She wondered whether he would lose her house keys down the seat or vomit on the floor, and the taxi driver would throw him out onto the pavement, an inert, stinking mass. She wondered whether to explain to Mrs Plummer that he wasn't her boyfriend but her brother and saw immediately how pointless, and even more how shameful, that would be.

When she went back to Belsize Park that evening, Jem was lying on her bed asleep. He opened one eye long enough to give her a whisky-fuelled grin, and say, 'A week's leave. Present for you, Romy. In my kitbag. Red paper,' and then he fell back on the bed, his eyes closed, snoring.

She opened his kitbag and drew out a parcel. Unwrapping the scarlet paper, she found a bottle of French perfume, and, curled up in a cotton-wool nest, a brooch. The brooch was in the shape of a swan, made of tiny pearls. They must be imitation pearls, she told herself, but there was something about their subtle gleam that made her uneasy. She stared at the brooch for a long time. The perfume smelt heady, intoxicating, voluptuous.

She slept on the floor that night, curled up in her coat. Rising in the morning, she had a dull headache and she tiptoed around the room, careful not to wake Jem as she got ready for work. There were things that needed to be said – such as why didn't you tell me you were coming home, and how dare you turn up like that at the hotel, especially when Mrs Plummer's in a foul mood because she's quarrelled with Johnnie – but she couldn't face saying them just now. She couldn't find her keys; she supposed they were in his pocket. Before she left, she scribbled instructions on a piece of paper and left it on the table. He mustn't make a noise, he mustn't smoke without opening the windows, and he must be in at six because she hadn't any spare keys.

When she got home that evening, Jem was out, and she had to sit on the top landing, waiting for him. Half an hour later, he arrived at the flat, carrying bunches of flowers and bottles of beer, and fish and chips, wrapped in newspaper. The smell of the chip fat mingled with the scent of the freesias and the stale smoke in her room. And with the French perfume, of course, the perfume that she couldn't see how Jem could possibly have afforded on a private's pay of less than two pounds a week.

She saw how the army had changed him. He was stronger, healthier, angrier. There were dark smudges around his eyes, but beneath the close-cropped hair his face was tanned, and he exuded physical competence. When he hugged her, he lifted her off the floor as though she were weightless. As soon as he finished a bottle of beer, he opened another, and there was always a cigarette in his hand. He talked constantly, his voice elated and brittle, his eyes always evading hers. When he had finished the chips, he hugged her again. He had to go out, he said, to see a friend.

She had more keys cut and bought a spare blanket.

During the day Jem's friends came to her bedsit. They were there when she arrived home from work, the men in leather jackets and jeans or striped suits of American cut, the women with platinum blonde hair, their lips cherry red, their blouses cinched tightly in at the waist and their narrow, clinging skirts showing the outline of buttock and thigh. They sprawled on her sofa, they ate her food and drank her coffee. Their cups and glasses left rings on the furniture, and the ash from their cigarettes drifted in silvery pyres across the lino. They stared at her as though she were an interloper, the men's eyes raking her up and down, the girls giggling, cherry mouths pursed.

There was no food in the cupboard; her things were no longer in the right place. She was late for work one morning because, in the disorder that had swept through her flat, she could not find her purse. Her clothes always seemed to be crumpled, and the headache that had begun on the first night of Jem's stay persisted. It was only for a week, she reminded herself, then Jem would return to Germany. How dreadful of her to begrudge him having fun during his week's leave. She wasn't going to spoil his stay by complaining about a little untidiness.

On the fourth evening her temper snapped. It had been a long, difficult day, with one of the guests complaining about a mouse in her room, and an outbreak of gastric flu among the chambermaids, and Mrs Plummer still short-fused and peremptory.

Romy heard the laughter as she climbed the stairs to her bedsit. When she opened the door, she saw that one of Jem's interchangeable, empty-headed, platinum blondes was wearing her blouse. Her best blouse, her new green gingham blouse that she had been intending to wear tonight when she went out with Tom.

'Take that off, you stupid cow,' she said and then, when the girl stared at her open-mouthed, she lunged and pulled. Buttons burst from their anchors, seams strained. The girl screamed, and one of the men laughed.

Romy found that she was clutching a button and a loose piece of thread. 'Get out,' she hissed. 'Just get out, all of you. Look what you've done to my *home*—'

One of the men said, 'Well, we're obviously not welcome here,' and rose from his seat. The blonde girl was crying as she shuffled off the blouse. Jem said, 'Romy,' and she turned to him.

'Go away. Leave me alone. I don't want you here.'

When she was alone, she sat down on the sofa and closed her eyes. After a while she got up and began half-heartedly to try to tidy up the room, but she soon gave up.

She and Tom were to have supper with Psyche and Magnus. At Magnus's flat, Psyche cooked while Magnus raged about the torpidity of the English middle classes and the grip of the establishment on the arts. Magnus had again forgotten to buy beer; Romy had to lend Tom money to get some from the pub. When Psyche served the supper, Magnus poked at his plate and said, '*Stew*. Seems symbolic somehow, doesn't it? So unutterably and depressingly British.'

'I had to do it on the hob,' said Psyche apologetically. 'The oven door seems to have got stuck. I always think stew's better cooked in the oven.'

'I think it's lovely,' said Romy. Chunks of kidney and gobbets of carrot bobbed in thick gravy. Her anger seemed to have solidified into a hard lump, lodged beneath her ribs, ruining her appetite.

'When I was in Brittany,' said Magnus 'we ate the most marvellous seafood every day. *Langoustines* and *crevettes* and *moules marinières*. *Stew.*' His lip curled as he picked up a dollop with his fork and let it fall back onto the plate. 'It sums up everything that's wrong with this country. So hidebound, dull and unimaginative.'

'It's delicious, Psyche,' repeated Romy stubbornly. 'Lovely.'

Magnus's eyes, shrunken and fishlike behind the thick lenses of his spectacles, eyed Romy. 'But then,' he said, 'you're a supporter of the status quo, aren't you? You pander to the idle rich in your smart hotel. In your world, I don't suppose anything ever changes.'

Romy jabbed her knife into a piece of steak and rather wished she were jabbing it into Magnus. 'Of course there are things that need to be changed,' she said, 'but you only seem to notice the bad things, Magnus. Nowhere's perfect.'

'OK.' Magnus leaned back in his seat. 'Name me one good thing about Britain.'

Psyche said, 'Well, I thought the coronation was jolly nice. The queen looked lovely.'

Magnus made a disgusted noise. 'The monarchy is the pinnacle of the establishment, Psyche. Without them, the entire edifice would crumble.'

'The countryside,' said Tom. 'Think of the poets who celebrated the English countryside. Wordsworth – John Clare—'

215

Magnus flapped his hands dismissively. 'It may have been presentable once, but now it's all being grubbed up to make way for roads and ghastly new towns. The whole of England will soon be covered with motor cars and hideous little red-brick boxes.'

Romy said smoothly, 'Perhaps you'd prefer people to stay in the slums, Magnus.'

'Of course not. I suppose it's too much to hope that some of the architects and planners could have a bit of taste, or even an awareness of the vernacular. All those dreadful rows of identical, hideous, semi-detached council houses are such an eyesore.'

Romy thought of Hill View. On the day they had moved into the house she had walked from room to room, dazed by the glory of living somewhere with an indoor lavatory and hot running water. 'Some people find those houses a godsend,' she said furiously. 'To plenty of families, moving into a council house is the best thing that ever happened to them. And, anyway, how can you criticize poor Psyche's cooking when she's gone to all this trouble? It's so unspeakably rude.'

Magnus gave his short, neighing laugh. 'You've all the bourgeois values, haven't you, Romy? So long as people say "please" and "thank you", you can ignore the things that really matter. That's what it's all about for people like you – papering over the cracks. And, anyway, Psyche doesn't mind what I say, do you, Psyche?' To Romy's intense irritation, Psyche shook her head.

'Psyche, you must mind.'

'I don't. Honestly. I know Magnus doesn't mean it.'

'See?' said Magnus smugly.

Psyche's big blue eyes focused on Magnus, their adoration naked. Romy felt furious: with Psyche, for being such a doormat, with Tom, for not standing up for her.

And yet, and yet. She thought of Jem. *Go away*, she had yelled at him. *Leave me alone. I don't want you here.* And all because of a silly girl trying on a cheap blouse. She felt ashamed of herself.

When she went home at the end of the evening she found that Jem had returned to the flat. The room was now clean and tidy, the lino swept and everything in its place. There was a black cat sleeping on the rug and a box of chocolates on the table.

Jem looked shamefaced, anxious. 'Sorry about the mess and everything. I'll go and sleep round at Barry's when I've finished here.'

'I don't want you to go, Jem.'

'I'd better.'

'Please.' She glanced at the rug. 'That cat.'

'She followed me here. Had a thorn in her paw but I took it out and I think she's all right now.' He stooped. and gently fondled the roll of fur around the cat's neck. He looked up at Romy. 'I bought you some Maltesers.' He offered the box to her. Then he said softly, 'I don't want to go back, Romy. I hate the army. There's always people around, yelling at you, getting on your nerves. I get so I can't think. Some bastard shouts at me, ordering me about, and I've forgotten what he's told me to do the minute he's shut up. So I'm always in trouble.' He took a deep, shuddering breath. 'They think it's deliberate, that I'm being bolshie, but I'm not, Romy, honest

I'm not. And they never leave you alone. And the noise ... the guns ... I hate it. Sometimes I think I'll just make a run for it.'

'You mustn't, Jem,' she said fiercely. 'You've got to stick it out. If you do anything silly they'll catch you, you know they will.' And then they'll lock you away, she thought, and shivered at the thought of Jem caged in a military prison.

She put her arms around him and hugged him. 'Only a few more months,' she coaxed. 'Promise me you'll go back, Jem.'

He seemed to make an effort. He gave her a bright smile. 'Course I will,' he said lightly. 'Always do what my big sister tells me, don't I?'

'And you can stay here.'

He shook his head. 'Better not. I'd only mess it up again, wouldn't I?'

'Jem—'

Fleetingly the hopelessness returned to his eyes. 'Oh, you know me, Romy. Never one for keeping good resolutions. Only the bad ones.'

At the weekend Tom and Romy went to a party in Suffolk, on the coast between Aldeburgh and Thorpeness. On the train their conversations sparked in little flurries, then died away. As though they couldn't hit quite the right note, she thought. As though they were out of tune with each other.

The house was owned by Susie's parents; it teetered on the seashore, poised between land and water. In the dunes rusted strands of barbed wire jabbed through the marram grass, remnants of sea defences put up during the war. Made of wood and glass, the house seemed to Romy too fragile for such a precarious situation. Picture windows at the back of the upper floor looked out across the North Sea. The sandbags heaped to one side of the house and the peeling, weather-worn shutters on the downstairs windows hinted at past battles with the elements. When there was a storm, thought Romy, the waves must beat at the back door.

Inside, the house was topsy-turvy, the living rooms on the upper floor, the bedrooms downstairs. In an upstairs back room they had put bottles of beer and cider on a table. A gramophone played, the music echoing on the wooden walls. Someone was opening beer bottles, dropping the caps into a metal bucket with a clunk, someone else was putting dollops of margarine on baked potatoes. And they were talking, always talking. Words and phrases drifted across the room to Romy. Class-consciousness and avant-garde and alienation. The words jostled in her head; she found herself longing for silence.

She drank a few glasses of beer in an unsuccessful attempt to dispel the gloom that had descended on her since Jem's departure, and then she went into the adjacent room. It was empty; when she shut the door, she could hear the hush-hush of the sea. Wind and damp seeped through the cracks around the doors and windows. Susie's father was a lecturer at Cambridge University, and the house bore evidence of his enthusiasms. A telescope mounted on a tripod pointed to the beach. Ornithological textbooks filled the bookshelves and photographs of seabirds were pinned to the walls.

Flotsam drifted across the tables and floors, as though deposited there by some long-gone tide: shells and strands of dried seaweed and the honeycombed papery egg-cases of sea creatures.

Through the window, she saw a figure walking along the seashore. Glimpsing a flash of red hair, she went downstairs and threaded through a jumble of old armchairs and broken-backed books. Standing on the porch, she called out Psyche's name. Psyche did not look up, but continued to move along the beach, jumping every now and then over the incoming waves.

Sea holly and cardoons raised ragged heads in the garden. There was a low fence made of driftwood; stepping over it, Romy ran across the pebbles.

Psyche was wearing a long navy cloak, like a nurse's cape. She clutched it around her, bunching it at her throat. A ragged moon showed between fast-moving clouds. In its soft light Romy could see the tears that sequinned Psyche's smooth, plump cheeks. She said gently, 'Are you all right?' and Psyche stretched her taut mouth in the semblance of a smile, and said, 'Fine. I'm fine.' She frowned. Then she said suddenly, 'It's Magnus. I went to see him yesterday and Susie was there.' Tears spilled from Psyche's eyes and trailed down her face, a river of grief.

'You mean – ' Romy trod carefully – 'they were—'

'*In bed*,' hissed Psyche. 'They were in bed together! Well, on that disgusting sofa of his. But they were ... you know ...' She wailed, 'She didn't even put her top on! And she's so *thin*, Romy! You can see her ribs!' Psyche blew her nose. After a few moments, she began to walk along the seashore, stooping every now and then

220

to pick up a shell or a pebble. 'And I know I'm not engaged to him or married to him or anything, but still, I thought . . .' The words trailed away. Water dripped from the clump of seaweed she gripped in her hand.

'How long have you been dating Magnus?'

'We never exactly *dated*. I mean, we didn't go out to the pictures or for supper, anything like that. It was more staying in than going out.' Psyche blew her nose again and then stuffed her handkerchief into the sleeve of her cardigan. 'I used to cook Magnus's tea for him. And I tried to tidy up the flat, but it seemed to get messy again so quickly that I gave up. And he didn't like me doing it when he was there. Fussing around, he called it. He said I reminded him of his mother.' Psyche's face jerked up; she stared at Romy. 'Do you think he thought that I was *smothering*? Do you think that put him off? Freedom's so important to Magnus, isn't it? It's just that I hated the mess. I hated not being able to find a clean knife or fork. And once, when we were in bed together, I stretched out and felt something cold and horrible touch my foot, and it was a piece of cheese on toast! A half-eaten piece of cheese on toast!'

Romy couldn't help it; the corners of her mouth twitched. 'I know,' said Psyche with a giggle. 'I was always afraid of what I might find after that – I never dared put my feet down to the end of the bed.' Wrapping her cloak around her, she stared out to sea. 'But I do love him, Romy,' she said sadly. 'I really do.' She looked back at the house. Lights showed in the window and there was a thin thread of music, just heard over the whisper of the sea. 'I'd better go back,' she said. 'I don't want them to think that I *mind*.'

They walked back to the house. Psyche went indoors, while Romy sat on a bench in the garden, listening to the sea pulling against the pebbles. It'll be all right, she told herself. Jem's only got a few more months in the army, and then he'll be discharged and he'll sort himself out. And I'm only cross with Tom because I'm tired and worried about Jem.

Tom came to find her. 'It's cold,' he said, shivering. 'Bloody July.'

'Beautiful, though.'

He sat down beside her. 'I thought you preferred cities.'

'I do, most of the time.'

He kissed her. 'Perhaps I should live somewhere like this. Perhaps then I'd be able to finish my book. I keep writing a bit and then tearing it up because it's no good, and then writing a bit more and realizing that's rotten as well. So it doesn't get any longer. I think the trouble is that I'm too ordinary. My life's been too uneventful.'

'Aren't you supposed to be making it up? Isn't that the point of writing?'

'But you have to have *lived*, don't you? That's what Magnus says. That I haven't enough material.'

'Oh, *Magnus*!' she said scornfully. She thought of Psyche, and the pain Magnus inflicted on her in the name of his half-baked existentialist philosophy. 'You wouldn't want to model yourself on Magnus, would you, Tom? So self-centred – so conceited—'

He looked taken aback. 'You don't mean that, do you?'

She stared at him. 'Well, I do, actually,' she said

222

coldly. Part of her knew that she should hold her tongue, let the subject drop, but instead she went on, 'Look at the way he treats poor Psyche. Like a drudge.'

'Magnus doesn't *make* Psyche do anything. She wants to. She likes looking after him. Some women like looking after men. There's nothing wrong in that, is there?'

'Why doesn't he marry her, then? At least then she could stop dancing in those awful clubs.'

'Magnus doesn't believe in marriage,' explained Tom earnestly. 'He thinks it's a bourgeois institution.'

'Magnus,' said Romy furiously, 'doesn't believe in anything that doesn't allow him to put himself first!'

'That's not true.' Tom sounded wounded. 'Think how good he was to me when I first came to London. He took me places – he helped me to find somewhere to live—'

'That's because he likes you admiring him. Running around after him.'

Her voice, cold and unforgiving, seemed to cut through the sound of the sea. She heard his quick inhalation of breath and then, when the silence had gone on too long, she turned to look at him.

'Tom,' she said. She could see the hurt in his eyes. She had the same feeling she sometimes had when she looked at him after they had made love, an uncomfortable awareness of his defencelessness and vulnerability.

'Sorry,' she muttered. 'I'm sorry. I shouldn't have said that.'

'It isn't like that.' He stood up and walked to the fence that bounded the garden. 'I'm sorry you think it is.'

'I just think you're nicer than Magnus, that's all.'

'If you weren't so touchy with him—'

'*Me*, touchy?'

'You never seem to agree with him.'

'He's so provoking—'

'That's just Magnus's way. He likes to talk, to set off a discussion.'

'So if he provokes me, he's starting a debate, but if I provoke him, I'm being touchy!'

'I didn't mean that.' He took a deep breath. 'I don't want to quarrel. I hate quarrelling. Especially with you, Romy.'

'Magnus is always borrowing money from you,' she pointed out. 'And you've hardly got any money.'

'I don't care about that. Money isn't important, is it?'

'Oh, it is, Tom, it is.' She stared out at the sea and said flatly, 'It is if you haven't got it. It is if you've never had it. There's not having money and not having money. If you were really desperate – if you had nothing to eat – then you'd go back to your family, wouldn't you?'

'I suppose so. But I wouldn't want to – it would seem like a defeat.'

'But you *could*. So all this pretending to be poor, it's just—'

She broke off. But his eyes hardened, and he said, 'Hypocritical? Was that what you were going to say, Romy? It's just hypocritical?'

'No ... more ... just *playing*.'

She knew, looking at him, that she had only made things worse. He walked away from her down to the shore. She watched him hurl stones into the water.

Gazing miserably after him, she found herself wondering why she had never told him about the grinding poverty of her own early life. Why had she never told him about her father or about Middlemere? The most terrible events of her childhood, the events that had set her family onto a darker course, and she had never mentioned them to Tom. Why? Because she was ashamed of what had happened? Or because she did not trust him?

Neither Tom nor Magnus could know the things that she knew. Coming from comfortable homes and loving families, only they might say that money didn't matter. But poverty wasn't romantic. Poverty wasn't starving picturesquely in a quaint little garret. She had realized years before, at the Pikes' party, that poverty was boring and mundane, that it gave you no choice. Poverty meant you never had anything nice, that you ate the same food day after day and wore the same clothes over and over again. That you couldn't cheer yourself up by going to the cinema or to the seaside, and even if you were invited to a party, you had probably better not go because you didn't look right. And if you didn't fit in, then people would look down on you, assuming that it was your fault.

She knew that there were things that she would never tell Tom. She would never tell him that her father had killed himself, just as she would never tell Olive or Teresa or Mrs Plummer or sweet, pretty Psyche. Some horrors she shared only with her family.

And with one other person, of course. For the first time in ages, she found herself thinking of Caleb Hesketh. How odd that a stranger should know her secrets when Tom, with whom she had shared her bed, her heart, did not.

A few days later, Mrs Plummer called Romy to her suite. There was an open suitcase on the bed and the doors of the wardrobes yawned. Mrs Plummer held up two dresses. 'Which do you think? The blue or the emerald?' Her eyes shone, her complexion glowed.

'The emerald,' said Romy.

Mrs Plummer nodded. 'The emerald's more youthful, isn't it?' She laid the dress carefully on the bed, smoothing tissue paper between its folds. She said, 'Johnnie and I are going to the cottage for a few days,' and Romy, understanding the cause of Mrs Plummer's altered mood, kept her features impassive.

'Yes, Mrs Plummer. Is there anything particular you want me to take care of while you're away?'

'Anton has still to show me the final menu for the reception next weekend. You can telephone it through to me, Romy. Last time we spoke, he had trifle down as one of the desserts, and I told him he'd have to think of something else. Trifle looks so unappetizing once you serve it. And I wasn't happy with the last lot of flowers from Dixon's. I've told them before I won't have red gladioli, they look common and they don't go with the decor. And you're to telephone the laundry and query that last bill they sent. Six pounds for the pillowcases is perfectly ridiculous.'

Half a dozen different-coloured pairs of gloves followed the dress into the suitcase. Mrs Plummer smiled.

'Now I'd like you to run me an errand, Romy. I need a few things from Harrods. You're to buy me half a dozen pairs of stockings – you know the ones I like. And can I trust you to choose a little gift for Johnnie? I saw some lovely silk scarves last time I was there. I think maroon would be nice, don't you? A little surprise for him. Tell them to put it on my account.' She straightened and opened her jewellery box. 'Run along now, Romy. As quick as you can.'

In the gentlemen's department of Harrods, Romy chose a dark red silk scarf flecked with gold. Walking back to the Tube station, she saw the headlines on the newspaper hoardings announcing the hanging that morning of Ruth Ellis. Ruth Ellis's image, bleached-blonde, hollow-eyed and fragile, stared out from the front page of the *Evening Standard*.

In spite of the summer warmth, Romy shivered. She thought of Psyche and Magnus, Johnnie Fitzgerald and Mrs Plummer. And of Ruth Ellis and the man she had shot, her handsome, faithless lover, David Blakely. Weaving between the late-afternoon crowds, her thoughts drifted to Tom. Though they had patched up their disagreement, it seemed to her that something had changed. Or was it that she herself had begun to view Tom with a sharper eye? Was there something missing, something wanting?

What would she do for Tom? Would she marry him, or bear his children, or give up, if it did not suit him, the life she had clawed out for herself? Would she abase herself for him, would she forgive him time after time after time, as Mrs Plummer did Johnnie? Would she lie for him, steal for him, or kill for him? She knew that she would not. She wondered whether that mattered. Perhaps Tom's diffidence, his hesitancy and his willingness to be led, suited her. What need had she of passion? She knew too well how uncontrolled passion – for a lover, or for a house – could lead to misery and madness. Romy tucked the Harrods bag under her arm and ran down the steps to the Tube station.

The summer fête of the parishes of Swanton le Marsh and Swanton St Michael was held each August in the grounds of Swanton Lacy, as immovable a feast as Christmas and as inevitable as taxes. It was Evelyn's responsibility to oversee the fête, to provide tables and chairs for the stalls, and to contend with difficult, over-sensitive parishioners who took offence at the smallest misplaced word. Over breakfast one morning, Osborne announced that Mr Browne and Mr Lestrange, the vicars of the parishes, would be calling that afternoon to discuss the arrangements.

Evelyn helped herself to scrambled eggs. 'I think we should scale things down this year,' she said. 'It's all so time-consuming.'

'It's only a little village fête.'

'Osborne, it's like planning a battle. And what with having to visit Mother more often and doing all the cooking myself, it really is too much. And then there's the garden – they make such a mess of the garden. And all the roses have to be deadheaded and mulched or that frightful Lockhart woman makes comments.'

'I don't think we need worry about the doctor's wife, do we?'

'Last year, she offered to lend me her gardener. So patronizing.'

'The fête is a tradition, Evelyn. It can't be changed.' With a sharp flick, Osborne turned a page of his newspaper.

Evelyn found herself staring at the back pages of *The Times*, hot with the now familiar rage. 'Osborne,' she said, 'have you listened to a single word I've been saying?'

The paper was lowered. 'Of course I have.'

'I'm trying to explain to you that I can't cope this year. It was different, perhaps, when we had servants, but I really can't manage these days.'

His brows snapped together. 'Of course we can manage.'

We, she thought, when Osborne's only contribution was to make an opening speech and present the prizes. She put down her knife and fork. 'Have you any idea how much work I have to put in? Have you any idea how long I spend coaxing people who'd really rather not be bothered into knitting tea cosies and baking cakes? Have you any idea how long it takes me to clear up afterwards? People always say they'll help, but they never do – oh, there are a few stalwarts like Mrs Lestrange and Mrs Arnold, but they have families, remember, and can hardly be expected to stay up till midnight to scrub our floors. Last year it took me an entire morning just to clean the lavatories! And the *litter* in the garden—'

He said coldly, 'I'm sorry you find it so onerous, Evelyn, but the Swantons' summer fête has always been held here.'

'I'm not suggesting cancelling it. Just, as I said, scaling it down.'

'And what message would that give to our neighbours?'

She stared at him. 'Keeping up appearances ... does that matter so much to you?'

He folded his paper and stood up. 'It should matter to you also, Evelyn. We have a position to maintain.'

He had a way of pleating his hands together behind his back, one finger beating against his clenched knuckles, a clear signal that he believed the conversation to be at an end. It was a habit that had irritated her for years; now it enraged her.

'It must be obvious to everyone who knows us,' she said tautly, 'that we cannot keep up past standards. You are deceiving yourself, Osborne, if you believe otherwise.'

'Our situation is temporary.'

'Is it? It wasn't temporary for the Maxeys or the Longvilles, so why should it be so for us? David Maxey now earns his living by running a garage. And Hugo Longville demolished his family home. In what way are we different?'

'Because we *are* different,' he said. 'We are Daubenys.'

He left the room. Evelyn sat staring at her plate, her appetite gone. She felt a cold, implacable dislike, which seemed to her just then to be far more invidious and far more immutable than anger. Anger could be a part of passion; dislike, once seeded, was much harder to uproot.

They had made up, after a fashion. Or, rather, they

had gone on as though the quarrel had not taken place. A few nights later Osborne had made love to her. As was her habit on such occasions, Evelyn mentally planned her summer bedding. Yellow begonias, white ageratum, blue lobelia, she thought, as Osborne heaved and gasped.

The following month she was driving back from Newbury after a bridge evening when, heading down a narrow, twisting lane, she lost control of the car. It skidded into the verge, and when it came to a halt she sat for a long breathless moment, watching her shaking hands gripping the steering wheel, her heart beating wildly. When she was able to, she climbed out and looked at the punctured front tyre.

It was dark. It had been dry when she had left home that evening, and she had optimistically gone out without her mackintosh. Now rain was sheeting from the sky. The nearest village was more than two miles away. The thought of walking alone down the winding lanes to fetch help alarmed her. Through the pounding rain, she could hear rustlings in the undergrowth and, overhead, the beating of wings. Though the spare wheel was in its neat little cage on the back of the car, she had no idea what to do with it. Osborne, or, before the war, one of the servants, had always attended to punctures. Once, half a dozen or so years ago, that dreadful Hesketh woman's son had changed a tyre for her; now, trying to recall what he had done, she could remember only Caleb Hesketh's quick efficiency and his dark good looks, and his smile at her when he had finished – a winning smile, admittedly, though she had instinctively distrusted it, recalling his mother's reputation. But how had he changed the wheel? Evelyn gave the bolts a tentative twist, but they did not budge.

She heard a car heading down the hill towards her. Headlamps washed over the road; a Bentley drew to a halt and the driver's door opened, and she recognized Hugo Longville.

'Oh, *Hugo*,' she said. 'Thank goodness you're here.'

'What's the trouble?'

She told him about the puncture. He peered at the tyre and whistled. 'Flat as a pancake. Not to worry, I'll put it right in two ticks.' He glanced at her. 'Are you all right, Evelyn?'

'It was a bit of a shock,' she said.

'I bet. You poor thing.' He gave her a hug. 'And you're getting soaked – rotten weather to be standing about in the middle of nowhere. Why don't you sit in my car while I have a go at this?'

'Actually,' she said, 'would you mind if I watched? I should know how to mend punctures, shouldn't I? I can't always expect you to rescue me, Hugo.'

He opened the boot of his Bentley. 'Here.' He handed her a hip flask. 'Have a swig of this, you look like you could do with it. And take this—'

He stripped off his raincoat and placed it round her shoulders. She said, 'Hugo, I couldn't possibly – you'll get drenched—'

He took a jack out of his car. 'Of course you must. It'll get covered in oil if I wear it.'

She stood by the verge, watching him change the tyre. When she passed him the flask, he took a swallow and handed it back to her. She did not wipe the mouth of the flask before drinking. The raincoat retained his warmth. In the deepening darkness her face burned. There seemed such intimacy in those moments. She was aware of the weight of the raincoat on her shoulders, the raincoat that smelt faintly, indefinably, of Hugo. She was aware of the rain stinging her face. She could still feel the pressure of his fingers where they had brushed against her and the warmth of his arm around her shoulders.

There was a single hair on the lapel of the coat: she noticed its gold-brown sheen. When he stood up to put the damaged wheel on the back of her car, she had no idea how to change a tyre, but she knew that she was in love with him.

At the end of August Romy went home to Hill View. As always, butterflies flexed their wings in her stomach as she made her way up the path to Number 5. As always, Stratton seemed unchanged; she might have left it yesterday. Only Gareth, poking a stick into a puddle in the front garden, had altered since her last visit. Now a little boy, he was steady on his feet, with most of his baby plumpness gone.

She walked round to the back of the house. Martha was standing at the kitchen sink washing dishes. When Romy tapped on the window, Martha's pink-gloved hands flew to her mouth.

'You should have told me you were coming,' she scolded. 'I'd have got something in for tea.'

Indoors Martha rushed around, disseminating news, boiling the kettle, slicing bread, spreading margarine. 'I don't do a cooked tea when Dennis is away – doesn't seem much point when it's just me and the kids. We just have a bit of bread and jam. If I'd known you were coming, Romy, I'd have got some sausages.'

'It doesn't matter, Mum. Really. Bread and jam's fine.'

'I'm doing lunches in the Rising Sun now, did I tell you? Carol babysits. She's a good girl, Carol. Not clever like you, Romy, but she's a good girl. She's round the Belbins' now, with Ronnie. Here – ' Martha searched through the cupboard and took out a tin – 'd'you fancy a bit of corned beef? I meant to get into town, do a bit of shopping, but the wheel's gone on the pushchair and I can't manage Gareth and the bags. My back's been playing up something rotten.'

'You should go to the doctor, Mum.'

'Waste of time. Last time I went he told me to get more rest. Rest! Who does he think I am? Lady Muck? House doesn't look after itself, does it?' Martha gazed at her elder daughter and her tired face broke into an affectionate smile. 'You look so smart. Like in a magazine.'

'Do you like my hair, Mum? I had it cut in France.'

'France,' said Martha proudly. 'Well I never. Tomato sauce?' She wielded a bottle. 'All those years you grew your hair. You used to yell at the tangles. And then you go and have it all cut off. Looks nice, mind.' Red blobs obliterated the corned beef.

They ate at the kitchen table. Romy told Martha about the hotel; Martha told Romy about Sharon Belbin's premature baby and Ronnie's impetigo and Gareth's latest bout of tonsillitis.

'Doctor says he'll have to have them out. I had to

take him to the hospital last month to have 'em looked at. Three buses, Romy, and a half-hour wait between each of them.' Martha's nervous fingers stripped the crust from a sandwich.

After tea the boys went to bed and Carol went out and Martha curled up on the sofa with the cigarettes and sherry that Romy had brought her, while Romy washed up. She was drying tumblers when Martha called out, 'Haven't had a postcard nor nothing from that brother of yours. You heard from him, Romy?'

'Not since he went back to Germany.'

'I knew the army wouldn't suit him.' Martha scrabbled at the packet of Player's Weights. Anxiety pleated her forehead. 'He drinks too much.' She stared at the glass in her hand and gave a raucous laugh. 'Can't think who he takes after. But he never used to drink, Jem. Did every other thing he bloody shouldn't have, but he didn't used to drink.' Clumsily Martha refilled her glass. Sherry spilled onto the couch's worn floral cover. She said suddenly, 'He was never the same after we left Middlemere. That bloody man . . .'

Romy paused, tea towel in hand. She had a sudden memory of Caleb Hesketh standing in the foyer of the Trelawney Hotel. *Osborne Daubeny owns Middlemere*, he had told her. *He's our landlord. Your family's landlord, too, when you lived at Middlemere.* 'Who?' she asked. 'Mr Daubeny?'

'I meant your father.' Martha inhaled her cigarette and frowned. 'Though Sam always blamed Daubeny. Sam hated him, put all our difficulties down to him. We were always having trouble with the well at Middlemere – the water would run foul in summer because the stream had dried up. Some summers we had to fetch our water from the village. Sam was always on at Daubeny to do something about it. Said he had all his fancy cars and servants, and there we were paying all that rent and couldn't even get a clean glass of water. But he was wasting his breath.' Angry lines incised Martha's forehead. 'He never knew when to keep his mouth shut. And look where it got me. Tramping all over the country with a couple of kids in tow.' She took a gulp of sherry. 'Jem missed his dad, I suppose. He couldn't understand why we couldn't go home. Don't you remember?'

Romy put the glasses away in the cupboard. She shook her head. 'Not really.' From that time, she recalled a succession of homes, a succession of schools, and sometimes being hungry and often being cold.

'After Sam died he didn't speak for six months,' said Martha. 'Not a word. His teacher caned him once. Said he was just being bloody-minded. I gave the bugger a piece of my mind, I can tell you. Poor little kid, anyone with any sense could see he was upset.'

Martha's eyes sparked with fury and grief. Romy shut away the image of a mute Jem, and said, 'What do you mean, Dad wouldn't keep his mouth shut? Do you mean about Mr Daubeny and Mrs Hesketh? Did he know about that?'

'Shouldn't think so,' said Martha scornfully. 'Whole bloody village might have known about them, but not your father. Always had his head in the clouds. And living out there you didn't really hear much. Anyway, Sam wasn't interested in that sort of thing. Hated gossip. Had his principles, your dad. Ha! Fat lot of good they did him, his bloody principles. Lived in a world of his own, didn't he? Thought you could better yourself, reading books and that.' She gave a short, bitter laugh. 'Sam used to tell me that all men are made equal. Well, some are more equal than others, aren't they?' Martha's eyes narrowed. 'As if we could ever have been equal to the Daubenys. That house . . .' She shook her head.

'The Daubenys' house?'

'Swanton Lacy,' supplied Martha. 'That's what the house was called. Swanton Lacy. There was a lake in the garden, Romy. Fancy having a lake in your garden!'

'Where was it? Was it near Middlemere?'

'It was a couple of miles out of Swanton St Michael. I only went there a few times, mind, to pay the rent. Sam didn't like me paying the rent – he usually did it himself. Said he wouldn't have me kowtowing to the gentry.' Her eyes took on a dreamy expression. She said slowly, 'There were hundreds and hundreds of roses in the Daubenys' garden. I've never seen so many roses. All different colours and the most beautiful scent. You could smell them, coming down the road before you reached the house.' When she smiled, Martha's face looked younger, prettier. 'I took one for my buttonhole once. No one saw me. They could spare me a rose, couldn't they?'

Then her expression altered and, picking up the overflowing ashtray and the empty glass, she went into the kitchen. 'Anyway, that's all done and dusted, isn't it?' she muttered. 'Best forgotten. No sense in raking over the past, that's what I always say.'

*

That night Romy dreamed of Middlemere. The house was neither as she remembered from her childhood, nor as she had seen it in 1953 when she had met Caleb Hesketh. In her dream the woods on the hillside had grown into a large forest that covered the valley. The trees encroached on the house, towering over it. Creepers snaked along the walls and planted their tiny tendrils on the windows, sticking like glue, darkening the interior of the house. Inside the rooms had become vast, cavernous, crumbling. Stone flags had cracked open to reveal black chasms plunging down into the earth. High walls, from which all plaster and paint had long since fallen, soared up into a dark sky, and puddles lay in the corridors. There was a sour smell of earth and decay and dank water, as though the land was reclaiming the house, seeping up through the foundations, tearing the stones apart, one by one.

When she awoke there were tears in her eyes. She was filled with a sense of dread, and of tasks incomplete. She tried to remember exactly what Caleb Hesketh had said to her two years ago. Scratching away at her recollection of that short, angry encounter, she recalled that Caleb had told her that he had spoken to Annie Paynter. Now she remembered hiding in the green cupboard, listening to Annie Paynter's father shouting up from the garden. For years afterwards she had nurtured a hatred of Mr Paynter. But the name of Osborne Daubeny had been unfamiliar to her until Caleb Hesketh had spoken it. *Osborne Daubeny owns Middlemere. Your family's landlord.* She tried to picture him, this tyrant she had never met, imagining him the red-faced, fat-bellied squire, swaggering through his demesne. She wondered what it was like, his house, Swanton Lacy with the beautiful garden, which had so long ago enraptured her mother.

She sat up in bed, the quilt wrapped around her, chilled in spite of the balmy August night. Well, she thought. There was only one way to find out.

Romy left Stratton the morning before Dennis was due home. A succession of trains and buses took her north through Hampshire towards the Berkshire border. In the preceding days temperatures had soared and the air was hot and humid.

By the time she reached Swanton St Michael clouds were bubbling up, towering, anvil-shaped edifices, blanking out the blue sky. She asked directions of a shopkeeper and started out of the village. Strips of coppiced woodland grew on either side of the road; beyond, she could see fields. Soil curled from a plough; not far away men struggled to peg a tarpaulin over a haystack. The black material flapped and billowed in the rising wind.

The rain began as she came over the brow of a hill and headed down into a valley. Drops of rain cast black dots the size of pennies on the narrow asphalt road. A thin grass verge, overgrown with docks and nettles, divided the road from the ditch, and when occasionally a vehicle rounded a corner towards her Romy had to leap, her small suitcase clutched in her hands, onto the verge.

The road twisted around corners and split into junctions and crossroads. Tall beeches and elms replaced the coppices. The sky had darkened to a dull purplish-grey, and rainwater had begun to gather in the ditches and at the side of the road. She wasn't sure whether she had remembered the directions correctly. Left at the first crossroads, or right? Take the second turn after the bridge or the third?

Then the road seemed to fade away, the tarmac melting into an unsurfaced track. The puddles between the rutted chalk were the colour of milk chocolate. She heard a crack of thunder and gave a small, involuntary cry. The soles of her shoes slipped on the mud and rainwater soaked through her mackintosh and her cotton dress. Her mac was too thin and her shoes more suited to the city, and she didn't have an umbrella. She never, she thought crossly, seemed to have the right clothes.

There was another rumble of thunder. She stepped off the track and looked out over the fields. Through the thick curtain of rain, she could see no grand house, no beautiful garden. She knew that she was lost, hopelessly lost, that Mr Daubeny's gleaming car would never take this mean little road to his palatial home. She put down her suitcase and sat on it it for a while, staring out at the fields. Rain streamed down her neck and ran in rivulets down her bare legs.

How many of her friends, she thought bitterly, would set out on such a fool's errand? Would soft, childlike Psyche, or composed, assured Susie? Would Teresa or Olive, Jake or Camille? People like Magnus and Tom cherished the idea of being thought of as outsiders. People like herself longed only to be accepted. She desired the things that Tom and Magnus despised.

She wanted nice clothes and a home that no one could ever take away from her. It seemed to her that a gulf yawned between her aspirations and Tom's.

A fork of lightning divided the sky, followed by a drumroll of thunder. She picked up her suitcase and headed back the way she had come. All she had to do, she told herself, was to take the opposite turnings to those she had previously taken and she would soon be back at Swanton St Michael.

But the narrow, winding roads confused her, and she began to have a frightening vision of herself wandering around this maze of woods and valleys and byways, becoming increasingly lost. The sky was dark grey, all light drained out of it, and her wet fingers slipped on the handle of the suitcase.

She reached a crossroads. Gazing at each road in turn, she tried to decide which direction to take. From behind her she heard the sound of a car engine. Spinning round, she flung out a hand to catch the driver's attention. The blue van slid to a halt a dozen yards up the road. Romy grabbed her suitcase and ran.

And, peering into the van, found herself face to face with Caleb Hesketh.

He spoke first. 'It *is* you,' he said, as he opened the passenger door. 'Get in. Dear God, you'll be soaked to the skin in this.'

Climbing into the van, her teeth were chattering and her heart was pounding. 'I'm sorry,' she said. 'I'm making your car all wet.'

'What on earth are you doing?' he asked. 'Were you looking for Middlemere?'

She shook her head. 'What, then?' he said. 'Where are you going?'

'Swanton Lacy. I was looking for Mr Daubeny's house.'

He made a scornful sound. 'You're going in completely the wrong direction. It's the other way out of the village.'

She felt foolish. She stared out of the window at the rain. Then she heard him say more kindly, 'All these little lanes are so confusing, aren't they? I still get lost sometimes. Here.' He took an old towel from the glove compartment. 'I put it over the seats when I'm carrying plants in the van, but it's quite clean. You could dry your hair a bit.'

She leaned forward, towelling her hair. Covertly she watched Caleb as he drove. He had a strong face, with a high forehead and prominent cheekbones and a hawkish nose. His black hair was curled by the rain. She thought at first that his eyes were brown, but then she saw that they were a very dark bluish-grey. Just now their expression was concentrated, rather severe.

'If you'd drop me at the bus stop,' she said. 'I have to get back to London.' She looked at her watch. 'There's a bus due soon.'

The windscreen wipers beat the rain from the glass; in no time at all they were among the scattered thatched cottages of Swanton St Michael. Caleb drew up at the side of the road. As Romy reached for the door handle, he said, 'It's still pouring. You'd better sit in here till the bus comes.'

'It's all right. I won't keep you.'

'Don't be daft. There's no shelter.' He looked at her curiously. 'You don't still hate me, do you?'

Her embarrassment deepened. She gave a sharp little shake of the head. 'That time you came to the hotel—'

'Not one of my better ideas.'

'I didn't know about Mr Daubeny till then, you see. Those things you told me ... Afterwards, I looked for Annie Paynter in the phone book, but I couldn't find her. There were lots of Painters with an "i" but hardly any with a "y". And she was always most particular.'

'She was engaged,' he said. 'She'll have married, changed her name.'

'Oh.' She was cross with herself for not having thought of that. 'Of course.'

'And her father was moving house. I can't remember where to.'

Suddenly there was so much she wanted to ask him. She said in a rush, 'What's Mr Daubeny like? And Annie – what did she tell you about Middlemere? And when you said that Annie's dad had been in Mr Daubeny's pocket, what did you mean?'

He glanced into the side mirror. 'There's your bus.'

Headlamps made smudged orange circles in the rain.

She climbed out of the van. There was something more she needed to say to him. She spoke quickly, to get it over and done with. 'When you came to the hotel, I was so horrible to you. That evening ... I was upset about something. But that's no excuse and I'm sorry. That was such a dreadful thing I said about your mother.'

'But true,' he said. As the bus slowed for the stop,

he handed her the suitcase. His wintry smile did not touch his eyes. He repeated softly, 'It was true.'

The conductor took her case from her as she climbed onto the bus. Standing on the platform, she called out, 'Caleb, about Anita Paynter—' and she heard him shout back, 'I'll get in touch. Are you still at that hotel?'

The bus pulled away from the stop. Viewed through the smeared, muddy windows his features seemed blurred, as though he was under water. She called out his name once more. But he was already lost in the falling rain, and though she waved she was unsure whether he could see her.

Chapter Eight

Caleb was now living in lodgings in Reading. His landlady was called Mrs Talbot; she had a sixteen-year-old daughter, Heidi. There was no sign of a Mr Talbot; Caleb imagined him gradually fading away to a wraith, worn to a shred by the proximity of his large, disapproving wife and sullen daughter.

In Caleb's room there were a bed, a table and chair, a chest of drawers and a paraffin heater, whose usage was strictly rationed. He shared a bathroom with the family; he had got into the habit of rising at six in the morning to avoid the awkwardness of colliding with the Talbots in their capacious pink candlewick dressing gowns. Mrs Talbot had a way of looking at him that made him think she suspected him of spending the night leafing through dirty magazines, or worse.

He had left home soon after his discovery of his mother's affair with Osborne Daubeny. Although they remained on good terms, since that day there had been a distance between him and his mother which time had not fully mended. He had done his best not to think about his mother and Daubeny, and had on the whole, he thought, managed pretty well. Only when he could find nothing else to occupy his mind – on a long journey, for instance, or while potting up a thousand geraniums during his stint with the parks department – had his thoughts drifted and settled on that uncomfortable little piece of the past.

Since leaving Broadbent's he had had several jobs. He had worked for six months for the town council in Reading, washing clay pots and planting up borders of blue salvias and red begonias. He had spent another year in a nursery in Earley, acquiring an encyclopaedic knowledge of plants. Some months ago he had started work for a man called Freddie Bartlett. Freddie ran a garden design and maintenance business and was kind and vague and disorganized. Caleb had taken to him instantly. Freddie's paperwork was chaotic and his time-keeping appalling, but there was about his horticulture a quintessential romantic Englishness that galvanized Caleb, and made him remember why he had abandoned a safe career in an office for the grubbier, and far less prestigious, business of gardening.

Gone were the ordered arrangements of alyssum and lobelia, geranium and salvia, so favoured by the parks department. Freddie sowed drifts of blue flax beneath the roses in a formal garden, and planted great swathes of wisteria and clematis against old brick walls. There were no hard edges or sharp corners in Freddie's gardens. To the untrained eye they looked like glorious accidents, fortuitous conjunctions of colour and shape. But Caleb knew the work that went into that pleasing carelessness: the planning, planting, digging, shaping and pruning.

Most days Caleb worked from dawn till dusk. He had calluses on his hands and the muscles of a navvy. In the evenings he studied for his Royal Horticultural

Society qualifications by correspondence course, and had supper with Mrs Talbot and Heidi. Freddie was a generous employer, allowing Caleb a free hand with a border, a stab at a design for an informal pond. Freddie taught him the importance of structure and surprise. They shared the routine, necessary work of digging, planting and pruning. 'Have to get your hands dirty,' gasped Freddie, an extraordinary sight in size eleven wellington boots and bright yellow oilskins, as they hauled stones to construct a rockery, or dug out a quarter of an acre of ground that in the war had grown potatoes and was now being converted back to a topiary garden. 'Don't feel I've done a day's work unless I've got my hands dirty.'

When the weather was at its worst, they drew up designs and put in orders for plants and seeds and grew seedlings and cuttings in Freddie's extensive greenhouse. Recently, in a rash moment, Caleb had offered to go through Freddie's books. Well, not *books*, exactly: Freddie's record keeping consisted of stuffing bills and invoices into a row of dusty glass jars kept on a shelf at the back of the potting shed. 'Help yourself, dear boy, help yourself,' Freddie had murmured, his normally jovial countenance downcast at the mere thought of addition and subtraction.

Now, driving back to Middlemere, Caleb found himself wishing he was in Freddie's shed, smoothing out all those grubby scraps of paper, writing figures in neat columns. He felt confused. He could not work out why on earth he had offered to keep in touch with Romy Cole. Digging up all that again – what had possessed him? Some irrational sense of inherited guilt?

An imagined responsibility for the tragedy that years ago had overtaken the Cole family?

When the figure at the roadside had hailed him that afternoon, he had braked automatically. It was only when he had looked back that he had recognized Romy. His sudden rush of resentment had taken him by surprise, a leftover, he supposed, from that memorable meeting at the hotel two years ago. For a fraction of a second he had considered driving on, leaving her to her own devices.

But he had not done so, of course, because some other emotion had immediately followed the anger – pity, he supposed. Lost in the thunderstorm, she had looked so small, so bedraggled. When she had sat beside him in the car, she had ceased to be the furious harridan of his recollection, and he had recognized her for what she was: very young and cold and rather frightened. Rain had dripped from her clothes and hair. He had had a sudden ridiculous impulse to take her hands between his own and warm them.

And besides, he had quite some time ago managed to see their previous interview from her point of view. He had turned up at the Trelawney out of the blue, clumsily meddling in affairs that must inevitably cause her pain. He should at least have phoned or written beforehand. Instead, he had given her no warning at all and, looking back, he suspected that some of her vindictiveness that night had been due to shock.

The van bumped and rattled on the muddy track. The rain had eased, and a shaft of sun cast a brilliant light through the parting clouds. Fragments of a rainbow glimmered over the hills. As Caleb took the rutted

248

path down the valley to Middlemere Farm, he found himself imagining a much younger Romy here, playing in the barn, perhaps, or running down the hillside. And he thought of the previous times they had met, and thought also how odd it was, how very odd, that he had not noticed that she was pretty.

'Somewhere,' said Freddie. 'I know I put it somewhere. Ah, here we are.' Beaming, he extracted a scrap of paper from the teetering tower on the window sill.

The papers were on the window sill because there wasn't room for them on the desk. The other rooms in Freddie's house were a sanctuary of tidiness, kept just so by Freddie's very efficient housekeeper, Mrs Simpson. Freddie did not allow Mrs Simpson to clean his study.

Freddie put on his reading glasses and unrolled the piece of paper. 'Mrs Zbigniew.' He spelt it out. 'I have no idea how to pronounce it. I addressed her as Irena. She has a nice little house in Hampstead with a disastrous little garden. I said you'd have a go at it, make it into an earthly paradise.'

Caleb was perched on the arm of a chair. More books and papers and Freddie's King Charles spaniel, Oscar, filled the seat of the chair. He looked up, surprised. 'Me?'

'Why not? I'm feeling rather jaded, to tell you the truth, dear boy. Peter and I have been thinking of a little jaunt to the south of France. Just a week or two. Recharge our batteries.' Peter was Freddie's friend, ex-navy and as gaunt as Freddie was stout.

Caleb began, 'I'm not sure if I'm ready—'

'Course you are.' Freddie was confident. 'Nothing too ambitious, no ha-has or cascades. Something pretty. She's a dear lady, you'll like her. You can pop up to town tomorrow, take measurements. Draw me up a sketch and I'll cast my eye over it before we head off to jolly old Antibes.'

The following morning Caleb caught an early train to London. Mrs Zbigniew lived in a mews house between the Tube station and the Heath. She was tiny and wizened; her head, swathed in plaits and combs, did not reach Caleb's shoulder. Her house was a treasure trove of richly coloured rugs and throws and intricately carved little cupboards decorated with painted flowers. There were also a great many cats: curled up on cushions, draped across sofas, arching their backs with a flash of emerald eye as Caleb made his way through the house.

The garden was, as Freddie had said, a disaster. The decaying remains of an Anderson shelter, its roof caved in and its floor awash with rainwater, stood outside the back door. There wasn't an intact pane of glass in the greenhouse, and half the small patch had been given over to an attempt at a kitchen garden. Onions, long since gone to seed, protruded leggily between rotting cardboard boxes; lettuces, their leaves turned to lace by marauding grubs, sprouted beside the blackened remains of a bonfire.

Mrs Zbigniew clutched Caleb's sleeve. 'It's terrible, isn't it, darling? Terrible. But you will make it lovely for me.'

He spent the day taking measurements and deciding whether any of the existing plants were worth keeping.

Variegated ivies scrambled up the walls, a white lilac filled the far corner of the garden, and a witch hazel hid beneath a sprawling mass of old man's beard. In the coldest months of the year its yellow flowers would be like small sunbursts.

At midday Mrs Zbigniew fed him bread and sausage and sweets and showed him photographs of her son, who had flown bombers for the RAF in the war, and now lived in Rotherham with his wife and three children. 'Laszlo is very tall, like you, dear Caleb,' said Mrs Zbigniew, stretching a tiny hand towards the ceiling. 'But fatter than you. Much fatter.'

He worked late into the evening and did not get back to his lodgings until twenty past ten. He was supposed to be in by ten: it was that sort of lodging house. He tried the front door, but it was bolted. He was deliberating between a night in the garden shed or knocking on the door and enduring Mrs Talbot's wrath when he heard the bolts slide open.

The landlady's daughter, Heidi, was standing in the doorway. She put a finger to her mouth. 'Sshh.'

She bolted the door quietly behind him and beckoned him into the parlour. That was what Mrs Talbot called it, the parlour. Which made Caleb think of lace tablecloths and old maids in mob caps.

Heidi whispered, 'I waited up for you.'

'That was kind of you. Thanks.' He added, in explanation, 'The train was late.'

'Do you want some supper?'

'It's all right, I'm not hungry.'

But she said, 'I made you something specially,' and produced a plate and a Thermos flask. Beckoning him to a chair, she put the plate and flask on a spindly-legged table.

He was obliged to express his gratitude once more and to sit down and eat. Heidi stood beside him, watching him. It was hard to swallow. The sandwiches were egg, rubbery and resistant, and besides, something in her prominent brown, heavy-lidded eyes made him feel uneasy. She was a strong-looking, well-made girl, with mousy hair scraped back into a severe ponytail. Her large breasts strained against her school-uniform jersey: one day, he thought absently, they'd join into a vast, single shelf, and she'd look like her mother.

He said, 'It's all right, Heidi, you don't have to stay up. You must be tired,' but she remained where she was, standing like a sentinel.

'I'm not tired. I never go to sleep before midnight. I write my diary.'

'Do you?' He imagined her, breathing heavily, tongue between teeth, laboriously scribbling down her adolescent fantasies.

'Do you keep a diary, Caleb?'

He shook his head. 'Wouldn't be much to write in it.'

'Have you got a girlfriend?'

He said carefully, 'Not at the moment.'

'Have you had lots of girlfriends?'

It crossed his mind, horribly, that her interest in him was not merely friendly, landlady's daughter to lodger, but something more particular. He rejected the idea almost immediately. She was only sixteen, after all. At worst, she had a bit of a crush.

Yet he had a sudden unpleasant vision of her peeling off her jersey and releasing her lank hair from the prison of its rubber band, so he choked down the last sandwich, screwed the top back on the Thermos and stood up. 'That was great, Heidi,' he said in a hearty elder-brotherly way. 'Shall I put these in the kitchen?'

'I'll do it.' Her pale, waxy fingers brushed against his as she took the Thermos from him.

Several weeks later Caleb had completed most of the structural work in Mrs Zbigniew's garden and was left with his favourite part, the planting.

There was more than a hint of autumn in the air, in the slant of the sun and in the leaves that drifted from the branches of the lilac. Clearing up when the light went at the end of a Friday afternoon, Caleb felt reluctant to return immediately to Reading. He needed company and conversation; he needed to celebrate the slow birth of his garden. And besides, Heidi had taken to bringing him cups of milky tea in his room during the evenings and perching on his bed in a predatory fashion, watching him as he drank.

From a call box at the corner of the street, he phoned Alec and Luiz. Alec was going to the theatre with his fiancée; Luiz was melancholy and not in the mood for company. Mentally Caleb ran through the list of his other London friends. His hand hovered over the telephone receiver. Get it over and done with, he told himself. It hadn't been preying on his mind, exactly, it was more a niggling awareness of something unfinished, like a sinkful of washing up, or an unwritten letter.

Romy could not understand quite what had gone wrong between her and Tom. It was not that they quarrelled – Tom hated to quarrel and would back down or walk away to avoid doing so. But what had once endeared had begun to irritate. She suspected that it was her fault, that he was simply too nice for her. That his idealism and lack of materialism were wasted on someone like her. She found herself exasperated by the qualities in him she knew she should admire: by his patience, his tolerance of other people's failings, his unselfishness. Sometimes, when he gave his last shilling to one of his friends or to a tramp on the Embankment with blood-shot eyes and a smoker's cough, she wanted to scream at him: *Your elbows are sticking out of your jacket. You haven't had a decent meal for days. Look after yourself, Tom, before you weep for the whole world.*

She told herself that she was feeling touchy because she was tired and because the summer had ended. Soon things would come right again. Yet she found herself short-tempered, disagreeing with Tom about unimportant things. The late-night conversations that she had once enjoyed so much now irritated her. She heard herself, cranky and querulous, seizing on some casual comment of his and tearing it to pieces. When she saw the hurt in his eyes, she muttered, 'Sorry, Tom, I'm sorry,' and kissed and coaxed him till he smiled again.

To make up for her uncertain temper, she bought him doughnuts and Chelsea buns from the bakery, and found him an old coat that no longer fitted Jake. When he wasn't looking, she fed coins into the meter at his bedsit; when he had a bad cold, she brought him aspirins and oranges. It was when she found herself replacing the missing buttons on one of his shirts that she stood back to look at herself and was horrified at what she saw. Here she was, ambitious, independent Romy Cole, who had promised herself never to wait on a man, never to become mired in domesticity, and she was *sewing on buttons*. Wary of marriage, she had nevertheless slipped into a wifely role.

When she looked around her, it seemed to her that a great many other women had fallen into the same trap. There was Psyche, of course, cooking and cleaning for a man who professed to despise marriage but was content nevertheless for a woman to carry out the day-to-day tasks that he felt were beneath him. In Soho itself, how many of the artists and writers that she encountered were women? She could think of hardly any. Most of the women were defined by their relationships with men. They were wives or mistresses, muses or whores. Only a few, like Mirabel Plummer, preserved their strength and independence. Mrs Plummer had used men as stepping stones to fulfil her ambitions, marrying a rich old husband here, taking a wealthy lover there. Yet even Mrs Plummer was not, of course, immune to woman's fatal need for love.

Caleb Hesketh telephoned just before Romy was due to leave the hotel for the Fitzroy. She wondered whether to put him off, but in the end agreed to meet him at the pub. Her pride demanded that he see her in a more civilized light. He had a knack of finding her at her worst. Each time they had met she had been angry, offensive, or dripping wet. Just the thought of their three encounters made her blush.

In the hotel cloakroom she combed her hair and carefully redid her make-up. She was wearing a black skirt, which flared out to just above the ankles, and a jade-green, short-sleeved angora jumper. She checked her reflection in the mirror. There were no ladders in her stockings and her shoes were polished. If she could only get through the evening without losing her temper or getting soaked, then she might put an end to her brief acquaintance with Caleb Hesketh with at least a semblance of dignity.

The pub was crowded. She was sitting between Jake and Tom when she saw Caleb standing in the doorway. In his muddy boots and patched corduroy jacket, he looked, she thought, out of place. In comparison, she felt gratifyingly sophisticated and urban.

She introduced him to the others. 'It's Magnus's birthday,' she explained.

Caleb offered to buy Magnus a drink; Magnus asked for a double Scotch. As Caleb disappeared into the thicket of people around the bar, Tom said, 'Friend of yours?'

'An acquaintance.'

'You haven't mentioned him before.'

'That's because,' she said lightly, 'he isn't important.' And he wasn't. After this evening she need never see him again.

Caleb came back with the drinks. Magnus made a great show of peering at his muddy boots. 'Are you a farmer?'

'I'm a gardener.'

Magnus's brows rose. 'How extraordinary.'

'I've only got a window box,' said Jake. 'Romy looks after it. Tells me off when I forget to water it.'

'Well, it's only one little window box, Jake. The poor plants had gone brown.'

'I could give you a lot of guff about being too absorbed in my art, but the truth is I've never got into the habit of looking after things. Plants and cats – kill 'em all off. Too forgetful, I suppose.'

Camille snarled. 'Too selfish.'

'You're probably right, my darling. I'm far too selfish. I prefer painting to gardening. When you're painting it may be bloody boring and miserable, but at least you're indoors most of the time and not freezing your arse off in some field.'

'You don't really find painting boring, do you?'

Jake lit a cigarette. 'Well, I do, Tom, to tell the truth; quite often I do.'

Tom looked pained. 'You don't mean that, surely. I would have thought it was marvellous to be able to express yourself through your art.'

'That's because you are very young and you still have some ideals. I suppose I was the same when I was an infant, but I really can't remember, it's so long ago. Gardening,' Jake continued thoughtfully. 'You must have seen a thing or two. It all sounds rather *Lady Chatterley*.'

'Who?' Psyche looked up.

'Dirty book, darling. Can't buy it here.'

'I'd lend you my copy,' said Magnus superciliously, 'but I don't think you'd get through it because it's in Italian.'

'Bloody boring anyway,' said Jake. 'You read about one couple copulating and you've read 'em all.'

'I should imagine,' said Magnus loftily, 'that gardening is in reality quite a *mundane* occupation.'

'Oh, it has its moments.' Caleb, who was standing on the outside of the circle, eyed Magnus. 'A woman I worked for last year used to sunbathe nude on the lawn while I did the flower beds.'

Jake guffawed. 'Bet that put you off your pruning.'

Romy drew Caleb away from the crowd. When they were alone, she asked curiously, 'Was that true?'

'About the woman sunbathing? Certainly. Only she was seventy. A naturist.' They went to stand in the pub doorway. 'People can be so dismissive about gardening. I mean, I can see it's not everyone's idea of how to get on in life, but still ... Most of the time I don't mind, but every now and then it gets my goat.'

'Oh, Magnus sneers about everything,' Romy said lightly. 'You should hear him talk about the hotel. You'd think I was single-handedly responsible for the survival of the class system.'

The corners of his mouth curled in a smile. Then he said, 'Anyway. Middlemere.'

'Of course. You'll want to get home.'

'Not really. I'm living in lodgings in Reading now. My landlady's daughter, Heidi, has taken to waiting up for me and making me rather poisonous sandwiches.'

'*Heidi?* Dirndl and plaits?'

'Something like that. Don't laugh. It's no laughing matter having to eat rubbery egg sandwiches at midnight.'

'I can quite see that.' She looked out at the street. Half a dozen Africans, their blue-black outlines melting into the shadows, were making their way up the road. They were carrying saxophones and tambourines. She said, 'Your mother and Osborne Daubeny—'

'They had an affair. It didn't last long, my mother said. I suppose she was lonely.'

She could see how much he hated talking about it. She said awkwardly, 'I shouldn't have said anything. I should have kept it to myself.'

'Should you?' He frowned. 'That's a tricky one, isn't it? Would I rather you knew and I didn't? I don't know. I don't think so. How did you find out?'

'My mother told me.'

'How did she know?'

She began, 'Oh, she'd heard—' and then she bit her lip.

His eyes narrowed to blue-grey slits. 'She'd heard what? Gossip? Everyone in the village knew – was that it?'

'I don't know about that,' she said. 'We weren't really a part of the village, living out at Middlemere. It must have been the same for you, surely. And my father ... he had his own ways of doing things, his own ideas. And he spoke his mind about things. That doesn't always make you friends. But my mother talked to people, I suppose. And when I told her that you were living in Middlemere now, well—'

'She drew her own conclusions?' He looked grim.

The Africans had turned the corner; from the other end of the street raised voices drew Romy's attention.

Two men and a woman were silhouetted against the night. Recognizing one of the men, she turned back to Caleb.

'Was that why you left home? Because of what I told you about your mother and Mr Daubeny?'

'Partly.' He shrugged. 'But only partly. I was drifting. I'd been in the army, then I had a job I didn't much like. I realized I had to sort myself out, find something I really wanted to do.'

'And you have now?'

'Yes. So, you see, you did me a favour. I needed a kick.'

'I didn't mean—'

He spread out his hands in a gesture of conciliation. 'Call it quits, shall we? After all, it was a long time ago. It's all done with, isn't it? Finished with.'

'Quits,' she echoed. She glanced back at the little group across the street. The men's voices were angry. Fingers jabbed, fists clenched. The woman stood on the sidelines, watching. The streetlamp caught the scarlet folds of her evening dress and the sheen of her auburn hair.

Romy said, 'You told me you spoke to Annie Paynter.'

'I met her by chance when I was working for a removals firm. The Paynters were moving house. Anita showed me round their bungalow. That was when I started to think that something was a bit off-key. Not quite right. Some of the things she said ... Daubeny blamed Paynter for what happened, but both Daubeny and Paynter were on the County War Agricultural

Executive Committee, and Daubeny, being gentry, had far more clout than Paynter, of course. On any important issue Paynter must surely have waited for the go-ahead from Daubeny. And then I found out that Paynter's shop in Swanton St Michael had been owned by Daubeny, and that Daubeny had helped the Paynters out after they left Swanton. Anita told me that her father fell ill after your father's death – he had a breakdown and couldn't work. Yet he seemed to have profited, if anything. And she said – I remember her exact words – that Mr Daubeny had been good to them. So I wondered whether there had been bad feeling between your father and Daubeny. I wondered whether that was why Daubeny had got rid of your family. It wasn't that at all, though, was it? I'd got it all wrong. It was because of my mother.'

On the far side of the road, one of the men was walking away. The other man yelled curses after him and then slouched against the wall, offering his cigarette case to the woman. Romy heard the rasp of the match scratching between the sound of the passing cars.

'Annie and me,' she said, 'we used to get into fights at school. She wasn't like me. Annie always had pink dresses and bows in her hair. She was May queen one year. You had to have yellow curls to be May queen. She always thought herself better than me. Well, that's what I thought then. You can't be sure, looking back, can you? I suppose we just rubbed each other up the wrong way. But I can remember Mr Paynter quarrelling with my father. Mr Paynter came to the house one day. I'd done something wrong – I'm not sure—'

'You pushed Anita into a horse trough.'

'She told you? Oh dear.' She felt embarrassed, then curious. 'What's she like now, Annie?'

'Pink dresses and bows in her hair.' He grinned. 'Dull as ditchwater.'

There was something rather satisfying in hearing Anita Paynter, queen of the village school, so dismissed. She looked at Caleb. 'Pretty, though?'

'I suppose so. Not my type.'

She wondered what Caleb Hesketh's type was. But she said, 'Tell me about Mr Daubeny. What's he like?'

'Full of himself. You must have met the sort. Expects *deference*.'

The couple across the road were embracing now. His hand caressed her body, then gathered up great hanks of her flame-coloured hair. His mouth pressed against her face, her neck, and her bare white shoulder.

'There's guests at the hotel like that,' said Romy. 'I was a chambermaid when I first worked there and I couldn't believe what some of them expected. The mess they'd leave their rooms in ... the things they'd leave lying about, personal things, for anyone to see, for us to pick up. As though we wouldn't mind. As though we weren't *people* – or weren't people who mattered.'

'Whenever I'm with Mr Daubeny, I find myself wanting to do something shocking. Swear a lot or pick my nose.'

'But you don't?'

'Wouldn't do, would it, the lower orders getting out of line? Anyway, he owns my mother's house, doesn't he? Better not get on the wrong side of him.'

She shivered. He glanced at her. 'Are you cold? Shall we go inside?'

She shook her head. Looking up, she saw that the red-haired woman had hailed a taxi and that her lover was weaving unsteadily across the road, cigarette in hand. As he reached the doorway of the pub, he stumbled, almost knocking into Romy. She said coolly, 'Good evening, Mr Fitzgerald,' and Johnnie snarled and staggered inside the pub.

Caleb said, 'Friend of yours?'

'He's my employer's lover.' She thought of the passion in Johnnie Fitzgerald's eyes as he had kissed the red-haired woman and the way his hand had clawed at her, as though he wanted to devour her.

She had found out two things, she thought, as they went back into the pub. The first was that Osborne Daubeny had rewarded Mark Paynter for evicting her family from Middlemere. The second – and equally surprising – was that Caleb Hesketh wasn't so bad after all. In fact, he was really quite nice.

It was the first time Evelyn had visited the home that Celia now shared with Gerald. The house was in Bayswater, in a small crescent which had the air of being slightly down-at-heel. Paint peeled from the window sills, and, though it was midday, milk bottles still lingered on doorsteps.

Celia kissed Evelyn and showed her into the hall. 'So lovely to see you. It's been ages. And I've so much to tell you.'

The kitchen was in the basement. There were a great many dusty whitewashed pipes and a large boiler that now and then emitted a wheezing sound. The floor was laid with differently coloured and randomly shaped pieces of a pock-marked stone, which must, Evelyn thought, be impossible to clean.

Celia made coffee. 'I know it's not as nice as the Hampstead house,' she said. 'Gerald let Laura have their house, otherwise she'd have made such a stink. And university lecturers don't get paid a great deal of money, and his family hasn't a bean.' She put cups and saucers on the table. 'But there's the sweetest little garden. A handkerchief tree, would you believe, in Bayswater! There's plenty of room for the children, that's the important thing. Kate and Sarah have the back room and the boys share the attic.'

'How are Miles and Charlie?'

'They're very well. They'll be here in a couple of weeks, at half-term. And Gerald's boy, Jamie, is coming too. We only saw him for a few days in the summer. Laura is being quite mean with him.'

'Still,' said Evelyn encouragingly, 'so lovely to have a houseful.'

'Oh, absolutely.'

'And so nice for Miles and Charlie to have a ready-made friend.'

'Yes,' said Celia, rather distractedly. She handed Evelyn a cup. 'Though Miles was so frightful the last time they were all together. Showing off. Boasting.'

'It's probably just a phase,' said Evelyn. 'I'm sure they'll get on like a house on fire.'

'Of course.' Celia looked doubtful.

'And Henry?' asked Evelyn. 'Have you seen Henry?'

'Well, one has to.' Celia lit a cigarette. 'That's the ghastly thing about it, one can't just cut and run.' She gave a little laugh. 'Sometimes I think I see more of Henry than I did when we were married. What with the visits to the lawyers and sorting out arrangements for the children and money things.' She drew on the cigarette, frowning.

There was a silence, then Celia asked after Osborne and the garden and then conversation died away once more. Then Celia said suddenly, 'I suppose you think that I've made an awful mistake. All the others do. My mother. My friends.' She had gone rather pink. 'And I suppose you think I've changed. For the worse. That I've gone down in the world.'

Celia had changed, thought Evelyn. She had never been a beauty, but she had always been well turned out and beautifully groomed. Evelyn had not been able to help noticing that there was a mark on the hem of Celia's skirt and a ladder in the heel of her stocking. Celia wasn't wearing any make-up and her hair was unkempt, her thick, dark waves, which had always been strictly tamed, had been left to run wild. Yet there was about her a sort of *glow*. She looked, Evelyn thought with an affectionate pang, ten years younger.

'Of course you've changed,' she said gently. 'Something like this – one could hardly be the same. But you look so well. So – so pretty.' She stabbed at the sugar bowl with her coffee spoon. 'Please don't think I disapprove, Cee. It's not that at all. I'm sorry I'm being rather . . . rather dull, but I've things on my mind.'

'Your mother?'

265

'Mother, of course. She's getting so frail.' Evelyn paused. She had to tell someone, she thought. Sometimes she thought she might explode.

'It's Osborne,' she said. She made herself meet Celia's gaze. 'I don't know whether I still love him, Cee. Often I find that I rather dislike him.'

Celia's brows rose. 'You're just going through a bad patch. Everyone hates their husband sometimes.' She gave Evelyn a hard look. 'Perhaps we could do with a proper drink.' She rose and went to the fridge.

Evelyn whispered, 'Sometimes I imagine leaving him, Cee.' It was the first time she had voiced out loud the treacherous, frightening thought.

Celia put a wine glass in front of her. 'Darling, do think very carefully about this. It's not so easy, you know, to leave one's husband.'

'You did it.'

'Yes—'

'And you're happy, aren't you?'

'Very.'

'And you don't regret it?'

'Oh, I do,' said Celia softly. She sat down beside Evelyn. 'I regret it enormously sometimes. Evie, my mother doesn't speak to me any more. A great many of my friends don't either. Not one of them has come to visit me here – you're the first. And the children ... well, Kate has had a string of unsuitable boyfriends, and Miles's housemaster had a word with me last weekend about his behaviour. Apparently he has taken to tormenting new boys. So shaming to be told that one's younger son has become a bully. And Sarah's asthma has started up again, and as for Charlie, dear old

Charlie, he just looks at me with his spaniel eyes and I feel such a *heel*.' She paused. 'Osborne may not be the most exciting man, but excitement can be overrated, you know.'

Evelyn drained her wine glass. 'He hardly notices I exist. And he's always so sure of himself. And so proud. If only he'd just for once admit he was wrong, Cee! If only he'd just once admit some human frailty!'

'So he's a proud man and a bit pompous. Plenty of men are like that.'

'You sound like my mother!' cried Evelyn irritably.

Celia poured Evelyn more wine. 'Osborne has always been faithful to you,' she said quietly. 'Now isn't that something to cherish?'

'Lots of men are faithful—'

'Are they? I wouldn't know.'

Evelyn stared at her. It took a while for the implications of Celia's remark to sink in. The wine seemed to be making her woolly-headed. 'Celia,' she said. 'You don't mean . . . ? I'd no idea . . .'

'Well, one hardly boasts about such things, does one?'

'You never said . . .' Her voice trailed away.

'That's because I felt ashamed.' Celia crushed her cigarette in the ashtray. 'As if it said something about *me*. As if it meant that I wasn't up to scratch.' Catching Evelyn's stricken gaze, she said crisply, 'Henry has had three mistresses that I know about. I suspect there have been others. I learned to tell. He'd start staying out late or I'd catch him making phone calls and he'd put the receiver down as soon as I came into the room. Once, I found a letter in his pocket. So unoriginal . . .' She paused, her eyes full of hurt. Then she said, 'The worst thing was that he would always be so *happy*. He was always so much more pleasant when he had a mistress. Light-hearted ... fun ... When there was only me he could be so grumpy and dull.'

Evelyn felt ashamed. 'I should have guessed. I feel awful. You poor thing – I haven't been much of a friend.'

'I didn't want you to know. Our lunches were always a refuge from all that.' Celia ran a fingertip round the rim of her glass. 'Some of Henry's friends knew. That was one of the most humiliating things. I expect they thought it was a bit of a joke. That he was a bit of a rogue. Of course – ' Celia grimaced – 'those same friends haven't spoken to me since Henry found out about Gerald. But then, it's different for women, isn't it? Different rules.' She patted Evelyn's hand. 'Osborne's a faithful husband and a good provider. I'm not sure that one can expect much more. Unless ...' She gave Evelyn a searching glance. 'You haven't met someone else, have you?'

Evelyn gave a quick shake of the head. Her face felt hot. She hoped that Celia would think it was the wine. She mustn't think about Hugo. Not now. Except that she thought about him all the time.

Celia rose and went to the back door. 'Henry's seeing someone now. She's one of the secretaries at the House. She's half my age and ten times prettier. All his friends are terribly sympathetic. Poor Henry, they say, he deserves some happiness.'

She opened the back door. Light flooded in from

the garden. 'I've often envied you, Evelyn,' she said. 'Your life has always seemed so settled, so serene. Nothing to hide, no dirty little secrets.'

Travelling back to Paddington, climbing off the escalator, Evelyn stumbled and cannoned into another traveller. He was youngish, scruffily dressed, his chestnut curls attractively tousled. Someone's gardener, she thought, or perhaps a garage mechanic. He helped her gather up her bag and umbrella. As they both rose to their feet, she caught a flicker of interest in his eyes. She wondered whether they showed, these feelings that threatened to overwhelm her, whether her happiness and longing were naked in her eyes, as they were in Celia's. For a fraction of a second she wondered whether the different, other Evelyn might befriend this stranger. But she only murmured thanks and staggered off in search of her train, her belongings clutched to her chest, slightly drunk, rather dishevelled.

In the carriage, pinioned between two bowler-hatted businessmen, she allowed herself to think about Hugo. The luxury of this short suspension of time, when she could sit back and close her eyes, heavy-limbed and elated with alcohol, and enjoy the brief passage of anonymity between the friend who had known her most of her life and the old, worn-out marriage.

There were two Evelyns now, she thought: the older one, with her anxieties and unfulfilled longings, and a new, different Evelyn, who expressed anger and felt love, and who sometimes seemed to be struggling to emerge, like a plant pushing between paving stones, into the light.

'I'm going to be away from the hotel for the next ten days, Romy,' said Mrs Plummer. 'Just a little operation. I've told Jack Starling, but I don't want the rest of the staff to know. They are such gossips, and it's really nothing, nothing at all. Jack knows how to run the hotel inside out and you can manage the office, so I daresay no one will notice I'm gone.' She handed Romy a sheaf of papers. 'This is a list of things that need to be dealt with, and that's the telephone number and address of the nursing home in case anything important comes up. Oh, and I haven't said anything to Johnnie. I've told him I have to go away on business. I don't want him to worry, poor love.'

'Yes, Mrs Plummer.' Romy paused, then took the plunge. 'Is it—'

'It's not polite to ask, dear, about someone else's ailments. If a person doesn't volunteer the information it's probably because the complaint is of an embarrassing nature. Now did you look out those laundry bills for me?'

A few days later Romy took the afternoon off and headed for the nursing home in Portland Place. Fluted columns framed the tall, black door. There was a brass plaque and a bell push. Inside, her stomach lurched at the smell of disinfectant. The silence, which was interrupted every now and then by bells ringing and the clacking of feet, made her heart flutter. She had never liked hospitals. It was the combination, she supposed, of authority and death.

A nurse showed her to Mrs Plummer's private room. The French windows were chintz-curtained; through them Romy could see a small garden. You could breathe a bit in here.

'Romy,' said Mrs Plummer. She was propped up on pillows.

'The hotel's fine,' she said. 'Jacqueline's keeping an eye on the office. I thought you might like a visit.' There were no flowers, no bunches of grapes or boxes of chocolates. Olive had said: *She hasn't got any family of her own.* 'I brought you some chrysanthemums, but the nurse took them.'

'How very thoughtful of you, Romy.' Mrs Plummer's pale face seemed to sink into the pillowcase. She looked smaller, older. She looked like someone who needed protecting, looking after. An uncomfortable thought.

Romy asked all the questions you were supposed to ask in a hospital. *How are you?* and *Are you feeling better?* and *Can I get you anything?* Then there was a silence, and the walls of the room seemed to close in. She was aware of her own inadequacy: that she was failing Mrs Plummer, that she was neither entertaining nor distracting. If she had had an operation and been confined for ten days in a place like this she would want to be entertained, to be distracted.

So she told Mrs Plummer about the guest who had walked in his sleep and had had to be led back to his bed by the night porter, and about the gentleman who had demanded an obscure American breakfast cereal that could only be bought in Harrods, and about the lady who had thought she had dropped a diamond earring on the stair carpet.

'We had to go through all the vacuum cleaners. We didn't find the earring. She found it later at the bottom of her handbag, but we did find all sorts of other things. Buttons and money and a medal – can you believe it? A French campaign medal.'

Mrs Plummer smiled. Her hands, denuded of the rings she usually wore, pleated the topsheet. 'And Johnnie?' she said. 'Have you seen Johnnie?'

'Jake saw him at the club.' *Draped around a rather pneumatic redhead*, Jake had said. Romy remembered the white skin against the scarlet dress. But she went on, 'Jake said he looked fine.'

'He doesn't like *change*.' Mrs Plummer looked fretful. 'He doesn't like having his routine upset. Some men are like that. My first husband was the opposite. He was very easily bored. Not like Johnnie. Johnnie's more sensitive.'

There was a pink flush to Mrs Plummer's cheeks, as though the blood had begun to flow again. Distract and entertain. Romy asked about Mrs Plummer's second husband.

'He was called Vernon. He was a gentleman, Vernon. Didn't care for women, though. Not really. Hid it well, mind – I'd no idea when we married, and I can usually sniff 'em out, queers.'

'Why didn't you get divorced?'

'Reputation, Romy,' said Mrs Plummer severely. 'A woman's nothing without her reputation, you must always remember that. It's a man's world. One rule for them, another for us. It's hard enough for a woman to succeed, without making life more difficult by having a messy divorce splashed over all the papers. I wouldn't get the clientele I have now if I'd divorced poor Vernon. We had an arrangement and it worked well enough. I'd learned by then that it didn't matter what you did so long as you kept it to yourself.'

Romy was curious. 'Which of your husbands did you like best?'

Mrs Plummer paused. 'Light me a cigarette, would you, dear?' There was a packet of Churchman's King Size on the bedside table. Romy lit one and gave it to Mrs Plummer.

'To tell the truth, dear – ' Mrs Plummer inhaled her cigarette – 'I'd had enough of the pair of them within a year. Nice enough in their way, but I didn't love them. That's the trick, not to love them. Then you keep the upper hand.' Her eyes darkened. 'Didn't think I could fall in love till I met Johnnie,' she said slowly. 'Thought it was a lot of nonsense. But you'd do anything for them when you love them, wouldn't you? Anything.' She began to cough, holding herself rigid, fearful of jarring the stitches, the wound.

That evening the wind got up. Outside a chip shop in Kentish Town Road sheets of newspaper darted across the street, twisting themselves around lamp posts.

In Tom's room they made love. Romy had grown accustomed to the brown, shiny couch. Tonight it felt cold and hard beneath her back. Sometime in the spring, when they had first become lovers, she had begun to understand, to feel the first flickers of pleasure, to see why women risked everything – heart, reputation, independence – for this. Now, six months later with winter just around the corner, she felt as though she were made of stone. Flesh grated against flesh, skin rubbed against skin. His touch seemed too tentative, too uncertain. As though he had not yet learned to know her, as though he would never really know her. Something seemed to be missing – passion, perhaps, the passion that she had always shied away from, seeing only its destructive side. Yet, without passion, love seemed shallow and half-hearted.

Afterwards Tom lay back, his eyes closed, as she pulled on her clothes. 'You're in a hurry,' he said.

'I'm hungry. I haven't eaten today.' Yet that was not the real reason that she was hurrying into skirt and blouse. For the first time she felt uncomfortable at being naked in front of him. As though, without her noticing it, he had become something less than a lover. A friend, perhaps. Or someone she might have been close to once.

'There's some bread,' he said 'and some paste.'

There was a packet of white bread in a waxed paper wrapping and an open jar of fish paste sealed with a greyish crust. 'For God's sake, Tom,' she said, exasperated, 'you don't have to starve yourself. It's all so bloody *monastic*.'

'Hardly,' he said, grinning, failing to catch her mood. He was pulling his trousers on.

'We'll go out. I've got some cash.'

'Romy—'

'I was paid extra this week. The overtime I did, with Mrs Plummer being away.'

'I don't like taking money from you. You work so

hard.' He crossed the room to her, his shirt unbuttoned, and put his arm round her. Beneath her blouse, his fingertips ran up and down her spine, soft and pressureless. 'You look tired,' he said.

Tears pricked without warning behind her eyes. She thought how thin and white he was, as though he was indoors too much. His lips nuzzled her neck and she ran her fingers through his thick, fair hair. Of course I love him, she thought. How could I not love him?

Outside, the wind stung her face and made her coat billow out. In a cafe along the road they ordered egg and chips. Her favourite dinner and she couldn't eat it. The yolk stared up at her, a viscous yellow eye, and the chips congealed in a pool of beef fat. She cut them up, trying to make the food look less, afraid that he'd notice.

He talked about Evelyn Waugh, Graham Greene, Dylan Thomas. He gestured with his hands, his features animated. She thought what different worlds they lived in, she with her laundry lists and invoices, he with his metaphors and allusions. She shovelled chips onto his plate and, still talking, he devoured them hungrily, unthinking.

They caught the Tube to the river and walked along the Embankment. They leaned their arms on top of a wall and looked out to where boats bobbed on the choppy water and the wavelets divided the reflected lamplight into diamonds.

'I've given up on my novel.' Tom's eyes were narrowed, and the wind ruffled his hair. 'It's no good. I know it's no good.'

'Oh, Tom,' she said.

'It doesn't matter.'

'What will you do? Get a job?'

'That would be giving in, wouldn't it?'

He was wearing the old coat of Jake's that she had given him. The sole of one shoe had come away from the upper. When, in the cafe, he had emptied out his pockets to search for change to tip the waitress, he had found only a half-crown, a sixpence and two ha'pennies. Which was, she had guessed, all the money he had in the world.

She felt a sudden surge of anger and was immediately ashamed of herself. It was Tom's choice, after all. If he chose poverty, if he chose not to have a proper job, to wear down-at-heel shoes and eat rotting fish paste, then he harmed no one but himself. Or was she ashamed of him? Was that the root of her irritation, of this repetitive and exhausting see-saw of mood? Was she, Romy Cole, who had known what it was to be judged for her second-hand clothes, ashamed of her shabby lover? Was that why she felt this persistent unease, this nagging dissatisfaction?

In a pub in Blackfriars, Tom spent his last half-crown on a couple of beers. Drinking, he fell silent, his fingers twisting a loose button on his coat. Though Romy cast her mind around for something to talk about, her thoughts seemed tired and barren.

An old couple were sitting at the next table. The woman was small and square, and she wore a flannel coat and a knitted beret. Her husband wore an overcoat, a muffler and a cloth cap. They talked incessantly, a hotchpotch of words and phrases, each completing the other's sentences. Romy imagined the wealth of love and experience that must lie behind these mutually understood, half-told stories. Her fingers pleated the folds of her coat; once more, tears gathered in the corners of her eyes. She stood up, knocking against the table; the glasses trembled.

In the ladies' room she blew her nose and combed her hair and redid her lipstick. Staring into the small square of mirror, she thought: it's because we are too different. It's because I'm ambitious and he isn't. It's because of Magnus, his best friend, whom he loves and I can't stand. It's because I'm touchy and pushy and I fly off the handle.

Yet she knew that it was all of these things and none of those things. *You'd do anything for them when you love them*, Mrs Plummer had said. The spaces that yawned between Tom and herself were there because she did not love him. It was as simple and as unanswerable as that. Overtime, she thought. Tom and me, we've been doing overtime for too long now.

She went back into the bar. As she sat down, Tom said, 'Magnus's advance has come through at last. He's going to Paris. He wants to live there. Says he can't face another English winter.' He looked away. 'I might go with him.'

'With Magnus?' Her heart fluttered.

'Yes.'

'Oh.' She felt breathless.

There was a silence. Then he said, 'I was going to say that you could come with us if you wanted, but there's not much point, is there?'

'Tom—'

He said softly, 'I can see it in your eyes.'

She folded her hands together, her fingers entwined,

clenching them until the knuckles hurt. 'I didn't say . . .' The words faded, trickled away.

'You don't have to. I'd follow you to the ends of the earth if you asked me to. You know that, don't you, Romy? But you don't feel the same way about me, I know you don't. And I'd rather not be hanging around when you do find someone you really care about.'

She felt dazed. It's over, she thought. It really is over.

'When will you go?' she whispered.

'In a few weeks.' He frowned. 'I'm going to go home for a while to see my people. I thought I'd go soonish.'

'Tom—'

'I couldn't bear to bump into you, you see. I couldn't bear to have to pretend we were just friends. Or that I hated you.'

'You don't, do you?'

'I don't know,' he said honestly. 'I suppose I do a bit, sometimes. When I see that you don't feel the same as me. Oh, don't cry, Romy. Please don't cry. That would make it unbearable.'

She blinked the tears back. She heard herself say, 'It's my fault. I'm just tired, Tom, because I'm working hard. Maybe if we tried again—'

He stood up, shrugging on his coat. He looked down at her. 'And I don't want you to stay with me because you're sorry for me. Or because you don't know how to say goodbye.' There was a pride and bitterness in his eyes of which she had not thought him capable. 'Come on, I'll see you back to the hotel.'

She shook her head. 'I'll get a taxi.'

She watched him leave the pub, watched her tall, beautiful Tom, her first lover, walk out of her life. But she thought, sitting in the bar, listening to the gentle chatter of the old couple beside her, that she had been wrong, that she had loved him after all. It was just that she had not loved him enough.

The garden was taking shape. Caleb had laid a small brick terrace immediately behind the house, where Mrs Zbigniew could sit in the sun. From either side of the terrace, irregularly paved paths led to the back of the garden, enclosing a lawn. He had planted conifers and climbers against the walls, the conifers to give shape and winter colour, the climbers – golden hop, clematis, honeysuckle and roses – for their flowers and foliage and scent. He had filled out the beds with quince and cotoneaster, lavender and hostas, and had found pots and urns in salvage yards, which he had planted with box, sculptured into balls and cones. In the summer pink cranesbills and the chartreuse flowers of lady's mantle would spill over the path, softening the edges. As a final touch, he created a shady seating area at the bottom of the garden beside a tiny pool. He couldn't put goldfish in the pool because of the cats; instead, white waterlilies floated like stars in the cool, dark water.

One morning, he was digging a border when he cut his hand on a piece of broken glass from the old greenhouse. In the casualty ward of the nearest hospital a doctor put in half a dozen stitches. After that, there wasn't much point in going back to Mrs Zbigniew's house – you couldn't do anything useful with your hand wrapped up in an enormous bandage. And besides, he felt rather light-headed.

He caught the train back to Reading. He would have a bath and something to eat, he decided, and then work on the final details of the garden. He had expected his lodgings to be empty – Heidi was at school and Mrs Talbot worked in a shop during the day – but when he opened the front door he saw Heidi's school blazer and beret on the coat stand in the hall. Hearing her heavy footsteps plodding down the stairs, he looked up.

'Caleb,' she said.

He held up his bandaged hand. 'Bit of an accident. Shouldn't you be at school?'

'I had a headache.' She took his hand in hers and stared at it, touching the bandage with an exploratory fingertip. 'Shall I make you something to eat?'

'No thanks. I'm going to have a bath.' He went upstairs, and felt the relief of escaping her pursuing gaze.

In the bath he lay back and closed his eyes. He could almost have slept. After a while the water cooled, so he dried himself and pulled on a clean pair of trousers and slung the damp towel around his neck and went back to his room.

Heidi was in his bed. The part of her that was not covered by the sheet showed a greying brassiere beneath a frayed Chilprufe vest. He said something inadequate like, 'Heidi, for God's sake,' and she patted the pillow.

'I was waiting for you.'

His heart was racing. 'Heidi, get out.'

'It's all right, Caleb.' Her protruding brown eyes latched on to him. 'I want to give myself to you.'

'Right . . .' he said faintly. 'No. Please. You have to go.'

'I love you, Caleb.'

He imagined Mrs Talbot returning to the house. He said, 'What would your mother think if she found you like this?' but he knew damn well what she would think: that he, Caleb Hesketh, a grown man, had seduced her innocent, sixteen-year-old daughter.

'Mum won't be home for ages,' said Heidi complacently. 'She's always late on a Friday. She does the takings.'

'Heidi, you have to go.'

'Why?'

'Because—' He stared at her. She was pulling her ponytail out of its rubber band. 'Don't do that—'

She shook out her hair. It lay in mousy rat's tails on her strong white shoulders. 'Don't you want to go to bed with me, Caleb?'

'No.' He could think of a great many things, in fact, that he'd rather do just now. Such as find himself on the other side of the earth. Or be in a similar situation with almost any female other than Heidi Talbot. Or be boiled in oil. Or maybe not that. On the other hand – his gaze fixed once more on the Chilprufe vest – perhaps he'd prefer the oil. 'No,' he said. 'No, I don't.'

Her eyes narrowed. 'Why not? Aren't I pretty?'

'Of course you are,' he lied, 'but you're too young. Much too young.'

'Girls get married at sixteen.'

His back to her, he yanked open a drawer, looking for a shirt. 'I want you to go, Heidi,' he said, with an attempt at authority. 'Now.'

281

'I expect that if my mother knew I'd been in your bed then you'd have to marry me.'

His mouth was dry. 'Heidi, don't be ridiculous.'

'I'd say you'd made me do it. She'd believe me, Caleb.'

And she would, too. At best, she'd think them mutually to blame, and he'd get the worst of it, being older. He imagined standing at the altar, Heidi to one side of him, breasts straining against white satin, Mrs Talbot to his other, with a shotgun in her hand.

He pulled on the shirt and sat down on one end of the bed. 'Heidi,' he said 'this is very ... very arresting ... but it really isn't going to work.'

'I would do it,' she said. 'Don't think I wouldn't.' Her eyes were hard and dark, like bottle glass.

'Yes,' he said. 'I do understand that. It's just that – ' he sighed – 'at any other time—' He held up his hand.

She looked suspicious, but she said, 'Does it hurt?'

He nodded. 'It's pretty hellish.'

'I could get you an aspirin.'

'That might help. And – ' he smiled at her – 'I am hungry, actually. I didn't think I was, but I am. I'd love a sandwich or something.'

Her brow lowered and she glared at him narrowly, but then she said, 'All right then,' and clambered out of bed. She was wearing navy blue gym knickers. She pulled on her discarded blouse and skirt. 'What would you like – ham or sardine?'

'Sardine.' It would take longer, he thought. All those little bones to be laboriously picked out. He pictured her breathing heavily, eyes peeled, poking the unlucky little fish with a knife.

When she was out of earshot, he grabbed his ruck-sack and hurled all his possessions into it. He didn't have much, just a few clothes and books. He found some change and left it on top of the chest of drawers in lieu of unpaid rent. Then he tiptoed downstairs.

He could hear Heidi in the kitchen, sawing bread, opening cans. Very quietly he turned the latch on the front door. Once outside, he ran.

He caught the train to London, partly because he needed to put as many miles as possible between himself and Heidi Talbot, and partly because he couldn't think where else to go. Alec would let him sleep on his sofa, perhaps. Or Mrs Zbigniew had a soft spot for him, he thought, and might let him have a bed for the night.

He found himself at the Fitzroy, where he downed two Scotches in quick succession to steady his nerves. He was halfway through the third when a hand clapped his shoulder and a voice said his name. Turning, he saw Romy Cole's friend, Jake.

Romy felt off balance, out of kilter. It took her by surprise that she minded so much. After all, she had been about to finish with Tom when he had finished with her. As the days passed, she found it hard to remember what she was doing, where she was supposed to be going.

Mrs Plummer came back to the hotel. She too had changed: she seemed quieter, paler, more fragile. For three nights running they worked late, catching up on the letters that had had to wait for Mrs Plummer's return. On the fourth evening Mrs Plummer shooed her away, telling her that she should go out and have some fun. Mrs Plummer, too, was dressed for fun, in a new outfit in pale yellow, with matching gloves and shoes. In the Trelawney's bar, Johnnie Fitzgerald waited for her, lounging on a stool, drinking whisky and soda, and letting his lazy, sulky gaze trail over the barmaid.

Romy went to Chelsea, to Jake's Apollo Place house. As soon as Jake opened the front door she saw the wreckage. Pieces of crockery, spilt packets of tea and sugar and broken-backed books were strewn across the hallway. Great arcs of yellow, red and green paint soared over the walls.

'Camille,' explained Jake. 'She's left me. Her parting gift.'

'Tom's left me,' said Romy.

'How symmetrical. Caleb, on the other hand, has run away from home.'

'Caleb?'

'I found him in the Fitzroy. He offered to help me clear up.'

She peered into the studio, and there he was, Caleb Hesketh, a large white bandage around his right hand, a cloth in his left. He was trying to scrub paint from the wall.

Then she saw the paintings. There were long diagonal slashes across each of the canvases. 'Oh, Jake,' she said. 'Your *pictures*.'

'She did a thorough job, didn't she? Not that they were up to much. A blind alley I won't explore again. But canvas is so bloody expensive. Drink, Romy? We might as well drown our sorrows. Go on, Caleb,' prompted Jake, looking suddenly more cheerful, 'tell Romy what happened to you.'

Caleb dropped the cloth in a bucket. 'I've cut my hand and can't work for a few days, and I've nowhere to live. That's all.'

'Oh, spill the beans, dear boy,' roared Jake. 'Might as well get some fun out of it. Cheer us all up.' He tipped back the last of his whisky, and said gloatingly, 'Caleb's been propositioned by a teenage nymphomaniac.'

Caleb looked gloomy. 'It's true. My landlady's daughter.'

Romy remembered their conversation in the pub. 'Heidi?'

'Mmm. Wanted to give herself to me.'

Jake sniggered. Caleb said, without rancour, 'Go on, laugh. I could see my life closing in on me. It was like a nightmare. Sharing the semi with Heidi and her mother. I'd have an allotment, I suppose, and in a few years' time I might be able to afford a second-hand car. Oh, and there'd be a brood of little Heidis, all with stringy hair and beefy shoulders.'

'Little bitch tried to blackmail him,' said Jake. 'So I said he could come here for a while, if he hadn't anywhere else to go. Sleep on my sofa. Only she's had a go at that too.'

Horsehair sprouted from the knife cuts in the sofa cushions. 'Camille must have been really fed up with you, Jake,' said Romy wonderingly. 'What did you *do*?'

'Nothing at all. Cross my heart. Only she *thought*. She always *thought*. I couldn't look at another woman without her going for my throat. The galling thing is that she was a bloody good model. So damned lazy she could lie still for an hour without moving a muscle. All this – ' Jake's gaze slid over the ruins of his studio – 'it's the most energetic thing she's ever done.'

'Where's she gone?'

'Haven't a clue. Got her teeth into some poor sap who'll put a ring on her finger, I daresay. That was what she wanted. Marriage. Told her from the beginning it wasn't on, that once was enough for me, but she kept trying.'

'I didn't know you were married, Jake.'

'Years ago, before the war. It was a bloody disaster. She ran off with a vacuum-cleaner salesman, thank God. Never again. That's the point. Never again.'

Caleb muttered, 'Why is it that the women you want to sleep with don't want to sleep with you, and the women you wouldn't in a million years want to sleep with won't leave you alone?'

'That,' said Jake, 'is one of life's great ironies.' He glanced at Romy. 'Tom buggered off, has he?'

'He's gone to Paris with Magnus.'

'Cheer up. Plenty more fish in the sea.'

She shook her head. She felt desolate.

'Nonsense,' said Jake bracingly. 'Girl like you. Poor old Tom's the first of many.'

She said miserably, 'They're not exactly queuing up, are they? And I do miss him.' Her eyes stung.

'Now don't howl. You know I can't stand it when women howl. Always makes me snivel as well.' Jake frowned. 'I suppose the trouble is that you actually liked old Tom. Whereas me and Camille – well, there was sex, of course, but I don't think we ever much liked each other. And you weren't exactly besotted with Heidi, were you, Caleb?'

'God, no.' Caleb put aside the cloth and bucket and came to sit beside Romy. 'Just think of all the advantages of not being in love.'

'That's the spirit,' said Jake approvingly. 'Cheaper, for one thing. Fewer drinks to buy. Fewer bunches of flowers for when you've cocked up.'

Romy thought of Magnus. 'And you don't have to pretend that you like their friends.'

'And you don't get paint sprayed over your walls.'

'And you don't have to eat bloody awful inedible sandwiches,' said Caleb.

Romy giggled. 'Or mouldy fishpaste.'

'See? Much better not to be in love.' Jake sloshed whisky into their glasses. He raised his tumbler. 'To not being in love,' he said. The glasses chinked in a toast.

Chapter Nine

Romy was never quite sure afterwards how she and Caleb became friends. He was just *there*, she supposed, and she was at a loose end, what with Tom having gone to Paris and Jem not yet having turned up, even though he had finished his national service.

One cold Sunday in November they were in a bar in Soho when Jake caught sight of one of his creditors and made a hasty retreat through a back door, leaving Caleb and Romy alone.

Caleb asked her what her plans were for the afternoon. She thought of her bedsit, and the chill, quiet air it had taken on since Tom's departure for Paris. 'Well, there's my ironing,' she said. 'And I should do some housework ... and write some letters ...'

'It doesn't sound too enticing.'

'We used to go out on a Sunday, Tom and I,' she explained. 'I work five and a half days a week at the hotel so Sunday was our day. Not being in love with someone is all very well, but it does leave ... gaps.'

She managed quite well, really, she thought, except for Sundays. The first day of the week had become greyed with a sense of failure: that she had lost Tom, that there was no one to replace Tom.

'It's all such a blow to the ego, isn't it?' said Caleb. 'Being given the push.'

'Oh yes,' she said fervently. 'You wonder whether it was your fault. Or whether there was something wrong with you.'

'Whether you've got cross eyes and bad breath and you just hadn't noticed. Or whether you're just boring.'

'Or whether you're just not the sort of person that people fall in love with.'

His gaze rested on her. 'You don't really think that, do you?'

'Sometimes.' She looked down at her drink.

'That's ridiculous, Romy.'

'Is it?' She had wondered recently whether she was in some way different, odd, lacking. 'I don't even look like girls are supposed to look, do I?'

He stared at her, eyes wide. 'What on earth do you mean? How are girls supposed to look?'

'You know.' Now she felt embarrassed.

'Well, I don't. Enlighten me.'

'Like they do in films or on magazine covers. Blonde hair and – you know – *curvy* ... and—' she broke off. 'You musn't laugh, Caleb!'

'I'm not, honestly.' He made an effort to rearrange his features.

'I did think of bleaching my hair, but—'

'You mustn't.' The vehemence in his voice took her by surprise. 'You've got lovely hair, Romy. A really unusual colour. Like falling leaves.'

'Dead leaves,' she said, with a sigh. 'So romantic.'

'Romy, you're mad if you think you'd prefer to look

like Jayne Mansfield or Marilyn Monroe. You're different.'

She wailed, 'But I'd rather look the same! I'd rather look like other girls!'

'You wouldn't, not really. And if you're as plain as you seem to think you are, why do you think Jake wants to paint you?'

'Oh,' she said dismissively, 'Jake paints the most peculiar things. He painted a picture of a tractor once.' She sighed. 'Tom's the only boyfriend I have had who's lasted more than a few weeks. And even he got fed up with me in the end. Plenty of girls of my age are married with children of their own.'

'Is that what you want?'

'Certainly not.' Of that, at least, she felt sure. 'But maybe that's what puts men off. Maybe men prefer girls who want to stay at home and get them their pipe and slippers when they come home from work, that sort of thing.'

'Some of them, perhaps. Not all.'

'Are you the pipe and slippers sort, Caleb?'

'God, I hope not. It sounds like a death sentence.' He said curiously, 'If you don't want marriage and babies, Romy, then what do you want?'

'I'd like Mr Starling's job,' she said. 'He manages the Trelawney.'

'Really?'

'Are you shocked? Do you think that's ... *unfeminine*?'

'Of course not. Think of all the women in the armed services in the war. Think of your Mrs Plummer.'

'And if you're the boss, you can plan, can't you? Everything can be how you want it to be.'

'And you're safe,' he said. 'Invulnerable.'

It jolted her that he had read her so easily. 'What about you, Caleb? What do you want to do?'

'I want to make a garden,' he said. 'A garden that enraptures ... that *entrances*. The sort of place that, when you're there, you forget everything else.'

'Are there gardens like that?'

'Oh yes. Chatsworth ... and Sissinghurst ... and Freddie has told me about wonderful gardens in the south of France ... And before the war Swanton Lacy was magical, of course.' He frowned. 'Jake once told me that every time he starts a painting he thinks that it's going to be the best thing he's ever done, but when he finishes it he never wants to see it again. None of his paintings ever lives up to his expectations, so he always has to do another to try and get it right. Gardening's a bit like that. Often, I can only see the mistakes. But sometimes I can almost see my garden – *here*.' He tapped his head, and she was caught by the expression in his eyes, a mixture, she thought, of passion and apprehension.

They fell into the habit of spending Sundays together. To fill in the gaps. Romy noticed that people took to Caleb; she supposed she was no different. She wasn't sure why that was at first – after all, he wasn't especially clever like Magnus, or handsome like Johnnie, or funny like some of Jake's friends, or wildly extrovert like Jake himself. Instead he was an odd and sometimes infuriating mixture of the easy-going and the stubborn.

When they argued, he'd let her have her head for quite a long time and then he'd suddenly and profoundly disagree with her. It was as though she had reached a brick wall. It was maddening, frustrating. You're so opinionated, she once yelled at him, before moments later collapsing into giggles. After all, it wasn't as though she hadn't an opinion or two herself.

The most annoying thing was that he was often right. She'd see him pause and know that he was thinking things through, taking the cool judgement she still found so difficult. After a while she began to realize that he was, in fact, rather clever – it was just that, unlike Magnus, he didn't care to broadcast it. Caleb had read every book she had read and a few more besides. He knew about politics, too, which had always bored her. In the pub one day he drew a map out of spilt beer on the table to show her where Israel, Egypt and the Suez Canal were. She explained to him that she couldn't read maps, had never been able to read maps, and he said: Well, think of the Mediterranean like a long, squashed balloon. Israel is up one end, near the tip, and Egypt and the Suez Canal are most of the way along one side.

She discovered that he could be funny, if he chose, and outgoing when the occasion required it. If he wasn't as handsome as Johnnie, then there was something about his sharply carved features and those eyes the colour of wet slates that made you look twice. You couldn't know Caleb at first glance, she decided. There were layers to be mined through before you caught a glimpse of all the different strands. She guessed that his work must suit his nature, which was an unusual mixture of the sociable and the solitary, and sensed also that Caleb Hesketh was one thing on the surface, but something far more complex beneath. Romy wondered what had made him like that, and also sometimes wondered why he bothered with her, who always had to struggle not to wear her heart on her sleeve.

At New Year they went to a party at Freddie Bartlett's house. Romy wore a dress of bronze silk that she had found in Selfridges. It was the most expensive dress she had ever bought; the bodice was boned, which meant, she thought, as she looked in the mirror, rather pleased with her reflection, that she even managed to have a bosom. Caleb wore evening dress; used to seeing him in cords and a donkey jacket, the transformation startled her. On the long drive out into the countryside she huddled in the front seat of his van, wrapped up in rugs.

Freddie's house was large and elegant. The garden, even on an ice-cold winter's night, was ravishing, the trees and seed heads filigreed with frost. Inside the house Romy let her fingertips trail over the figured-silk covering of a chaise longue and the carved back of a delicate Regency chair. Her gaze feasted on glassware the colour of cranberries and rugs whose intricate patterns caught and held the eye.

'Like living in Harrods!' she whispered to Caleb. 'Lucky, lucky Freddie!'

'Would you like to live in Harrods?'

'It's my favourite shop. I just walk round and look. It's my second favourite place in London, actually, after the Trelawney.' She glanced at him. 'I suppose that makes me rather shallow.'

There was laughter in his eyes. 'Terribly shallow.'

'One day I mean to be rich enough to do all my shopping in Harrods. Do you disapprove, Caleb?'

'Should I?' He took a couple of glasses of champagne from a tray and handed one to her. 'It's hardly surprising that you should want things. I mean – we haven't had things, have we, you and me. There was the Depression, and then there was the war and then there was rationing, and then there was austerity. We haven't exactly spent our lives surrounded by idle luxury, have we?' He raised his glass. 'Here's to idle luxury.'

Later they danced, and Romy was aware of a sudden feeling of contentment, one of those rare, unexpected moments when everything seems to fall into place and she wanted for nothing, hungered for nothing. The beautiful house, she thought. The music, the champagne.

When, at midnight, Big Ben chimed from Freddie's radio, she saw Caleb looking at her speculatively. 'Well,' she said, rather robustly, 'I don't see why stopgaps shouldn't kiss just once, do you?' So they did.

Leaving the hotel one cold January afternoon, Romy looked across the road and saw Jem, huddled on a bench in Parfitt Gardens. She called and ran across the road to him.

She hugged him, not wanting to let him go. If she blinked, he might disappear again. There was always this dizziness, this elation, when Jem returned to her from his wanderings. As though she had rediscovered some missing part of herself.

'Jem, where've you been?'

'Brighton,' he said. 'I was working in Brighton.'

'*Brighton?* I could have visited you, if I'd known. I've missed you.'

'Place is a dump.' He scowled. 'You think someone's doing you a favour and then you find out they just want you to jump whenever they snap their fingers. Like the bloody army.'

She threaded her arm through his as they walked out of the gardens. 'Most jobs are like that,' she said comfortingly. 'They get better, honestly, Jem. When you've stayed in the same place for a while—'

'It wasn't that sort of job.' There was a touch of mockery in his dark eyes. 'Not like you have, Romy. Not going to work and being paid at the end of the week, not like that. They don't give jobs like that to people like me.'

'What was it, then, Jem? What were you doing?'

'Oh,' he said vaguely. 'Running errands. Doing a bit of driving.'

They went into a cafe. She sat down at a table while Jem went to the counter. When he came back, she said, 'What sort of driving?'

'Delivering things.' He put down the tray. 'And moving things.'

'What sort of things?'

'*Romy.*' He sat down and took out a tin of tobacco and lit a roll-up. 'Oh, come on, Romy,' he said softly. 'You're supposed to be the brainy one.'

He was looking into the distance as he smoked. She saw the shame in his eyes. She whispered, 'You weren't thieving were you, Jem?'

He closed his eyes. Then he said quietly, 'Some blokes I met in Hamburg when I was in the army told me they had a business in Brighton. They said they needed someone, someone who could drive. I was working for a bookie at first. It was OK.' He seemed to take a moment to gather his courage, and then he went on in a rush, 'But there was ... other stuff going on. I didn't think much about it to begin with. I was shifting bottles of spirits from restaurants. I knew it was dodgy, but it didn't seem so bad. And then –' he took a deep breath – 'they wanted me to help them take stuff from a warehouse. They wanted me to drive the car. When I said I wasn't interested, they hit me about a bit. So I went along with it.' He leaned forward, drawing on the cigarette. 'I was scared, Romy.'

'Oh God, Jem, what did you do?'

'Did a runner, didn't I? Came to London a month ago. Been sleeping on park benches.'

'You should have come to me,' she said fiercely. 'You know you can always stay with me.'

He sat up straight, looking her in the eye. 'I wanted to sort myself out a bit first. I wanted to make you proud of me, Romy. I haven't done much to make you proud, have I? I came to tell you that I've got a job. A proper job. It's at a coal merchant's in Blackfriars. I'm looking after the horses. Nice horses, they are, not worked to death like some of them. And –' Jem's eyes gleamed – 'and I've met a girl.'

'Jem.' She squeezed his hand. 'Go on, tell me. What's she like? Is she pretty?'

'She's beautiful,' he said simply. 'She's called Liz. We met on the top deck of a bus. I had to go up top because of Sandy, my dog. Poor old Arthur died, but Sandy's a cracker. Liz was sitting on the front seat. We got talking – Liz loves dogs but she can't keep one because she lives with her family and the house is too small.' He laughed. 'We were talking so much I ended up going way past my stop.'

A few days later Romy met Liz. Jem's favourite sister had to meet his girlfriend. They had supper together in a small cafe in Soho, one of a number of new places that had sprung up recently. Inside, the room was lit by candles in straw-covered Chianti bottles. A couple of sombreros dangled from a hook on the ceiling in one corner and large photographs of foreign beaches, the sea and sky speedwell blue, decorated the walls.

Liz was a little dark scrap of a thing. Only seventeen years old, her black hair was tied back in a ponytail and her blue eyes were wary and nervous, except when she was looking at Jem. She gestured with a cigarette in one hand and twisted a loose button on her poplin blouse with the other, while the words poured from her in a soft, fast, jerky flood. 'Pretty tablecloths. I made myself a skirt out of gingham like that. The menu's all in French ... I can't make head or tail of it. *Creeps* – what's that?'

'Pancakes,' Romy explained. Liz's fingers fluttered over the cutlery and she looked at Jem, seeking reassurance.

Romy thought that Liz seemed good-hearted. Her devotion to Jem was unmistakable. Her small, thin fingers constantly reached out towards him, touching an arm or a cheekbone, curling into the hollow of his palm.

The naivety and nervousness that would quickly drive Romy herself to distraction would only endear Liz to Jem. Having something or someone to look after always brought out the best in Jem, the more defenceless and fragile the better.

Bournemouth that winter was sometimes still and cold and sometimes shaken by storms. Venetia seemed to become frailer as the months passed, as though the cold and wind wore at her ageing frame. Just after Christmas she had a fall and fractured her wrist, and was briefly hospitalized with suspected pneumonia. Evelyn packed a suitcase and drove to Bournemouth, where she settled herself in a large, light bedroom looking out to the seafront. Slowly and steadily Venetia's health improved.

It was Venetia herself who first broached the difficult subject of her future. 'I shall look for a suitable nursing home,' she announced to Evelyn at supper one evening. 'Somewhere refined and quiet. A seaside town.' When Evelyn demurred, Venetia silenced her. 'I have taken you away from your home and husband for too long, Evelyn. I appreciate everything you've done for me, but you have a life of your own. I've always promised myself that I would never be a burden to you.' Venetia then made it plain that she considered the subject to be closed.

At first Evelyn felt only relief. The decision was inevitable: her mother could no longer manage on her own, and as she refused to move to Swanton Lacy, and as Evelyn herself could not decamp permanently to Bournemouth, there really was no alternative. Evelyn

visited nursing homes, enquiring about fees and routines, making notes in a little book about the buildings
and their inmates. But as the days passed she became
aware of a deepening unease. No matter how hard she
tried, no matter how clean and bright the homes, it was
impossible to imagine her mother living in such places.
Impossible to imagine her happy in such places. Venetia
would try to oblige, she would put on a brave face, but
her proud, independent spirit would never, Evelyn saw
increasingly, adapt to institutional life.

With a sigh, Evelyn put away her notebook and
placed advertisements in local newspapers and in shop
windows. A succession of females arrived at the house
to enquire about the position of companion. All were
lacking, many were hopelessly unsuitable. One or two –
heavy, bovine women, whose cheap clothes smelt of stale
cigarettes – reminded Evelyn horribly of Mrs Vellacott.

Eventually only one candidate remained for interview. Evelyn had no great hopes of Miss Mitchell,
picturing another stout, unimaginative matron who
would talk of routines and boast of her skill in cooking
bland, easily digestible dishes for the elderly.

But Miss Mitchell proved to be neither stout nor
matronly. Young, curly-haired and bright-eyed, she
swept into the house, her duffle coat wet with rain,
apologizing for being a few minutes late as she collapsed
her umbrella and slid it neatly into the hall stand. She
had spent years looking after her own sick mother,
she explained to Evelyn. She wasn't squeamish, and she
knew some practical nursing. She wasn't the best cook
in the world, she admitted, but she could follow a recipe
and she would improve with practice. She had applied

for the position because she liked the elderly, enjoyed their company, and – her honesty disarmed Evelyn – her digs were small, uncomfortable and expensive and a job that included accommodation would suit her just fine. 'Call me Jeanette,' she said to Evelyn, before asking to meet Venetia. Which settled it – not one of the other applicants had asked to meet her mother; not one had given Venetia the dignity of individuality, all had lumped her into the grey, indistinguishable mass of the old.

If Evelyn was aware of some reservations – Jeanette's youth, and a slight puzzlement as to why an attractive young girl should choose to become a companion to an elderly woman – none seemed overly important. Talking to Venetia, Jeanette was neither condescending nor impatient. There was a sticky moment when Jeanette laughed uproariously at one of her own jokes, but then Venetia's stern features relaxed into something approximating to a smile, and all was well. Evelyn herself felt an immediate liking for Jeanette and, after consultation with her mother, offered her the position of housekeeper and companion.

A few days later Evelyn drove back to Swanton Lacy. Her spirits lowered as she headed into the driveway. It had been a wet winter and large yellow puddles spotted the gravel. To the rear of the house, the level of the lake had risen several feet the previous month, swamping the lawn and inundating the half-built stables. Overnight, rain had pounded between the stables' as yet untiled rafters and the unfinished walls had slid into the mire. Osborne's builder, a shifty-looking man called Woolmer, whom Evelyn suspected of robbing them (things had disappeared during Mr Woolmer's tenure – a marble urn, a set of spanners from the garage, a pair of stepladders), had left the site sometime in the middle of the chaos and had not been seen since.

Indoors it was impossible to keep at bay the mud, which swilled through corridors and up the stairs, impossible also to keep track of all the drips that found their way through the roof. Swanton Lacy's roof had always been prone to leaks. The fault was in its design, an over-complicated, late-Victorian assemblage of peaks and gables and Gothic turrets. In most years a few strategically placed buckets resolved the problem. This year, thought Evelyn, as she made her way into the house, there probably weren't enough buckets in the south of England to catch all the leaks. Osborne had prowled around the attics, adjusting tiles, placing bowls. Another builder had visited the house, had peered at the roof and sucked the long drooping hairs of his walrus moustache, before telling them that the entire structure needed replacing, for which he named an astronomical fee. Evelyn suspected him of being a relative of Mr Woolmer; Osborne had sent him packing.

Now the damp seemed to eat into the house. There was a pervasive smell of mould, and of hopelessness, she thought. She touched a radiator: it was cold. In the kitchen, opening the door to the range, she saw that the fire had gone out. The ashes were grey and there was no coal in the scuttle.

She found Osborne in his study; he went to fetch coal. Upstairs, she washed in icy water and put on her thickest jersey. The cold and damp seemed to have got into her bones. She wished she possessed a pair of trousers. Trousers must be warmer than skirts and stockings. Osborne disliked women wearing trousers, which was why she had none, but then, Evelyn thought with a rush of irritation, women had been wearing trousers for decades; even Princess Elizabeth had worn them during the war.

Downstairs, in the kitchen, Osborne was feeding coal into the stove. Evelyn had a sudden perception of the pair of them as an outsider might see them, leftovers from another era, with their outmoded clothes and manners and their way of life, untenable now.

But she made herself say, 'How was your day, Osborne?'

'I had another look at the plans for the stables.' He jabbed the coal with the poker. 'I think the drains were part of the problem. I'll probably have to resite them.'

She stared at him. 'You still mean to rebuild the stables?'

'Of course.' He dusted his hands, struck a match.

Unable to stop herself, she muttered, 'That's ridiculous,' and he stilled.

'I'm sorry you think so, Evelyn.'

'Osborne, this house is falling about our ears.'

Newspaper crackled and flared, kindling caught. 'You are exaggerating, Evelyn.'

'The roof—'

'The roof has a few leaks, that's all. You'd find the same in any old house.'

'A few leaks?' Her voice rose. 'Osborne, it's like a colander!'

'Nonsense—'

'You know that it's true.' She tried to sound a conciliatory note. 'Perhaps it's time to admit defeat.'

'*Defeat*? I don't consider myself *defeated*.'

'You've tried so hard. We both have. But this house is too big for us. What need do we have of a place like this when we have neither children nor grandchildren?'

'Where would you prefer us to live, Evelyn? A suburban villa, perhaps? Or should we move into one of the council houses in Swanton St Michael?'

'Of course not—'

'And if I were to attempt to sell Swanton Lacy, whom do you imagine would buy it?'

She began, 'There must be people . . .' Yet her voice trailed away as she remembered what Hugo had said. *Clarewood was just another nice little country house, and they're ten a penny these days.*

'The fact remains,' she said briskly, 'that we don't need stables. Or a water garden. Or a *bridge*.'

Closing the door of the range, he stood up. 'It's not about need. If my grandfather's life had been ruled by need, then Swanton Lacy would never have been rebuilt. It would have been left a heap of ashes.' He struck his hands together, shaking off the soot.

'Perhaps that would have been better,' she said bitterly. 'Perhaps, then, we wouldn't have become trapped so.'

'Evelyn, this is our home.'

'Home?' She looked around, at the great clanking pipes, at the antiquated stove, at the row of bells on the wall, bells to call servants who no longer existed. 'Home? This isn't a home. It's a mausoleum.'

303

He seemed to look at her properly for the first time. 'You seem upset. Perhaps your mother's getting to be too much for you. Perhaps you are unwell.'

'I'm feeling perfectly well, Osborne.'

'Maybe you should have a word with Dr Lockhart.'

She wanted to throw something at him. 'Oh, for heaven's sake!' she hissed. 'Don't be such an idiot, Osborne! I'm not ill! And it's not Mother. It's *you*! You won't listen. You never bloody well listen to me!'

She found herself wanting to laugh at the expression on his face. It was the first time in their entire married life that she had sworn at him. She had to put her hand over her mouth and leave the room, yet the giggles seeped out through her fingers as she ran through the corridors, and the carved wooden figures on cornice and rafter seemed to cheer her on, their laughter mimicking her own.

Since Mrs Plummer's operation, Romy's responsibilities had increased. A junior had been engaged to type letters and do the filing, which left Romy free to carry out some of the tasks that Mrs Plummer had formerly taken care of herself. Had she not felt a faint but persistent anxiety, Romy would have welcomed her new responsibilities wholeheartedly.

Her anxiety centred on Mrs Plummer. Recently she had lost weight and tired more easily. Difficulties that had once provoked in her anger or sarcasm were now met with weariness or resignation. It was as though she knew that she must conserve her strength, which came now from a limited store. It seemed to Romy that Mrs

Plummer had also lost some of her resilience – to the day-to-day problems of the hotel and to her stormy love affair with Johnnie Fitzgerald. Romy blamed Johnnie for Mrs Plummer's pallor and loss of spirit. In the New Year, Mirabel Plummer had discovered what Romy and Jake and all Soho had known for months: that Johnnie was having an affair. His lover was the tall, voluptuous, red-haired Irishwoman Romy had seen him with outside the Fitzroy. Norah O'Neill was in her early thirties; she could be seen, most nights, in the Colony Room or the Gargoyle, the centre of a circle of male admirers, where her rich, throaty laugh would cut through the chatter of the crowds. Norah did not appear to single Johnnie out or to offer him special favours. Which accounted for the attraction, perhaps. Johnnie Fitzgerald was the sort of man who would always want what he couldn't have.

Romy had been visiting her family in Stratton when Mrs Plummer discovered Johnnie's infidelity. They had had an almighty row, Teresa confided to Romy when she returned to the Trelawney, and Mrs Plummer had thrown Johnnie out. To begin with the separation had followed its usual pattern. Johnnie had drunk and whored and gambled, while Mrs Plummer had gone about her business as usual. Then the roses, the orchids, and the bottles of champagne had begun to arrive at the hotel. This time, to everyone's surprise, Mrs Plummer sent them back to the suppliers. Johnnie Fitzgerald, she snapped to Max, the doorman, was not to be admitted to the hotel. Johnnie roared and cursed and whined. Howling drunk, standing beneath Mrs Plummer's bedroom one night, he shouted up insults at her, each more vile than the last, until Max and Lawrence, the tattooed, ex-navy commis chef, hauled him away.

On an evening of clouds like iron and sudden, fitful winds, Romy was making her way through the crowds in the French pub, looking for Caleb, when she found herself face to face with Johnnie.

'Romy,' he said. 'It is Romy, isn't it?' He was smiling at her. Which surprised her; he had a way of looking through her, as if she were beneath his notice.

'Mr Fitzgerald.'

'There's no need to be so formal. We've known each other for ages, haven't we? You must call me Johnnie.'

'Johnnie, then.' She thought his smile reptilian, untrustworthy.

He moved in front of her, barring her exit. 'Don't be in such a hurry. It's time we had a little chat. Let me buy you a drink, Romy.' He clicked his fingers and ordered two gins and tonics. 'Lots to talk about,' he said. 'You and me, we've got lots to talk about.'

When he leaned towards her, she could smell the alcohol on his breath. 'There's the hotel, for instance,' he said. 'You like working at the hotel, don't you, Romy? And there's Mirabel, of course.'

Close up, Johnnie Fitzgerald's eyes were a deep, dark brown, almost black. She wondered what he wanted of her. He seized his glass and swallowed half the gin in a single gulp. There were small black hairs on the back of his hands. He was like an animal, she thought, a sleek, predatory animal.

'How's Mirabel?' he asked. His tone was casual, but his eyes, beneath their heavy lids, watched Romy carefully. 'She's well, I hope?'

'She's very well, Mr Fitzgerald.'

'*Johnnie*,' he said, pained. 'I told you to call me Johnnie. I thought we were going to be friends.' He reached up a hand, and his fingertip touched her cheekbone and then slowly traced her jawline. 'You and I should be friends, shouldn't we, Romy? You work for the woman I love, don't you? That's a sort of kinship, isn't it?'

She said, 'I thought you loved Mrs O'Neill,' and an angry flush suffused his face.

'My, my,' he said. 'She bites.' Then he smiled again. 'You're very young, Romy, aren't you? You don't understand, do you?'

'Don't understand what?'

'About men and women. You don't understand about love. You don't understand how it is between Mirabel and me. Norah — Norah isn't important. We men —' he gave a little laugh — 'we're weak creatures, I'm afraid. If a woman makes a play at us, we find it hard to resist. But it doesn't mean anything. You do believe me, don't you?'

She shrugged. 'It doesn't matter what I believe.'

'I know how fond Mirabel is of you, Romy. And I know how loyal you are.' His eyes fixed upon her, hot and hungry. 'That's why you and I need to get to know each other. Because we both care about Mirabel's happiness. You wouldn't want her to be unhappy, would you?'

'Of course not.'

'And she's not happy at the moment, is she?' He seemed to take her silence for assent. He laid his hand over hers. She could feel the pulse beating at his wrist, drumming out its tattoo of greed and need. 'So you'll help me out,' he said, 'won't you?'

She echoed, 'Help you out?'

'I need you to give Mirabel this.' He took a letter out of his jacket pocket. Mrs Plummer's name was written on the envelope.

There was something hypnotic about his eyes, his touch. 'I can't,' she muttered. 'Mrs Plummer said—'

'I'm just asking you to deliver a letter, Romy.' His voice coaxed. 'That's not much to ask, is it? She won't see me, won't answer my phone calls. It's driving me mad. I can't take it much longer. It's making me ill.'

'I'd lose my job.'

'Nonsense. You know Mirabel's only really happy when she's with me, don't you? And you'd like to see her happy again, wouldn't you? You could tell her I'm ill, then she'll be worried about me. Tell her how much I'm missing her. She'd listen to you, Romy. She trusts you.'

He was proposing to use her as a conduit to Mrs Plummer. Proposing that she should lie to Mrs Plummer for him. She seemed to snap out of her trance. She snatched her hand away from his. 'Sorry,' she said. 'No. No, I can't do it.'

His features seemed to alter, something menacing flickered beneath the beautiful exterior, Dionysus peeking out from behind Apollo. He said coldly, 'Now don't be a silly little girl.'

She felt a sudden wave of revulsion. The smell of him choked her. She had been taken in, if only for a moment; she felt foolish. She found herself wanting to claw at his self-conceit, to puncture his vanity.

'Was that what you thought?' she said softly. 'That you'd talk nicely to me, buy me a drink, butter me up a bit, and I'd do whatever you wanted? Did you think I'd be like all the other girls, Johnnie? That I'd fall for your big brown eyes? Well, sorry, but no. You're going to have to find someone else to run your errands.'

She turned away. She heard him mutter, 'Bitch,' and she paused, biting her lip. She looked back at him. 'What did you say?'

'I said that you're a bitch. Always suspected you were. Now I know. You're a frigid little bitch.'

Her glass of gin and tonic stood untouched on the bar. Seizing it, she dashed it into his face. She hissed, 'Run your own errands, Johnnie! I hope you never see Mrs Plummer again! If it was up to me I'd make damn sure you never saw her again!'

'You little tart—' Gin dripped from the cowlick of dark hair that fell over his face. The front of his jacket was wet. He grabbed at her, his fingertips digging into her arm.

Then a familiar voice drawled disgustedly, 'Oh, for God's sake, pick on someone your own size.' Looking up, she saw Caleb.

He had been watching them, watching them ever since he had glanced across the crowded bar and seen Romy with Johnnie Fitzgerald. He had watched Johnnie speak to her, and at the touch of Johnnie's hand on her face he had felt something uncoil inside him, something dark and ugly. When she had thrown the drink, he had

309

pushed quickly through the knots of people, knowing Johnnie's type, Johnnie's temper.

Now Johnnie seemed to draw himself up like a cobra, aiming his venom this time at Caleb. 'What the hell's it to do with you?'

Caleb didn't answer. He just hit him. Didn't think about it, just hit out. There was the crack of his fist on Johnnie Fitzgerald's jaw, and then Johnnie was sprawled on the floor of the bar, blood flowering at the corner of his mouth.

Johnnie, veteran of a thousand bar-room brawls, recovered himself quickly and lashed out at Caleb. Caleb locked his arm around Johnnie's neck and they staggered around the floor in a grotesque parody of a dance. There was the sound of breaking glass, and he was dimly aware of catcalls, protests, cheers. Shaking Johnnie off, he was seized by a rage so intoxicating that he seemed, literally, to see red, a scarlet haze that coloured the air. Then Johnnie's fist struck him in the eye. As he collapsed to the floor, Johnnie kicked him in the ribs. A blackness began to replace the red.

And then he was being hauled to his feet and slung out of the pub door. The frosty air brought him round; he tasted the dust on the pavement. The only thing he could hear, through the singing in his ears, was Romy yelling at him.

'What did you think you were doing? Why did you have to interfere? I didn't need you!'

'Oh, come on, Romy,' he said thickly as he shuffled into an upright position. 'He deserved it.'

'It was *my* business! Nothing to do with you! So stupid, *fighting*!'

310

If he concentrated, he could stand up, he was sure that he could. He managed to get to his feet. When he touched speculative fingertips against the side of his face they came away red. 'He's an arrogant, obnoxious bastard,' he mumbled. 'He needed taking down a peg or two.'

'And you think – you *really think* – you did that?'

His face hurt, his ribs hurt. He hoped Johnnie Fitzgerald hurt more. 'At least I rumpled up his suit a bit,' he said defensively.

'And you, Caleb? What about you? You're a bit worse than rumpled, aren't you? Just look at you!' She was standing on the pavement in front of him, arms akimbo. Her face looked greenish white.

'I'm fine. Just a few bruises.' He tackled the difficult business of walking. Heading off down the pavement, he swayed and had to reach out a hand to the wall to steady himself.

'Oh, for heaven's sake!' she hissed. 'You'd better lean on me. Here, put your arm around me.'

She hauled him off to the Marrakesh. In the club's spidery, clanking little bathroom, she dabbed at his face with a handkerchief and lectured him on his shortcomings.

'I don't know what you were thinking of. Fighting like that. Do you think I can't cope with vermin like Johnnie? Because I can, you know.'

'That's not,' he said quietly, 'the point.' He took her hand, stilling her. He saw how upset she was. He tried to explain, not an easy task when he didn't altogether understand himself.

'I just don't see why you should have to put up with

it. And I don't see why he should be able to get away with it. Men shouldn't get away with insulting women. They shouldn't be allowed to manhandle women. They should – they should—'

'Protect them?'

'Yes. Yes, I think so.'

'How chivalrous of you, Caleb,' she said scornfully. She ran the handkerchief under the cold tap. 'I've had to put up with worse than Johnnie Fitzgerald. Much worse.'

'Well,' he said, 'I guessed *that*.'

'What do you mean?' She sounded wary.

'You don't necessarily expect to be treated kindly, do you?'

She pressed the ice-cold handkerchief onto his eye with, he thought, unnecessary force, and he winced and fell silent. After a while he heard her say grudgingly, 'I suppose you were only trying to help.'

He felt sick and exhausted. 'Rather ineffectually, as you pointed out.'

'I just don't see why, Caleb. It's not like you.' Her voice shook. 'And you're such a mess.'

'Romy, I'm fine. Honestly.' Even smiling hurt.

Later, as he travelled back to his lodgings by Tube, his fellow passengers eyed him warily and avoided sitting next to him. And Romy's voice echoed. *I just don't see why, Caleb. It's not like you.* Because Johnnie deserved it, Caleb repeated to himself obstinately. Yet a series of images flickered through his mind: Romy in the rain, her cheeks flushed; Romy at Freddie Bartlett's party, the folds of her gold-brown dress showing the outline of her body, kissing him at the chime of the bells. And Johnnie Fitzgerald's long fingers, tracing her profile, as though he, Johnnie, had wanted to possess her.

Caleb groaned out loud, and several passengers moved even further away. He couldn't have fallen in love with her, could he? He couldn't have fallen in love with difficult, uncompromising Romy Cole, could he?

The train reached Hampstead Station. He had been lodging with Mrs Zbigniew since leaving the Talbots the previous year. Caleb got out of the carriage and limped up the stairs as fast as he could, suddenly needing to escape the dust and darkness of the tunnel.

A few days later Romy was heading for her office when Johnnie came out of Mrs Plummer's room.

His dark eyes caught her, fixed her. '*You*,' he said. 'What the hell are you doing here?'

Her heart was pounding, but she said calmly, 'I came to see whether Mrs Plummer wanted anything.'

He crossed the corridor to stand close – too close – to her. His palms struck the wall on either side of her, pinioning her, trapping her. 'Not from you,' he said. He smiled. 'We've just had a nice little drink together, Mirabel and I. Kissed and made up. And later on I'm taking her out to dinner. And I don't think,' he added coarsely, 'that she'll be cold in bed tonight, so you won't have to fetch her hot-water bottle and cocoa, anything like that.'

The malevolence in his eyes jolted her. His face was

flushed with triumph. She could smell the cologne that he wore.

At last he straightened. Then he whispered, 'She'll always take me back. She loves me. Just remember that, Romy. She'll always take me back.' As he turned away, his outstretched finger stabbed the air in front of her. 'And as for *you*,' he said, 'well, you'd better watch out.'

He strode away. It was a few moments before she could move, before she could shake away the smell of him, and the echo of his voice. *As for* you, *you'd better watch out.* What had he meant? What would he do? Would he tell Mrs Plummer that she had thrown the drink at him? Would Mrs Plummer, defending her paramour, give her the sack? Would Johnnie Fitzgerald, using his power over Mrs Plummer, try to take from her her job, her security, her home?

She felt suddenly frightened and very alone. She knew that she had made an enemy. She had a sense of corners having been turned, bridges having been burnt. And an implacable foreboding which, try as she might, she could not brush away. If she could have turned back time, she would not have picked up that glass, would not have thrown the gin into Johnnie Fitzgerald's handsome, insolent face. Of all the misjudgements she had made over the years, she found herself wondering whether that had been the most profound. It would have been better to have been tactful, perhaps, better to have played up to his vanity. The expression in Johnnie's eyes had been perfectly clear. It wasn't hard to read hatred.

*

Romy spent Saturday afternoon with Jem, walking in the park near his lodgings in Blackfriars. The dog made little darting runs into the pond, and the ducks stabbed at the crusts of bread Jem threw to them. Jem walked fast, his head down, and his shoulders hunched. A breeze rustled the leaves on the trees and swirled the sand in the children's playpit.

Jem talked about Liz. 'I love her,' he said. 'I'm mad about her, Romy. Only she was engaged before, to a bloke called Ray Babbs.' He picked up a stone and threw it into the water. The ducks, and the round leaves of the waterlilies, rocked. 'Liz only told me a couple of days ago. She thought I'd be angry with her. Well, I wouldn't, Romy. I'd never be angry with her.'

'Jem, you're giving me a stitch,' she said. 'Let's sit down.'

They sat on the sparse grass beneath the horse chestnuts. Tiny blossoms detached themselves from the candelabra of flowers, drifting through the air like pink and cream snow.

'Ray's been in the army for the past couple of years,' said Jem. 'Liz was just a kid when she went out with him – she was only fifteen. She said he had a temper on him.' He stared at Romy, his brown eyes wide. 'It wasn't a proper engagement. He didn't get her a proper ring – just a cheap thing he found in a pawn shop. Not a diamond or anything. When he went into the army, she thought he'd forget her, find someone else. She hadn't heard from him for more than a year.' Jem had taken out his pocket knife and was sharpening a stick into a point.

'And he – Ray – is out of the army now?'

'A few weeks ago.' The knife cut at the wood, slicing away pale shavings. Jem's gaze latched on to her again. 'Ray's a bit of a tough nut. Used to slap her around a bit, the bastard. A bit like Dennis.'

'Has Liz told him about you?'

'She tried. He got all het up. Told her she had to stop seeing me.'

Romy frowned. 'Maybe you should ease off a bit. Just for a while. Give Ray the chance to get used to the idea of Liz being with someone else.'

'I can't do that.'

'Why not?'

He stabbed the stick into the earth. 'Liz thinks she might be pregnant.'

She stared at him. 'Pregnant?' she whispered. 'Oh God, Jem. Is she sure?'

'She's a few weeks late.'

'How many weeks?'

He looked away. 'Six.'

'Jem, you idiot—'

He groaned and ran his hands through his thick, dark curls. Scuffing the tip of his shoe in the sandy soil, he muttered, 'We were going to get married anyway. It was just that we were going to wait a while, till I'd saved up a bit.'

Liz, not much more than a child herself, was going to have a baby. Jem would have to support the pair of them on the wages he earned from the coal merchant. Romy imagined Jem, Liz, the dog and a baby living in the small room that Jem rented.

'Just when you were sorting yourself out,' she said. She felt furious with him and sorry for him at the same time. 'Just when you'd found a job you like and some-where decent to live.'

Jem whistled to the lurcher. The dog bounded out of the pond and shook itself. The spring sun made prisms in the droplets of water.

'It'll be all right,' he said with a sudden burst of optimism. 'Liz likes babies. And I love Liz. We'll be all right, won't we, Sandy?' He grinned, caressing the dog's narrow neck.

Evelyn always looked for Hugo. At cocktail parties and dinners, on the train or out shopping, her gaze always homed towards a golden-brown head and a set of broad shoulders. There was that glorious second of hope before disappointment set in and she turned away, knowing that it was not him. She hadn't seen him for months: she had become used to realizing it was not him.

So when, shopping in Hungerford, she saw Hugo Longville coming out of the newsagent's in Bridge Street, she thought at first that she was mistaken. Then he turned and, seeing him clearly, her heart leapt. She waved, calling out to him, a crow's croak of delight.

'Evelyn,' he said. 'How are you?'

'I'm very well.'

'No more punctures?'

She shook her head. 'How lovely to see you, Hugo. Such a pleasant day. Are you shopping? I thought you'd be at work.' She knew that she was red-faced and she had to force herself to stem the flood of words.

'I've been let out of school early,' he said, with a

smile. 'I've been hoping I might run into you. There's something I've been meaning to tell you, Evelyn.'

Her heart lurched. She had fantasized about this moment a dozen – a hundred – times. They would meet, and he would tell her that he loved her. *There's something I've been meaning to tell you, Evelyn.*

It took her a moment or two to grasp that he was talking, of all things, about *Canada.* 'Such a marvellous opportunity,' he was saying. 'Morwenna, of course, was brought up in Canada. And we've never really settled in Berkshire. There have been compensations, of course. Friends – ' a warm smile – 'and it's been convenient for work, but it's never felt like home. And then, when Pagett suggested the post in Toronto ... well, I have to admit, I was bowled over. I never imagined ... It's so easy, once you turn forty, to start thinking your life's over, isn't it?'

In the course of his speech, hope died. Her brief access of joy faded and shrank, and was replaced by a familiar greyness. He was telling her that he was going away. He was telling her that he was to leave England and travel thousands of miles across the ocean to start a new life in a new continent. He was telling her that she would never see him again.

He had stopped speaking. He was looking at her, waiting for her to say something, but in the desert of her heart she could not find a single word.

He looked concerned. 'Are you all right, Evelyn?'

Just for once, she said to herself fiercely, just for once find the courage. The courage to salvage your own dignity and his friendship.

'I'm fine,' she whispered. 'Fine.' She pasted a smile

onto her stiff, tired face. 'It's marvellous news, Hugo. Absolutely marvellous.'

Driving back to Swanton Lacy, a headache gripped Evelyn's temples and her heart was clogged with despair. She opened the car windows wide, battling against exhaustion. Reality stared her in the face, unforgiving and unmalleable. She would never see Hugo Longville again. Her feelings for him would never be reciprocated. They had been, she thought harshly, a symptom of her own illusions, her own failure.

She had fallen in love with Hugo Longville because he had been kind to her. So needy was she for both kindness and love that she had become obsessed with a man to whom she had meant nothing. Though, in her daydreams, Morwenna Longville had been erased with slick convenience, she knew of no man more happily married than Hugo.

She wondered whether the kindness, gentleness and protectiveness that had so beguiled her were a consequence of Hugo's love for Morwenna; wondered whether, surrounded by love, satiated by it, he could afford to give some away. She wondered whether those who had been well loved could afford to be more generous with their love. The thought depressed her: deprived of parents throughout her childhood, denied the solace of children in her adult life, was she herself unloving, ungiving? Could her loneliness be read in her face, in her speech, her gestures? Bleakly it occurred to her that Hugo Longville had been kind to her not because he liked her, but because he had felt sorry for her. Parking in the courtyard at Swanton Lacy, she had to sit for a moment in the car, struggling to regain control of herself, before she was able to go into the house and greet Osborne.

Late one evening, after the Trelawney had hosted a wedding reception, Romy found Mrs Plummer asleep at her desk. Papers were scattered on the floor around her. There was a pallor, a graininess, about Mrs Plummer's skin that alarmed Romy. She poured out a measure of brandy and touched Mrs Plummer's arm, and said, 'You should go to bed. You look tired. It's all right, I can manage,' and was briefly alarmed by her own temerity. Yet Mrs Plummer smiled and whispered thanks.

She worried about Jem, too. Liz – fragile, seventeen-year-old Liz – was pregnant. In moments of optimism, she thought that Liz and the baby might be the making of Jem. That they might give him purpose and something to love. In darker moments she knew that poverty and cramped housing can destroy love, that Liz seemed barely able to look after herself, let alone a child, and that Jem, who had so many demons of his own, might lack the simple powers of endurance necessary to support a wife and child at so young an age. She had never doubted that Jem was capable of love; she had often feared that he lacked the tools for survival.

On Friday night she lay on the sofa in her bedsit, too tired to read, too tired to eat. Warm air gathered in the small room. She had pulled back the curtains and opened the windows; every now and then she cracked open her eyes to look out to where a sickle moon hung in the navy blue sky. Pigeons rustled their wings on the chimney pots. Through the open windows she could hear in the distance the driving beat of 'Rock Around the Clock', playing on the juke box in the milk bar on the far side of the road.

She was drifting off to sleep when she heard footsteps running up the stairs. Then a fist hammered on the door, and a voice called out her name over and over again. When she opened the door, Jem half-fell into the room.

'I've killed him,' he said. His face was as pale as the moon. 'Romy, I've killed him.'

Chapter Ten

She made him sit down. She put a blanket around his shoulders because, in spite of the heat, he was shivering. There were cigarettes in his pocket; she lit one and put it between his trembling fingers. She wished she had brandy; instead, she made tea, stirring several spoonfuls of sugar into both cups.

He began to talk again while she was boiling the kettle. 'I didn't mean to, Romy. It was an accident, he hit his head. But I've killed him.'

'Who?'

His head jerked up. 'Ray Babbs.'

'Liz's fiancé?' she whispered. 'Oh God.'

'He started it. It wasn't my fault. You believe me, don't you, Romy? Jesus, what'll they do to me? You've got to help me!'

It took a while to worm the story out of him. Phrases jerked and jolted, interspersed with pleas for help.

Jem had been drinking in a pub in Blackfriars when Ray Babbs had come in, looking for a fight. Ray, who had had a few drinks, had found out about Liz's pregnancy. There had been an inconclusive scuffle and, while Ray was dusting himself down, Jem had managed to slip out of the pub. He had been heading down a

322

narrow alley a few streets away when Ray had caught up with him. Ray was looking for blood, for vengeance.

'I couldn't get away from him, Romy. I tried to, but I couldn't. He's a mean bastard. I thought he was going to kill me.'

'So you hit him?'

'He was yelling at me. The things he said ... And he was hitting me ... It got on my wick, Romy. I had to make him stop.'

'Jem.' She knelt down on the floor in front of him. As she looked into his eyes, she felt sick inside. 'Jem, did you lose your temper?'

His gaze flicked away. 'Just for a minute,' he muttered. 'That's all. But he started it, Romy! He started it!' He exhaled sharply. 'He fell backwards. There were metal railings. He hit his head on them.' He stared at her, his eyes wild. 'I didn't think I'd hit him so hard! I thought he was kidding at first. I thought he was trying to frighten me. I kept thinking he was going to get up! But he didn't, he just lay there!' He struggled with shaking hands to light another cigarette. 'You've got to help me, Romy. I can't go back to my lodgings, they'll be looking for me.' He searched through his pockets; coins spilled on the sofa and rolled to the floor. 'I haven't any money ... there's a fiver in my flat, I won it on the horses, but I can't go back there. You have to lend me some money, Romy—'

'Where will you go?'

'Anywhere.' He ran grazed fingers through his tousled hair. 'Scotland, maybe. Or Germany – I know some people in Hamburg—'

'Where's your passport?'

He stared at her, and groaned. 'At my lodgings. I can't go back there. They'll be waiting for me.'

'Jem, you can't just run away.' If he ran away this time, he would never come back. Of that she felt certain. She would never see him again.

'I have to. What'll they do to me? He's *dead*.' His voice rose.

'Are you sure?'

'The way he was lying...' He made a quick, despairing gesture. 'And the blood...'

'Did you touch him? Did you feel his pulse?'

He shook his head. 'It made me feel sick. I just ran.'

'Head wounds always bleed a lot.' She felt a sudden return of hope. Perhaps Jem had only knocked Ray Babbs out. Perhaps Ray was back on his feet already, roaring vengeance.

Or perhaps he was lying in the gutter, bleeding to death. She shuddered. 'We have to find out what's happened to him. We have to make sure he's all right. We might have to get him to a hospital.'

'I can't go back there.' Jem rose to his feet, panic in his eyes. 'Don't make me go back there.'

'Jem, we have to. Don't you see?'

'I can't, Romy—'

She took his cold, clammy hands in hers. 'Jem, if what you say is true—'

'It is, Romy! I swear it! Every word!'

'Ray Babbs started the fight?'

'Yes! I didn't want to get into an argument with him, Romy! That's why I left the pub.'

'Then it was an accident. Self-defence.'

'Nobody'll believe me, will they?' he said bitterly.

'I've got to get away! Please, Romy, just help me get away—'

She said, 'And Liz? And the baby?' and he sank back onto the sofa, covering his bruised face with his hands.

'Oh God, Romy. What am I going to do?'

She couldn't think clearly. Jem needed her, needed her as he had never needed her before, and she must not let him down. Yet if she gave him money, helped him to run away, then Martha might never see her son again and Liz's baby would not have a father. Jem would never make the new start Romy had always told herself he one day would. Instead, he would be condemned to a hand-to-mouth existence, living with fear, without a home or even a name.

She took a deep breath. 'First, we have to find out what's happened to Ray Babbs. He might be all right, Jem. He might not be hurt as badly as you think.' She attempted a reassuring smile. 'Then,' she said, 'then we have to go to the police and tell them the truth.'

'The police?' He shook his head violently. 'I can't. I just can't.'

'You have to, Jem. You have to think of Liz and the baby. What use are you going to be to them, on the run?'

He fell silent, hunched forward, his head in his hands. Then he gave a great sigh and said, 'If that's what you think's best, Romy. But I'm afraid . . .'

'I know,' she said. And thought, but did not say, *I'm afraid too, Jem. I'm afraid too.*

*

On Saturday morning, Caleb was up early, moving quietly around Mrs Zbigniew's kitchen, making toast, when he looked out of the window and saw Romy. There was, at first, shock, and that odd little stab to the heart that afflicted him nowadays whenever he saw her or thought about her. And then, looking at her, he was suddenly concerned. Her gait was peculiar, stumbling, as though she was unwell or had lost her way.

He opened the front door. When he called out to her, her eyes slowly focused on him. 'Caleb,' she said. She paused, halfway across the road. 'I couldn't think where else to go.'

'What's happened?' he said sharply. Possibilities raced quickly through his head. She was ill . . . she had lost her job . . . Johnnie had hurt her . . .

'It's Jem,' she said. Her face was drained of colour. 'Something awful's happened.'

Jem. Romy's younger brother. Caleb had met Jem Cole once, briefly, in Romy's company. A charming, hopeless loser, he had decided, keeping the thought, of course, to himself.

'You'd better come in.'

She shook her head. 'I'd rather walk.'

She looked, he thought, as though she had been walking all night. He took his jacket from the hall stand and shut the front door behind him. As they headed up towards the heath, an early morning mist drifted over the shrubs and lawns in the gardens of the grand houses that lined the road. A milkman's dray climbed the hill; there was the clink of bottles, the clop of horse's hooves.

She told him that Jem had been involved in a fight with a man named Ray Babbs. 'Jem thought he'd killed him, but he's still alive. He's unconscious and badly concussed. We went to the hospital to try to find out what had happened to him.' Her voice was low, lacking in timbre, and Caleb had to strain to hear her. 'The police were at the hospital. They arrested Jem. I tried to tell them what had happened, that it was an accident, but they wouldn't listen to me. They just took him away. I've been up all night, at the police station and the hospital. No one'll tell me anything.' She paused in the deep shadow of a row of sycamores, chewing her knuckles, her anguish etched into her face. 'He might die, Caleb! Ray Babbs – they said he might die!'

He put his arms around her. After a while, she began to speak again, the words darting from her, fast and tremulous. 'The police said that if he dies then they'll charge Jem with murder. They could hang him, Caleb!'

The phrases dissolved, fell apart. When she sobbed, her entire body shook. She cried like a child, gulping for air. His jacket was wet where it pressed against her face.

She pulled away from him, blowing her nose, struggling to regain control of herself. He asked, 'When did you last eat something?'

Her head jerked up, her red-rimmed eyes blank. 'I don't know . . .'

'Come on. There's a place that does breakfasts.' He took her hand, led her across the road.

'I couldn't eat a thing.' She sounded angry.

'You have to eat. You won't think clearly if you don't eat. And you won't be able to help your brother if you can't think properly.'

He took her to a cafe and ordered tea and toast. He made her drink the tea, eat the toast. When a little colour had returned to her face, he said, 'You said it was an accident?'

'Jem told me he tried to get away. Ray Babbs wouldn't leave him alone. He didn't mean to hurt him.'

'What was the fight about?'

She crumbled a crust of toast between her thumb and finger. 'Jem's girlfriend used to be engaged to Mr Babbs. She – Liz – is pregnant, you see. Ray Babbs had just found out.'

'The police have probably arrested Jem while they try to find out what really happened,' he said. 'As a precaution. Just to make sure he doesn't do a bunk.'

'Do you think so?' For the first time, he saw hope in her eyes. 'And then, when they find out that he's telling the truth, they'll let him go?'

Yet it seemed to him muddy, full of bad possibilities. A pregnant girl, involved with both men, and a fight in which one had come off so much worse than the other. He said carefully, 'You have to wait and see, Romy. Take one day at a time. And in the meantime you have to make sure Jem has a good solicitor.'

'A solicitor?' She looked frightened again.

'It's best.'

'I don't know any solicitors.'

'I'll ask my friend Alec, if you like. He's training to be a lawyer. He might know someone.'

'Would you, Caleb?'

'Has Jem any money?' He had to ask, though he guessed the answer. She shook her head.

'Has your mother?'

'Oh God,' she said. She was biting her knuckles again. 'Should I tell Mum?'

'It might be an idea.'

'Maybe I should wait.' Her eyes were panicked. 'If they let him go in a day or two ... There's no point worrying her unnecessarily, is there?'

'Whatever you think is best. A solicitor ... ?' he prompted.

'Mum hasn't any money. I've got my savings, though.' She stared at him. 'I've got almost a hundred and twenty pounds, Caleb. Do you think that'll be enough?'

'Probably.' He hadn't a clue, only a suspicion that lawyers were very, very expensive. He glanced at his watch. 'I'll phone Alec in a couple of hours.'

'Thank you, dear Caleb.' Her fearful eyes focused on him again. 'And you didn't mind—'

'Mind what?'

'Me coming to you?'

'Of course not.'

'Only,' she said quickly, 'I had to talk to someone.' She touched his hand and for a fraction of a second a smile flickered across her face, but then it died. 'Oh, Caleb,' she cried, 'I couldn't bear it if anything happened to Jem!'

'Nothing's going to happen,' he said, with a confidence he did not feel completely. He stood up. 'You should go home now, Romy, get some rest.'

In the doorway of the cafe, she paused. She said bitterly, 'I made Jem go to the police. He was going to run away, but I made him go to the police. I thought it would be all right. Why did I think that, Caleb, after what happened to my dad? The police didn't help Dad, so why should they help Jem?'

'You must try not to worry,' he said. 'It'll be all right.' And wondered, again, whether he was telling her the truth.

Caleb waited until nine and then he phoned Alec, who, after grumbling about his hangover, was useful and constructive. He promised to ask around and to get back to Caleb as soon as he could. Caleb thanked him. Then he phoned Bow Street police station and Bart's Hospital. Both were unhelpful, but by the end of the day, though Jem was still in police custody, he had a solicitor, a hollow-eyed, ponderous man called Mr Rogers. 'He's a crashing bore,' Alec told Caleb, over the phone, 'but he's a good solicitor. Thorough. Good at unpicking the strands.'

After everything practical had been done, Caleb found himself with no option but to think about Romy. In the weeks since the fight with Johnnie Fitzgerald, some of his assumptions had begun to seem increasingly facile and self-deceiving. He liked Romy, he had told himself, as a friend. He liked her because she was bright and spirited and generous, and because she was good company and she wasn't the sort of woman who fussed about her clothes or made a scene when her hair got a bit wet. And she was a survivor. She had started with nothing and was making something of herself. The early years of her life had not been kind to her, and yet, though the events of the past had crushed others in her family, Romy had hardly allowed herself to falter. Caleb had worked out some time ago that it had been Romy who had kept the Cole family together, propping up her mother and brother both financially and emotionally.

If he had fallen in love with Romy, he certainly hadn't intended it to happen. Yet it would explain – wouldn't it? – why he had hated to see Johnnie Fizgerald touch her. If he were attracted to Romy, it might even explain why, years ago, when he had first met her at Middlemere, he had been unable to forget her, why that small, angry figure had lingered in his mind's eye, like the after-image of a firework. Love at first sight . . . Or if not quite that, a fuse that had sparked love, slow burning at first, yet persistent and inextinguishable.

On Monday morning, Jem was formally charged with grievous bodily harm with intent. At the magistrates' court, the police opposed bail and Jem was driven away to Pentonville Prison.

Romy talked to Jem's solicitor, Mr Rogers. 'It was self-defence,' she pointed out. 'That's the important thing, isn't it? Ray Babbs hit Jem first.'

Mr Rogers frowned. 'The more significant question is whether the jury will consider your brother to have used only reasonable force. *That* is the salient point.'

She stared at him blankly. Mr Rogers explained, 'If the jury considers Jem to have intended to use excessive force, then they may find him guilty as charged. And Mr Babbs undoubtedly came off worse. Your brother suffered only cuts and bruises.'

'But Ray Babbs hit his head on the railings!' she cried. 'It was an accident!'

'And we will endeavour to make that point very clear.'

She said desperately, 'Plenty of people in the pub must have seen Babbs start the fight.'

Mr Rogers shuffled papers. 'The difficulty is, Miss Cole, that there appear to be few witnesses who claim to have seen the *start* of the fight, though there are many who saw its progress. And no one at all witnessed the later altercation in the street, the one in which Mr Babbs was injured.' He peered at her over the rims of his glasses. 'And you must bear in mind, Miss Cole, that Mr Babbs has a great many friends in the area. His family have lived in Blackfriars for several generations. People have ... *allegiances*, you understand.'

Leaving Mr Rogers's office, the sick, frightened feeling that had been with her ever since Jem had knocked on the door of her bedsit seemed ingrained in her now, as though it would never go away. She wondered whether it made her look different, whether her fear showed in her face, marking her. She found herself wanting to put up the hood of her raincoat, even though it was fine; wanting to hide, to run away.

She was late to work after seeing Jem at the magistrates' court. 'I had a stomach ache,' she explained to Mrs Plummer, on her return to the hotel.

Mrs Plummer was sitting at her desk, checking accounts. She eyed Romy and said briskly, 'You'll have to do better than that, dear, if you're going to take time off without a by your leave.'

Romy bit her lip. Mrs Plummer put down her pen. 'I seem to remember telling you before, Romy, that I'm not easily shocked. Whatever it is that's troubling you,

you can be sure that I've seen worse.' She took her cigarettes and lighter from her handbag. 'The hotel comes first with me, you know that. If your problems are going to get in the way of your work, then I need to know.'

So she told Mrs Plummer about Jem. As she spoke, she felt ashamed, diminished, as though the events of the weekend had somehow sucked her back into the chaos of her upbringing. But when she had finished, Mrs Plummer said only, 'Make sure you let me know beforehand if you need to take time off. You can make up the hours at the evenings and weekends. And I shall be discreet, of course, Romy. The rest of the staff don't need to know about this. We'll say that your mother is unwell, shall we? A minor operation ... hospital appointments ... that sort of thing.'

That evening Romy went to see Liz in the Morrises' small, terraced house in Blackfriars. Surely Liz, she reasoned, could tell the police what Ray Babbs was really like: a violent man, the sort of man who would pick a fight.

She found Liz distraught, almost hysterical. The elfin brightness that had made Jem strike up a conversation with her on the top deck of a bus had vanished. Though her pregnancy was not yet visible, she looked thin and ill. 'Jem should never have got into a fight with Ray,' she sniffed as tears oozed from her eyes. 'Now look what's happened – Ray's going to die and then they'll hang Jem!'

Romy's palm itched to slap her, but she managed to squeeze out some words of comfort and offer a hand-kerchief instead. 'But you'll tell the police what Ray's really like, won't you? You'll tell them that he used to slap you around?'

Liz mumbled something inaudible.

Romy said, 'You will, won't you, Liz?'

Liz looked away. 'I'm not going to the police,' she muttered. 'You don't know what you're asking. I'm not telling tales on no one.'

'But Liz – you have to—'

'Well, I'm not.' Liz's chin jerked up. There was defiance in her eyes. 'You're just like everyone else, aren't you? Everyone's telling me to do this, do that. You don't know what it's like. Ray's mum's friends with my mum. Best friends. Been friends ever since Ray and me were born. They'd kill me if I said anything bad about Ray.' She twisted her hands together. 'You don't know what it's like for me,' she repeated. 'I feel ill all the time and my mum's cross about the baby and she says she'll throw me out if Jem doesn't marry me! And I'd even chosen the pattern for my wedding dress!' She began to cry again. 'And now I'm going to be left all on my own! And everyone's staring at me in the street, talking about me!'

Of her friends, Romy told only Caleb and Jake about Jem. She knew that Jake, normally an inveterate gossip, would not tell a soul about Jem's imprisonment. As for Caleb, she didn't know how she would have managed without him. It was Caleb who drove her to Stratton so that she could let her mother know what had happened to Jem. She couldn't have borne making Martha receive that sort of news in the grubby call box by Stratton post office. Caleb had started work a few months earlier on a garden near Newbury, which was no distance, he pointed out to her, from Stratton. He'd give her a lift down and she could take the train back.

He sat in the van while Romy spoke to her mother. Afterwards, with the memory of her mother's expression scouring her, she hunched in the passenger seat, staring out of the window as Caleb drove her to the station. He talked to her about small, unimportant things. Eventually the sound of his voice began to soothe her.

Working on the Newbury garden, Caleb often stayed overnight with his mother at Middlemere. He and Romy made an arrangement: each evening he would be in the phone box in Swanton St Michael at seven o'clock. They would talk for ages some nights, the conversation interrupted by the shovelling in of coins, the pressing of buttons and the operator's distant voice. There was the hot airlessness of the phone box and the cigarette ends and sweet wrappers on the floor and her breath on the glass. Every now and then they would have to break off when someone tapped on the door, demanding to make a call. When the phone was free again, they would pick up their conversation where they had left off. First, they would talk about Jem: what Mr Rogers had said, and whether Ray Babbs was showing any signs of recovery. Then the conversation would drift to the hotel or to Caleb's work. Afterwards she couldn't always remember everything they had talked about. Sometimes it seemed to her that they had spoken for an hour about nothing at all. Sometimes, by the time she put down the receiver, the knots of the day would have untwisted inside her. If they talked long enough, she might even sleep at night.

On the night that Ray Babbs's condition took a turn

for the worse, Caleb met her in a pub in Belsize Park. It was a dark-interiored, old-fashioned little pub. No one she knew ever went there. She wanted that; she wanted anonymity and privacy. And she needed a drink; a drink might blot out the worst of her thoughts. A young woman drinking alone would attract unwelcome attention, so she accepted Caleb's offer of company, realizing that he was the only person she could bear to be with just now. He had a knack of knowing when she wanted to talk and when she did not. He was the least intrusive person she knew, a person who could cope with silences, who did not seem to feel impelled to fill them.

He had picked her a dozen irises from the banks of the river that flowed along the perimeter of the Newbury garden. They lay on the seat beside her, their colour brash against the scuffed brown moquette. Always afterwards the sight of yellow irises would recall to her the unreality of that night, and the fear that had tainted it. The same thought hurtled repetitively round her mind like a bird trapped in a cage. What if Ray Babbs died? Would they hang Jem? She could not let go of a distant memory of Combe Gibbet, standing like a baleful sentinel on the crest of Inkpen Hill. There was that old feeling of the world being out of joint, unpredictable, everything familiar set awry. Every nerve ending screamed. She was afraid that if someone jostled against her, or even said the wrong thing to her, she would fall apart.

The whisky and soda burnt her throat. She hadn't the knack yet, she thought, of ploughing through drink after drink, erasing the darkness that way. But she persevered, searching for a blurring of pain. It took her two drinks to be able to voice the thought that had haunted her for days. 'I keep thinking,' she said to Caleb, 'that's it's my fault. That maybe I was cross with Jem when I should have been kind to him. Or maybe I was too soft with him – bailed him out when I should have insisted that he stand on his own two feet.' It seemed to her that some people bounced through life, nothing touching them, and that other people, people like Jem, always seemed to find the sharp angles, the bruising corners.

At closing time Caleb saw her back to her bedsit. Alone again, her eyes were heavy, but she was afraid that if she closed them, she would find herself in the green cupboard again, watching that circle of light, the circle that contained all the bad, frightening things. Perhaps Ray Babbs is dying, she thought. Perhaps he's just taken his last breath. She was so tired, she thought, of being frightened.

She remembered Jem, a little boy, happy at Middlemere. Middlemere, she thought bitterly. Always, always, she came back to Middlemere. She could see in her mind's eye the path along the edge of the field, the short cut that she and Jem had taken to school. She could see the waving corn, the scarlet poppies and the stile, fringed by nettles and brambles, which had bridged the boundary between the copse and the track.

She drifted off to sleep. When she woke in the morning, she thought: *Jem*, and ran out of the room and downstairs to the phone box. She was oddly unafraid as she dialled Mr Rogers's number, as though, overnight, something had altered, had clicked into place.

There was better news, Mr Rogers told her. Ray Babbs was on the mend: he had opened his eyes that morning and demanded bacon and sausages for breakfast. Romy put down the receiver. She seemed to have walked out of a very dark place. Leaving the phone box, she felt the warm sun on her face.

Returning from an afternoon's shopping, Evelyn saw Dr Lockhart's car parked in front of the house. She murmured pleasantries to him and offered a cup of tea.

'Oh, don't put yourself to any trouble for me, Evelyn,' he said cheerfully. 'Although I was just saying to Osborne that it's a long time since I've seen that lovely rose garden of yours. Would you have a few moments to show me around?'

Aggravating man, she thought: as if it wasn't far more trouble to show him the rose garden than to make a cup of tea. And the roses weren't even out yet. But she gave a polite assent.

The rose garden was at the front of the house. Bordered by a seventeenth-century wall that had survived the fire, it lay to one side of the drive. Climbers and ramblers grew against the walls and crawled over trellises; shrub roses and standards flowered in the beds. The paths that threaded between the beds were made of brick laid in a herringbone pattern. There was a large stone urn in the centre of the garden, placed there by Osborne's mother in memory of Osborne's elder brother, who had died in the First World War.

Dr Lockhart said, 'It's been quite a while since I've seen you, Evelyn.'

'Christmas – and at church—'

'I meant in my professional capacity.'

Pompous man, she thought, and said rather snappily, 'That's because I haven't been ill.'

'Well, I'm glad to hear that, Evelyn, but Osborne's been a bit worried about you, I'm afraid. He thinks that you've seemed a bit tired.'

She was taken aback. 'Well, my mother—'

'A bit . . . unsettled.'

'Unsettled?'

'Mmm. Rather up and down.'

'Well, I—'

'He felt you hadn't been coping with things too well lately.'

She said robustly, 'I've been coping perfectly well!'

'Have you, Evelyn? Are you sure?' His eyes, the pale grey-brown of oysters, examined her in a way she suddenly found disturbing. 'The housework. Osborne feels you have been neglecting the housework.'

'That's ridiculous,' she said hotly. They had reached the darkest, dankest corner of the garden; she noticed a spot of mildew on a rose leaf and made a distracted mental note to remind Fryer to spray. 'What's the point of doing housework when you know that you'll just have to do it all over again the next day?'

She realized immediately that she had said the wrong thing. He gave a little laugh and said patronizingly, 'Well, I'm afraid that's the nature of the beast, Evelyn. It's much the same in my line of work, you know. Saying the same thing over and over again to women who seem to have no idea how to look after one child, let alone six. But we all have to do our duty, don't we?'

'So my duty is to mop up the mess that Osborne's workmen make?'

Again, that measuring look. 'How have you felt in yourself, Evelyn? A bit moody, perhaps?'

'Fine,' she said furiously. 'I've felt fine.'

'I hope you feel that you can talk to me, my dear. After all, we've known each other for years, haven't we? Both as a doctor and, I hope, as a friend. If there's anything on your mind, if you're troubled in any way, then you can always come to me.' He paused beside a lichened statue. 'I see a lot of women in my surgery like you, Evelyn. Women who are finding things a bit difficult. Women who've been carrying out their duties satisfactorily for years and then suddenly run into trouble. I always tell them – ' that little laugh again – 'to imagine themselves as a train running into the buffers. A little oil, a bit of repair work, and they'll soon be back on track again.'

She had to turn away so that he would not see the betraying twitch of her lips at the incongruous image he had conjured: herself, transformed into some lumbering railway engine, a string of pearls, perhaps, slung around her iron neck.

She heard him go on, his monologue echoing against the garden's old walls, 'Now you mustn't get upset. There's plenty of help we can give you nowadays if the usual things don't work. We're not in the dark ages any more, Evelyn. You don't have to suffer in silence.'

'You think I'm ill. But I'm not – I've no fever – no pains—'

He smiled. 'There are other sorts of illness, you know. Housewives' neurosis, we call it, but there's no need for you to trouble yourself with long names, my dear.'

She stared at him. 'You think I'm mad? Did Osborne tell you I was going mad?' Her voice fluttered, croaked.

'Osborne just suggested we have a little chat. And, as I said, there's nothing to worry yourself about. There's plenty we can do to set you up again. I always say to my ladies that they should try having a day in town. Buy themselves a new hat, something pretty. Joan tells me that a new hat can work wonders. And if that doesn't help then modern medicine can work its magic.'

He was taking something out of his pocket. 'In fact,' he said, 'I've brought something along.'

He held out to her a small bottle of pills. She let it slip into her hand, felt the cool glass against her palm. 'They should do the trick,' he said. 'And if they don't there are other things we can try.'

After she had seen Dr Lockhart back to his car, Evelyn went upstairs to her bedroom. She stood in front of the cheval mirror. Her reflection stared back at her: pale face, tweed skirt, cardigan, pearls. Her bust and hips were larger than she would have liked them to be, and there was a substantial sprinkling of grey in her fair hair.

She sat down on the bed. She felt exhausted and drained and profoundly humiliated. She was a caricature of a middle-aged, upper-middle-class Englishwoman, she thought bitterly. She had believed that she was keeping her feelings to herself, yet if even Osborne, who was hardly the most perceptive of men, had known something to be wrong, who else might have noticed the violent see-sawing of her emotions? Might the vicar or the daily woman? Might Josephine Maxey or Anne Radcliffe? Might – God forbid – Hugo himself have detected some lack of restraint in her?

She remembered bursting into tears in front of Hugo not once, but twice – at that awful dinner party when Mrs Vellacott had flicked her cigarette ash in the soup and later, at the railway station, saying goodbye to Kate. What must he have thought of her, this large, ageing, over-emotional woman, with her nakedly obvious need for attention and kindness? Had she amused him or had she embarrassed him? Had he thought her pathetic or merely laughable? How could she even for a fraction of a second have believed that he might return her love for him?

There was, she thought, looking critically in the mirror, a rather mad look about her, in the wildness of her eyes and the tautness of her skin. And she had had mad thoughts, hadn't she? – an inability to accept her lot in life and, for heaven's sake, falling in love, at her age!

She took the bottle of pills out of her coat pocket. They rattled in time with the trembling of her hand. *They should do the trick*, Dr Lockhart had said. *And if they don't there are other things we can try.* What had he meant? Would they send her to a psychiatrist or a sanatorium? Would they attach electrodes to her skull, and jolt mind and body once more into placidity and obedience?

She opened the bottle, took out a pill and swallowed

it. There was the temptation to take another and then another, anything to blot out her awareness of her own folly, so she screwed the lid back on and put the bottle in her bedside cabinet, then sat down on the bed.

She had let herself drift, she thought. She had become caught up in a fantasy world and had jeopardized her safe, comfortable life. Teetering on the edge of a cliff, she had only just stopped herself from tumbling over. She should count her blessings. Though Osborne might be dull, though he might sometimes be infuriating, he had always, as Celia had pointed out, been faithful to her. She needed Osborne and she needed Swanton Lacy. She was bound to them: how foolish of her to have thought she could possibly survive without them.

Martha came to London to visit Jem in Pentonville Prison. Jem was thin and edgy. He had acquired a habit of glancing over his shoulder as though afraid of what might lie behind him. His mood veered between bravado and terror. Sometimes he bragged about what he would do when the trial was over, when he had been acquitted. He'd leave London and go and live in the country, he said. He didn't want any kid of his brought up in the city. At other times, his eyes would lower and he'd mutter, 'I can't take much more of this. You've got to get me out of here, Romy. I can't breathe in here.'

Afterwards Romy bought Martha tea in a cafe on the Caledonian Road. Martha chain-smoked. Phrases, aching with bewilderment, jerked out between puffs at her cigarette.

'He never means to hurt a soul, Romy, you know that. Whatever he's done – and I know he's no angel – he never means to hurt anyone. I know he loses his temper, flies off the handle, but there's no real *badness* in him. He was always such a gentle little boy. A bit of a dreamer. Remember how long it used to take him to get ready for school in the mornings? It drove me mad. You used to have to tie his shoelaces for him.' Martha began to cry, tears trailing unchecked down her face, ash falling from the cigarette into the teacup. 'I'm afraid,' she muttered. 'If they put him away, I don't think he'll be able to cope with it. I'm afraid that if they send him to prison, he'll do something silly, like Sam . . .'

Romy saw Martha back to the railway station. When she returned to Belsize Park she found Jem's dog tied up outside her lodgings. There was a note, in Liz's looping, childish writing, affixed to the lurcher's collar. 'My mum won't let me keep him no more. If you can't have him he'll have to go to the Dogs' Home.'

She smuggled Sandy upstairs when no one was looking. In her bedsit the cat hissed and the dog cowered, his eyes mournful. When she sat at the table to write letters, the cat curled possessively in her lap. When she tried to make something to eat, the lurcher darted around her ankles. She was afraid of making a false step, knocking against its spindly legs. She wondered what it would cost to feed her growing menagerie; she wondered, her heart pounding, whether she would have enough money to pay Mr Rogers's bill.

Two wedding receptions were to be held at the hotel the following weekend. Mrs Plummer and Romy checked off lists and placed countless telephone calls. The first bride wanted white flowers; the florist sent pink. The mice that always plagued the Trelawney's kitchens nibbled the icing on the cake. The hotel had been told that two hundred guests were to be invited to the second reception; on Wednesday morning, the figure was revised to two hundred and fifty. Romy spent the day looking out extra chairs, tables, cutlery, cloths and napkins.

It was six o'clock, and she was ticking off the last item from her list when she heard a sound from the adjacent room. When she knocked on the door, there was no reply. Pushing open the door, she saw that Mrs Plummer was crouched over the desk, her face contorted with pain. Pens and papers had spilled onto the floor beside her; the telephone receiver had fallen from its cradle.

Mrs Plummer's eyes were screwed shut, her face waxen. 'My pills,' she gasped. 'My pills – in my bag—'

There was a plump navy leather handbag on the desk. Romy unclasped it. Scrabbling beneath purse, compact, handkerchief and address book, she found a pillbox.

'Two,' whispered Mrs Plummer. Her hand clawed the air; Romy slid two pills between her chilly fingers.

When she had swallowed them and sipped some water, Romy said, 'I'll get the doctor.'

'No. No doctor.'

'That's ridiculous,' she said angrily. 'You're ill.' She seized the door handle, prepared to defy Mrs Plummer.

'They can't do anything.'

There was a calm finality in Mrs Plummer's voice that made Romy pause. 'That can't be true. Please, Mrs Plummer, please let me call you a doctor.'

Slowly, her hand clutched to her middle, Mrs Plummer sat up. There was pity, as well as pain, in her eyes. She said levelly, 'That last operation, they told me they couldn't do anything more for me.'

'You said it wasn't anything important. You said it was just something embarrassing. You said—'

'Romy, dear, I'm dying.' Mrs Plummer frowned. 'There, I didn't mean to tell you like that. I didn't mean to tell you at all. You've got enough on your plate to worry about.' She closed her eyes, trying to breathe steadily. 'Romy, my dear, sit down. Listen to me, please.'

Romy sat down. 'You're not dying,' she said. Her voice shook. 'You can't possibly be dying. You're too young.'

'Sweet of you to say so, but I'm afraid that's not true.' Mrs Plummer's eyes opened, and her gaze caught and held Romy's. 'I've known that I had cancer for several years now. I had the first operation not long before I met you. That was why I made my will. I've been lucky really. I'd begun to think I might have beaten it.' She paused, gathering her strength. 'But then, last Christmas, I began to feel unwell again. I thought it was indigestion at first – too much rich food. But when I went to the hospital, they told me it'd come back. Don't look like that, my dear,' she said gently. 'It's not a tragedy. I've had a good life. A full life. I'd have liked a bit longer, but then I suspect I'd always want a bit longer.' She touched Romy's hand. 'Now, my dear, you must promise not to tell anyone.'

'But – Johnnie? Surely you've told Johnnie?'

A little colour had returned to Mrs Plummer's cheeks. 'Johnnie mustn't know,' she said. 'Sickness frightens him. Repels him. His mother took an age to die.' Opening her powder compact, Mrs Plummer stared into the mirror. 'I'm nearly ten years older than him, Romy. For a long time, that didn't matter. I kept myself young for him. Never told him my true age. Why should he want an old, sick woman?' The compact snapped shut and her shrewd, tired eyes settled on Romy once more. 'I wish you and Johnnie would be friends. He told me you'd had a little . . . disagreement.'

Romy muttered, 'I didn't mean to – I'm sorry – I lost my temper—'

'Your besetting sin, my dear. Mine, too, when I was younger. I always found it a struggle to keep myself in check. But I wish you'd get on with Johnnie, for my sake.'

She managed to squeeze out, 'I'll try.' She looked anxiously at Mrs Plummer. 'But you're not cross with me?'

'Why would I be cross with you? Because you threw a drink over Johnnie?' Mrs Plummer gave a wry smile. 'I've done it often enough myself. I know he can be . . . difficult.' The smile faded, was replaced by a look of utter weariness. 'I'm not blind to his faults, Romy. Whatever my feelings for him, I've always done what was best for the hotel. Johnnie has no say when it comes to the hotel. And you're good for the Trelawney, Romy. You love it, don't you? You feel the same way as I do about it, don't you?'

'Yes, Mrs Plummer.'

347

'It's not just a business, is it? Not just a way of making a nice living. It's a home.' There was pride in Mrs Plummer's voice. 'It's something special.'

She fell silent, exhausted. 'You have to help me,' she muttered. 'You have to help me keep this place going. I'd hoped that Johnnie . . . I need you, Romy. I can't do it on my own any more.'

She said, 'Why does everything have to happen at once? One thing would be bad enough. But first Jem – and now Mrs Plummer—'

They were walking through Soho. Romy's mood matched the unseasonably cold, raw evening. She had told Caleb about Mrs Plummer's illness because she had to tell someone and, of all people, Caleb wasn't a gossip. She had noticed how, though he fitted into several crowds, he belonged to no particular group.

They rounded a corner. 'She can't be dying,' she said angrily. 'She can't, can she, Caleb? Not really. People don't die just like that, do they? She's still working. If she were dying, if she were really ill, she'd be in bed, wouldn't she?' Yet she recalled the greyish tinge of Mrs Plummer's skin, and the way her hands had clawed at the air, searching for the painkillers.

She paused outside a delicatessen, scuffing the ground with the sole of her shoe. 'If Mrs Plummer dies, then Johnnie will inherit the hotel. And then he'll fire me because he hates me.'

'There's other jobs. Other things to do.'

'I don't want another job! I want to stay at the

Trelawney!' She began to walk again, hurrying through the busy streets.

'And anyway,' he said, 'that's not the point, is it, Romy?'

'What do you mean?'

'It's not the *job* you're upset about.'

'Easy for you to say that,' she said scornfully. 'You've always had work – money – somewhere to live—'

He shrugged. 'We should eat,' he said.

'I'm not hungry.'

He looked down at her. His eyes glittered. 'Fair enough. But it's raining. And we might as well quarrel in comfort, don't you think?'

There was a cafe on the other side of the road. She followed him inside. Raindrops slid from the sleeves of her mackintosh. The most annoying thing was that Caleb was right. If she thought about Johnnie, if she thought about the unfairness of Johnnie inheriting the hotel and putting her out of work, then she wouldn't have to think about how fond she had grown of Mrs Plummer and how unbearable it was that she might lose her.

Caleb went to the counter to order coffee. A thin, ponytailed girl was scrubbing tables and sweeping the floor. It was almost closing time and there were only a few customers in the small cafe. The espresso machine hissed and rain trailed down the windowpanes.

Romy said suddenly, 'Everyone I care about ... everyone who cares about me ... something awful always seems to happen to them.'

He turned towards her. 'Not *everyone*,' he said.

'Jem ... Mrs Plummer ... Dad ...' There it was again, that treacherous stinging behind the eyes, that betraying tremulousness in the voice.

He said, 'Come here.'

She crossed the room to him. His hands rested lightly on her waist as he began to kiss her. 'Not everyone,' he said again. 'I care about you, Romy Cole, and I've no intention of letting anything awful happen to *me*.'

At first, she let him kiss her, she supposed, because she was too shocked to stop him. He had only kissed her once before, at Freddie Bartlett's New Year party. And then she let him kiss her because she was enjoying it. And then, when she became aware of the stares of the ponytailed girl and the women sitting in the corner, eking out their cups of coffee, she drew back, saying shakily, 'Caleb. *Silly.*'

He shook his head. 'Not silly at all. Most sensible thing I've ever done.'

'But we're *friends*.'

'Course we are. I forgot.' He turned away, picked up the coffee cups and carried them to a table.

She found herself staring at his back. '*Caleb!*'

'What?'

'Don't do that!'

'Don't do what?'

'You know,' she hissed. She sat down opposite him. 'Kissing me and then pretending nothing's happened!'

He said, 'Has something happened?'

'Well –' her face was burning – 'I meant – you know—'

He leaned across the table and took her hands in

350

his. When he pressed his lips against the palm of her hand, a shiver ran up her spine.

She snatched her hand away. 'I wish you wouldn't do that!' she said furiously. 'You're making things *complicated*!'

'It's not complicated. It's very simple. I love you, Romy.' For a moment, he looked serious. 'I realize it may be . . . inconvenient, but I do.'

'I don't want you to say things like that! I don't want to talk about things like that!'

'If you say so—'

'There are too many other things to think about! Far too many!' She scowled. 'You have to wait, Caleb.'

'Ok.' He dropped a lump of sugar into his coffee. 'We'll talk about something else. *Frightful* weather we've been having.' His eyes danced.

He had been joking. Teasing her. Of course he had.

Later that evening, as she took Sandy for a walk around the block, as she fed the cat and ironed a blouse for work the next day, she could not stop thinking about what had happened in the cafe.

He had been teasing her. He must have been. Yet he had told her that he loved her. Would someone like Caleb joke about something like that? She found it hard to convince herself that he would. And she remembered the dark intensity of his gaze. *I love you, Romy*, he had said. The recollection of his words, and of the imprint of his lips on her palm, made her heart pound.

But then, she thought, he had changed the subject, had not afterwards referred to love, had not touched her apart from the usual kiss on her cheek at parting. But, she reminded herself, that had been at her own insistence, hadn't it?

There was a smell of burning; she whipped the iron off her blouse, saw the scorch mark on the sleeve and swore. With a sigh, she sat down on the sofa. The cat nudged her hand, seeking caresses; the lurcher sat at her feet, looking up at her with pleading, soulful eyes. They all wanted something of her. *Inconvenient*, Caleb had said. Well, she thought irritably, you could say that. She needed all her energy just now to support Jem and to relieve Mrs Plummer of as much of the burden of running the hotel as possible. She had no time to spare for love. It was ridiculous of Caleb to have made such a declaration at such a time. Love was a distraction; she could not even consider it just now. And, since Tom, she had no wish to be troubled with love. She had only to recall how miserable she had felt after Tom to avoid courting *that* again. And men, even more than dogs and cats, tended to want things of you. They wanted your time, your attention, your energy. They wanted you to go to bed with them. Some of them wanted marriage and babies. She resolved to put that unexpected kiss out of her mind, to pretend it had not happened.

She went through her clothes, looking for a clean blouse. She seemed to have forgotten to do any washing that week. She poured hot water from the kettle into the washing-up bowl and scattered in a handful of Lux flakes. Something niggled at her: she felt unsettled and restless. Would she have preferred that she and Caleb had walked and talked – about anything and everything but that – and had parted, as usual, as friends? It was not a question, she found, that she particularly wanted to put to herself. Her answer might not be the one she expected. And if he had meant what he had said – *if* – then did she care for him?

Over the years, Caleb had been at first an intrusive stranger, a usurper. Then, he had become an acquaintance and then a stopgap, someone to pass the time with until something better came up. But nothing better had turned up and it occurred to her that it never would. Did she want him as anything more than a friend? Did she want Caleb Hesketh as her lover?

She paused, squeezing the fabric in the soapy water. She remembered the cafe, the hiss of the espresso machine, the rain on the window. She remembered the hollow of his throat, the weight of his hands on her waist, the touch of his mouth. She let the blouse fall back into the water and she straightened, gripping the edge of the table. If he were here now, she asked herself. If he were here now, what would she do?

She would go to him, and, soap bubbles dripping from her hands, she would unbutton her blouse and step out of her skirt. Oh God, she thought. What have you begun, Caleb Hesketh? What have we begun?

She got a grip on herself. She knew that she was right, that she hadn't time for love just now. She'd think about it later, after the trial.

After the trial. After the trial, Jem would be free again, and everything would be all right again. Well, almost everything. At the Trelawney, Romy did not refer to their conversation, sensing how much Mrs

Plummer would hate it. Instead she tried unobtrusively to lessen Mrs Plummer's workload, dealing with as many problems as she could by herself, fetching and carrying files, letters, messages, cups of coffee. She could not think why she had not noticed before how ill Mrs Plummer looked. Such an unobservant person, not to notice that her employer was dying, not to notice that her best friend was in love with her.

She attended the committal proceedings, which were held at the magistrates' court. Mr Rogers had explained to her that the purpose of the hearing was to establish that there was a case to be answered. He had also told her that Ray Babbs had recovered sufficiently to be a witness at the trial. 'Constitution of an ox, it seems,' Mr Rogers had said, and had steepled his fingers before adding, 'we must consider the likelihood, Miss Cole, that Mr Babbs will testify that your brother started the fight.'

At the committal in the magistrates' court, the police called the witnesses for the prosecution, who were then cross-examined by Jem's barrister, Mr Stokes. It was the first time Romy had seen Ray Babbs. Watching him in the witness stand, her heart sank. He was not the lumbering brute, a younger version of Dennis, whom she had pictured in her imagination, but a pleasant-looking young man, in spite of the large, white bandage that encircled his forehead. His open features were set off by bright blue eyes and a slightly florid complexion. Babbs's demeanour was calm and considered as, in his deposition, he stated that Jem had started the fight in the pub and that Jem had later waited for him in the

354

alleyway, where he had been subjected to a vicious and unprovoked attack.

Later, leaving the court, Romy found herself in streets full of afternoon shoppers. How nice it would be, she thought, if your only concern was whether to buy the carrots or the peas, the blue shoes or the red. How nice it would be to be worrying about whether you would miss your bus or be late for a date.

That evening she went to see Liz again. Liz was in the kitchen, ironing. The iron swooped at the cloth; Liz's eyes evaded Romy's.

'You weren't at the committal hearing this morning,' said Romy.

'I had to go to work.'

'Jem said you hadn't visited him for a while, Liz.'

'I hate that place. The prison. It makes me feel ill.'

'He misses you.'

Liz looked close to tears. 'Can't go in there,' she muttered. 'It gives me the heeby-jeebies.'

'He's worried about you. He just wants to know you're well.'

'*Well?*' She looked down at her belly. There was a hysterical edge to her voice. 'I was as sick as a dog for the first three months and now the doctor says my blood pressure's gone up. He says I've got to rest. Says I'm worrying too much. How am I supposed to stop worrying, what with Jem and Ray?'

Romy's mood, which had lurched since Jem's arrest between hope and despair, became, as the days went on, muted by exhaustion. She worked long hours at the hotel, she walked the dog, she kept in touch with her mother in Stratton and Mr Rogers in Bermondsey, and she visited Jem. After the trial, she repeated to herself, then everything'll be all right again. If she said it often enough, surely it must come true.

She was returning from her lunch break one day when Jackie, the receptionist, stopped her in the hotel lobby. 'I'd keep your head down if I were you, Romy,' she whispered.

'What's happened?'

Jackie's eyes gleamed. 'Mrs P's just found out lover boy's still seeing that Mrs O'Neill. He'll be lucky if he comes out of there in one piece.'

She heard the raised voices as soon as she turned into the corridor. Pausing outside the office, her fist bunched to knock on the door, she heard Mrs Plummer scream, 'How can you lower yourself by going with that cheap little tart?'

'Cheap little tart?' Johnnie's voice. 'You'd know about that, wouldn't you?'

An audible gasp. 'What do you mean?'

'Wouldn't the patrons of your precious hotel like to know the truth about you, Mirabel? Shall I tell them? Shall I tell your ever-so-respectable guests that you were a nightclub hostess? They'd all know what that meant, wouldn't they?'

'Johnnie—' There was fear as well as pain in Mrs Plummer's voice. 'Johnnie, you wouldn't do that.'

'Wouldn't I?' A crack of laughter. 'Just you watch me!'

'You promised me!'

'Shall I tell them you're nothing but a whore? An

old, ugly whore! I should be ashamed to be seen with you. Once a whore, always a whore—'

There was a sound like a gunshot. The door trembled with the impact of a missile ricocheting against it. 'You bastard!' cried Mrs Plummer. 'You bastard!'

A jangle of broken glass and a muffled gasp from Johnnie. When he spoke again, the timbre of his voice had altered. Romy only just caught the low, angry words.

'You bitch. You vicious old bitch—'

And then Mrs Plummer, pleading now. 'Don't hurt me, Johnnie. Please don't hurt me.'

Romy opened the door. Johnnie's hand was at Mrs Plummer's throat. Blood was trailing from a cut on Johnnie's forehead. There was broken glass on the carpet.

'Leave her alone.' Romy took a step forward. 'Let go of her.'

Johnnie's hand fell away from Mrs Plummer.

'Now get out. And don't ever come back.'

For a moment she thought he was going to refuse. Then he turned on his heel, dabbing the blood from his forehead. As he reached the door, he whispered, 'You shouldn't have interfered. You really shouldn't have interfered.' The door slammed behind him.

Romy managed to catch Mrs Plummer and steer her into an armchair before she collapsed. Mrs Plummer's smart Hardy Amies suit was askew. The torn ends of a necklace dangled around her neck. 'My pearls...' she whispered. She clutched at the broken thread.

Romy crawled around the carpet, searching for pearls. She heard Mrs Plummer mutter, 'He could ruin me if he chose to. The only thing is I probably won't live long enough.'

'Of course he can't ruin you.' Romy knelt up, pearls rolling in her palm. 'He was just making threats, trying to frighten you.'

'No.' She only just caught the whispered word. She stood up. Mrs Plummer's face was stricken.

'I know he was lying,' said Romy.

'It was true.' Slowly Mrs Plummer shook her head. She repeated, her voice a little stronger, 'It was true. In the Twenties I worked in a nightclub. I had to serve drinks and talk to the customers.' She closed her eyes and took an audible breath. Then she said wearily, 'And I was young and pretty and I did what women have done since the beginning of time. The men had the money and I had something they wanted, something they were willing to pay for. And they paid well, God help me.' Mrs Plummer opened her eyes and looked at Romy. 'Give me a cigarette, dear,' she said more calmly. 'I need a cigarette. Are you shocked, Romy? Do you despise me now?'

Romy remembered running away to London and looking for Jem and being unable to find him. She had had only a few shillings in her pocket and nowhere to go. She remembered her sense of panic, her fear of destitution. What might she have been driven to if Mrs Plummer had not helped her? What might she have done to get her through that night and the next and the next?

She shook her head. Then she let the pearls trickle

out of her palm into an ashtray. 'How did Johnnie find out?'

'Oh, I told him,' said Mrs Plummer softly. 'Like a fool, I told him. It's what you do when you're in love, you tell your secrets. I told Johnnie because I loved him. And because I thought he loved me.' She touched the remains of the necklace. 'He bought me these. It was when he was courting me. He said I was his pearl. His pearl without price. But he never loved me, did he?' Her eyes glittered with tears. 'I don't think he's ever loved anyone. Maybe his mother. No one else. Some people don't know how to love, do they? In the beginning he wanted me because I was beautiful. All the men wanted me then. And Johnnie always wants whatever everyone else wants. And then he wanted me because of the money. And now ... he hates me. I have a hold over him, and he hates me for that.'

She drew on the cigarette. 'I've been a fool,' she muttered. 'An old fool. I've known for a long time that he didn't love me. After Norah, I was sure. He was seeing her when I was in hospital, wasn't he?' She looked away and added softly, 'I've never loved any man the way I loved Johnnie. He's the man I loved most, and he'll be the man I love last. I knew there wasn't going to be anyone else, not the way things are. So that's why I took him back, because I knew I had so little time. I thought I could go on pretending. Thought I could go on putting up with the tantrums, the lies. Thought it was better than being alone. Well, it isn't.' Her face crumpled. 'When he came to me this afternoon, I could *smell* her on him. Smell her scent. Smell the sex. He'd come from *her* bed to me.'

She crushed the cigarette into the ashtray. Then she said, 'He's not to be allowed into the hotel. I won't see him again. Not ever, this time. You're to tell Jack Starling and Max.' Her features were ravaged, agonized.

Romy stood up. 'I'll get a dustpan and brush and clear up the glass.'

But Mrs Plummer's hand shot out, gripping her wrist. 'No. Don't go. Don't leave me, Romy. I don't want to be alone. Not yet.'

On Saturday afternoon Romy saw Jem for an hour in Pentonville. Afterwards she went shopping for an engagement present for Psyche and her fiancé, Dave. Dave was a friend of Magnus's; he and Psyche had been dating since Magnus had left for Paris. Wandering along Oxford Street, Romy felt dazed and tired and curiously out of kilter. It took her the remainder of the afternoon to choose a set of spotted tea plates in Selfridges. Later, wrapping the present, her hands seemed clumsy and unpractised, so that the package was lopsided and lumpy, the ribbon twisted into a small, hard knot.

To the party that evening she wore a flared black skirt with a close-fitting, coffee-coloured top, cinched at the waist with a wide black belt. She made up her face carefully. Clothes and make-up were a bulwark against the world. Getting ready to go out, she thought of Mrs Plummer, perfectly turned out in Hardy Amies and Elizabeth Arden, while she was dying of cancer, dying of love.

In Psyche's tiny flat guests crushed into the rooms and overflowed into the back garden. The air was thick with cigarette smoke and Romy had to shout to be heard over the record player and the loud hum of conversation. Food – bread and cheese and pickles – was laid out on a trestle table. There were crates of beer and cider; the empty bottles were left anyhow on the floor. The guests had a scruffy, unkempt look; the girls' long fringes drooped over their pale faces and their eyes were framed with thick black liner. They wore jeans and baggy black jumpers; threading between them, Romy felt out of place and overdressed. From the crowd she picked out familiar faces: Soho friends and Fitzrovia friends and people whom she vaguely recognized as once a part of Magnus's circle, or Jake's.

She found Psyche in the kitchen. Psyche ripped open the wrappings and screamed with pleasure at the spotted plates.

'We were going to have a register office wedding,' she explained to Romy, 'but Mummy's insisting we get married at home, and I couldn't say no, could I, she'd have been so disappointed, and anyway the parish church is so pretty, and all the cousins are queuing up to be bridesmaids. If you count up all the relations, there are almost a *hundred*! So I suppose it'll be a big wedding, even though we hadn't meant it to be.'

Romy tried to imagine what it must be like to have so many brothers and sisters and aunts and uncles that you had to invite a hundred people to your wedding. Her own family – scattered, dysfunctional, or incarcerated – would number less than a dozen. Which of them would she ask to her wedding? Would she invite Dennis, who would drink too much and slobber kisses over the bridesmaids? Would she invite Jem, who would forget the date, the time, the address? For such scarce, unreliable guests would it be worth her while dressing in white satin or opening champagne?

She went outside into the back garden. Someone had put a Frank Sinatra record on the gramophone, and the slow, silky ballad drifted out over the hot little square of grass. She felt brittle, as if she was made of the thin, silvery glass of Christmas decorations. None of the things the other celebrants in this house took for granted – the comfortable homes, the supportive families, the money and love – were hers. Her home was the Trelawney, which within months, maybe a year at most, she would lose. She would lose Mrs Plummer, too. She must earn her own financial security or do without. Her fractured family was far too preoccupied with its own problems to notice any of hers. And as for love . . .

Any stable, enduring love had vanished from her life when she was eight years old, snuffed out by a single gunshot. Since then she had made do with Jem's mercurial affection, with her mother's exhausted loyalty, and with Tom's half-formed passion for her, which had seen only the parts of her he had wanted to see.

Someone touched her shoulder; turning, she saw Caleb and felt immense relief. 'I thought you weren't coming.'

'Got held up. Sorry.' He kissed her cheek. 'How was Jem?'

'A bit down in the dumps. Worried about the trial, I think.' She stared at her drink. After a few anxious enquiries about Liz, Jem had hardly said a word to her the entire visiting hour. There had been a desperation in his eyes that had alarmed her. She had remembered what her mother had told her: *after Sam died, he didn't speak* ... A seven-year-old child, he had had, she now realized, some sort of a breakdown. It frightened her to think that history might repeat itself.

He said, 'You look like you've had enough,' and she nodded.

'Take me home, would you, Caleb?' She was weary, suddenly, of crowds. She could bear only to be with him. 'Please take me home.'

Chapter Eleven

Caleb had started work on the Rolands' garden at the beginning of the year. Freddie had given him a free hand in the design, backed up with generous offers of help and the occasional piece of constructive criticism. It was a large plot, his biggest project so far, and, seeing it for the first time, he had felt a thrill of excitement, closely followed by a shiver of apprehension. He had wondered whether that was how Jake felt, looking at a blank canvas. That sense of possibility, that here you were, poised on a mountain top, with a long branching road of choices before you. You hoped that you were beginning something that would be marvellous, magical. You were afraid you might mess it up completely.

He had kept his nerve, though, taking time over the initial drawings. Mr Roland worked in the City, commuting from Newbury to London each day; Mrs Roland was angularly elegant and seemed to divide her time between drifting around the house and garden wearing colourful sundresses and driving out at great speed in a new Vauxhall car. Their house, which was recently built, looked down a long slope to a tributary of the River Kennet. Caleb had realized early on that the garden's incline was both a challenge and an opportunity. It would probably have to be terraced, and the section nearest to the river would be difficult to drain and might well flood in winter.

He had tramped around the plot, getting to know every sapling and hillock; after a while he could see it whenever he closed his eyes, saw it even in his dreams. The Rolands gave him a free hand, Mrs Roland only insisting that the garden should include a fountain. 'We saw something absolutely marvellous in Italy last summer,' she told him. 'Little stone fishes ... and nymphs ... and a statue of Neptune.'

Over the spring and summer Caleb saw the slow transformation of his vision into reality. They had had to bring in earth-moving equipment to level the ground and to lay pipes to feed the fountain. In his mind's eye, he could see the fountain as it would look when the garden was finished: the stone fishes and naiads encrusted with lichen and the lilies floating on the surface of the water. At midnight, moonlight would make the pale old stone luminesce.

Often it took him over. The garden was his other world, his vision, his obsession. He had another obsession, of course. *There are too many other things to think about*, Romy had said, when he had told her that he loved her. And he could quite see that she might feel that just now.

So he tried to be patient. And yet, away from her, he longed for her. With her, he wanted to touch her pale gold, finely grained skin, and to trace with the palm of his hand the curve of breast and waist and thigh. Yet he knew that if he rushed, if he demanded what she was not yet able to give, he would lose her. And even the torture of waiting was preferable to that.

On the Sunday before the trial he took Romy to see the Rolands' garden. The dog, Sandy, ran ahead as they walked along the river bank. Reeds and bulrushes pierced the water, and a kingfisher, an iridescent flash of blue and russet, swooped through the air, following the line of the river. Though it had rained as they had driven out of London, there was now the beginning of a heavy warmth. Trees – willows and rowans and silver birches – straggled up the far side of the garden towards the house.

Caleb watched Romy walk ahead of him to the uppermost terrace. She was wearing jeans and a cotton shirt and a borrowed pair of overlarge wellingtons because of the muddiness of the site. He thought she looked beautiful. *You have to wait, Caleb*, she had said, and he had understood that she had meant until after the trial. And then what? She had made him no promises, had given little indication of whether she cared for him as anything more than a friend. There was only the recollection of that kiss in the cafe. She had returned his kiss, and he had sensed a fire in her that matched his own.

He gave himself a shake, as if to clear away the memory. She was peering through the windows of the house, staring into the turquoise depths of the Rolands' swimming pool. He called to her, 'Are you hungry?' and she nodded.

'Do you like bacon sandwiches?'

'Love them.'

'I'll make you some, them.'

'We're going back to London?'

He shook his head. 'Middlemere. It's only a few miles away.'

'Caleb—'

'My mother's away for the weekend, so we'll have the house to ourselves.'

'It's not that—'

'That was then and this is now,' he said firmly. He held out his hand to her. 'Come on, Romy. Let's try and lay a few ghosts.'

While Caleb fried bacon, she prowled around the house. Testing herself, she went upstairs. There were the bedrooms and there was the landing. There was the window and there was the cupboard. She opened the cupboard door and peered into it. It seemed so small, so cramped. She closed her eyes, wondering whether she would still hear the clink of metal on wood as her father laid the shotgun on the sill, or whether she would still smell the gunpowder from the spent cartridges.

But there was only the cawing of the rooks from the topmost branches of the trees, only the smell of floor polish and frying bacon. The blurring of the boundaries between past and present that had so disturbed her the last time she had been to Middlemere, the time she had first met Caleb, was absent. It puzzled her – how had the house lost the power to hurt her?

She leaned her arms on the sill, looking out of window, down to the garden, trying to work it out. She thought of the garden they had visited that morning and how it had showed her a different side to Caleb.

They were both in the business of realizing dreams, she thought: she with the hotel, he with his gardens.

There was a flicker of movement below and, looking down, she saw Caleb picking salad stuff from the rows in the vegetable garden. She watched the sweep of the knife as he cut the lettuce, watched him turn and walk back to the house. Caleb alone shared her history, knew all that had made her what she was. Though experience had taught her to rely on herself and no one else, she had valued Caleb's company above all other during these last, awful months. She had turned to him when she could tolerate no one else. Was it because he was here that she felt at peace? Was it because of him that the house no longer haunted her? Such a sea change, such an immense turning away from the past.

She went downstairs to the kitchen. He was standing at the stove. 'Beer with your bacon sandwich?'

'Please.' He handed her a glass.

'I was looking at our path,' she told him. 'Jem's and my path, by the edge of the field. We used to walk along it to school. I suppose you must've, too, Caleb.'

'I didn't go to the village school. After Dad died I went to boarding school.'

'Ah,' she said.

'What do you mean: *Ah*?'

'Explains it, doesn't it? You're a bit posh, aren't you?'

'Rot.'

'Course you are.' She perched on the edge of the kitchen table. 'I bet you never starved because you couldn't remember which knife and fork to use for fish. I bet you never made a fool of yourself starting to eat before everyone else had sat down. And I bet you never fell on your bum because you weren't expecting the waiter to pull your chair out.'

'I suppose not,' he admitted.

'When I first started at the hotel, I had to learn everything. Lots of the time I felt a complete idiot. I had to learn to be like everyone else.'

He said mildly, 'You'll never be like everyone else.'

'Caleb—'

'It's true. You won't.'

'Oh dear,' she said. 'And I try so hard. I can't think why you put up with me.'

He crossed the room to her. 'Can't you?'

She shook her head. The room — the house, and time itself — seemed to have stilled. 'Well then,' he said. 'I'll try to explain.'

This time, when he kissed her, she did not pull away. His fingers wove into her hair. She could feel the pounding of his heart.

After a while, he stepped back. 'Does that make things any clearer?' he asked.

Then he put a plate in her hands and she stared down at the sandwich, wondering why she didn't feel hungry any more.

Or, at least, not hungry for that.

'I must talk to you, Evelyn,' said Venetia mysteriously over a rather crackly telephone line. 'I'm sorry to trouble you when I know that you are so busy, but if you could find the time on Sunday, perhaps . . .'

Evelyn had been gardening. There was earth

beneath her fingernails and a rose thorn in the ball of her thumb. She sucked at the thorn furiously and then, when Venetia failed to elucidate further, said, 'Are you unwell, Mummy? Have you had another fall?'

'I'm perfectly well,' said Venetia.

'Then—'

'It isn't something I can discuss over the telephone,' said Venetia firmly.

Driving away from Swanton Lacy on Sunday morning, Evelyn was aware of the familiar feeling of relief. Though she had tried to buckle down, to become once more a good wife, to scrub floors and cook dinners, her efforts seemed unconvincing and amateurish even to herself. There were smears on the tiles, and she forgot to salt the potatoes and burnt the pastry. She worried that Osborne observed her with a condescending, wary eye, as if she were unstable, capable at any moment of tipping into some unstoppable chain reaction.

In the Bournemouth house, Venetia sent Jeanette out to the newsagent's before beckoning Evelyn into the drawing room.

'Well?' she whispered. 'I'm not mistaken, am I?'

'Mummy?'

'*Jeanette*,' said Venetia darkly. Then, when Evelyn looked confused, she whispered, '*Evelyn*. Oh dear. I am afraid ... I am very much afraid ... that Jeanette is in the family way.'

'In the family way ...' Evelyn repeated. She stared at her mother. '*Pregnant*? You think Jeanette is *pregnant*?' She felt rather cross that her mother had brought her all this way to confide such a preposterous suspicion. 'Of course she isn't pregnant.'

Venetia regarded her with a cool, intelligent eye. 'I fear that she is.'

Evelyn opened her mouth to protest again and then shut it. In her mind's eye she saw Jeanette, dressed, as always, in baggy jerseys or men's shirts over her blue jeans. She had noticed, in a vague sort of way, that Jeanette had put on weight during her months in Bournemouth. Evelyn had put it down to her cake-making.

'You don't think,' said Evelyn hopefully, 'that she's just a little overweight?'

'The other night, when my spectacles fell beneath the bed and she came to help me, she was wearing her nightgown – and, well, I'm afraid there's no doubt. I have had my suspicions for some time.'

Evelyn felt rather floored. She sat down. 'Have you said anything to her, Mummy?'

'I thought it might be better if you spoke to her, Evelyn. After all, you are nearer to her in age.' Momentarily Venetia looked bewildered. 'When I was a young woman, one did not speak about such things. I'm not sure that I would know how to broach the subject.'

Not long afterwards Evelyn found herself in the kitchen, struggling not to stare at Jeanette's middle, which seemed recently, to her newly aware gaze, to have thickened alarmingly. She was aware of a mixture of emotions: despair at the prospect of having to search once more for a suitable companion for her mother, just when everything seemed to be going so well, and envy that this young girl seemed to have achieved – without even wanting to, presumably – what she herself had always longed for.

And distaste, of course, for the inevitable embarrassment of the forthcoming interview. She heard herself falter, 'My mother wondered . . . Of course, she may be mistaken . . . and I don't mean to be intrusive . . .' Evelyn took a deep breath. 'I wondered whether you had anything to tell us, Jeanette.'

Jeanette had gone rather pale. There was a silence as she upended a bag of flour into a jar. Then she said drily, 'I am pregnant, if that's what you're trying to ask me.'

'*Oh*,' said Evelyn.

'Six months pregnant, actually.' She gave a crooked little smile. 'I was afraid you'd guess ages ago.'

'Six months . . .' Evelyn did the maths. 'Then you knew when you came here?'

'That was why I needed the job. I needed somewhere to live.' Momentarily she shut her eyes. 'I'm sorry. You must think it a rotten trick. A rotten thing to do. I'll pack my things after dinner.' She emptied potatoes into the sink and began to scrape them.

Evelyn noticed how the knife shook and how every now and then one of the potatoes would slip from Jeanette's fingers and fall into the water with a splash. She said, 'Really, I've no intention of throwing you out onto the street, Jeanette. There's no need for you to leave today. And where would you go?'

'I'll find somewhere.' She added suddenly, fiercely, 'I'll miss Mrs Seymour. I don't want you to think it was all pretence, all to get a roof over my head. It wasn't. I've enjoyed working here.'

Evelyn tried to imagine what it must feel like to be young and pregnant and unmarried. For the coming baby to be a source of fear rather than joy. She said, 'I think we should talk, don't you? The dinner can wait.'

They sat in the garden, beneath the lilac tree. Evelyn prompted, 'The father . . . ?'

'He's not interested. He's married, if you want to know.'

'I don't mean to pry, Jeanette. Only to understand. And to see what's to be done.'

'I'm sorry, Mrs Daubeny.' Her defiance evaporated; Jeanette scrubbed at her eyes with the back of her hand.

'My mother and I may have been very unobservant,' said Evelyn, 'but you can't have thought that we wouldn't notice eventually. What were you planning to do when the baby came?'

Jeanette shook her head. 'I don't know. I kept hoping I'd think of something.' She sounded despairing. 'Or I suppose I thought it would put off having to think of something. There isn't an answer, is there? You get pregnant and nine months later there's a baby. There's no way out of it and everyone thinks you've done something awful, and that you're a bad person.'

Evelyn looked out to the flower beds. *You get pregnant and nine months later there's a baby.* Not for me, she thought bitterly. Not for me.

Jeanette said, 'The baby's father was my boss. I used to work for a firm of insurance brokers in South-ampton.' She looked down at her knotted hands. 'We worked late one evening, and afterwards he took me out for a meal to say thank you. And later . . . when he was driving me home . . . well, I didn't know I could feel like that. I didn't know that I could want someone like that. All those things people say to you – not letting men go all the way and not kissing on a first date – just didn't seem important.'

Bees whined among the hydrangeas; there was a tang of salt in the air. Jeanette frowned and raked back brown curls from her forehead. 'I'm not making excuses. I knew it was wrong. But I thought he understood me. He seemed to think the same way as me. And he made me feel . . . oh, important. *Beautiful*. I thought he loved me. When I told him about the baby, I thought he'd leave his wife. Stupid, wasn't I? It's not just about *love*.'

Tears were trailing down Jeanette's face. Evelyn thought she had rarely heard anyone sound so bleak. 'I suppose there are other considerations,' she said carefully. 'If he had children, for instance.'

'He had a boy and a girl. And he certainly didn't want any more.' Her voice lowered. 'He said . . . he said that I should get rid of it.' She glanced at Evelyn, as though defying her to disapprove. 'He said he'd give me the money. And when I refused, he said that he'd done everything he could and that I was on my own. A couple of days later I lost my job. I suppose I should have expected it. I mean, I could hardly go on working for him, could I?'

Dashing the tears from her eyes, she went on, a little more firmly. 'So there I was – no job, no money. When I told my mother, she had one of her turns. She said I could stay with them for as long as it didn't show, and then I must go to a mother-and-baby home. After the baby was born, I was to have it adopted. I realized that what my mother and father care most about is respectability. I realized that their reputation – our family's reputation – is more important to them than my happiness.'

'I'm sure that's not true—'

'Oh, it is. As long as no one knew about it, as long as my baby could be hidden away, forgotten about, they'd help me. When I told them I couldn't do that, they washed their hands of me.'

'Perhaps,' said Evelyn hesitantly, 'perhaps the home wouldn't be too bad.'

'Have you ever been to one of those places? I went to look at one. It was awful. People telling you what to do every moment of the day. You're supposed to feel ashamed of what you've done. You spend all your time washing linen and scrubbing floors and going to church. The one I visited, there was a girl cleaning the parquet with a toothbrush! It's as though they want to punish you. And after the baby's born, they take it away. You don't know where it's gone or anything. And I thought: Why should I give it away? It's mine, isn't it? I don't have much, but I will have this baby.' She rested her palm on the curve of her belly. 'We'll be all right,' she said defiantly. 'We'll manage.'

'But . . . *money*. And a place to live—'

'I've been saving,' said Jeanette proudly. She stood up. 'I'd better get on with dinner.' She went back into the house.

Evelyn remained sitting on the bench for a few moments and then she slipped out of the side gate and walked down to the beach. It was a warm day and the sands were sprinkled with day trippers. Children paddled in the shallows. Further out to sea, heads bobbed above the water and arms scythed through the waves.

She sat down. To one side of her a toddler was shovelling sand into a bucket. When she looked at him, he smiled a wide, gap-toothed smile. Just for a moment she sank into her old fantasy and let herself believe that he was hers. This little boy was one of her five lost babies. She had named them all, those children she had never known: Stephen, John, Richard, James and Alice.

But the dream dissolved, washed away by the relentless dictates of nature. Over the course of the last year her periods had become erratic, spaced wider apart. She suspected that she was approaching the menopause, which explained, perhaps, some of her moodiness. Soon even hope would be gone. She would never carry a child to term, would never hold her baby in her arms.

She put her hands over her face, as though trying to press the tears back to their source. Through her fretwork of fingers, she glimpsed the sea, the sunlit waves fractured into shards by her sobs. She felt as though she, too, were splitting apart.

Eventually she managed to pull herself together. *Crying on the beach!* she scolded herself. *Everyone is staring at you, Evelyn.* The paroxysm of grief subsided and she wiped her eyes and blew her nose. She sat quietly, waiting for the pain to fade to the familiar dull ache. How long, she wondered, would she have to bear these repetitions of an old grief? And if it ever stopped hurting, even if her longing one day disappeared, wouldn't that, in some way she could not quite put her finger on, be even worse?

With a huge effort of will, she tried to turn her mind to Jeanette's problems. Was it wrong of Jeanette to wish to keep her baby? Many people would say that it was, for practical as well as moral reasons. There was a time, not that long ago, when Evelyn herself might have judged and condemned Jeanette. Into her mind came an image of Betty Hesketh, sluttish in her bright, cheap clothing, always with a man in tow. Evelyn, like everyone else in the Swantons, disapproved of Betty. More than disapproved – Betty provoked in her distaste, even repulsion.

Yet it seemed to her now that there was little enough love in the world. She herself had hardly been overburdened with it. Why should Jeanette have to give up a baby she would undoubtedly love and care for just because it was born out of wedlock? The rebellious little voice that had recently struggled to be born now refused to be stifled, telling her that in this instance convention was faulty. Years ago, to her suggestion that they consider adoption as a solution to their childlessness, Osborne had said dismissively: *You wouldn't know what you were getting, Evelyn.* As though a child's value must be limited by its blood, its lineage and by the circumstances of its birth.

Love was a precious commodity; love transformed and redeemed. Loving Hugo, the world had, for a while, taken on a different cast. For a brief but glorious period of time, she had glimpsed possibility and hope. Had that been wrong? The vicar might remind her that she had coveted someone else's husband. To Dr Lockhart both her happiness and her blind burrowings towards some sort of freedom had been a disease rather than a revelation. And recently she had attempted to force herself back into the mould, afraid of the consequences were she to do otherwise.

But she did not seem to fit any more. What had once seemed a comfortable, if unexciting life, now seemed to jar. Her existence now seemed without either purpose or motive. How little difference she had made to the world, she thought, immured in her crumbling castle, with its roses and its lakes!

Once more she thought of Jeanette. If she could not be happy, then perhaps she could at least help secure someone else's happiness. And, after all, she herself knew better than most what it was to long for a child, to lose a child.

The toddler had tired of his bucket and spade; tottering across the sand towards her, he presented her with the gift of a pebble. Evelyn thanked him and curled her fingers around it, clinging to its smooth, cool surface as if it were a talisman as she walked back to the house.

Venetia was in her bedroom, writing letters. Closing the door behind her, Evelyn said baldly, 'You were right, Jeanette is pregnant.'

'Oh dear.' Venetia blotted the letter. 'And when is the baby due?'

'In about three months.'

'And there is to be no husband?'

Evelyn shook her head. 'He's married.'

Venetia tutted. Evelyn said, 'Jeanette has nowhere to go. I think we should let her stay. Her parents won't have her, you see.'

'Evelyn—'

'After all, it's not a crime, is it, to have a baby?'

'An affair with a married man is hardly something of which one can approve.'

'Of course not, Mummy. But it seems to me that if we don't let Jeanette stay here then everyone will suffer. You'll have no company again, and we'll both miss her. And she'll end up in some awful bedsit, living on a pittance, and even if you believe she deserves that, the baby certainly doesn't. If she stays here, at least she'll be among people who care about her.'

In spite of her best efforts, her voice shook. Evelyn sat down on the edge of the bed, her face turned away from her mother and ran a hand across her eyes.

She heard Venetia say, 'Evelyn, my dear, are you all right?'

She took a deep breath. 'Of course I am, Mummy. I'm just a bit tired.'

There was a silence. Evelyn watched Venetia fold her letter and try to put it into an envelope.

'Can I help you with that, Mummy?'

'Thank you, dear.' Venetia passed her the letter. She frowned and said, 'And, of course, Jeanette must stay. We are not *Victorian*, after all, to throw the poor girl out of the house because she is in trouble. Just until the baby is born, mind. Then we will think what to do.' Pausing, she glanced down at her hands, as though the age spots and fingers clawed by arthritis had taken her by surprise. Then she said, 'I always consider that Donald and I were happily married. But, when I look back, I believe that the happiest months of my life were the ones that we spent together, just the two of us, when I took you to England, Evelyn. Of course, there was the shadow of separation, but perhaps that made me value the time we had together more. When I left you with Ernest and Marigold to return to India, I felt as though

I was leaving a part of myself behind. A cliché, but it's true. I was forty-three years old, and I never felt young again. It was like this – ' again she looked at her hands – 'another little piece of yourself gone, chipped away.'

The trial was held at the Old Bailey, near St Paul's. The monumental stone edifice seemed to tower over Romy as she entered the building. As the hours passed, her thoughts would flick back every now and then to the day that she and Caleb had spent together. The lingering happiness of those memories seemed out of step with the arcane and ponderous procedure of the court. Her strongest emotion was one of bewilderment. She was bewildered by the rules and the delays and by the ritual of the trial. She was sometimes cowed by and sometimes resentful of the bewigged and gowned lawyers, with their cut-glass accents and their cold, mocking humour.

Jem sat hunched in the dock as the clerk of the court read out the indictment, then the jury was sworn in, and the prosecution barrister, Mr Notley, made his opening statement. Mr Notley was tall and thin and dark. His black hair was cropped very close to his head around the back and sides, where it was peppered with grey, and his small black moustache was threaded with a few white hairs. He bore a slight air of decay: if she bumped into him in the corridor, Romy thought, she might find herself scattered with flecks of dust.

The months in prison had made their mark on Jem. He had lost weight and his skin had an unhealthy pallor, and he fidgeted constantly, biting his nails and twisting a button on the sleeve of his jacket. The expressions that flickered across his face, as Mr Notley summarized the evidence against him and listed the witnesses to be called, were familiar to Romy. She had seen that mixture of anger and fear and hurt before, when Jem had been dismissed from yet another job, or when Dennis had without warning lashed out at him.

Ray Babbs was the first witness. Neatly dressed in suit, collar and tie, his demeanour was, as at the committal hearing, steady and controlled. Under oath, he testified that Jem had started the fight in the pub and had afterwards waited in the alley, where he had beaten the surprised and defenceless Ray almost to death. And as for Liz – they had been childhood sweethearts, Ray explained. Ray had first asked Liz to marry him when he was sixteen and she thirteen. They had become engaged two years later. He still loved her – he would always love her. And he believed that Liz loved him. Hadn't she visited him when he was sick in hospital? Hadn't she, on his discharge, called round frequently to his home? Hadn't she said that she'd marry him if she weren't afraid of Jem? If she weren't afraid of Jem's anger, Jem's temper?

Jem's fist slammed against the wooden edge of the dock, and he sprang to his feet. 'You're a liar!' he shouted. 'You're a rotten, bloody liar! Liz would never say that!'

The court was hushed, Jem was reprimanded. Ray Babbs swayed slightly and gripped the witness stand. The judge asked him whether he would like an adjournment, but Ray shook his head. Though Mr Stokes, in his cross-examination, tried to cast doubt on his version of events, Ray Babbs did not falter. At the end of the cross-examination, after Mr Notley had told the judge that he had no further questions, the judge asked sympathetically, 'And are you sure that you are fully recovered from your terrible ordeal, Mr Babbs?' and Ray Babbs produced a brave smile and thanked the judge for his concern.

A succession of other witnesses were called during the afternoon. Pressing the publican of the Prince of Wales during cross-examination, Mr Stokes secured an admission that the pub had been exceptionally busy on the night of the fight – it had been someone's stag night, and the boot-blacking factory across the road had just closed down so many of its employees had been drowning their sorrows – but was unable to shake the publican's conviction that Jem had come into the pub after Ray, that Jem had been looking for Ray. Several people who had been drinking in the Prince of Wales that night were then called to the stand. Romy's spirits rose as one young man, questioned by Mr Stokes, admitted that, because of the crowds in the pub, it had been hard to be sure exactly what was going on. They plummeted as a woman wearing a check headscarf described how she had seen Jem running from the alleyway. 'Blood dripping from his hands and looking as if the hounds of hell were at his feet,' she finished ghoulishly.

At home in her bedsit that evening, Romy could see how it all might look from the outside. There was Ray and there was Jem, and it was a question of choosing between them. Ray was confident, contained, articulate. He had worked on the docks between leaving school and doing his national service. His family – known and respected in the area — had lived in Blackfriars for generations. He had been smartly — but not too smartly — dressed. He had given an impression of honesty and courage. In the fight he had come off worst. He was the victim, the underdog. The British, thought Romy miserably, always sided with the underdog.

And then there was Jem. Jem, whose father had committed suicide, and whose violent stepfather had had the occasional minor brush with the law. Jem, who always seemed to fall into the clutches of those who would exploit him or corrupt him, in Stratton, in Germany and in Brighton. Whose two years of national service had included petty pilfering, who had never stayed in the same job for more than a few months, and whose former employers could testify, if asked, to his short temper. She should have bought him a new suit, she thought desperately. Though she had washed his shirt and pressed his jacket and tie, she knew that, compared to Ray, he had looked down at heel, slightly disreputable. Chasms seemed to have opened up all around Jem, chasms that were black and deep and into which, always unwary, always lacking the instinct for self-protection, he might all too easily tumble.

She took the dog for a walk and fed the cat. She caught up on the ironing and made a list of things for Mandy, her assistant at the Trelawney, to do over the next couple of days. She tried to eat some supper, to read a book, to listen to the radio. She read the same sentence over and over again, failing to understand it, and the babble of the radio irritated her, so that she soon switched it off. The food seemed to lodge in her gullet, choking her: she tipped it uneaten into the bin.

She phoned her mother and tried to sound reassuring, but did not wait at the phone box for Caleb to call. She felt tainted, as if the events of the day had wound a grey, sticky, shameful web around her. Though she tried to cling on to her memories of Caleb's garden and of Middlemere, they suddenly seemed fragile and slippery. Fear erased love, allowed it no place. The tension of the last few months had accumulated to such an extent that she struggled now for even the appearance of normality. *When the trial's over*, she said to herself, as she lay in bed that night, trying to sleep, *when it's over and everything's all right again.* Yet she had lost her confidence in the mantra, had lost confidence in the future. With each chime of the distant church clock – two o'clock, three, four – the core of fear inside her seemed to grow and blossom.

The following morning the police gave their evidence. Outside the sky was cloudless, and along the corridors and staircases of the Old Bailey the hot air seemed to gather, stale and lacking in oxygen. The tension of the previous day had been replaced by torpor and weariness. In the dock Jem looked tired and heavy-eyed. Romy's head ached, the result of the sleepless night. Her mind would keep drifting to inconsequential things. She must remember to buy dog food and to collect her jacket from the dry cleaner's. She must remember to tell Mandy to check the number of guests for the Variety Club dinner on Saturday . . .

Something the policeman was saying broke through her scattered thoughts. In his original statement, given on the night of the fight, Jem had admitted that he had

384

lost his temper during the altercation in the alleyway. Romy's head jerked up. The policeman flicked over the pages of his notebook. Mr Notley questioned him more closely. The defendant, said the policeman ponderously, had stated on the night of the crime that he had fled the alleyway in which the fight had taken place because he was frightened. When asked why he was frightened, Cole had admitted that he had believed that he had killed Mr Babbs. Under questioning, Cole had then become distressed and violent.

'Violent?' enquired Mr Notley in silken tones.

'Yes, sir. Two officers had to restrain him until he calmed down.'

Jem, she thought, sickened. Jem, you *fool*.

'Please continue, officer.'

'When questioned further, Cole admitted that he had lashed out during the fight with Babbs.'

'His exact words, please, officer?'

The policeman read from his notebook. 'Cole said, "I didn't mean to hurt him. He just made me mad and I flew off the handle. I didn't mean to hurt him."'

There was a shuffling upright, a sharpening of attention, as if a ripple of electricity had run through the courtroom, dissipating the heavy languor of the day. As Mr Stokes cross-examined the policeman, securing an admission from him that the defendant had revised his statement the following day, Romy could hardly bear to look at Jem.

The policeman stepped down from the witness box. Romy pressed her knuckles against her teeth as Mr Stokes and Mr Rogers spoke quietly to one another, and then Mr Stokes approached the judge and asked for an adjournment.

She sat in the waiting room. There were a dozen or so other people there, most of them concerned with different court cases. Romy's gaze drifted from one to the other. On the seat opposite Romy a young girl was crying. Romy tried to smile at her, to cheer her up, but either the girl was beyond comfort or the smile betrayed the despair in Romy's heart, because the girl continued to sob quietly, mopping her eyes every now and then with a handkerchief.

In another corner a couple pored over *The Times* crossword. The other inhabitants of the waiting room seemed to have abandoned all hope of distraction. Newspapers, magazines and paperbacked books lay discarded beside the benches. Men smoked pipes or cigarettes; a woman had unwrapped a bar of Fry's Chocolate Cream and was slowly breaking off pieces and placing them one by one in her mouth. Time was measured out by the minutes it took to smoke a cigarette or suck a sweet. Romy could feel the moments shrinking, shrivelled by the unbearable heat. Somewhere in the hour of waiting hope had died and had been replaced by dread. By dread and by the beginnings of a gathering and implacable rage.

Her rage was for Jem. It seemed to Romy that the process of the law had not revealed the truth. She and Jem were as voiceless as they had always been, as voiceless as Jem had once literally been in the dark months that had followed their father's death. Through the high, dusty windows, the bright, white sun still burned in a cloudless sky. Her head ached and the palms of her hands were clammy. When she looked down, she saw that she had twisted the ends of her chiffon scarf into a greyish string.

The door opened. Mr Rogers came into the room and sat down beside her. He had come to warn her, he explained, that he had advised Jem to offer the prosecution a plea of guilty to the less serious charge of grievous bodily harm. And that he would not have done so were he not convinced that there was a very real possibility that the jury would find Jem guilty of the original charge. The judge had made it plain that his sympathies were with Babbs; this would influence his summing up. Babbs's statement to the police was consistent with his evidence in court; Jem's was not. And he could not be confident that Jem would not further damage his case if he were to give evidence.

He had noticed, Mr Rogers said gently, that Jem had a tendency to panic or lose his temper under pressure. And Mr Notley would be sure to apply the greatest pressure. He anticipated that if Jem were to offer to plead guilty to the less serious charge at this juncture, halfway through the trial, the prosecution might well accept it. Whereas, if Jem were to perform poorly in the witness stand, then the prosecution might feel confident of a conviction under the original charge and refuse to accept a change of plea. And – Mr Rogers touched her arm reassuringly – if the prosecution were to accept Jem's plea, he felt sure that the judge would impose a sentence of no more than two years' imprisonment.

'*Two years?*' she repeated and heard her voice rise.

'Miss Cole,' said Mr Rogers, 'the maximum sentence for grievous bodily harm with intent is life imprisonment.' As he left the room, she began, in spite of the sun and the heat, to shiver.

After the tortuously slow, grinding procedures of the previous months, the end came with a speed that left Romy shocked and breathless. The court was reconvened, and another count – that of grievous bodily harm – was added to the indictment. Jem was arraigned and the charge was reread. Jem gave his plea of guilty and Romy squeezed her eyes tightly shut. As Mr Stokes offered to the judge a list of mitigating circumstances – Jem's youth and his lack of any previous convictions – she tried to cling on to the last few shreds of hope.

Yet the judge's summing up quickly crushed her fragile optimism. Phrases echoed in the courtroom. *Vicious and uncontrolled ... youth no excuse for unprovoked violence ...* And then, with a last, disdainful sniff, the judge was saying: *I have no hesitation in imposing a custodial sentence of two years*, and Jem was led back down to the cells.

She was allowed to speak to him for a few minutes. 'I'm sorry,' she heard herself say, over and over again, as she clung to him. 'I'm so sorry. I shouldn't have made you go to the police. I didn't think this would happen.' And Jem shook his head and smiled his wide, familiar smile, and said, 'It wasn't your fault, Romy. And it's not long, is it, two years? Just like doing national service again.'

Then she was out in the street, stumbling past shops, cafes and offices. She walked, choosing streets at random, directionless, all at sea. Every now and then she had to pause and sit down on a wall or a bench, to wait for the nausea and dizziness to pass. Though the heat was pitiless, her cotton jacket seemed too thin to warm her. She wondered whether she was ill; she wrapped her arms around herself, trying to give herself comfort. Then she thought, *Caleb*, and she stumbled to her feet and headed for Waterloo Station.

On the train, leaving London, she rested her head against the seat and closed her eyes. Dark shapes, red and brown and black, danced behind her lids. Her temples pounded in rhythm with the wheels of the carriage. Her rage endured, grew. With the force and inexorability of a steamroller, the trial had completed the obliteration of a person who had been fragile since childhood. Jem hadn't needed supercilious lawyers or lying witnesses to destroy him: he was more than capable of carrying out the task himself. The Jem whom the prosecution had painted had not been her Jem. This other Jem was unschooled and unreliable, capable of striking out at the least provocation. She had not been allowed to show the jury the events that had made Jem the way he was. She had not been able to make them see the other Jem, her Jem, the Jem who could be so gentle to a bird with a broken wing or a brutalized dog. Her Jem had no intimacy with arrogance and little knowledge of hatred. Her Jem was bewildered by spite and unkindness and always vulnerable to those more calculating than himself.

Each time the train slowed, she opened her eyes

briefly to check the name of the station. She couldn't remember how to find the Rolands' house, so she remained on the train until it reached Hungerford. She would go to Middlemere, she decided, and wait for Caleb there.

At Hungerford she emerged from the shadow of the station into a late afternoon of blinding sunshine. The hot air stilled the leaves on the trees and the flowers in front gardens so that they drooped limply, motionless. She seemed to be pushing against some invisible force, and the other passengers – women with shopping bags and small children in tow, and men in pinstriped suits – seemed also to encounter resistance, their feet dragging along the dusty pavements.

She saw a bus and hailed it, and went to sit on the upper deck. The road narrowed as the bus heaved and sputtered out of the town. There was the smell of hot rubber and diesel and stale cigarettes; feeling queasy again, she rested her forehead against the cool glass of the window. The wheels brushed against the verges in the narrow lanes and the outstretched branches of the tall trees banged against the windows of the upper deck. From the front seat Romy could see the countryside spread out around her, with its patchwork of fields and hedgerows and hills. She did not recognize the narrow lanes or the thatched cottages or the small, sleepy hamlets. There were no familiar landmarks; she might have been travelling in an unknown country, her compass set at random, north, south, east or west.

The bus rattled down a long incline, its jolts and lurches and the hot, stale air stirring her stomach. Dizzily recalling that you should look straight ahead if you felt travel-sick, she stared out of the window. Amid the blur of green and gold fields, she saw a house and the gardens that surrounded it. Flower beds and orchards, paths and trees, swept back towards the hills. A lake glittered, pale and cool and distant, amid green velvet lawns.

A voice echoed in her head. *There was a lake in the garden... Fancy having a lake in your garden!* Her stomach lurched; she pressed her hand against her mouth, dashed down the stairs, and rang the bell to ask the driver to stop the bus. She heard the conductor scolding her for ringing the bell between stops, and she glared at him and said loudly, 'If you don't let me off, I'll be sick all over your bus.' The bus ground to a halt and she jumped off to find herself in a countryside of woodland and verges thick with buttercups and cow parsley. As the bus disappeared around a bend in the road, she stopped and closed her eyes, then took several deep breaths. She knew that she had found the Daubenys' house, Swanton Lacy.

The nausea retreated and she began to walk, yet her limbs still moved with the sticky inertia of a nightmare. The trees parted and thinned. She reached a long wall, built of old red bricks blotched gold with lichen. At the end of the wall a wrought-iron gate swung open. Romy stood in the aperture, looking up the driveway. Her first sight of Swanton Lacy left her breathless and awed. Turrets and belvederes grew from the house's roofline, and the dozens of windows – oriel, rose and lancet, grilled and latticed and mullioned – divided the sunlight into diamonds. In front of the house was a gravelled forecourt. To either side of it, tall, graceful trees cast dark shadows on the grass. A flower border ran the length of the driveway. Bees hummed among the blue and white and yellow blooms.

As she looked, her awe turned to anger. You could have fitted 5 Hill View into that house a dozen times. All that she could see – this great edifice, this wide-acred garden – spoke of unshakeable confidence, of permanence and of continuity. The Daubenys had never known what it was to be homeless; they had never known the humiliation of poverty. They had not only wealth, they also had history, and the power and authority that stems from the ownership of money and land.

Fourteen years ago Osborne Daubeny had used that power to crush the Coles. Now, remembering, Romy would have liked to seize a stone from the driveway and hurl it through one of the windowpanes, or, taking a stick, to run alongside the herbaceous border, knocking the heads of the flowers from their tall stems. Giddy with anger, she closed her eyes and noticed for the first time the scent of roses.

She walked a few steps along the driveway and heard the click of secateurs. To one side of her, a garden was enclosed by the red-brick wall. Peering through the open gate, Romy saw the roses, hundreds of them, scrambling along walls and up trellises, spilling their fat, blowsy blooms over archways and obelisks. Petals tumbled to the ground, cream and gold and blood red against the emerald grass. Their heavy, sweet scent made her stomach churn once more.

In a corner of the garden stood a woman. Her secateurs clipped the blossoms and stripped away leaves. She was fair haired, and she was wearing a tweed skirt and a cream silk blouse, and there was a single strand of pearls around her neck. How serene she looked, how untouchable. Romy pictured Martha, in her cheap synthetic clothes, her face prematurely lined with worry. Martha, who would shortly receive the news of her eldest son's imprisonment. There it was again: that urge to break, to destroy.

She must have made some sort of sound because the woman turned towards her. 'Can I help you?' she called out. 'Are you lost?' She crossed the garden to Romy.

'Are you Mrs Daubeny?'

'I'm Evelyn Daubeny, yes.'

'Osborne Daubeny's wife?' She had to be sure.

'Yes.' Mrs Daubeny looked puzzled. 'He's not at home just now. Can I give him a message?'

Osborne Daubeny had given Middlemere to his mistress, and in doing so had been instrumental in causing the death of her father and the destruction of her family. Had it not been for Osborne Daubeny, her father would not have died, nor would Jem's life have been knocked off course.

'Yes,' she said. 'Yes, I'd like you to give him a message.' Her voice was low and unsteady. 'I'd like you to ask him how he could take away our house. And whether he ever thinks about it.' Seen through a fog of rage, Evelyn Daubeny seemed to shimmer and drift. 'People like you,' she whispered, 'you have so much, and yet you still want more, don't you?'

Evelyn Daubeny made a quick, uncomprehending gesture. 'I think you must have made a mistake – I think you must have come to the wrong house—'

Romy shook her head. 'No. No mistake.'

'Who are you? What's your name?'

'My name's Romy Cole.' Staring at the bewildered expression on Evelyn Daubeny's face, she felt an urge to laugh. 'You don't know me, do you? Why should you? Your husband only threw my family out of our home so that he could give it to his mistress. He only destroyed my family.' She pressed the heels of her palms against her face.

'I don't understand,' Evelyn Daubeny whispered. 'House? What house?'

'Middlemere, of course,' she said contemptuously. 'I'm Romy Cole, and Middlemere was my home.'

There was silence. Then Mrs Daubeny said, 'Mistress . . . ?'

Chapter Twelve

She watched the girl walk away. When she was out of
sight, Evelyn looked down at her hands and saw that
she was still holding the secateurs. She picked up the
trug containing the roses and fetched her gardening
gloves from where she had left them, and walked back
to the house. In the scullery she filled the vases with
water and arranged the roses. Yet the stems would not
seem to stay as she wanted them and she realized that
she felt rather sick, and that she was shaking. Shock,
she supposed. Soon, she told herself, soon Osborne
would come home, and she would tell him about the
girl, and he would say in that uninterested manner of
his: *Who? Romy Cole? Never heard of her.* And then he
would disappear into the study to inspect his latest
building plans.

Abandoning the roses, Evelyn sat down on a stool.
The girl must have been lying to her, she told herself.
Yet if she peeled away the layers of memory, she had a
distant recollection of a tragedy that had taken place at
Middlemere Farm. It had been during the war years,
she thought; she could not remember exactly what had
happened.

And the Heskeths were indeed tenants of Middlemere now. In her mind's eye, Evelyn pictured Betty's

curled, bleached-blonde hair, her powder and lipstick and her tight, brashly coloured clothing. There was always a smile on Betty's lips, always a glint in her slightly slanting, cat-like eyes. Betty's appearance advertised her sexuality and availability. Everyone in the village knew what sort of woman she was. When, years ago, Osborne had first suggested that he offer the Hesketh boy holiday work at Swanton Lacy, Evelyn had found herself wanting to say no, afraid that the child would take after his mother, that he would carry with him that aura of lawlessness and carnality. Ridiculous, she had realized almost immediately; you should not, of course, penalize a child for the sins of his mother.

Osborne and Betty Hesketh ... It was impossible, ridiculous. Yet the girl had been so credible, so sure of herself. Fourteen years ago, she had said. Evelyn counted back and reached 1942. She had lost the last baby in the summer of 1942 – Alice, the only girl. The remainder of the year had been blurred by grief and depression.

She was not an innocent, Evelyn thought angrily, as she stood up and began to ram the remainder of the flowers into the vases. She knew that some men were attracted to sluts and that some men strayed. But Osborne wasn't that sort of man, was he? Whatever his faults, he had always, as Celia had pointed out, been faithful to her, hadn't he?

She heard the car draw up outside the house. She felt hot and rather sticky: her blouse had become untucked, and there were splashes of water on the front of her skirt. She stared at the flowers. They looked as though they had been arranged by a madwoman. The blooms stuck out from the vase at all angles, their heads in disarray, their leaves jostling for space. She needed a cup of tea, thought Evelyn. Or a large whisky, or one of Dr Lockhart's magic pills.

She went to meet Osborne. Although she murmured mechanical greetings, the clamminess and unease persisted, intensifying as the afternoon's encounter repeated itself over and over again in her head, like a jammed loop of film. She was in the kitchen, filling the kettle, when Osborne said sharply, 'For goodness sake, Evelyn. What's wrong with you? The kettle.' And she looked down and saw the water bubbling out through the spout and lid.

At the tone of his voice, something seemed to snap inside her — that *he* should criticize *her*. She heard herself say, 'We had a visitor today, Osborne. A girl called Romy Cole. She asked for you.'

When he did not reply, she looked round. He had turned away, but not quickly enough. She just caught the shock in his eyes.

'Osborne?' she said, suddenly hesitant.

He seemed to make an effort. 'The name is familiar . . .'

'You know her?'

He gave a little laugh. 'Hardly *know*. But the family—' He broke off.

'Used to live at Middlemere?'

'Yes.'

She felt jarred, as though she had lost her footing and was struggling for balance. Osborne went to the sink; she watched him turn on the cold tap and place his hands beneath the stream of water. 'So hot,' he muttered. 'So bloody hot.'

Osborne never swore. Evelyn put the kettle on the hob and said, 'Why did they leave?'

'Who?'

Another stab of annoyance. 'The Coles, of course.'

He ran his wet hands over his face. 'They were evicted.'

Your husband threw my family out of our home. 'You evicted them?'

'They were evicted by the War Ag. Cole wasn't running the farm efficiently.'

'But you—'

'Yes, yes,' he said irritably. 'I sat on the committee. It was all above board, Evelyn, I assure you. And Cole was impossible. Wouldn't do a thing he was told. We gave him every chance.'

She might almost have been reassured. Romy Cole's father had lost his farm, yes. But with justification. As for that other, terrible charge, there was a rational explanation, wasn't there? Perhaps, a loyal daughter, unable to accept the true reason of her father's incompetence, Romy Cole had invented a different motive for the Coles' eviction.

She spooned tea into the pot. 'What happened to the Coles?'

'The mother and children? I don't know. They left the area. Samuel Cole—' Again he paused. Then he said, 'You must remember, Evelyn. Samuel Cole shot himself.'

Tea leaves scattered over the draining board. 'Shot himself?' she echoed.

'At the house. It was unfortunate, but the man was unbalanced. Unhinged. Had been so for some time. For

heaven's sake, he proved that himself, didn't he? Turning the shotgun on himself ... Don't you remember?'
He was staring at her. 'Do you really not remember?'

Mutely she shook her head.

'Cole refused to plough when he was told to plough
and wouldn't plant what he was told to plant. He
disputed every order. The fields were always too boggy
or too stony. Any excuse. And he was offensive. Argued
with me. Made a fool of me, do you remember? That
time at church ... Make no mistake, he deserved to be
evicted.'

He sounded resentful, she thought. Almost indig-
nant. The kettle was screaming on the hob, but she did
not yet pick it up. She struggled to remember what she
was supposed to be doing, had to remind herself how
you made a pot of tea. She couldn't get out of her mind
the image of a man turning the shotgun on himself and
pulling the trigger.

Though she had spent most of her life in the
countryside, she had always been revolted by the violence that seemed an inescapable part of it. She had
never hunted, had never taken part in the pheasant
shoots that had taken place on the estate before the war.
Now she found herself remembering the birds' iridescent feathers and the sweet, sickening smell of blood
and raw flesh.

She said, 'The family—'

'Yes, yes. But it was wartime, Evelyn, remember.'
He added pompously, 'We all had to make sacrifices.'

She picked up the kettle, scalding herself on the hot
handle. Like an automaton, she made the tea and put
the cups on the table. Osborne was red-faced, perspiring.

A small muscle beat at the corner of his eye. His demeanour lacked the confidence of his words; it betrayed him, she thought.

'Cole was a difficult man,' he said suddenly. 'He had few friends in the village. I don't recall many tears being shed for him.'

The heat seemed to have gathered in the high-windowed, badly ventilated room. A trickle of perspiration ran between Evelyn's breasts. She knitted her hands around her cup. The tea tasted sour; she wondered whether the milk was off. They should buy a fridge, she thought. Everyone else had a fridge: even Celia, in her little house in Bayswater, had a fridge.

Osborne said suddenly, 'What did she want?'

She realized that he couldn't let the subject drop. That he felt the need to defend himself, to justify himself. His forefinger was beating a tattoo on the table top. *Your husband only threw my family out of our home so that he could give it to his mistress.*

She said, 'Why did you give Middlemere to the Heskeths, Osborne?'

'They were tenants of mine ... Their cottage was very dilapidated ...' The tic at the corner of his eye had speeded up.

'Betty Hesketh had been widowed not long before, hadn't she?'

'I think so ... I can't remember.' He gave a little laugh. 'Really, Evelyn, you can't expect me to remember every detail of our tenants' lives.'

She put down her cup and stared at the scum on the surface of the tea. 'I just thought,' she murmured, 'that you might particularly remember Betty Hesketh.'

'What do you mean?' he said sharply.

'She's a rather noticeable woman, isn't she?'

'Do you think so?'

'*Men* seem to notice her.'

'Do they?' Glancing at his watch, he half rose from the table. 'You must excuse me—'

'You haven't finished your tea, Osborne.' He sank back into his seat. 'I meant, why Betty Hesketh and not one of the other tenants?'

'I don't know.' He pulled at his shirt collar. 'I can't remember.' He said again, 'What did she want? What did Romy Cole want?'

Evelyn's heart was beating very fast, yet she knew that she sounded calm, almost disinterested. She said slowly, 'She wanted me to ask you whether you ever thought about the Coles. You see, she told me – ' and she made herself look at him – 'she told me that you had had an affair with Betty Hesketh, Osborne.' There was a stillness about him, a sudden vigilance. 'Is it true?'

He made a protesting sound. 'Of course not. That's preposterous.'

'That's what I thought at first. But then she – the girl – told me that Betty Hesketh herself had admitted that it was true.'

'Betty—' The bluster died away; he looked alarmed.

'That's what Miss Cole said.'

'I don't see why you should believe—'

'And I don't see why she should lie. And I did believe her, Osborne. I'm afraid she was rather convincing.' Frowning, she looked down at her cup. 'It is true, isn't it?'

He was silent. She said, 'Tell me the truth, Osborne.

You have to tell me.' The unreal calm had gone: her voice faltered.

Eventually he said, 'It was a long time ago. And it was only once or twice.'

She felt stunned, as though he had inflicted on her a physical blow. Yet in Osborne himself she sensed relief, the relief of the confessional, perhaps, as though he were letting go of something that had haunted him for years.

'It wasn't important,' he said.

Her fury reignited. 'How could you?' she hissed. 'That woman – that *slut*—'

He seemed to begin to recover his confidence. 'I told you,' he said, 'it was a long time ago. Twenty-five years. I'd almost forgotten about it.'

Intermingled with the shock of his admission, she was aware of confusion. 'Twenty-five years?' she repeated.

'Yes.' He added angrily, 'The woman's a tart. You know that, Evelyn. You know her reputation.'

She almost wanted to laugh. 'Are you trying to tell me that Betty Hesketh seduced you, Osborne?'

He pulled at his collar again. 'She was always *there*. And you were so ill – it was after the first baby—'

'I wasn't available, but Betty was? Is that what you're saying? Does that justify what you did?'

'*No*. I mean – ' standing up, he gripped the back of the chair – 'she made it clear that she wasn't averse. Every time I saw her. And it wears you down ... You don't mean to, and then – ' his eyes were tortured – 'she was attractive, as you said. No – it was more than that. There was something magnetic ... You wanted to resist but you couldn't.'

'So you went to bed with her? Or perhaps bed wasn't the place.' The words tumbled from her, vile and uncontrolled. 'Where did you and Betty fornicate, Osborne? Was it in the fields? Or in a haystack? Or perhaps in the back of the car?'

She had to turn away, to clamp her hand over her mouth. She heard him say, 'She didn't mean anything to me. I didn't – I didn't even much like her. She was common. Pushy. *Brazen*. She had no shame.' A little of his self-assurance had returned. 'For God's sake – how long should one have to feel guilty for – for a *lapse*, a momentary lapse? Surely it doesn't matter now? Surely it's just – just—'

'Water under the bridge?' she supplied. She pushed aside her cup. She couldn't have drunk any more, it would have choked her. 'Is there a moratorium on such things, Osborne? Does infidelity only matter if it's recent? And how long before it ceases to count? A year? Five? Ten?'

If he would only say sorry, she thought. If he would only admit that he had done wrong. Perhaps then her anger, which was so intense it made her feel light-headed, would cool.

She said slowly, 'Was that why you evicted the Coles? So that you could give Middlemere to Betty Hesketh?'

'Of course not! It was Cole's fault. If he hadn't been so obdurate, so proud, so *above* himself!' He added, the clincher to the argument, 'The man was a bloody socialist!'

'Tell me what happened.'

'Evelyn—'

'Tell me. Tell me everything.'

She saw him glance out to the garden, to the lawn and the lake and the ruined stanchions of the bridge. Then he sighed and said, 'We had to survey all the farms. Orders from Whitehall. We got to Middlemere in the early autumn of forty-two. Paynter was the district officer, so he went to see Cole.'

'And Middlemere wasn't up to scratch?'

'There was a history of non-compliance. Cole simply wouldn't do what he was told. At first, he wouldn't let Paynter on the land. He was offensive, threatening. I had to insist. There was derelict land that hadn't been reclaimed ... and some of the soil was waterlogged.' Osborne dabbed at his forehead with his handkerchief. 'You had to classify each farm A, B or C, according to the state of the place. Middlemere was classified C.'

'On what grounds?'

'Personal failings.' He shut his eyes tightly. 'That's what we put on the form. Personal failings.'

'*Personal failings* . . .'

'It was a difficult job,' he said angrily, 'and someone had to do it. For heaven's sake, Evelyn, there was a war on! Hitler was only a few miles over the Channel, trying to starve us out. I couldn't afford to be sentimental. Surely you can see that?'

She said slowly, 'So Middlemere was classified as a failing farm—'

'Cole was told to change his methods. Told to work according to the committee's direction. But he still refused to toe the line. So then . . .' He looked up at her, defiance in his eyes. 'It was in the regulations. We had every right to evict him. When we told him to quit, he refused to do so.' He paused, then muttered, 'It didn't have to be like that. It should have been ordered – civilized—'

'I'm not sure,' she murmured 'that one can evict a family from their home in a civilized manner.'

'I meant – I didn't intend—'

'You meant just to throw Mr Cole out of his home and deprive him of his livelihood. Not to kill him. Was that what you meant, Osborne?'

'For God's sake—'

'The eviction. Tell me what happened.'

He had covered his face with his hands. After a while he said more quietly, 'I'd given him notice to quit. Paynter went up to Middlemere in the morning to make sure everything went smoothly. But Cole was still in the house. He'd barricaded himself in. When he fired a shotgun, Paynter fetched the police. One of the policemen tried to get into the house through the skylight in the roof, and Cole shot him. That's the sort of man he was, Evelyn! He shot a policeman!'

'Did he kill him?'

'No.' He frowned. 'The fellow was wounded in the shoulder.' Another pause. 'But perhaps Cole thought—'

'What?'

He twisted his hands together. 'That he *had* killed him.'

She was aware of an overwhelming feeling of horror. She understood what Osborne implied. That Mr Cole might have believed that he had lost everything – his home, his livelihood, his liberty. And his life, of course: if he had killed the policeman, then he would have expected to receive the death penalty. Judges and juries were unlikely to be sympathetic to the murderer of a policeman.

Osborne had closed his eyes. He whispered, 'The little girl was hiding in the house. We didn't realize. When the police broke into the house, they found her with the body.'

The image of the child with her dead father was almost unbearable. She heard him cry out, 'It wasn't my fault, Evelyn! You do see that, don't you?'

She saw that he was asking her for forgiveness, for absolution. She said, 'Could you have prevented it, Osborne?'

'I had a job to do.'

'Yes, but could you have intervened on Mr Cole's behalf? Could you have handled him more tactfully, perhaps?'

His eyes were wild. He whispered, '*Evelyn*,' and she repeated, '*Could* you?' and at last he said quietly, 'Yes. Yes, I suppose so.'

His short grey hair had become dishevelled and a pallor had replaced the reddening of his complexion. She was aware of a feeling of revulsion. A revulsion that was directed also at herself.

'All the work I did for the War Ag,' Osborne said suddenly, angrily. 'The long hours, from dawn to dusk. I was proud of what I did. I wanted to do my bit, and I did, didn't I? And then Cole ... It tarnished me ... It was never the same afterwards. People used to look at me ... And Paynter ... Paynter had a breakdown after it happened. I helped him out, helped him make a new start. You see – ' he looked up at her, his eyes pleading – 'you can't accuse me of callousness. I made sure Paynter was all right.'

She hardly heard him. They had had a responsibility, she thought, a responsibility to their tenants, who depended on them. *People like you ... you still want more*, Romy Cole had said. Yet Osborne's faults – of self-righteousness, of arrogance, of impatience with those he believed to be fools – were not, Evelyn thought bitterly, her own. Her faults were different in nature.

She said slowly, 'And after the Coles had gone you gave the farm to Betty Hesketh?'

He flinched. 'Not the land,' he muttered. 'Just the house.'

She gathered together the cups and saucers and carried them to the sink. Tipping out the cold tea, filling the sink with water, she said quietly, 'But don't you see how you are compromised, Osborne? Don't you see that even if what you say is true, that the eviction of the Coles and your affair with Mrs Hesketh were not connected, then they must inevitably appear to be?'

'But they weren't!'

'A man died, Osborne.' Her voice was harsh. 'Mr Cole died.'

He groaned. He sat down at the table, his shoulders bowed, his defiance gone. A strong, powerful man, he looked suddenly old and defeated. He had never before seemed weak to her.

'I never meant it to happen,' he muttered. 'I never thought he'd take his own life.' He closed his eyes. 'You have to believe me, Evelyn.'

At the sink she rinsed cups and saucers and laid them on the draining board. He said again, pleading, 'I didn't mean it to happen,' but she did not reply, only stared into the soapy water, watching the twist and turn of her hands.

Romy went back to Stratton. She couldn't face Middlemere, not just yet. Couldn't face Caleb, needed an hour or two to catch her breath before she could meet his eyes. The sense of dread that had been with her throughout this long, terrible day had intensified. She could not shake off the fear that, in speaking to Evelyn Daubeny, she had done something very wrong, something that might have unforeseen consequences. *Mistress?* Evelyn Daubeny had said, and Romy had realized that Mrs Daubeny had known nothing of her husband's affair with Betty Hesketh. She had had no need of sticks or stones, then; she had inflicted her wounds with words. As she had spoken, as she had watched the blood drain from Evelyn Daubeny's face, she had felt a wild, vengeful joy.

And yet now, if she could have turned back time, she would have glanced into the rose garden just once and then walked away. One question haunted her throughout her journey to Stratton. Continued to haunt her as she told Martha about Jem, then tried to comfort her, and later helped Carol cook supper. Stayed with her, making her stomach squeeze and her head pound as she and Carol washed up.

Whom had she hurt most in telling Evelyn Daubeny of her husband's affair with Betty Hesketh? The Daubenys or Caleb or herself?

Carol was talking to her about her boyfriend and about her dead-end job in an ironmonger's in Romsey.

Darren fools about a bit, but he's all right really. And my job's so boring and at least we have some fun. He's got a motorbike, Romy. He wants us to get engaged, only Mum won't let me.

Romy found herself distracted for a moment from her own preoccupations. She seemed to hear her younger self, eighteen years old and railing at the narrowness of her life.

'Do you love Darren?'

Carol paused, tea towel in hand. 'I dunno. But it's so boring here, Romy. If I married him at least I might have a place of my own.'

Carol put Gareth to bed; Ronnie went out to play. Martha had dozed off on the couch. Romy went outside. She was picking up toys from the front garden when she looked up and saw the blue van turning the corner into Hill View. Her heart fluttered. He mustn't know, she resolved. He mustn't ever know what she had done. He had no need to know and there was no reason why he should ever find out.

She watched the van pull up outside Number 5. The bats and balls and Davy Crockett hats slid out of her hands; she ran down the path to meet him.

'Caleb,' she said. She was crying. 'Jem—'

'I know. Jake told me.'

'Jake?'

'I phoned him. He heard. Jake always knows things, you know that. He tried to find you, but you weren't at your bedsit or at the hotel. I guessed you might have come here to see your mother.' He frowned. 'Poor Jem. I'm so sorry, Romy.'

Swanton Lacy and Evelyn Daubeny slipped out of

her mind at last and were replaced by an image of Jem as she had last seen him in the cell, a smile on his face and defeat in his eyes.

'It was my fault,' she said. 'If I hadn't made him go to the police—'

He took her hand. 'Is there somewhere where we can be alone?'

She glanced around wildly. Neighbours were standing at their garden gates, every now and again giving them interested glances. Romy thought of 5 Hill View's shabby living room: Martha drinking herself into a stupor on the couch and Dennis home from the pub any minute.

'There's a place I sometimes go to,' she said.

As they walked out of the cul-de-sac and down the hill, she told him about the trial. The police, the witnesses, the distorted picture they had painted. 'Jem didn't have a chance, Caleb!' she cried. 'They wouldn't let him explain anything! Ray Babbs lied – I know he lied!'

They reached the copse where, years ago, Liam Pike had offered to take her for a drive. In the summer heat the circular pool had shrunk, a dark mirror to the trees. A thicket of hawthorn and bramble screened them from the road. Jackdaws cawed, rising from the treetops.

'It was my fault,' she repeated. 'I should have known what would happen – should have known what everyone would think. I keep thinking of him, Caleb. Jem hates being shut in. He can't even bear to work in an *office*. So *stupid* of me—'

'Stop,' he said firmly. He held her upper arms. 'Stop,

Romy. It wasn't your fault. You did everything you could. You did nothing wrong.'

'That's not true——'

'You did nothing wrong,' he said again.

She thought of Evelyn Daubeny and turned away. But she felt him kiss the curve of her neck and she closed her eyes, shutting everything else out. 'Jem will get through it,' he said. 'He will, Romy.' His hands were running up and down her spine; his mouth brushed against her cheek. 'And you don't have to think of it now. There's nothing more you can do now.'

He drew her to him. His body moulded into hers. She felt the heat of his skin through her palms, and the hard outline of muscle and sinew, felt something inside her ignite and begin to burn, something fierce and bright enough to wipe from her mind the events of the day.

Buttons snapped from their anchors, zips jammed, and her stockings snagged on twigs and acorns. She was wearing a pink floral nylon bra and corset beneath her cotton dress. She peeled them off, not bothering about the way they squeezed and clung and left red marks on her skin, caring only to rip away the layers of cloth that prevented the joining of flesh. She heard him say, 'I always imagined somewhere different ... A moonlit garden ... a suite at the Savoy ... I wanted the best for you, Romy.'

'This is the best,' she whispered. 'Absolutely the best.'

Limbs pushed against dead leaves; pebbles pressed into her spine. The sun was cut into lacework by the canopy of leaves overhead. When he was inside her, when she felt her pleasure gather and soar, she finally knew the answer to the question that had always puzzled her: why women gave so much of themselves to men. It was because of this, because of this glorious, intoxicating delight. And because she now knew that she wasn't alone any more, that she need never be alone again. And because passion muted even loss and regret. And when at last, exhausted, they fell apart, her hand still drifted against him, unable to bear separation.

There were things that Evelyn had always tried to avoid thinking about. Things she had never faced up to.

Fourteen years ago terrible events had occurred at Middlemere. An eviction, a suicide, the destruction of a family. And she had hardly been aware of them. Osborne attempted to deny his complicity in the death of Samuel Cole, but Evelyn saw hers clearly. The fault was not only Osborne's.

She had never taken a proper interest in the welfare of the tenants. It was an aspect of her life as mistress of Swanton Lacy that she had always shrunk from. She had failed to befriend them, not because she disliked them, but because she was ill at ease with them, nervous of them. She had never completely lost the shyness of her girlhood. A young bride, she had found her social responsibilities an ordeal. Entertaining Osborne's friends had been bad enough; meeting the tenants had been much worse and had made her heart pound, her stomach cramp. She knew that they in turn thought her proud and stand-offish. She remembered once, long ago, trying very hard at some local event – judging a vegetable show or opening a sale of work – yet as she had left the village hall, she had heard one woman mutter to another, 'Well, *she's* a friendly type!' Those few words – disparaging, contemptuous – had been such a blow to her fragile self-confidence that afterwards whenever possible she had avoided the company of those of a lower social class.

Some responsibilities she had been unable to escape: the fête, the Women's Institute and her various wartime committees. Though she had enjoyed her contact with the village children, she had always found their fathers – farmers of few words and awkward manner – intimidating. To herself she had used the reason of her miscarriages. As though unhappiness excused you from responsibility.

Now she felt tainted, tarnished. *Cole was so obdurate, so proud*, Osborne had said. He might have been listing his own failings. She imagined the two men, both refusing to back down, locked in a combat to the death. If she had known what was going on then, she could have reasoned with Osborne. Perhaps she would have been able to make him see the possible outcome of the course on which he was set; perhaps she would not. But she should at least have tried.

Her thoughts shifted back to her discovery of Osborne's affair. While she had been enduring the grief that had followed the loss of her first baby, Osborne had been bedding Betty Hesketh. If it had been anyone else, she thought savagely. Anyone but her. Betty was the sort of woman Evelyn had always despised; was she also the sort of woman men really wanted? Did men claim to admire chaste, virtuous women while secretly desiring sluts like Betty?

Osborne's passion for Betty Hesketh, together with her own lack of engagement, had distorted the past, clouding it, so that now it slipped through her fingers, evading easy judgement. Did you abandon a marriage because of a fleeting, long-ago infidelity? Or was there, as Osborne had seemed to imply, a statute of limitations on such things? And if she left him, where would she go? It might be easier to appear, at least, to forgive him. Osborne had told her that the affair had meant nothing to him. Men and women thought differently about sex, didn't they? Men enjoyed sex more than women did, yet it meant less to them. And besides, as Osborne had said, it was a long time ago.

A long time ago ... Standing at her bedroom window, looking out at the garden, Evelyn absently picked up a small Meissen statuette as she considered the discrepancy that niggled at her. Osborne's story didn't fit with Romy Cole's. Romy Cole had told her that Osborne had evicted her family so he could give Middlemere to his mistress. The Coles had been evicted from Middlemere in 1942. Yet Osborne had made it plain that the affair had taken place in 1932, just after the loss of their first child. Ten years earlier. If the affair had been as short-lived and unimportant as Osborne had claimed it to be, then why had he given the house to Betty Hesketh so many years later? *I didn't even like her*, he had said. So why favour her? Why rent her Middlemere? Why such disproportionate loyalty to a supposedly meaningless and transitory coupling?

Evelyn thought back to 1932, the year in which

Osborne had shared Betty Hesketh's bed. It was a year which, in her memory, was blackened by the loss of her first son. She had been ill for months after the birth. Far worse than the physical pain, however, had been her mental anguish. Her grief had almost destroyed her. So much had reminded her of her loss. An infant sleeping in a pram, the swings at the recreation ground in Swanton le Marsh. She could not pass the little shop in Hungerford that sold babywear without a pang of longing and loss. The sight of a pregnant woman or a woman pushing a pram had induced in her a mixture of bitter envy and despair.

Betty Hesketh had been pregnant that year, she recalled. Evelyn had a sudden, clear memory of driving back from Hungerford one day and overtaking Betty Hesketh on the road into the village. Betty had been in the latter stages of pregnancy and she had been carrying heavy shopping bags. Evelyn should have stopped the car and offered Betty a lift, but she hadn't. Her rage had almost blinded her: that Betty Hesketh's belly should grow when her own was empty. That Betty Hesketh's child would survive when her own had died.

It had always surprised her that Osborne had taken an interest in the Heskeths' child. He wasn't a sentimental man, wasn't given to such attachments. He had little interest in children and felt, if the experience of the evacuees had been anything to go by, repelled by the offspring of the lower classes. Yet after Betty Hesketh had been widowed Osborne had made sure that Caleb always had work in Swanton Lacy's gardens in his school holidays. And in the war years and in the years of rationing that had followed the war Caleb had taken home fruit and vegetables from the kitchen garden. Years later, after Caleb left the army, Osborne had helped him find work.

Evelyn turned the Meissen statuette over and over in her hands. In her imagination, she pictured Caleb. Tall, broad-shouldered, dark-haired, with those unusual slatey eyes. She paused, seized by a sudden, terrible suspicion. She found herself reaching out, unable to find anything to hold on to. The statuette slipped out of her grasp, the shepherdess and her bucolic swain shattering on the floor. The events of a quarter of a century ago rattled through Evelyn's head, concertina-ing into a dreadful possibility. She had lost her first baby and then Osborne had had the affair with Betty. And then Betty had given birth to Caleb. When, exactly, had Caleb Hesketh been born? She tried to remember, but in her mind's eye saw only tall, dark Caleb and petite, blonde Betty. She could not remember what Archie Hesketh had looked like.

She clamped her hands over her mouth to stop herself crying out. The past fractured as if she were looking down a kaleidoscope, reassembling into hideous patterns. *You're being ridiculous*, she whispered. *You're letting your imagination run away with itself.*

Because she must be mistaken. It was not possible that Osborne had given Middlemere to Betty Hesketh so that his only son might have a decent home.

Mirabel Plummer's luck had almost run out. One evening she collapsed in the bar of the Trelawney. Her doctor was called and she was taken to a nursing home.

A few days later she returned to the hotel, to her private suite, but she knew that the game was almost over, knew that she was dying.

She approached death in the same practical spirit that she had dealt with life. She put her affairs in order, paid her debts, evened a few old scores, and tried, as far as possible, to avoid pain and humiliation. One thing bothered her; one thing would not let her rest. At night it prevented her from focusing her mind on keeping the pain, which was now her constant companion, at bay.

She had always intended to leave the Trelawney to Johnnie. Years ago, in the exhilaration of the early days of their affair, she had told him that he would inherit the hotel. Of course, back then, love and passion had made her feel immortal, and death had seemed a distant prospect. Johnnie had been flattered, grateful. She had seen that the idea excited him. And who else would she leave the Trelawney to, if not to the only man she had ever loved?

She had thought that Johnnie would start to take an interest in the hotel, had imagined him eventually taking over Jack Starling's position as manager. Yet that had never happened. His existing business interests took up too much of his time, he told her; he had far too much on his plate. *Later*, he had said – pacifyingly at first, and then, when things had begun to go wrong between them, angrily. *Later*, when he got round to it.

And now she had run out of time. Now, lying awake at night, she faced up to the fact that if Johnnie were to inherit the hotel, then he would sell it. That was all the Trelawney had ever meant to him: a source of capital to fund his racing cars, his drinking, his mistresses. He didn't love the hotel as she loved it. He hadn't nursed it from ramshackle infancy, hadn't transformed it into a successful business, didn't feel a thrill of pride and belonging every time he walked through the Trelawney's elegant portico.

She hadn't seen Johnnie since the quarrel. She wouldn't have wanted him to see her now, wouldn't have wanted him to witness how illness had hollowed out her face and yellowed her skin, how it was making her weak and vulnerable. As time went by, she found that she missed him less and less. It was as though she no longer had the strength for love. One sort of pain was being replaced by another. She didn't need passion any more, didn't need the extremes of pleasure and jealousy that Johnnie Fitzgerald had given her. She needed something to get her through this last, difficult sliver of her life. She needed, on the days when she was not too tired, company to keep away the darkness. She needed kindness, comfort and distraction to lift her out of the black moods that every so often came upon her.

She found that there were fewer and fewer people she wanted to see. Many whom she had believed to be her friends had stayed away from her since her illness had been made public. She frightened them, she supposed, frightened those who prided themselves on their defiance of convention. But there was only so long you could defy death: she suspected that she reminded them of that uncomfortable truth.

A few true friends remained. A handful of women she had known since her days working in nightclubs, and Jake Malephant, and Romy. During the days of Jem Cole's trial, the hotel hadn't seemed to run as smoothly in Romy's absence. Mrs Plummer had noticed that Jack Starling was becoming slapdash, his mind not on the job. She put her ear to the ground, made enquiries, and discovered that he was putting out feelers for another position. Didn't fancy working for Johnnie, she thought cynically. It was one of the many frustrating things about being ill, not being able to keep a proper eye on the hotel. She thanked heaven for Romy, who had a flair for the job and a natural aptitude. She was a quick learner, Romy; she had speedily rid herself of the manners of the gutter and was metamorphosing into a beautiful and accomplished young woman. Sometimes Mirabel worried about what would happen to Romy when she was gone. Her family were more trouble than they were worth; there was the boyfriend, of course, a good-looking lad who seemed to Mirabel nice enough, but then, she had never had much faith in men. The world could be hard on girls like Romy, who were bright and ambitious, but had no money and no connections. Mirabel knew all too well how hard it could be.

Almost imperceptibly Romy had become something more than just an employee. Mrs Plummer thought Romy looked thin and tired: that wretched brother of hers, of course. She had the waitress bring biscuits and cakes when they shared their morning coffee, to stop her looking so peaky. She insisted Romy take a proper lunch hour, insisted she go out and get some fresh air, no matter how busy they were. Her concern made her laugh at herself. She had never wanted children, had never been the maternal type. And yet here she was, fussing over the girl, making sure she ate her greens and went to bed at a proper time. Whatever next,

Mirabel, she asked herself. Isn't it a bit late to discover that you'd have liked to have a daughter? Because it wasn't at all her usual style, this concern, this affection – this, damn it, *love* – for an urchin who had happened to come into her life by chance.

The idea came to her a couple of days after Romy's return to the hotel. It was mid-morning, her best time these days. Romy was pouring out the coffee; Mirabel reached out and touched her hand, stopping her.

'I want you to telephone Mr Gilfoyle,' she said. 'He's to come and see me. Today.'

She was standing in the middle of the track. Caleb braked; the van bounced and rattled. It was early evening. The weather had turned that day, puffy grey clouds breaking up the blue skies. The rain showers had not yet softened the flinty, impacted mud that made up the track to Middlemere.

It was raining hard now, yet the woman standing on the brow of the hill was wearing only a short-sleeved blouse and skirt. It took Caleb a moment or two to realize who she was; at first he thought that she was one of his mother's customers, come to Middlemere to buy a lipstick or a tin of talcum powder. Then he squinted and recognized Evelyn Daubeny.

He drew up beside her, wound down the window. 'Mrs Daubeny?' he said. 'Are you all right?' Knowing from the first glance that she was not all right, not all right at all.

Her clothes were dishevelled, her hair glued to her head by the rain. He wondered what on earth she was doing, wandering about miles from home. She must have had an accident, he thought. Or perhaps she was ill.

He climbed out of the car. 'Mrs Daubeny,' he repeated gently, 'can I help you? Can I take you anywhere?'

He had rarely exchanged more than a few words with Mrs Daubeny – about the garden, mostly, and once, years ago, he had changed a punctured tyre for her. He knew that she was shy, guessed that she found talking to all but her intimates an ordeal. But he had always liked her. She had always seemed to him a kind, gentle person.

She didn't look gentle now, though. The expression in her eyes unnerved him. She was staring at him as though she hated him.

He tried again. Smiled, and said, 'Mrs Daubeny, can I help you?'

The smile seemed to set her off. She hissed, 'Don't laugh at me!'

'I'm not laughing at you, Mrs Daubeny.' He put a hand on her arm, but she flung him off.

Her eyes narrowed. 'You and your tart of a mother,' she said.

He took a step back towards the van. 'Mrs Daubeny—'

'You've all been laughing at me for years, haven't you? You and that slut and Osborne. Silly old Evelyn, who couldn't see what was going on under her nose!'

Something cold was uncurling in his stomach. She *knew*, he thought. Knew about his mother and Mr Daubeny. How had she found out?

Then she said, in that same taut, vindictive tone, 'But I've been thinking about it. I've worked it all out. I'm not stupid, you know.'

'No,' he said. 'Of course not.'

He wanted to get into the car, to drive away. A sense of danger made the hair on the back of his neck prickle and stand up. But he couldn't just abandon her. Couldn't just leave her standing there, ladders in her stockings and rain dripping from her clothes.

He coaxed, 'Why don't you let me drive you back to Swanton Lacy?'

'Swanton Lacy?' She gave a cackle of laughter. 'Why should I want to go there?' She rounded on him again. 'It's different for *you*. I suppose you feel you *belong*.' Suddenly she reached out a hand and gave him a shove. She had a surprising strength; his spine jolted against the open van door. 'Go on,' she whispered. There was loathing in her eyes. 'Why don't you go to Swanton Lacy, Caleb? Why don't you go and tell your father that I *know*? That I know every one of his dirty little secrets.'

In the end he did as she asked and drove to Swanton Lacy. Two reasons: to tell Osborne Daubeny that his wife was tramping around the lanes of West Berkshire, completely off her head. And the other reason . . .

The other reason he did not allow himself to think about as he sped through the village and out along the twisting byways that led to the Daubenys' house. He blanked it out, made himself concentrate on changing gear, on braking for crossroads, on not losing control and ending up in a ditch.

By the time he reached Swanton Lacy he had calmed down a little. Evelyn Daubeny was off her rocker: what she had just told him proved it. He could not possibly be Osborne Daubeny's son because the timing was all wrong. He was too old to be Daubeny's son, a decade too old.

He parked the van on the gravel forecourt and was about to walk round to the back of the house, to the tradesmen's entrance, when he caught himself. As he pulled the bell by the front door, he had a sense of crossing some invisible bridge, of transgressing unwritten rules.

Daubeny himself answered the door. 'Caleb,' he said. 'So long since I've seen you ... Is it rent day? I'd forgotten. You'd better come in.'

Caleb followed him into the house. He thought that Daubeny, like his wife, looked a bit ropy: older somehow, slightly bowed, and his skin slackening as though it didn't fit him properly any more.

Caleb said abruptly, 'I think Mrs Daubeny's ill. I found her on the path to Middlemere, just wandering about. I offered to drive her back here, but she wouldn't let me. So I thought I'd better come and get you.'

They were in the hall. The mullioned windows cast barred shadows across Daubeny's face. He saw Daubeny close his eyes for a moment and then open them again. 'Yes,' he muttered. Then, 'She hasn't been well, you see.' And, making an effort, 'I'm sorry you should be troubled, Caleb.'

Unexpectedly he felt a flicker of sympathy for the old bastard. There was something curiously neutered about Daubeny: he seemed stripped of the power and authority that Caleb always associated with him. He should warn him, thought Caleb. Give him some clue of what he was about to face.

Not the easiest subject to broach, though. In the end, he just said baldly, 'I think Mrs Daubeny's found out that you and my mother had an affair. I think that's what upset her.'

Daubeny's head jerked up. '*Caleb*—'

He said quickly, 'It's OK. Well, not OK, but I've known for years.'

Daubeny was searching through his jacket pockets. He brought out a set of keys. 'It seems so *disproportionate*,' he muttered suddenly, angrily, 'to make a public exhibition of herself like this. When I have explained to her that it was such a long time ago—'

At Daubeny's indignation, Caleb's sympathy evaporated. And he knew – that cold fear once more – that he had to ask. Just to make sure. And because, once someone said something like that, you couldn't just forget it, let it go.

'How long?' he said.

'Caleb, I really think—'

'How long?' he repeated softly.

A quick, dismissive shake of the head. 'Almost twenty-five years. So ridiculous to make such a fuss about something that happened twenty-five years ago. And it was not as though it was anything – anything important.'

He almost said, *Twenty-five years? Are you sure?* but managed to stop himself, seeing how ludicrous that would sound. *Twenty-five years.* He didn't need to do the maths. He felt knocked off balance, his certainty erased. Daubeny took another set of keys, for his car presumably, from a salver on the hall table. He couldn't have forgotten when the affair had taken place, could he? Daubeny wasn't that old, that barmy? Surely people didn't forget things like that?

But why should his mother lie? And yet, with a jolt, he recalled that she hadn't lied. He had just assumed. 'I don't mean now,' he had said, that time he had asked her about Daubeny. 'I meant ages ago, when the Coles had to leave Middlemere.' And she had not corrected him. Why not? Because she had hated to talk about it? Or to hide the fact that the affair had taken place while Archie Hesketh was still alive? Or for another, darker reason?

Daubeny prompted, 'If you wouldn't mind taking me to my wife, Caleb.'

'Yes,' he said. He felt dazed and rather sick. He saw that Daubeny was impatient to bring the conversation to an end, saw also that there was no going back, that he had to find out, because it was, after all, perfectly possible that Evelyn Daubeny might have by now broadcast her accusations around the entire county anyway.

He said to Daubeny's tweed-clad back, 'Mrs Daubeny seemed to think that I—' He broke off. Just couldn't get the words out. He saw Daubeny pause, his hand on the doorknob, his face suddenly stricken.

Anger took the place of fear. Anger that the lying and cheating of a quarter of a century ago should come back to haunt him like this. He said coldly, 'She said that I was your son. Is it true, Mr Daubeny?'

*

After work on Friday Romy went to see Liz. 'I won't be left on my own,' Liz told her. 'I'm not having everyone looking down on me because I've had an illegitimate baby. If I can't have Jem, then I'll have Ray.'

They were to marry after the baby was born, she said defiantly. She would have it adopted. It was the best thing; she had never wanted a baby anyway. And Ray wasn't the sort of man to put up with another man's child.

Travelling home, Romy tried to work out what best to do. She wasn't going to let Jem's child be given away to a stranger, of course. Most of all, Jem needed a reason to keep going, to get him through the next two years. Romy did not intend to let him slip away from her as her father had done. Jem needed to know that there was something good out there, waiting for him when he came home. She didn't know what she'd do yet, but she'd think of something.

As she turned the corner of the street in which she lived, she saw Caleb. She called out his name and waved to him; though he straightened, he did not wave back.

She ran to him, put her arms around him. She felt him return her embrace, heard his quick, indrawn breath. Then, standing back, he said, 'Can we go inside?'

She led the way up to her room. 'Would you like some tea? Or we could go out, get something to eat.'

'We need to talk.' She noticed how tired he looked. And there was something else: a guardedness, perhaps, in the set of his mouth, in the way that he was looking at her.

426

She said, 'Caleb, are you all right?'

He sat down on the sofa. Absently he scratched the dog's long, thin head. 'Thing is,' he said, 'I had a little chat with Mrs Daubeny.'

Thing is, I had a little chat with Mrs Daubeny. Romy felt her stomach twist. She remembered her, of course, so vividly. The fair hair, the open, pleasant face. The shock that had gathered in her eyes as she, Romy, had spoken.

Caleb said, 'Mrs Daubeny knew about my mother's affair with her husband. Told me some other stuff as well, but we'll get to that later. Anyway, I went to see Daubeny.' He paused. 'One thing I forgot to ask him. How did she find out? Who told her?'

She sat down beside him. It'd be all right, she told herself. He'd be cross, justifiably cross, but he'd understand in the end, forgive her in the end.

'Do you know, Romy?' he said, and she nodded.

'How, then?'

Her mouth was dry. 'I told her.'

'*You* told her?'

She whispered, 'I'm sorry, Caleb.'

'*Why?*'

'I didn't intend to—'

'You didn't intend to? What was it then? An *accident*?' His voice was heavy with sarcasm. 'Some sort of slip of the tongue?'

'No. No, of course not.' She knotted her hands together.

'I shouldn't have said anything, I know that. And I'm so sorry, Caleb. It was after the trial. I was coming to see you and I ended up at Swanton Lacy instead. Mrs Daubeny was in her garden and it all looked so beautiful, so perfect. I felt so *angry*. I couldn't stop myself.'

He was staring at her, disbelief in his eyes. He said softly, 'Did you think at all about what you were doing? Did you think at all – or care at all – about how much you'd hurt her – and how much you'd hurt *me*—'

'I never meant to hurt you, Caleb!'

'Didn't you?' His voice was cold. 'Avoiding it wasn't exactly high on your list.'

She flinched. 'As soon as I'd told Mrs Daubeny, I wished I hadn't.'

'Really?' His lip curled. 'Well, she was heading for the loony bin the last time I saw her. Poor old Evelyn – you certainly got her right where it hurts.'

'Her marriage—' She faltered.

'Not her *marriage*. I don't suppose she's ever got much fun out of *that*. I mean – quarter of a century living with Osborne Daubeny – who would? I meant *children*. After all, she's spent the last couple of decades trying to produce a sprog that'll last more than five minutes. But I don't suppose you knew that, did you, Romy?'

'I don't see what that's got to do with it.' She stared at him, confused. '*Children?*'

'*Ah*. Well. I was getting to that.' He gave a humourless smile. 'We thought we'd got it all worked out, didn't we, you and me? Daubeny has an affair with my mother, then takes Middlemere off your family so that he's got somewhere nice and quiet to romp with his mistress. *Almost* right. Just a few minor corrections.'

'Caleb,' she whispered. 'Please. You're frightening me—'

'Daubeny and my mother were certainly at it, shall we say, but a bit earlier than we'd assumed. My poor old dad was still alive and Mrs Daubeny was recovering from the first of many failed attempts to produce a son and heir. And then along comes Betty, the village slut, and does the job as easy as shelling peas.' His cold, contemptuous gaze slid to her. 'Oh, come on, Romy. *Think*. I'm Osborne Daubeny's bastard. That's why he rented Middlemere to my mother. To get his only surviving offspring out of the rat hole we were living in.'

I'm Osborne Daubeny's bastard. She shook her head slowly. 'I don't believe you. You're making it up.'

'Now why should I do that? D'you think I'd rather be Osborne Daubeny's brat than Archie Hesketh's? Lots of people might, I suppose. Blue blood, and all that.'

'Don't say that, Caleb. Don't tease me. I said I was sorry.'

'*I'm not making it up.*' His eyes were dark with anger. 'It doesn't all revolve around *you*, Romy. All that – Daubeny, Middlemere – it didn't only affect *you*.'

'You can't be Daubeny's son,' she whispered. 'You can't be.' She pressed her knuckles against her mouth. 'You must have made a mistake. Or he's made a mistake—'

He crouched on the floor in front of her. She felt him unpeel her hands from her face. 'No mistake,' he said savagely. 'I've had it on the best authority, you see. After all, my mother should know, shouldn't she?'

'Oh God, Caleb—'

'It's all right,' he said. 'We've just both been a bit naive, haven't we? And you live and learn, don't you? But the thing I've come to realize,' he went on softly, 'is that nothing is quite how it looks on the surface. There's Daubeny, the respectable landowner, who everyone's meant to look up to. And there's my mother, with her supposedly happy marriage. Even my *school*. Daubeny had a word in someone's ear – that's how I got my scholarship. Nothing to do with my stunning powers of intellect. Couldn't have a kid of his learning the three Rs in that dump of a village school in Swanton le Marsh, could he? Good enough for all the kids who'd end up labouring on his farms, but hardly adequate for someone with Daubeny blood.'

With his thumb, he gently traced the outline of her jaw. 'And what about you, Romy? So beautiful, so spirited.' The thumb paused at the corner of her mouth. 'You were everything I wanted, did you know that? I thought I knew you. But what are you *really*?'

She was crying now. 'Caleb—'

Suddenly he moved away from her. 'Of course, I feel rather – rather *stupid* – not to have worked it out before. What an idiot to think that Daubeny was helping me out because of the charm of my personality. Or because, under that appallingly pompous exterior, he still had a soft spot for my mother.'

'Don't. *Please*.' She had clapped her hands over her ears. 'I didn't know. Don't you see, Caleb, that I didn't know?'

'Too bad. Light the blue touchpaper and –' he

spread out his fingers – '*boom*. And you've certainly got the hang of lighting touchpapers, Romy.'

She cried desperately, 'But it doesn't change anything! You're still the same person!'

'Am I?' Just for a moment, the bitterness and anger dropped from his face and were replaced by a terrible bleakness. 'But I don't even know my own name any more, do I? It's all rather ... rather bewildering. One day I'm the son of a man everyone admires – a war hero, a decent sort of bloke. The next day I'm the bastard offspring of a member of the landed gentry I've always despised. The son of the man who dispossessed your family. How does that feel, Romy?'

'It doesn't make any difference.' Tears were pouring down her face.

'I don't believe you. Of course it does.' A quick shake of the head. 'And it sure as hell makes a difference to *me*.'

He turned to leave. She ran after him, seizing the sleeve of his jacket. 'Caleb! Please—'

He spun round. 'Well, you got your revenge at last, didn't you, Romy? You certainly waited long enough for it. I hope it makes you happy.'

Her hands clawed at him. 'You can't just go! I need you, Caleb!'

'You?' he said. He shook his head. 'You've never needed anyone.'

Her fingernails tore into the cloth. 'But I love you!'

His face seemed to still. 'Do you, Romy?'

'Yes!' She gripped his arms and pressed the side of her head against his chest. 'I don't want you to go,

Caleb. I really don't want you to go. I'm so sorry. I didn't know—'

With the tip of his finger, he lifted her face towards his. He said more gently, 'I used to think that the truth was the most important thing. But I don't think I do now. I think I preferred the lies.'

Her arms fell away from him. She watched him leave the room, heard his footsteps on the stairs. Then she was running down after him, hurrying to catch up with him as he walked fast along the pavement.

'Caleb!'

He kept on walking. She called out his name again and he paused.

'Caleb, you can't leave me!' She was gasping for breath.

He frowned, scuffing the pavement with the sole of his shoe. 'I think I must. You see, Romy, the thing is that just at this moment I wish I'd never met you. That first day I saw you at Middlemere, I wish I'd just walked away and never seen you again.' He gave a crooked smile. 'Sorry. Harsh, I know. But that's how it is.'

He walked away, disappearing around the corner, out of sight, out of her life. After a while, she went back upstairs to her room. She sat on the sofa. The dog sat at her feet; the cat curled on her lap.

She remained there until the room darkened and the moon replaced the sun. When eventually she stood, knowing that his parting words to her would echo through the days and weeks and years, through her dreams and her nightmares, her limbs felt stiff, as if she were ill or old.

She fed the animals, put away crockery, checked figures in her savings book. *I am Romy Cole*, she whispered to herself, *and I shall start again, and I shall have something different, something better.*

Only she couldn't think of anything better than Caleb and, no matter what she did, no matter how hard she tried, the tears would keep sliding from her eyes, trailing down cups and saucers, splashing into the washing-up water, blotting the neat columns of figures in the book.

Chapter Thirteen

Jake was working on Romy's portrait in early November when all the talk on the streets and in the bars was of war. 'Nasser nationalized the Suez Canal in July,' he explained to Romy. 'You must have noticed *that*, surely.'

'I had other things on my mind,' she said. Though an image came into her mind of Caleb drawing a map in spilt beer on a table in a pub: *That's Israel, and that's Egypt, and that's the Suez Canal.*

'Such an extraordinary ability,' said Jake, studying her, 'to live in your own little world. I envy you.' He peered at the painting. 'Anyway, Nasser – he's the president of Egypt, you know, Romy – didn't take kindly to our ultimatum demanding that he stop military operations, so we – that's the British and the French, I hope you're concentrating – have invaded Egypt. And no one's very pleased with us and it's all going to end in tears.'

She thought of all the young men she knew, all the young men who had done national service and who could be called up if war broke out again. Jem and Tom and Magnus. And she thought of Caleb, of course, but then, she thought of him most of the time.

'Do you think there will be a war, Jake? A proper war, like the last one?'

He shook his head. 'I don't think so. The Americans don't want war and they call the tune these days. All this nonsense is a last roar of the lion, Romy. A last roar of a rather moth-eaten, tired old lion.'

Jake looked, she thought, rather tired and moth-eaten himself. There were bags under his eyes and deep lines scored to the sides of his mouth. 'I think we'll call it a day,' he said suddenly and put aside his brush and palette. 'Can't seem to concentrate...' He went to the window and took out his cigarettes. 'It just makes me so angry,' he said. 'All these strutting colonels manqués who think that because we won the war we should call the shots. Can't they see? Can't they see that we count for nothing these days?' He looked depressed rather than angry. 'And, of course, there's always the worry that things will get out of hand and some maniac will push the button.'

Romy thought of mushroom clouds and twisted, blackened bodies at Hiroshima. Jake assumed her indifferent to the world, yet she knew that that was no longer so. She was changing, her priorities altered by the upheavals of the last six months and by her proximity to love and loss and death.

Jake changed the subject. 'How's that hotel of yours?'

She smiled. 'It's splendid, Jake,' she said. 'And it's going to be even more splendid by the time I've finished with it.'

He had begun the portrait in the summer. She had had to tell Jake about Caleb, about why Caleb had left her, had left London, and to explain all that she had to tell him about Middlemere. And when she had finished, she had discovered that there didn't seem to be anything more to hide, and that she wasn't afraid of what he might see in her.

The sessions were short because she had never been much good at sitting still, and because Mrs Plummer was dying. Summer merged into autumn and the hours that she sat with Mirabel Plummer seemed to mingle with the pungent smell of linseed and turpentine. She felt both grief and rage. The rage had been that she should lose yet another person whom she loved.

In September Johnnie Fitzgerald came to the hotel. Got past Max, the doorman, and ran into the foyer yelling that he'd been abroad, hadn't heard, and that someone had told him that the woman he loved was dying. Jack Starling and a couple of others manhandled him out into the street. From her office, Romy heard Johnnie shout, 'But I love her! I'm going marry her!'

A week before she died Mrs Plummer moved into a nursing home. She would have preferred to die in the Trelawney, she explained to Romy, but that sort of thing wasn't good for business. And Romy wasn't to visit. She'd die alone; people always did die alone, she'd learned that a long time ago. And, besides, she needed Romy to keep an eye on the hotel.

On Mrs Plummer's strict instructions they neither put up black nor closed the hotel to mark her passing. Instead, they ran a free bar at the Marrakesh, the best champagne all round, and the pianist playing all Mrs Plummer's favourite songs. They remembered that night in Soho for years afterwards. They drank the bar dry. They jived on the table tops. A hundred of them yelled out the chorus to 'Heartbreak Hotel' from an upstairs window, and the two young policemen who were patrolling the streets below turned tail and ran. When, the next day, they unlocked the narrow blue door at the bottom of the stairs, they found half a dozen mourners tumbled in the stairwell, sleeping off the after-effects of the night before.

A few days later Mr Gilfoyle telephoned Romy and asked for an appointment to see her. That was when she discovered that, although Johnnie had inherited the Marrakesh and the cottage by the Thames, Mrs Plummer had left the Trelawney Hotel to her.

Posing for her portrait, she wore the pale blue Paquin coat that Mrs Plummer had given her. She remembered the time that she and Mrs Plummer had travelled to Nice. Her first trip abroad; she had worn the Paquin coat. She had walked along the Baie des Anges and had looked out to sea and had thought: I'm Romy Cole, and that sea is the Mediterranean Sea. Which had seemed to her a miracle.

Now she owned the Trelawney Hotel, which was even more miraculous. The first few weeks she was unable to believe in her good luck, in the generosity of Mirabel Plummer's extraordinary gift. A part of her remained guarded, half-expecting someone to take it away from her.

But you could get used in time to the most outlandish turns of fortune, and an acceptance of her good luck began to settle in, to become a part of her. And she remembered what she had learned a long time ago: that wealth and security gave you choices. Some things she couldn't change, no matter how much money she had. She couldn't buy Caleb back, for instance, so there was still that to be endured, to be shoved into the green cupboard along with all the other bad things, to be looked at only when she had the strength to face her shame and her guilt and her knowledge of the pain that her need for revenge had caused.

And she couldn't, she discovered to her surprise, persuade Martha to leave Dennis. 'He's a stupid old sod,' said Martha, between puffs on a cigarette, 'but I'm used to him and, besides, what would I do in London when all my friends are in Hill View?'

But, remembering how she had seen her own longing to escape in her stepsister, she could find Carol a job at the hotel. And she could care for Jem's infant son until Jem came out of prison.

Sometimes she couldn't help laughing at herself. Here she was, Romy Cole, who had always promised herself that she wouldn't go through life with dependents hanging round her neck, and yet she had landed herself with a dog, a cat and a newborn baby. And a teenage stepsister and a hotel.

She found a nanny for the baby and had an attic room at the Trelawney – the little room with the sloping ceiling that she had stayed in when she first came to London – decorated for Carol. She visited Jem, in Pentonville, and told him about his son. 'He's such a good baby, Jem – he has his feed and then he goes to sleep and he doesn't wake up till four hours later, when his next feed's due. He's no trouble at all.' And Jem smiled for what seemed like the first time in months, and said, 'You're a star, Romy. A star.'

Jake wouldn't let her see the portrait until it was finished. On the day that it was complete, he made her close her eyes as he led her into his studio to stand in front of the painting.

'You can open them now.'

She opened her eyes, saw her own image on the canvas. Small, pointed face, nut-brown hair, large cinnamon-coloured eyes and the pale blue coat. She smiled and reached out a hand to touch herself. *I am Romy Cole*, she whispered, *and I shall have something different, something better*.

PART FOUR

A Sense of Direction

1958–60

Chapter Fourteen

Later, when she looked back, it seemed to Romy that
her recollection of the months immediately following
Danny's birth and Mrs Plummer's death were almost
blank, as if she had been too exhausted at the time to
consign events to memory.

Liz had wanted nothing to do with her infant son.
She had relinquished all rights to the child, agreeing
that Romy could care for Danny until Jem, his natural
father, came out of prison. In spite of having helped her
mother look after Ronnie and Gareth, Romy quickly
discovered that though she knew how to change nappies
and how to feed and bathe and wind, she was in other
ways completely unprepared for caring for Jem's baby
son. It took her by surprise how greatly she felt the
weight of responsibility. Danny was so small, so helpless.
His skinny little limbs seemed to slip from her grasp
when she held him. She, who had once thought herself
afraid of so little, now seemed to be afraid of everything.
She was afraid of accidents, of germs and, most of all,
of her own inadequacies. When Danny cried, she felt a
profound despair. She was not his mother, so how could
she comfort him? Danny's purple face and flailing arms
seemed to express his anger and loss. A part of Romy
suspected that Danny sensed that she was fraudulent,

lacking. After all, she had never wanted children, had never thought of herself as the motherly sort. She envied the nanny's brisk practicality. When Danny cried, Sarah would pick him up and say, 'Wind, I expect,' and put him against her shoulder, patting his back until he fell asleep, plagued by none of the doubts that tormented Romy.

It seemed to her that they came to an understanding, she and Danny. At eight weeks old he settled and began to feed and sleep with more regularity, as though he had accepted his lot in life and forgiven her fumbling efforts to fill in for the parents he lacked. A robust baby, he was rarely unwell. Bald and blue-eyed at birth, his eyes gradually darkened to brown, and by the time he was six months old the first black curls had begun to cluster in the nape of his neck. As the months passed, Romy herself became less fearful, less afraid of not being up to scratch, she needed to check his cot only once or twice a night instead of half a dozen times. She began to believe that he might survive, that they might escape disaster, that this fragile little creature might endure until Jem was free again.

And she began to love him. His smile and his uncritical pleasure in her company worked their magic. No one else had ever loved her in such an undivided fashion. As time passed, she realized that, though Danny bore a physical resemblance to Jem, he seemed to have been born with a greater resilience. His instinct was to laugh rather than cry. The touch of his small fingers and the scent of his skin delighted her. She could have sat by his cot for hours, just watching him sleep. She was immensely proud of his every small achievement: his first step, his first word, his first scribbles with a wax crayon. Danny restored her optimism, so battered by Jem's imprisonment and Mrs Plummer's death. Danny began to fill in some of the gaps left by too many absences.

In early 1958 Jem was released on parole. Prison had changed him, making him quieter, more guarded. He found work loading vans at a department store and rooms with a pleasant woman a few streets away from the Trelawney. He kept himself to himself, never spoke of his months in prison, never mentioned Liz and avoided his former friends. An air of defeat clung to him; in his eyes there was a deadened look that cut Romy to the heart.

Yet he adored Danny, pushing him on the baby swings in the park, watching him play in the sandpit, taking part in the repetitive play that bored Romy and she was glad enough to leave to the nanny. Jem was endlessly patient with his small son and on his days off took Danny for outings to the zoo or to see the boats on the Thames. Yet Danny continued to live in Romy's flat at the hotel. 'If you don't mind, Romy,' Jem said, scuffing his foot, not quite meeting her eye. 'I'd be afraid of doing something wrong, you see.'

When Danny was two years old, Jem left London to work on a farm in north Yorkshire. He needed a change, he told Romy, needed to get away from his old haunts. He needed to go somewhere where no one knew him and where no one knew what he had done.

The day before Jem was due to travel to Yorkshire

they were in Romy's sitting room, when she said, 'I could bring Danny up to see you most weekends, if you like, Jem. Or Sarah could, when it's difficult for me.'

'You know I'll always be pleased to see you.'

Her back to him, she was looking into the mirror as she put in her earrings. 'I meant, if you wanted him to get more used to being with you. For when he comes to live with you.'

'Oh, I don't think that would be a good idea, do you, Romy?'

Startled, she fumbled, dropping a pearl. 'I know Danny's very young now.' She scrabbled on the floor for the missing earring. 'But in a few months – a year, maybe—'

'He's better off with you.'

'For now, perhaps. But—'

'Always. He'll always be better off with you.' Jem's voice was flat and matter of fact.

She stood up, the earring clutched in her palm. 'That's not true, Jem.'

'He will. You know he will. If you don't mind, that is.'

'Of course I don't mind. I love having him here. But it's what we always said, that Danny would come and live with you when you'd sorted yourself out.'

He looked up at her. 'What *you* always said.'

'Jem,' she whispered. 'He's *your* son.'

'I know.' He frowned. 'And he's a great kid. And that's why I want the best for him. And you're the best, Romy, you always were. Not me.'

She tried once more to put the earring in. As she stabbed herself with the pin, she swore and threw it back into the jewellery box. She went to sit beside Jem. 'I know things have been difficult for you. I know you've had ... false starts. And Ray Babbs lying about the fight – that was so unfair—'

'Sometimes,' he said slowly, 'I'm not sure what happened then. Whether it was him or whether it was me. Whether I wanted to hurt him, like they said I did. It all tangles up in my mind and I don't know what's true and what isn't.'

She stared at him. 'Of course it was Ray Babbs's fault—'

'Even if all that's true, there's plenty of other things I've done that I haven't taken the blame for. Things I've never told you about, Romy. Things I'd be ashamed to tell you about.'

She touched his hand. 'But all that's behind you now, isn't it, Jem? You're different now.'

'I mean to be different.' He stared at her, eyes wide. 'But it's not always easy. And that's why I'm going away. A few days ago I met a bloke I knew in Brighton. He offered me work – well, work of a sort. Good money, Romy – twice what I'm earning now. Oh, I didn't take it,' he said quickly. 'Told him I was trying to sort myself out. But what if things go wrong with this job? What if I end up out of work again? Sometimes I do things I don't mean to. I might mean to go straight, but I can't be sure that I'll manage, can I?'

'You're not going to lose your job, Jem. There's no reason why you should.'

'Things can go wrong,' said Jem flatly. 'I might make a mess of things. Or the bloke I'm working for might find out that I've been in prison and decide to give me the push. And I don't want Danny to suffer if I foul up again.' He looked away. 'Just because you get a girl pregnant doesn't mean you're going to be a good father, does it? Think of Dennis. Think of our dad.'

'Dad wasn't like Dennis!' she said indignantly.

'He *left* us. He *chose* to leave us.'

There was a silence. Jem rose from the sofa. 'I'd rather Danny stayed with you, Romy. Sometimes I look at him and I think of all the things that might happen to him. That I might drop him and he'd hit his head. Or he might run out into the road and get knocked down by a car. Or he might fall ill—'

'Jem,' she said desperately, 'everyone worries about things like that. Every parent. That's *normal*.'

His dark, shadowed eyes met hers. 'I know I'll never make anything of myself. But I don't want Danny to be like me. I want him to be like you, Romy.'

The next day Romy and Danny saw Jem off from the station. The guard's whistle screeched, steam hissed and there was a great plume of white smoke from the funnel of the train, masking Jem's face as the engine pulled away from the platform. As they walked away, tears blurred Romy's vision and she was aware of a feeling of emptiness, as though someone had gouged a hole in her heart. He'd change his mind, she told herself. A few more months and Jem would find some confidence in himself, and then Danny would go and live with him.

Apart from Danny, her other preoccupation was, of course, the hotel. The elation that she had initially felt when Mr Gilfoyle had told her of Mrs Plummer's bequest had been quickly overwhelmed by reality. Mrs

Plummer's money had been divided between various charities and the sisters, nephews and nieces whom few people had known to exist. Which meant that the Trelawney must continue to be profitable in order to survive. During the first six months difficulties often threatened to swamp her. Jack Starling resigned and Romy took over his job herself, partly to save paying a manager's salary, and partly because she wanted day-to-day control of the hotel. Teresa left to get married and Max retired. A flurry of other staff also handed in their resignations. Though not one admitted it, Romy guessed that they didn't want to work for a young woman who had only a few years earlier been a chambermaid at the hotel. Of the staff who had been at Trelawney when Romy had started work there, only a dozen or so remained.

She recruited new staff, though she left some posts unfilled. The Trelawney had always been overstaffed; they could make do with less. The first winter was difficult: Danny was so young, and it hurt her to think of Jem incarcerated in prison. At the hotel bookings were down because of the fuel shortage that had followed the Suez crisis, and she struggled with staffing problems and her own inexperience. And she seemed every now and then to glimpse Mrs Plummer's ghost on a dimly lit stairway, or in the shadows that pooled around her desk in the office. Often she worked twelve-hour days; often she felt exhausted and overburdened. Often, she was afraid that she was letting Mrs Plummer down, afraid that the Trelawney would fail and that she would betray the trust that Mrs Plummer had put in her.

She would find herself sitting at her desk late in the evenings, her head in her hands, the office door shut, in an attempt to escape the endless demands of the hotel. Eyes tightly closed, she would ask herself what Mrs Plummer would have done, faced with the same problems. Sometimes she could almost feel Mrs Plummer's presence, almost smell the familiar scents of her perfume, her cigarettes. Elizabeth Arden's Blue Grass and Churchman's King Size would mingle in her memory, calming her, helping her to think more clearly.

At first she made mistakes, double-booking the reception rooms because she was panicking about the hotel's falling income, and alternately over-ordering supplies so that they had more boxes of hotel stationery than they had cupboards to put them in, and then under-ordering, so that they ran out of soap and she had to send Carol out in a taxi to Selfridges to buy more. Yet she learned. And she had always been a quick learner. She drew on her own experiences of working in the hotel. She knew what it was like to be a chambermaid or a secretary and to work in the kitchen and the bar. She knew that to earn the respect of the staff she must treat them with respect. She never lost her temper with the staff or the guests: she had only to recall Evelyn Daubeny and the rose garden at Swanton Lacy, and to remember what a few angry words had cost her to avoid making that mistake again. She learned to impose her authority when it was necessary: dealing for the first time with a dishonest barman or a careless chambermaid, her knees might tremble beneath her desk, but she made herself imitate Mrs Plummer's icy grandeur and saw the barman pale, the chambermaid blush.

The Trelawney survived. More than survived – as the country's economic situation eased, profits began to grow again. Time passed, and Romy began to feel safer and not so haunted. She started to make changes – small, at first: the purchase of a television for the sitting room, a relaxation in the formality of the restaurant. Then she began to draw up more ambitious plans for the hotel, plans that would allow her to put her own imprint on it.

It still awed her that she, Romy Cole from the council estate in Stratton, owned the Trelawney Hotel. She still felt immense pride as she walked into the black-and-white marble tiled reception hall. She still, sometimes, found herself running her palm over a polished table or a gilt lamp as if only through touch could she convince herself that these things were really hers.

Like the hotel, she, too, was changing. She had moved out of her Belsize Park bedsit and into Mrs Plummer's former flat in the Trelawney. Now she had a drawing room and a bedroom and bathroom and a tiny kitchen, which seemed to her the height of luxury. She had given the other three rooms to Danny and Sarah. The flat had fitted carpets, deep, comfortable chairs and sofas, and swagged velvet curtains. She had a fridge and a television. She sent her clothes to the laundry or the dry cleaner's; a daily woman cleaned her flat and made her bed.

She let her hair grow out so that it could be swept

up into a smooth chignon. She threw out all her old clothes, replacing them with dresses, coats and separates bought in Selfridges and Dickens & Jones and, yes, Harrods. Now her evening dresses were made of silk and satin, finely embroidered or encrusted with tiny beads, with boned bodices and waists of not much more than a hand's span. Now she wore ten-denier nylon stockings and had gloves and handbags to match every pair of shoes. She wore jet beads at her throat, pearls in her ears. She didn't buy her lipsticks from Boots any more but from Helena Rubinstein and Elizabeth Arden.

Yet, if she were honest with herself, she had a sneaking fondness for the circular print skirts she had bought from Bazaar, in the King's Road. She felt more comfortable in them – so nice to be free of bones and elastic. They made her feel younger, somehow. Sometimes she imagined turning up at a smart party wearing a Mary Quant skirt, black leotard and ballet shoes. How brows would raise. How lips would purse.

At first, overwhelmed by the shock of losing Caleb and Mrs Plummer, bringing up Danny and inheriting the hotel, it was all she could do to get through the day and to collapse into bed late at night, thankful for the peace and for the absence of any demands on her. But gradually, as the months passed and life became a little easier, she began to notice, once again, gaps. Only this time the gaps seemed to be huge, yawning chasms. Those first few months after Caleb had gone she had thought she had seen him everywhere. In a crowded street and in the carriage of a Tube train, in the pubs and coffee shops of Soho: the Carriage and Horses, the Moka, the Heaven and Hell. Yet they had never been

Caleb, those dark young men who had fleetingly brought him back to her, and each disappointment had clawed at her, leaving a scar.

Eventually she had heard through Jake that Caleb had gone abroad. Some of the grief she had felt at their parting began, then, to be replaced by anger. That he should judge her so harshly. That he should be so unforgiving. That he should have left her just when she most needed him, left her to endure Jem's imprisonment and Mrs Plummer's death on her own. *You don't need anyone*, he had said to her. Well, maybe he had been right. She was managing fine, she thought. Managing perfectly fine without *him*.

And it wasn't that she was short of offers. She let herself be taken out, pampered, courted. It was nice to feel sought after, flattering to discover that men were vying for her attention and that ownership of the Trelawney had moved her several notches up the social scale. The men she now dated did not take her to smoky little pubs or for chilly tramps around windswept cemeteries; instead they took her to exclusive cocktail parties, or bought her dinners in discreet and extremely expensive French restaurants, or escorted her to the theatre, the opera or a concert hall. More things to learn: not to applaud after the first movement of a symphony, not to doze off, after a long day's work, through the soprano's lengthy aria. She learned to tell Gielgud from Olivier, Mahler from Mozart. She acquired a polish to go with the Jaeger dresses, the mohair coats.

She had everything she wanted, she told herself. Only sometimes nowadays did she wake in the night and hear a voice echo in her memory. *You got your revenge at last, didn't you, Romy? I hope it makes you happy.* Of course she was happy, she thought angrily, as she curled up in the blankets and tried to fall asleep again. Jem was free, and she had Danny and the hotel. She had a wardrobe full of new clothes and shoes, and she had bought her mother a washing machine and a television. *I'm a lady of leisure now*, Martha had told her. So how could she not be happy?

Because Danny's only borrowed, said the nagging voice. And because the hotel, and the time it takes and the obligations and authority it demands, have divided you from your friends and your family. And because you haven't even a steady boyfriend, let alone a fiancé or a husband.

It was true that none of the boyfriends lasted. Romy couldn't have said why: it was just that they never seemed to be quite right. She kept trying, though. She went to bed with one or two of her admirers because she was lonely, and because she wanted to prove to herself that she didn't need Caleb Hesketh, that she had forgotten him. But waking one morning in someone else's bed, she felt momentarily disorientated and rather frightened. She couldn't quite think how she had got here, to the wrong bed with the wrong man. He was rich, pleasant, good-looking, but she didn't love him at all. She wondered whether she had forgotten how to love, and why love still mattered to her when she had so much else. But it did, and, dressing, taking her leave of him, she was aware of a slight self-disgust.

And then, in the summer of 1958, she met Patrick Napier. Patrick was waiting for his date in the Trelawney's bar: she felt his eyes follow her as she crossed the room to give a message to the barman. Golden-haired, blue-eyed and patrician-featured, he was, she found herself thinking as she glimpsed him out of the corner of her eye, just her type. Such men hadn't always been her type in the past, but then you could change your mind, couldn't you?

He telephoned her the following evening. He had spoken to the barman to find out who she was, and had rung her up to introduce himself and ask her out for dinner. Ten out of ten for nerve, Patrick Napier, she thought. They had dated intermittently since then. Sometimes she didn't see him for weeks; often, parting from him, she was unsure whether she would see him again. She assumed that, in common with her, he was uninterested in marriage and was enjoying himself far too much to settle down. Assumed also that the glitter of the society he was introducing her to was a welcome contrast with his work. Patrick Napier was a doctor; his consulting rooms were in Harley Street. She had not lost her squeamishness; just the thought of a hospital made her heart flutter. She had never seen his consulting rooms, but she guessed that they were opulent and thickly carpeted, with soothing watercolours of seas and hills on the walls in an attempt to distract from the smell of antiseptic and the metallic gleam of medical instruments.

As he came back to the table, Patrick said, 'It's no use, I shall have to ask.'

Romy looked up at him. It was eleven o'clock; they were in the Chanterelle restaurant in Old Brompton Road.

'Ask what?'

'Your notebook. What do you write in it? I have a terrible fear that I'm being marked. Six out of ten. Compared, to my detriment, with all your other conquests.'

She laughed and slid the small gold notebook and matching gold pen into her handbag. 'And I thought I was being discreet. I'm not making notes about you, Patrick, I'm making notes about the restaurant. And it's not marks out of ten, it's just . . . ideas. Inspirations.'

'For what?'

'For my hotel.'

'So conscientious. I've never met such a hardworking girl.'

'That's because you usually date debutantes, Patrick. Or feather-brained blondes.'

'True.' He smiled. 'So our dates are just . . . research, to you?'

'Something like that,' she teased him.

She put on her coat; they left the restaurant. As they stepped out into the misty November night, Patrick said, 'Tell me your ideas. Tell me your inspirations.'

'The Chanterelle has a marvellous chef, of course,' she said enviously. 'Anton's wonderful, but he's just not in the same league. And the decor . . . all that pale wood and those gorgeous fabrics. Such lovely soft colours.' Such a contrast, she thought, to the Trelawney's dark mahogany panelling and richly patterned rugs and heavy, swagged curtains. So much more modern.

'Don't you ever stop thinking about your work?'

She considered. 'When I'm with Danny. Otherwise, not often, I suppose.'

He did not reply; she glanced at him. '*Patrick*,' she

said, 'you're not jealous, are you? You can't possibly be jealous of a *hotel*.'

He hailed a taxi. 'When you put it like that, I suppose not.'

'And I bet you think of ... *lungs* and things ... all the time.'

'Actually, no. I never think about my work while I'm off duty. I'm only too pleased to stop thinking about lungs and things, as you put it. And I certainly never think of my work when I'm with you, Romy.' He shot her a glance. 'When I'm with you, I think only of you.'

'I don't believe you,' she said, as she climbed into the taxi. 'Can you honestly say that it doesn't cross your mind to think – oh, whether you've had a good week—'

'Whether profits are up or down? It's not quite like that in the medical profession. Not so *blatantly*, anyway. Although –' he stared out of the window of the cab – 'there are no pea-soupers any more. That's spoiling business a bit.'

In the cab he took her hand in his. He had nice hands; long, elegant hands, the sort that doctors were supposed to have. They were one of the first things she had noticed about him.

He said, 'What are you thinking?' and she smiled and said, 'I'm thinking how utterly unsuited we are. We haven't a thing in common. I hate hospitals and you never stay in hotels.'

'I'm just lucky. I have friends in Paris, Nice and Rome, so why should I choose to stay in an hotel?'

They had reached the Trelawney. She offered him a

nightcap and he followed her upstairs to her suite of rooms on the second floor.

She poured him a Scotch and then, on the pretext of powdering her nose, peeked into the nursery. Danny was humped up in his cot, the bedclothes flung off as usual. Very gently she traced the plump curve of his pink cheek with her fingertip. She must buy him a bed, she thought; he was getting too big for the cot.

She went back to the drawing room. Patrick was examining the photographs on the mantelpiece. 'Family?' he asked.

She went to stand beside him. 'That's Danny, my nephew. And that's his father: my brother, Jem.'

'They look very alike.'

'Don't they?' She beamed. 'And that's Carol, my step-sister, who works here in the office. And that's my mother.'

'Have you a father?'

'Dad died when I was a little girl.'

'I'm sorry.'

'It's all right,' she said. 'It was a long time ago.'

'Do you still miss him?'

She shook her head and wondered whether she was telling him the truth. She knew that Patrick's father had died three months earlier.

'You must miss yours.'

He put down the photograph. 'I didn't think I would – we never exactly saw eye to eye. But sometimes I find that I even miss the rows.' He turned to her. 'Come here,' he said.

She let him take her in his arms and kiss her. She was wearing a knee-length, strapless evening gown with

a boned bodice: his mouth followed the curve of her
bare neck and shoulder. She felt his breath on her skin,
felt his short, fine, golden hair brush against her face.
His hands encircled her waist, then drifted down to her
hips.

She pulled away. 'No, Patrick. It's late. I have to be
up early tomorrow.'

'You could take a morning off.' He was still caressing her. 'You're the boss.'

She shook her head. His hands fell away and he
said, 'What are you waiting for, Romy Cole?'

'Nothing,' she said. 'I'm not waiting for anything.'

He frowned, looking into her eyes. 'I'm thirty-five.
Too old to play games.'

'I'm not playing games, Patrick.'

'If you're not interested, then you must say so.' He
picked up his overcoat. 'I can take it. I might howl like
a dog in private, but you wouldn't have to know about
that.'

'Dear Patrick.' She touched his arm. 'It's not that.'

'What, then?'

'I told you. I'm just tired.'

'You work too hard. You don't have to, Romy.' He
caught her and kissed her once more. 'Now, if you *were*
giving marks . . .'

'Ten out of ten,' she said lightly. 'Ten out of ten, of
course, Patrick.'

When he had gone, she poured another drink for herself
and ran a bath. Then, with a sigh of relief, she unzipped
and climbed out of her evening gown (mauve-pink silk,

embroidered with a trail of tiny black flowers across the bodice) and her corselette and stockings.

Sinking into the hot water, letting it cover her head, she knew that she had not quite told Patrick the truth. She was tired, she was always tired these days, what with Danny and the hotel, but she was not *too* tired. She had felt a flicker of desire as he kissed her, which was why she had pulled away.

So why hadn't she gone to bed with Patrick Napier? After a moment she sat up in the bath, gasping for breath, water streaming from her hair. At first, she thought, her refusals had been motivated by pride. She had recognized Patrick's type. A bit of a lady-killer. Handsome, rich, cultured and unattached, his attempts to seduce her had, to begin with, seemed almost perfunctory, almost motivated by habit. There had been a presumption about him that had reminded her sharply of Liam Pike all those years ago. She hadn't lost her virginity in the back of Liam Pike's car, and she wouldn't slip that easily between Patrick Napier's monogrammed linen sheets. She had an aversion to becoming just another conquest, another name on the list. Drawing the line at kisses and caresses, she had expected Patrick to drop her, yet he continued to phone her every few weeks or so to make a date. He didn't like to be turned down, she concluded. He wasn't used to girls saying no. Yet she enjoyed his company and didn't want to lose him. It wasn't that she was playing games, she thought, it was just simple practicality. Goal fulfilled, he would walk away. It wouldn't matter to him, but it might matter to her.

What are you waiting for, Romy Cole? Patrick had

asked her. I'm not waiting for anything, she thought crossly, as she stepped out of the bath and wrapped a towel around herself. I'm not waiting for *anyone*.

The following month Patrick took her to a cocktail party in Belgravia, in a tall, elegant house with fluted columns, which stood like sentinels beside the front door.

He had known the Harbornes for years, Patrick explained. 'They're old friends of the family. Minnie Harborne, James's mother, was at school with Bunny, my mother.'

Romy imagined them, Minnie and Bunny, plump, hearty, hockey-playing girls at a posh boarding school, characters from the Angela Brazil novels she had read when she was a girl.

'You must meet Bunny,' said Patrick. 'She'd adore you, I know she would.'

Inside the Belgravia house, waitresses offered drinks and trays of canapés. In another room couples danced in a restrained fashion to a three-piece band.

As Patrick led Romy onto the dance floor, he said, 'In fact, had you any plans for Christmas? I always spend Christmas at my mother's place in Suffolk and I'm getting a little party together. I wondered whether you'd like to come.'

'I'm sorry, Patrick, I can't. Christmas is one of our busiest times.'

He steered her round a corner. He was a good dancer; it was something she enjoyed, dancing with him. He said, 'But you could take time off, surely?'

She shook her head. 'Not possible, I'm afraid.'

He looked down at her. 'As I said before, you're the boss, Romy. Being able to take time off when you want to should be one of the perks.'

'It doesn't work like that.' She saw that he was put out; she had noticed this in him, a disinclination to be thwarted.

'Your staff should be able to cope, surely?'

She felt a flicker of annoyance that he should tell her how to run her hotel. She tried to explain. 'It's not a question of not being able to cope. All my staff are good at their jobs. But for me not to be there at Christmas would be disastrous. It would be – ' she searched for a simile – 'it would be like leaving an orchestra without a conductor. And besides,' she went on as the dance came to an end and there was a flicker of polite applause, 'I have to see my family at Christmas.'

'Your mother?'

She shook her head. 'I visit my mother in January, when things are quiet at the Trelawney. I meant that I have to be with Jem and Danny.'

Now he looked sulky. 'I should have thought it was about time your brother started to take responsibility for his own child.'

'It's not as simple as that, Patrick.'

He took out his cigarette case and offered it to her; she shook her head. He said, 'You mustn't let people take advantage of you, Romy. What happened to the child's mother, anyway?'

'I told you, they split up. She went off with someone else. And Jem was in the army.' She took a large gulp of gin and tonic. It wasn't even a lie, she told herself.

More a juggling of the facts and a by now habitual evasion of an uncomfortable truth. 'And now – well, it's taken Jem a while to get settled, that's all. It's hard for a man on his own to cope with a baby. When Danny's a bit older, then he'll go and live with Jem.' She looked down at her glass. 'And he's not taking advantage. I wanted to help him. I *offered*.'

'Hey,' he said. He brushed the back of his hand against her cheek. 'No need to be cross with me. I was only asking.'

'I'm not cross with you.' She made herself smile. 'I'm just a bit tired, that's all.'

'Poor little thing,' he said and kissed her forehead. 'I just think you take too much on yourself. At your age you should be having fun.'

'I am having fun. Lots of fun.' She held out her empty glass. 'Do you think you could get me another drink, Patrick?'

When he had gone, the smile slipped from her face and she threaded through the dancers to where tall French windows faced out over the garden. The wintry December air seeped in through the glass, and some of her irritation drained away and was replaced by weariness. It seemed impossible, she thought, to do everything well, to keep everyone happy. Even now she was worrying about whether the Rotary Club dinner being held at the Trelawney tonight would go smoothly in her absence. And whether Danny's cold was just a cold, or whether it would turn to something worse, such as flu or measles.

She sighed and looked out at the garden. A movement among the shrubs and trees told her that someone was out there, braving the bitterly cold weather. Ironically the band had now switched to 'Isn't This a Lovely Day'. It had been kind of Patrick, she thought, to invite her to his mother's place for Christmas. She imagined a beautiful old house and a Christmas tree and holly and paper streamers and his mother serving huge dinners of turkey and plum pudding. Just how Christmas ought to be. She found that she regretted not being able to go.

The figure in the garden had moved out of the darkness onto the terrace adjoining the house and was now standing, his back to her, in the patch of light that flooded from the windows. Something in his height and the set of his shoulders made her draw in her breath rapidly. She was being silly, she told herself. Soon the man in the garden would turn and she would see that her imagination was playing tricks again, and she would experience once more that familiar mixture of embarrassment and disappointment. Coupled this time with a feeling of foolishness: after all, she was long over him.

She moved away from the window. The small room had filled up. Couples jostled against each other, chachaing to 'Zambesi'. Then a voice said her name, and she froze.

It was the sort of party Caleb loathed. Bite-sized portions of unrecognizable food and the stiff shuffling that passed in these circles for dancing. He wouldn't have come – wouldn't have been invited – if it hadn't been for Diana. 'I could introduce you to lots of useful people,' she had said. 'I'd be pleased to help you out, Caleb.' He had suspected her of other motives, tall, dark

Diana, with her absent husband and her heart of stone. Yet she had had a point, and business was poor because it wasn't the time of year when people thought about gardens. So he had accompanied her to the Harbornes' party, where he had had quite a few drinks and eaten half a dozen fishy little vol-au-vents. And then he had seen Romy.

He hadn't recognized her at first. Her face was turned aside as she danced. She was wearing a gold dress with a close-fitting top and a floaty sort of skirt. Her light brown hair was twisted up in a knot. You couldn't not notice her; sophisticated, elegant and assured, and with that indefinable spark, she was the only woman worth looking at in the whole damn room.

Then her voice cut through the music – *It's not as simple as that, Patrick* – and he felt a shiver run up his spine. He had always known that it was inevitable that he and Romy should run into each other some day – London, they said, was a series of villages, and everyone knew everyone in a village, didn't they? But he hadn't thought it would touch him any more. Yet he found himself turning on his heel and heading out into the garden. He smoked a cigarette as he stared out at frozen fronds of Michaelmas daisy and the pale papery seed-cases of honesty. And thought how ridiculous he was being: after all, he wasn't some tongue-tied teenager and all he had to do was to exchange a few pleasantries with her and then take his leave.

When he went back into the house, she was walking across the dance floor. He said her name and she turned to him. She didn't smile; he noticed that.

'Caleb.' Her glance flicked around the room: he assumed that she was looking for that chap, Patrick. 'How extraordinary. After all this time—'

'Small world, Romy.'

'Of course.' A quick frown. 'Jake told me you'd gone abroad.'

'I've been back for about a year now.'

'How are you?'

'I'm fine. And you, Romy?'

'Terrific,' she said. 'Absolutely terrific.' Her eyes – that uncommon mixture of brown, hazel and gold – seemed to settle on him at last. 'What are you doing? Are you still gardening?'

'I've set up my own business. Garden design and maintenance.'

'Is it doing well?'

'Very well,' he said, rather heartily. There was a silence. Then he said, 'And you? Are you still at the hotel? Mrs Plummer—'

'She died two years ago.'

'I'm sorry.'

'She left me the hotel.'

'Ah,' he said. Now he understood the air of sleek prosperity that seemed to cling to her. He inclined his head in a small bow. 'Congratulations. I'm sure you'll be very successful.'

'Thank you, Caleb.'

Another silence. Then, 'And Jem . . . how is Jem?'

For the first time, she smiled. 'He's fine. He's working on a farm in Yorkshire.'

Romy's dancing partner returned, drinks in hand. 'Here you are, darling,' he said, as he handed Romy a glass. He glanced at Caleb. 'Are you going to introduce me?'

'Patrick, this is Caleb Hesketh. Caleb, this is Patrick Napier. Caleb and I knew each other ages ago,' she said.

Which put him neatly in his place. Caleb shook Patrick's hand then muttered an excuse and headed out of the room. Grabbing a couple of drinks en route, he made his way back through the house.

He had hoped to escape without seeing Diana. But she had positioned herself near the coats, so there was really no evading her. 'Had enough already?' she said, as she headed for him with the single-mindedness of a Minuteman guided missile. She was a mixture, he thought, of Diana the Huntress her namesake, all pale skin and Roman features, with just a touch, in the resolutely upright carriage and long, muscular limbs and the utter lack of sympathy in her large dark-brown eyes, of a PE teacher at a girls' school.

'The Harbornes' affairs are always so desperately dreary,' she said in an overloud stage whisper. 'It's as if they *court* dreariness.'

He fetched their coats. 'Well,' she said, as they left the house, 'did they come up trumps?'

'Mr Harborne said to call round in the New Year.' He pictured the Harbornes' neglected garden: lots of potential there.

'Then you'll let me give you a nightcap,' she said, as he hailed a taxi.

'Diana—'

'I won't take no for an answer, Caleb.' There was a hint of steel beneath the playfulness. 'The Harbornes have lots of friends. They could be very useful to you.'

Diana Coulthard lived in Chelsea. Diana's husband was a government scientist who was often absent from home on expeditions to remote research establishments throughout the British Isles. Caleb had met him only once, a quiet, slightly desiccated man.

Inside the house Diana poured him a drink and patted the sofa, commanding him to sit beside her. Then she said, 'Well, who was she, then?'

'Who was who?'

'That girl you couldn't stop looking at.' When he did not reply, she rolled her eyes. 'A gold dress. By Susan Small, I think. She was with the divine Dr Napier. Who is terribly well connected and has pots of money, of course. Though his mother's a nightmare.' Her eyes fixed on him. '*Well?*'

'She's called Romy Cole,' he said briefly. 'She works in – she *owns* – a hotel in Bloomsbury.'

'What I meant, darling, is, what is she to you?'

'She's nothing. Nothing.'

She smiled. 'Then I'm glad to hear it.'

He raised her hand and pressed his lips against the back of it. Her hands were strong and white and smelt of Pears soap. Then he kissed the inside of her wrist.

'*Caleb*,' she said. 'How naughty of you.'

He read the invitation in her eyes and found, suddenly, that he wanted her, wanted her long limbs and large breasts, so different from the slight, golden-skinned body whose memory had troubled him for years. He kissed the crook of her arm and the curve of her shoulder. Then he threaded his hand behind her back and began the time-consuming task of undoing the row of tiny satin-covered buttons that fastened her dress, and divesting her of cocktail gown, long-line bra, corset, stockings and petticoats.

Diana shooed him from the house an hour later. His bow tie was in his pocket, his overcoat and the top two studs of his shirt undone. After Diana's energetic love-making, he felt rather tousled and battered, as though he had been on a five-mile run.

He dozed intermittently on the Tube train home. Two months ago he had bought a flat in Canonbury, a very run-down part of Islington. Previously grimly working class and badly bombed in the war, during the last few years many houses in the area had been bought by professional people for renovation. Brass knockers now adorned hitherto neglected doors and blackened stonework had been repainted white. There was an excitement in the air, as though streets that had slept for centuries were being brought back to life.

Caleb's flat was the ground floor and basement of a Georgian town house. Inside the plaster was crumbling from the walls and many of the floorboards were rotten; colonies of woodlice, silverfish and earwigs lived behind dilapidated skirting boards and peeling wallpaper. The price had been good because of the flat's decayed condition, yet he knew, with an uncomfortable lurch of the stomach, that if he didn't get more work soon he'd be hard put to pay the mortgage instalments.

As he let himself in, Alison, who lived in the flat above, came down the stairs. 'There's a parcel for you, Caleb. The postman left it on the front step, so I thought I'd better take it in.'

He thanked her and took the parcel from her. 'Nice evening?' she asked, as he chucked his coat and tie on the sofa.

'No. No, not especially.'

'You look tired.'

He threw her a smile. 'Drunk, actually.'

'I'll make you some black coffee.'

She went into the kitchen. Alison was the ideal neighbour, kind and quiet and unobtrusive. She taught at an infants' school in Tufnell Park: Caleb imagined her, the long, rich, chestnut hair that was her claim to beauty, falling, as it always did, from its hair grips, her loose, slightly odd-looking clothes trailing from her as with infinite love and patience she coaxed twenty infants to learn the alphabet.

She came back a few moments later. 'There.' She put the cup on the table. 'It's very hot, so don't scald yourself. Oh, and you're almost out of sugar. Well, I'll leave you in peace now. Goodnight, Caleb.' She paused at the door, her gentle blue-grey eyes betraying a sudden uncertainty. 'The school dance—'

Preoccupied by the events of the evening, he couldn't for a moment think what she was talking about. Then he remembered that she had asked him, with a great deal of embarrassment and a flurry of disclaimers, to a fund-raising hop at her school the following night. 'Yes, of course,' he said. 'Sevenish?'

'That'd be perfect.' She closed the door quietly.

He heard her footsteps disappear up the stairs as he carried the coffee into the room he used as an office and sat down at the desk.

If the Harbornes commissioned him to redesign

their garden – *if* – then he would, he thought, just about manage. And Diana had said, hadn't she, that if they liked his work, then they'd recommend him to their wealthy friends. That was all he needed, half a dozen solid commissions, to feel more confident about his future.

But if the Harbornes changed their mind, if they decided after the extravagances of Christmas that they couldn't afford to redesign their garden, then – well, he wouldn't think about that. It wasn't as though he would starve: Freddie had told him that he would always give him work. But it might mean selling the flat, which he had grown fond of. And it would mean, also, an inevitable and galling loss of independence.

He had set up on his own eight months earlier, starting out with an optimism and determination that hadn't quite yet been battered out of him. He had chosen to return to London because of the new houses springing up on wasteland, and because of those, like his own, which were being renovated. Plenty of work for a landscape gardener, he had reasoned. He'd make his name with smaller projects, the bread-and-butter work, and then, in time, when he became established, he'd be able to pick and choose.

He turned the pages of the account book in front of him, running his eyes down the rows of figures. If he could just keep going till spring. Then the work would start to come in again, he knew it would. He started to scribble down numbers, to add and divide, but after a while the pencil fell from his hand, and he sat at the table, his eyes unfocused. He couldn't concentrate: too much to drink, he supposed. Nothing else. Most certainly not the lingering image of Romy Cole, lighting up the Harbornes' room like a pale gold flame.

Two and a half years ago she had torn his life apart. His decision to go abroad had been motivated by a need to escape all that was familiar. Or all that had seemed familiar: the revelation that he was Osborne Daubeny's son had cast him onto shifting sands. The foundations of his existence – his parentage, his history, his name – had been kicked away from under him. He had been afraid to look too closely at all the other things he had once taken for granted, for fear that they, too, might disappear in the blink of an eye.

The weather had been unseasonally bad during his ferry journey from Dover to Calais, grey skies and a gusty wind, November at the end of August. Caleb had stood on deck, watching the strip of sea between land and boat widen. He had found himself wondering what it would be like to slip between those jagged waves, to feel the water close over your head, cold and breath-taking, wiping away the endless, repetitive thoughts that had worn him down so these past weeks.

He hadn't jumped, of course; instead, he had gone back into the boat's interior in search of something to eat. And after they had docked in France he had been taken up by the business of surviving in a foreign country. He had discovered that his instinct to escape had been a good one, that the change of scenery and the sort of concentration you needed to find your way around in unfamiliar surroundings distracted him.

Exploring this new world, he had realized how narrow his life had been. The further he travelled from England, the freer he felt. He had been confined too long – a comfortable, civilized sort of confinement, made up of complacency and insular opinions, and weighted down with history and tradition.

Slowly, with many detours and pauses, he made his way south through France. He learned to drink wine instead of beer, to eat dishes whose contents he could not fathom, whose description he could not translate. He slept in tiny *pensions*, in flea-bitten ramshackle seaside hotels, and, not a few times, beneath the stars. When he ran out of money, he worked in restaurants and on farms, on fishing boats and driving delivery vans. He learned to rely on himself and not to think about tomorrow. He discovered skills he had not known he possessed, discovered that he could survive, alone and cut off from friends and family.

Sometimes he felt as though he was only just beginning to find out who he really was. In the past he had adapted himself to whatever the circumstances had required of him, putting on an amiable mask in order to fit in. He had been a different person at home, at boarding school and in the army. He could not, looking back, tell which had been the real Caleb Hesketh. He seemed to shift, amorphous and ill-defined. He had only rarely, when prodded by extreme circumstances, let his true self come through – at Broadbent's, after they had fired Pickering, or when his feelings for Romy had forced him to scrape away the artifice. Of course, he had been ignorant of the greatest pretence, the pretence which had had been stripped away by Evelyn Daubeny one rainswept afternoon. And after that he had no alternative but to start from scratch, slowly and painfully building up the layers, like the lining of a shell.

During the year he spent abroad, he did not send a postcard or write a single letter. It was a simple, pared-down existence, with no responsibilities except to feed and clothe himself. If certain faces – his mother's, and Romy's when he had told her that he was leaving her – appeared sometimes in his dreams, then in the morning he banished them by moving on to somewhere new. That year he made a hundred new friends, heard a hundred new stories. Some of those stories told him of dislocated or unlucky lives. In a dusty, sunlit square in Avignon a gnarled veteran of the First World War shared his memories of the Battle of Verdun. In a cramped little bar in Marseilles a pretty girl limped as she cleared the tables, her leg in a caliper. Polio, she explained when, to his embarrassment, she caught his glance. He began to acquire a sense of proportion, his own bruises seeming to fade and diminish as he travelled.

In the late summer of 1957, visiting the garden of La Mortola on the Riviera, he found himself thinking of England. It took him by surprise, his sudden longing. He hadn't planned, he supposed, hadn't set a time limit on his exile. Now, for the first time, the fierce, hot, southern summer and the parched grass and languid air seemed to grate at him. He began to miss the familiar, to long for soft rain and the green of English lawns. He began to miss his work, also, to feel restless and impatient, to feel that he was wasting his time.

A few months later he went back to England. Because he knew that he must, he went first to see his mother. Betty was now living in Southampton, working in a shop in the suburbs of the city. She had changed, some of the old bounce and certainty rubbed away from her. She seemed to Caleb to have become smaller, to have faded a little. The visit was awkward, stilted, far too many things lying unsaid. He told her about his travels and explained that he was going back to work with Freddie for a while. He stayed only one night in Southampton and, walking away from the cramped little flat the following morning, felt a sense of relief. There were questions he had not been able to bear to ask her, there were answers he was afraid of hearing. The memory of their last, awful meeting, the meeting in which she had admitted to him that Osborne Daubeny was his father, was still too vivid. That she had chosen Osborne Daubeny, who seemed to Caleb to personify hypocrisy, still ate at him. That, and the enormity of the lies she had told him. He knew that he wanted his forgiveness. He knew that he could not yet bring himself to forgive.

And Romy? Had he forgiven her? Objectively he wasn't even sure that there was anything much to forgive. All she had done was to reveal the truth. And she hadn't even intended to do that. Why should he blame her for the betrayals that had taken place so long ago?

Yet he did blame her. He blamed her for the carelessness with which she had used his secrets as a weapon, and for the burdens she had so thoughtlessly laid on him. She had shown him to be the son of the man responsible for her family's dispossession – he, who had once loved her. She had made him think of himself differently. He trusted himself less now, saw shadows in

475

his impulses, his desires. Science might appear to have confounded old theories of bad blood, yet they lingered, surely, in a different guise, making him wonder whether Osborne Daubeny had bequeathed to him a twist of darkness along with his DNA, making him wonder whether you could inherit guilt.

He recalled the vivid golden figure of earlier that evening. Romy appeared to have shaken off the past with hardly a backward glance. She had fallen on her feet; she exuded confidence, success and material well-being. God, she had changed: immaculately turned out, not a hair out of place, without a trace of the accent of her childhood, she had hardly seemed the same woman as the one he had first encountered in scuffed shoes and cheap clothes at Middlemere. You couldn't imagine that beautiful, sophisticated creature getting lost in a rainstorm, or deigning to wear wellington boots several sizes too big while she tramped round a garden. And as for that chap she had been with ... Caleb's lip curled as he pictured smooth, handsome Patrick Napier. *Pots of money*, Diana had said. Easy enough to imagine the attraction *there*, then.

Romy Cole had become someone he no longer knew. She had everything she had always wanted: money, property, success, authority. She moved in altered circles and carried with her an exclusive, impenetrable glitter. Caleb winced – his pounding head, and his memory of the halting awkwardness of their conversation. Well, he thought grimly, if nothing else, at least they had got that first meeting over and done with. If they met again, there need be just a smile and a conventional greeting.

In time even that would dwindle to a mere nod of acknowledgement. And that was just fine with him.

'Your last chance, Romy,' said Patrick. 'You can come to Suffolk with me and have breakfast in bed in the mornings and all your meals cooked for you and spend your time talking to interesting people or taking walks along the beach, or –' a quizzical raise of the eyebrows – 'or you can remain in London, working all the hours God sends.'

Romy laughed. 'When you put it like that—'

'You'll come, then?'

She shook her head. 'I can't, Patrick. I'd love to, but I can't.'

He sighed. 'Then you are going to have to be very nice to me because I shall miss you terribly.'

He put his arms around her and began to kiss her. It was the night before Christmas Eve; they had been to a party and were having a drink in Romy's flat at the Trelawney. Relaxed and happy after several glasses of champagne, she closed her eyes and gave herself up to the touch of his mouth, the pressure of his hands. It would be so easy, she thought dreamily, just so easy – and so *nice* – to go to bed with Patrick Napier.

Then there was a cry from the adjacent room and she pulled away. 'Danny,' she said.

'Surely the nanny—' Patrick began irritably.

Danny was standing up in his cot, his face wet with tears. He had dreamed that a snake was hiding under his pillow. Romy turned over the pillow to prove to him the absence of snakes, and then she rocked him till he became limp in her arms, then tucked him back beneath the blankets.

When she came back into the drawing room, Patrick said, 'I almost think that you do it deliberately. Give the child a prod or something, so that he wakes up at the worst possible moment.' He crossed the room to her. 'What about taking up where we left off?'

'Patrick, no.' She glanced at the clock on the mantelpiece. 'It's past midnight and I'll have to be up at six tomorrow. Christmas Eve—'

'I know, I know. It's your busiest time.'

'I'm sorry.'

'Not as sorry as I am, I fear.' He frowned, and picked up his coat. 'If you go on saying no, I might just have to marry you, Romy Cole.'

She laughed. 'You shouldn't make such rash statements, Patrick. Everyone knows you're a confirmed bachelor.'

He kissed her once, lightly, on the mouth. 'Promise you'll come away with me for a weekend in the New Year.'

'Patrick—'

'You owe me that, don't you think?'

His voice coaxed, his blue eyes cajoled. 'All right,' she said. 'January. We'll have a weekend in January.'

'Good.' He went to the door. 'Merry Christmas, Romy,' he said as he left the room.

Chapter Fifteen

Romy would have liked a white Christmas for Danny, blobs of snow dancing in the crisp air and a snowman in the back garden, yet Christmas Day dawned warmish and windy, the heavy grey sky clinging to the city like a lid on a saucepan.

In the afternoon they went for a walk. A sharp breeze tugged at the oily waters of the Thames and newspapers and sweet wrappings danced in the gutters. Romy found herself wanting to give London a brisk shake and tidy, to restore it to the pale clarity of the Christmases of films and books.

Jem went back to Yorkshire the day after Boxing Day. The next day Romy found Carol weeping in the office. Between sobs Carol gasped, 'It's *Tony*. I found him in the broom cupboard with *Sandra*.' Tony was a commis chef, Sandra was a waitress. Carol had been going out with Tony for three months. Carol wiped her nose on her sleeve. 'I thought he loved me.'

Carol went back to Stratton earlier than planned to escape the faithless Tony. Which left them short-staffed amid a sudden flurry of problems. There were all the usual difficulties – guests who mislaid belongings, or who fell ill having eaten too much turkey and plum pudding – and there was the sort of problem the hotel often encountered at this time of year, of high-spirited young men intent on celebration. Drunkenness, and the type of woman Romy didn't want under the Trelawney's roof. And then the band that had been booked for the New Year celebrations all went down with flu, so she had to find another at two days' notice when anyone decent had been booked up for months. At this rate, she said grimly to Anton, the cook, they'd both have to get up on stage and rattle off 'Cry Me a River' and 'Blueberry Hill' on kazoos.

They always put on a big New Year's Eve dinner-dance at the Trelawney. It had been one of Mrs Plummer's favourite traditions: Romy remembered her vividly, decked out in pale yellow or emerald green, foxtrotting around the room in Johnnie Fitzgerald's arms. Yet it seemed to Romy that this New Year's Eve failed to come alive. Parties were like that, she had discovered: however much you planned, you couldn't be certain of that spark. The band, who were a bit long in the tooth, worked doggedly through a repertoire of tired interwar standards. The food also seemed tired. She must have a word with Anton, she thought crossly, as she bit into a vol-au-vent. No one, but no one, wanted turkey on New Year's Eve. Even the guests seemed to lack sparkle, sitting around the perimeter of the room instead of dancing, punctuating their conversations with yawns and a wave of a gloved hand to cool themselves.

At last they put on the radio for the bells. There was a rather half-hearted cheer and a mumbled verse of 'Auld Lang Syne' and then a flurry of dutiful kisses. Romy found herself longing for it to be over, longing for the silence and sanctuary of her room.

Yet when, eventually, she was able to escape upstairs to her flat, she felt both restless and wakeful. She should be tired, she told herself; she had been up for eighteen hours. She took off her Jaeger dress and hung it in the wardrobe, and put on a dressing gown. Then she poured herself a drink and sat down in an armchair. There was the tick of the clock and, distantly, the sound of revellers making their way through the streets. Danny and Sarah were asleep, and there was no one to welcome her, or to share their hopes and fears for the coming year with her. The flat seemed both empty and impersonal, full of Mrs Plummer's furniture, Mrs Plummer's books and ornaments, which she had somehow never got round to changing.

It was New Year's Eve and she was twenty-four years old and alone with the slightly sour memory of a party she hadn't really enjoyed. She felt tempted to pour herself another drink, and another, to blur her sense of failure and isolation. Instead she picked up the phone and asked to speak to the concierge. Who was a sort of genius, and could find you anything.

Including, with a bit of luck, a taxi at one o'clock in the morning on New Year's Day.

She went to Jake's house in Apollo Place. Put on a black leotard and ballet tights, then her circular skirt from Bazaar and a mohair jacket, and hopped into the taxi.

Jake always gave a party on New Year's Eve. Jake's parties didn't get going until around three in the morning and tended to drift on long into the next day. The taxi rounded the corner of the street and Romy saw the light spilling out of the windows of Jake's house. As she paid the driver, a figure fell out of the front door and landed in a sprawling heap of arms and legs on the pavement. Romy stepped over him carefully.

The hallway was choked with people. She caught fragments of conversation as she elbowed and excuse-me'd her way along the corridor. A girl in a Sloppy Joe and jeans was saying, 'He painted it blue and green – supposed to remind you of the womb,' and a West Indian man said, confused, 'But I should have thought wombs were red.' And the girl replied earnestly, 'The womb as ocean, darling. The womb as a nurturing ocean.' Then a man in a pork-pie hat asked Romy for a light, and another man (holey jersey and paint-spattered cords) stared at her with eyes whose enlarged pupils almost blanked out the irises, and then seized her hand, hazily passionate, convinced they had once spent a weekend together. 'You must remember,' he yelled. 'Wales, wasn't it? Aberthingy. Or Llansomething.'

People clumped together on the stairs, passing round a messy-looking home-made cigarette. There was the smell of something sweet and exotic, not quite patchouli, not quite musk. A girl was sitting in the studio doorway. Tears trailed down her cheeks and fell unchecked onto her olive-green jumper. A glass trembled in her pale, thin hands. 'It wasn't that I didn't want the baby,' she was saying over and over again. 'I wanted it, Sheila, I really, really did.' Romy squeezed past her.

Cigarette smoke blurred the candlelight in the studio; the floor was a snowstorm of breadcrumbs and bottle tops and cigarette ends. A single branch of mistletoe hung drunkenly from a bare bulb in the centre of the room, Jake's sole decorative concession to the festive season. A gramophone was playing; Romy caught fragments of riffs whenever the crush of conversation and laughter and argument dipped. *You can't just assume, Bobby ... And I said to him, if you think I'm giving you that for twenty quid ... Hang down your head, Tom Dooley ... the most awful pains in my stomach ... men with dogs – I think it was my landlord ... Poor boy, you're bound to die ...*

A voice yelled '*Romy!*' and she ducked through the crowds to Jake, who was sitting on the sofa.

'Romy, my darling. Thought you'd be hobnobbing with the rich and famous in that hotel of yours.'

'I decided to slum it for a change. Happy New Year, Jake.' She kissed him.

A red-haired woman was sleeping open-mouthed to one side of Jake; Romy perched beside him on the arm of the sofa. Jake held up a bottle. 'Drink?'

'Please.'

'Everyone's here,' he said, applying a corkscrew. 'Psyche, Dave, Matty, Julian ... Everyone.' He gazed rather mournfully around the room. 'Most of 'em are only here for the free booze. Never underestimate, Romy, how far people will travel for a glass of plonk and a chunk of French bread.'

There were two rather grubby glasses on the hearth. Jake sloshed wine into both of them. 'Oh, and Caleb's here,' he added. 'Did I mention that?'

Caleb. Romy felt a rush of annoyance. She wished he would stop turning up like that, out of the blue.

Jake said, 'You should go and say hello.' He handed her a glass.

'I don't think so.'

'He'd like to see you.'

She gave a little laugh. 'What on earth gives you that idea?'

'Instinct,' he said, and she snorted.

'Honestly, Jake. Caleb and I have nothing to say to each other.' She caught the expression in his eyes and explained, 'I met him at a party a few weeks ago and it was simply awful.' She remembered their conversation with uncomfortable clarity, remembered the chill procession of clichés and platitudes. She said, 'He was different, Jake. Not like he used to be.'

'Rot. He's just the same.'

She shook her head. 'With you, maybe. Not with me.'

'Well, water under the bridge and all that . . .'

'He couldn't wait to get away from me.'

'Nonsense. You're imagining things. Always had an overactive imagination, Romy. You should do what I do, take things as they come.' Jake put back his head, tipped the contents of the glass down his throat and coughed. Drops of wine flecked his large belly. 'Damned cheap stuff,' he muttered. Then he yelled, '*Caleb!*' and she reached over and clamped a hand over his mouth.

'*Jake,*' she said furiously, 'I wish you'd mind your own business!'

'Your happiness is my business,' he said pompously, the words slurred by Romy's fingers. He drew in his breath to shout again, and she hissed, 'All right. I'll go and say hello. Will that make you happy?'

She found Caleb in Jake's tiny kitchen. He was with Psyche, who was hugely pregnant. Psyche was saying, 'I shall feed on demand, of course. I've just read *Child Care and the Growth of Love*, and do you know, Caleb, how bad it is for a baby to be separated from its mother? But do you think that means when I go to the *hairdresser's*—' Catching sight of Romy, she broke off and shrieked, 'Romy! Happy New Year!' and hugged her.

Disentangling herself, Romy said hello to Caleb. He was wearing a corduroy jacket over an open-necked shirt and jeans. Squeezed between the sink and the kitchen table, he gave her a nod. 'I didn't think you'd be here,' he said. 'Didn't think this was your scene these days.'

She said coolly, 'It was all rather spur of the moment.'

Psyche was shuffling into a voluminous wool coat. 'I'm going to have to head off, I'm afraid. My ankles are like balloons. Dear Romy, you must come and visit me soon. You must tell me about babies. I don't know how I shall be able to manage. It all sounds so complicated.'

She disappeared into the crowd. Romy, too, turned to go. Caleb said suddenly, 'What did Psyche mean, tell her about babies?'

'I suppose she thinks I've some idea, because of bringing up Danny.'

'You're married?' he said sharply. 'That chap – Patrick—'

'Of course not. Danny is Jem's son.'

She saw him blink and pause, as if reassessing something. 'Liz's child?'

'Yes.' He didn't know, of course. She said, 'Liz married Ray Babbs.'

His eyes widened. 'Good God.'

It was something Romy herself still struggled to come to terms with. 'I think she felt she had to marry someone. And Ray was free and Jem wasn't.' She could not quite keep the bitterness from her voice. 'When she told me she was going to have the baby adopted, I said I'd take him in until Jem came out of prison. That's all.'

She began to move away again, but her passage was barred by a very large man brandishing a saxophone. She heard Caleb say, 'So the child's with Jem now?' and she paused.

'No. Danny's still with me.' Depression seemed to settle around her once more like a heavy grey blanket.

'Jem's son – Danny –' Caleb frowned – 'how old is he now?'

'He was two in October.'

'A huge thing to take on, bringing up a child.'

'Danny's no trouble,' she said stiffly. 'He's such a good little boy.'

He was looking at her in a way that unsettled her. She remembered him saying to her: *Just at this moment I wish I'd never met you*, and she had to suppress a shiver. She hugged the mohair jacket around herself. 'I have to go,' she said quickly. 'I haven't talked to Jake properly for months.'

'I should have thought,' he said, interrupting her, 'that if any of you were going to look after the child, it would have been your mother.'

'No,' she said sharply. 'I couldn't even consider that. Not with my stepfather. Don't you see, Caleb? I couldn't let him do to Danny what he'd done to Jem. It would just ... *perpetuate* things. And anyway, Mum's only just got Gareth off to school. It wouldn't have been fair.'

He inclined his head, as if accepting what she said. Then she turned away, weaving through the crowd, dodging the discarded glasses and empty wine glasses on the floor.

She was almost out of earshot when she heard him call out her name. She looked back.

She had forgotten his smile; her heart gave an odd little beat. He raised his glass to her. 'Happy New Year, Romy,' he said.

Patrick said, 'There it is. There's Whitewaters.'

Whitewaters was the name of Bunny Napier's Suffolk home. Art Deco in style, pale and flat-roofed and many-windowed, it shimmered, Romy thought, like the sea that lay only half a mile or so behind it.

'It's beautiful,' she said.

'Isn't it?' Patrick swung the Jaguar around a bend in the road.

Romy felt suddenly nervous. She looked down at herself, checking coat, gloves, handbag, stockings. Patrick caught her glance, and laughed and said, 'There's no need to worry. Bunny's weekends are very casual. And I've told her all about you. She's longing to meet you.'

He parked in front of the house and then, their bags in hand, bounded up the steps two at a time. He was like a schoolboy, Romy thought indulgently, impatient to see his mother.

Inside the house the stone-paved reception area was empty. Patrick opened doors and called out his mother's name. A small, thin woman in a floral apron came bustling down a passageway.

'Mrs Napier isn't well, Mr Patrick. She's having a lie-down.'

Patrick looked worried. 'I'd better go and see her. My mother has migraines,' he explained to Romy. 'I'll show you to your room, shall I, and then you can have a bit of a rest, tidy up, that sort of thing.'

He took her to a room at the back of the house. Then he kissed her and said, 'Won't be a tick,' and disappeared along a corridor.

Alone, Romy hung up her dresses and brushed her hair and touched up her make-up. Then she explored the room. The furniture was of a pale blond wood, the floorboards a similar shade, waxed and polished and scattered with softly striped rugs. Cream-coloured hopsack curtains hung to either side of the windows, which faced out to the sea. Looking out, she saw that a group of tiny black stick figures was moving along the beach. Gulls soared on the slipstream or were tossed by the wind, and there were white peaks on the waves.

Time passed and she had run out of things to admire and had tired of the view. She glanced at her watch. It was almost an hour since Patrick had left her. He must be waiting for her downstairs, she decided. She left the room, but became confused, uncertain of her direction. The architecture of the house was peculiar, stairs and corridors branching off unexpectedly, rooms leading into other rooms, many of which had high, vaulted ceilings. All the rooms were sparely furnished. She didn't come across another soul until she found herself in a large room with tall French windows. The windows looked out over the terrace and garden. Small squares of coloured glass were inset into the window panes, so that blue and orange and yellow patches of light danced on the pale carpet.

A dark girl in a red dress was lounging on a huge white sofa, eating chocolates. She looked up at Romy.

'I thought you were Marian.'

'I'm Romy. Romy Cole. Hello.' She held out her hand.

Pale fingers drifted fleetingly against Romy's. 'I'm Christine,' said the girl, 'and I'm quite relieved you're not Marian, because these are her chocolates.' She waved the box at Romy, who shook her head.

'I was looking for Patrick.'

'Haven't seen him.' This through a mouthful of chocolate. 'He's probably on the beach with the others.'

'Do you think so?'

The girl shrugged, her fleeting interest seeming to wane. 'He can be awfully *busy*, Patrick,' she murmured.

Romy went outside. It was late afternoon and the sun hovered just above the horizon. Patrick might have thought she was asleep or having a bath, she reasoned, so it was perfectly possible that he could have gone out for a walk with his friends. He was, as the girl in the red dress had said, a very busy person, always on the go.

Outside, the terrace fell away to a lawn. Beyond the lawn there was a shrubbery of increasingly wind-bitten and salt-blasted plants, and then the garden seemed to peter out as the ground humped and rose into dunes. The dunes were threaded with sandy paths and scattered with tufts of tall, sharp grass. Emerging from their shelter, Romy found herself on the beach.

The wind hit her, biting and invigorating. She was wearing a thick jersey and a wool skirt, yet the cold air seemed to pierce through the threads in the fabric. She walked down to the sea, pausing every now and then to prise shells and pebbles out of the clammy grasp of the sand. At the waves' edge she stooped to trail her fingers in the icy water. The cold stung, whitening her skin, and she stood up, wrapping her arms around herself. The dying sun cast flashes of light on the waves, like the flickering shades from the coloured glass in Bunny Napier's drawing room. She took a deep breath of chilly air, braced by the emptiness of the scene and the glorious expanse of sea and sky. She felt free, liberated. It jolted her slightly that some of her relief and exhilaration was in being away, if only for a weekend, from the hotel.

She began to walk along the beach. She couldn't see Patrick, and the stick figures she had glimpsed from her bedroom window had vanished. The wind whipped at her hair and tugged at her clothes. When she reached the headland she looked around, struggling to see in the fading light. The beach was deserted; even the gulls seemed to have made for the shelter of the dunes.

Eventually she turned round and walked back to the house. It took her a while to find the right dune, the right path. It was dark now, the sky dimmed to indigo, and the only sounds were the hush of the wind in the grass and the distant murmur of the sea.

And another sound, coming from the house. She

began to feel uneasy, catching the distant laughter and chatter. Shapes shifted behind the tall French windows of the room which, when she had left it – not so long ago, surely – had been empty.

Any hope that she was mistaken evaporated as she neared the house. The room was full of people. Approaching the terrace, Romy paused, seized by an uncertainty she had not felt in years. Just for a moment, she was eighteen again, wearing the wrong clothes, doing the wrong thing.

She squared her shoulders and walked into the room. There were more than twenty people there now, twenty people drinking cocktails and eating canapés, and looking at her with interested, expectant eyes. Patrick was standing beside an older woman. It took Romy only a split second to realize how mistaken she had been, to know that Bunny Napier was not the comfortable, motherly woman of her imagination, but instead was tall and thin and beautiful. Her slight pallor emphasized her beauty. Her fair hair was pinned up in a French pleat and her face was perfectly made up. She wore a green silk evening gown with a closely cut bodice and a wide, full skirt. Pearls gleamed at her neck and in her ears. There was a sharpness in her eyes, which were the glassy grey-green of the sea and which were now focused on Romy.

Bunny's voice, a high, clear drawl, cut through the chatter. 'So you've turned up at last. We were beginning to worry about you. We thought we might have to send out a search party.'

A tinkle of laughter from the other guests.

'I'm sorry,' said Romy. 'I didn't realize—'

'It's quite all right, Miss Cole. We all enjoy a good walk. And we haven't been waiting long.'

Patrick was weaving through the crowds to Romy's side. He looked furious. 'Where were you?'

'I was looking for you.'

'Looking for me?' His eyes raked over her. 'You appear to have been on a five-mile hike.'

'I'll go and tidy myself up.'

'There isn't time.' He took out a cigarette and tapped it irritably against the box. 'The dinner gong went five minutes ago. You'll just have to do.'

'Patrick,' she said gently, 'I can't possibly come to dinner dressed like this. You go ahead – I don't mind if my soup's cold.' She touched his arm, trying to pacify him, but he moved away. 'I won't be a moment, I promise you.'

She ran upstairs. She had a moment of panic when she thought she had forgotten how to find her bedroom, but then, miraculously, she found herself at the right door. Inside her room, she pulled off her skirt and jersey. No time to change her thick stockings; she would have to hope that no one noticed them beneath her long evening gown. She was unbuttoning her blouse when she caught sight of herself in the dressing-table mirror. She paused, appalled. Her hair was a tangled bird's nest, her nose and cheeks crimsoned by the wind. Hurriedly she scrambled into her gown, twisting round at an untenable angle to do up the zip. She pulled a comb through her hair and coiled it up into a chignon, her fingers shaking, pins falling from her grasp. Then she dabbed at her nose with face powder and touched up her lipstick. Earrings, evening bag and gloves, she muttered to herself, and took a deep breath, and went downstairs.

Later she had no recollection whatsoever of what she had eaten for the first course. Soup or something, she assumed, but simply couldn't remember. She was halfway through the main course when the man to her right turned to her, and said, 'Well, have you got your breath back yet?'

She smiled at him. 'I think so.'

'I'm Nicholas Thirkettle. How do you do?'

She introduced herself. 'Romy *Cole*,' he said ruminatively. 'Do you know what your surname means? Coal black and swarthy. Rather inappropriate in your case. Mine, on the other hand, means Thor's cauldron.'

'How extraordinary,' she said politely.

'Isn't it?' He was fiftyish, and had a round, shiny face and a high, domed forehead from which his brown hair had retreated. His small, inquisitive eyes settled on her as he said, 'I always think that it should bestow on one a special fate, sharing a name with the gods, but I can't say that it has so far.'

She smiled. 'What do you do?'

'I have a stall at Bermondsey Market. I sell antiques and books.'

The man to Romy's other side made a snorting noise. 'Sell books! You keep all the best ones for yourself, Nick.'

'Let me introduce you to Neville Murray, Miss Cole. We shared a flat many years ago. Wouldn't do, of course

– Nev and Nick – sounded like some frightful turn at the London Palladium. Spinning plates or something.'

'I did that once,' said Neville gloomily. 'After RADA. Could never catch the bloody things.'

Neville was rather handsome, with slightly greying wavy hair and a Roman nose. Nicholas said, 'Neville's an actor. You may have seen him on the television. He was in *Emergency Ward 10.*'

'I broke my leg in a car crash,' explained Neville, 'and then died, rather tragically, of complications.'

'Goodness,' said Romy.

'Do you watch *Emergency Ward 10?*'

'I'm afraid not. But my mother loves it.'

'Miss Cole owns a hotel,' said Nicholas. 'Patrick told me,' he explained. 'I always like to come to these affairs armed with as much information as possible. One feels more able to cope.'

Romy glanced along the table to where Patrick was sitting between his mother and the dark-haired girl, Christine.

'It's your first visit to Whitewaters, isn't it?' said Neville. 'What do you think?'

'It's rather . . . rather *unusual.*'

'I loathe this house. It's so *exposed.* Rooms like bloody cathedrals and there's nowhere to go and hide. And one needs somewhere to hide, doesn't one? It always makes me think,' went on Neville, dabbing at his mouth with a napkin, 'of some frightful cavernous modern stage. Of course, that's the way Bunny likes it. Her own little performance, specially put on for her entertainment.' He glanced at Romy. 'So you're Patrick's latest, are you?'

'Neville, you are being terribly rude,' murmured Nicholas.

'Your immediate predecessors, Miss Cole,' said Neville, undeterred, 'were a nurse and an air hostess.' He gave a malicious smile. 'You should have heard Bunny on the subject of the air hostess. Glorified waitresses, she called them. A fleeting and ultimately doomed attempt to flee the maternal apron strings, *I* called it.'

'Neville, do shut up,' said Nicholas equably. 'You are annoying Miss Cole. He's had rather a lot to drink, I'm afraid,' he added, turning to Romy, 'he becomes loquacious. Do you know everyone here?'

'Only Patrick,' she said.

He told her the names of the guests and drew little thumbnail sketches for her. 'That's Leon Bradbury, he's a photographer, tells everyone he comes from Peckham and was in the merchant navy, but I think I remember him from Winchester. And that's Barbara Tully, terribly nice girl, helps me out some Saturdays, but she married an absolute swine, and they are Roman Catholics so she's stuck, poor thing. And Peter McNeish, beside her, was a friend of Patrick's father. Decent sort of chap, but so *dull*. And Marian – white dress with sequins—'

'Looks rather bridal,' said Neville, with a snigger. 'Never quite gives up hope, poor old Marian.'

'Marian used to date Patrick,' explained Nicholas. 'Years ago. Everyone began to think they might get engaged. Bunny approved.'

'The right sort,' muttered Neville. 'Well-bred, simple and utterly malleable.'

'As for Christine—'

'I wouldn't say Christine was *malleable*. More supine.'

'She used to be a model for Worth. Pretty girl. Was terribly broken up when Patrick finished with her.'

'Wouldn't fit into many of Worth's dresses any more.' Neville eyed Christine's ample figure and patted his stomach.

Romy said, 'Are there any women here who aren't old flames of Patrick's?'

'Hush.' Nicholas patted her hand soothingly. 'Patrick is madly in love with you, Miss Cole. A ridiculous expression comes in his eyes when he speaks about you.' He went on with a sudden swift apparent change of subject, 'Have you spoken to Bunny?'

'Just now – when I was late—' She felt herself redden. 'Not a good start, I'm afraid.'

'Oh, I wouldn't feel too bad. These things happen.'

'I really didn't mean to inconvenience everyone.'

Nicholas Thirkettle's eyes gleamed. 'Miss Cole, I suspect you did exactly what you were meant to do.' She stared at him, confused, but then the housekeeper appeared to take away the plates, and Neville began to tell them about the radio play he was starring in.

It was midnight before Romy managed to speak properly to Patrick. After dinner Marian plonked herself resolutely on the sofa beside Patrick, and Bunny sat to his other side. Then a short, ginger-headed man played the piano, something long and rather discordant. Nicholas Thirkettle made comments sotto voce throughout.

And then, after a little polite applause, Bunny put her hands to her forehead and excused herself and went upstairs. Patrick followed her.

There was some desultory conversation among the remaining guests, and someone suggested cards and someone else charades, but soon, amid a flurry of yawns and goodnights, they went upstairs to their rooms.

Romy was unpinning her hair when there was a knock at her door. She opened it. Patrick said, 'Sorry. Bit of an evening.'

'And *I'm* sorry. About earlier.'

He had taken off his bow tie and undone the top button of his shirt. 'Bunny's rather a stickler about mealtimes, that sort of thing,' he said. 'I know it must seem rather old-fashioned to you, but—'

'No, it was my fault. I was looking for you.'

His eyebrows rose. 'On the beach?'

'I couldn't find you in the house.'

'I was with my mother. I told you.'

She almost said: *For an hour?* but managed to stop herself. 'Anyway, as I said, I'm sorry. I'm afraid your mother was quite annoyed.'

He said rather huffily, 'I thought she was terribly gracious.' He went to the window and stared out.

'Patrick—' She sat down on the bed. 'Don't let's quarrel. This is such a wonderful place. Such a lovely change for me. I've hardly ever been to the sea.'

He turned to her. 'You're joking.'

'It's true. About half a dozen times, I suppose.'

She had totted them up. A couple of day trips to Bournemouth as a schoolgirl and the party with Tom at Thorpeness, not far from here. She had managed a few days on the south coast with Danny in the last two summers: no more, because of the hotel.

Patrick sat down beside her. 'Where did your people take their holidays, then? Scotland?'

She had a sudden incongruous mental picture of Dennis, Martha, herself, Jem, Carol and the boys trooping off to some turreted Scottish hotel and had to suppress a smile. She said lightly, 'No. We went ... oh, here and there. What about you, Patrick?'

'We spent summers down here, of course.' He was running his fingertip along the curve of her cheekbone; at the fold of neck and shoulder he paused and bent to kiss her shoulderblade. 'Before the war, we went to Switzerland every winter. My father loved to ski. Do you ski, Romy?'

Tobogganing down a hill on a tea tray was about the limit of her winter sports, she thought, and shook her head. She returned his kiss. 'One day, when I'm rich,' she said dreamily, 'I shall buy myself a house by the sea.'

His lips brushed against her throat, her breast. She threaded her fingers through his short, fair hair, which smelt of salt and the sea. She whispered, 'Undo my zip, would you, Patrick?'

He pulled down the zip. 'Such lovely soft skin,' he murmured. 'That was the first thing I noticed about you, Romy. Your skin. I just wanted to touch you ...' He moved the narrow straps of her dress over her shoulders, and ran his palms over her breasts. In the pit of her stomach, she felt desire uncoil and flower. So long, she thought, since she had shared a bed with a man. Far too long.

Suddenly he sat up. 'Oh, *damn*!'

'What is it?'

'I promised I'd get my mother some Seconal.' He sounded irritable. 'She's run out and she won't be able to sleep a wink without it.' He was flushed. 'I'm so sorry, Romy.'

When she was alone, she stripped off her clothes and curled up in bed, half-expecting him to return. Yet he did not, and after three-quarters of an hour had passed she pulled on her nightdress and put out the light. It was a while before she slept, though. She couldn't quite put her finger on what was troubling her, but she was aware of a sudden discomfort at the unfamiliarity of the house and the solitariness of the landscape. And the wide, cold, empty bed, which she had believed herself used to.

He brought her breakfast in bed the next morning. Tapped on her door and placed a tray on the bedside table. Then he drew back the curtains and Romy saw that the weather had changed overnight. The skies were grey and heavy, the rain battering against the window-panes.

Sitting beside her in bed, Patrick fed her pieces of toast and honey. There was a single red rose on the tray. 'A rose in January!' Romy said admiringly. His mother always had roses in the house, Patrick explained, whatever the season. They were her favourite flower.

After she had bathed and dressed, Patrick showed her round Whitewaters. Somewhere there were twenty other guests, yet they did not come across any of them.

They must still be in bed, Romy supposed, or they had all assembled in some huge, angular room she had not yet discovered.

A door at the gable end of the house led into a conservatory. A high glass roof framed the sky and glossy leaved plants in terracotta pots threaded up the wall. There was the warm, sourish smell of damp earth and lush vegetation.

'Bunny calls this her jungle,' said Patrick. He put his hands round Romy's waist. 'About last night ... I seem to remember that we were in the middle of something.' He began to kiss her.

Then the door opened and Patrick sprang away. Bunny said, 'Patrick! Darling. I've been looking for you *everywhere*.'

'Just showing Romy the house—'

'You've been hogging her. So naughty of you, Patrick, when you know how I've been longing to talk to her.' Bunny's smile settled on Romy. Bunny was wearing a cream wool two-piece. Her hair was scooped back from her forehead and pinned at the back of her head. Arpege blotted out the earthy scent of the plants.

'Now run along, Patrick darling.' Bunny kissed her scarlet-enamelled fingertips and then pressed them against Patrick's cheek. 'I want to have Romy all to myself.'

Patrick left the room. Bunny said, 'I'm so sorry we didn't get the chance to talk to each other yesterday, Romy. It's always such a rush when there are so many people in the house and I felt so wretchedly ill.'

'I hope you're better now, Mrs Napier.'

'Bunny. Everyone calls me Bunny. Mrs Napier

sounds so *forbidding*. And I'm perfectly well, thank you. Patrick is such a marvellous doctor. I always say to him that he has a healing touch. Now has Patrick showed you my wonderful house?'

'Well—'

'He loves this house as much as I do.'

'It's very beautiful,' said Romy politely.

'Isn't it? Let me show you round.' Bunny put her hand through Romy's arm as they left the conservatory for one of the adjacent rooms. 'Everything in White-waters is so important to me. I don't think my late husband ever quite understood that. To him a vase was a vase and a chair was a chair. But for me it's essential to have the right vase and the right chair. It grates if things aren't just so. I feel an almost *physical* pain. Are you the same, Romy? Do you like to have things just so?'

'Well, I—'

'Patrick takes after me. He likes everything to be just right, nothing out of place. That vase for instance – ' Bunny indicated a green glass vase on a side table – 'we found it in a gallery in London. We were browsing, not even looking, but we both saw it at once and simply knew that we had to have it.' Bunny gave a little laugh. 'I think that we both said "Whitewaters" at exactly the same time! Isn't that extraordinary?'

Two large black-and-white spaniels had come into the room; one nuzzled at Bunny's free hand. Bunny said sharply, 'No, not now, Clara,' and the dog whined. 'My late husband's dogs,' she explained. 'Jonathan used to take them out for long walks every morning.' Another laugh. 'Sometimes I used to say to him that he spent more time with the dogs than with me! But I really can't be expected to trudge miles along a beach.' She sounded irritated.

'It must be very difficult . . .'

'Jonathan and I were married for thirty-seven years. It is rather a *shock* to find oneself on one's own after so long. I know that some women seem to do very well by themselves these days, but I have never been that sort of woman. I'm afraid that I am only really content when I'm making others happy. Can you understand that, Romy? And I've always been a *man's* woman. Not that I don't enjoy female company – ' a squeeze of Romy's arm – 'but men seem to enjoy being with me. And I've always preferred men. I find them more straight-forward, more *honest*. Some of our sex can be rather devious, rather manipulative, don't you find? Do you know, if I had to pick out a quality that is most important to me, I believe that it would be honesty.'

In the next room the dogs, who had followed them, began to root through the log basket. Bunny said, 'You mustn't think that I disapprove of independence in women, Romy. Patrick told me about your hotel. You must be terribly clever.'

'Not really, I—'

'Is it a family business?'

Romy explained. 'It was owned by a lady called Mrs Plummer, who left it to me.'

'Rather a burden for a young woman like you.'

'I don't think of it like that.'

'Don't you? How industrious you must be.' The spaniel nuzzled at Bunny, who gave her a little shove. 'Run along, Clara, *please*. Patrick is terribly devoted to his work, of course. Such a demanding profession, medicine.' The grey-green eyes flickered. 'Between you and me, I don't doubt that my husband's work contributed to his untimely death. I wouldn't say that to Patrick, of course. Even now he can hardly bear to talk about it.'

'Was your husband a doctor, Bunny?'

'Jonathan was in banking. But the two professions have a great deal in common, don't you think? They are both such a great responsibility.' Bunny smiled, a wide, tight smile that showed her teeth but did not touch her eyes. 'I always say that my marriage and my child were my career. And with one's child, one's work is never quite finished, is it? Children never stop needing you, do they?'

There was a silence. Bunny's fingertips, still gripping Romy's arm, seemed to increase in pressure. Bunny murmured, 'I believe you have some experience in such matters.'

'Patrick told you about Danny?' Romy could not keep the disbelief from her voice.

'You don't mind, do you?'

She couldn't speak. She managed to shake her head. Though she did mind, rather a lot.

'Patrick tells me *everything*. We are very close.'

'Danny is my nephew,' said Romy shortly. 'He's staying with me until my brother is able to look after him.'

'I do admire you modern girls. You seem to manage to do so much. Of course, when Patrick marries he'll need a good, old-fashioned stay-at-home wife. Someone who'll look after him. Someone who'll *cherish* him.'

The spaniel gave another whine and looked up at

Bunny with pleading eyes. '*No*, Clara,' said Bunny sharply and gave the dog a smart smack on the rear.

Driving back to London, they quarrelled. 'I had no idea,' Patrick said angrily, 'that it was a secret.'

'It's not a secret.' Yet there was the old fear, that she would find herself judged, condemned, excluded. That she would be dragged back down to the gutter.

She had pulled off her leather gloves and was twisting the fingers into knots. 'It's just private.'

He changed gear rather noisily. The Jaguar snaked through the narrow country lanes. She knew that she should let it go, but she didn't seem to be able to. 'Danny is a part of my family,' she said tightly. 'I don't see that my family is anyone else's business.'

'Bunny is hardly anyone.'

'I meant – ' and she could feel rage boiling up inside her, rage that she had been unable, in the aftermath of her interview with Bunny Napier, to quell – 'you should have asked me, Patrick. You shouldn't have just *assumed*—'

'I can't think why you are making such a fuss,' he said shortly. 'There's nothing to be ashamed of in bringing up your nephew. There's no reason why Bunny should disapprove.'

She muttered something under her breath and folded her arms and stared out the window at the fast slipstream of high verges and leafless hedgerows.

Patrick glanced at her sharply. '*What?*'

'Of course she disapproves of me.'

'Nonsense—'

'She does. She made it very plain.'

'That's utter nonsense—'

'Patrick, the *road*.'

He tugged at the steering wheel, pulling the car in towards the verge as a van rattled past with a blare of its horn. 'Bunny told me how much she liked you,' he said. 'How pretty she thought you were – how much she enjoyed talking to you—'

'Really? Yet she made sure to keep me well away from you almost the entire weekend, didn't she, Patrick?'

'That's ridiculous.' He shot her a furious glance. 'You got off to a bad start, that's all, turning up late for dinner. Just because you felt foolish, there's no need to interpret that as Bunny finding fault with you.'

She said obstinately, 'I still don't see why you had to tell her about Danny.'

'Don't you? I suppose that just about sums it up.'

'What do you mean?'

'Danny's important to you, isn't he?'

'Of course he is.'

'Has it crossed your mind that what's important to you might also be important to me? No? I thought not.' Patrick braked sharply for a crossroads. Then he said, 'You like to dole yourself out in little portions, don't you, Romy? A piece here, a snippet there. Never too much. Sometimes I wonder whether I know you any better than on the day we first met.'

'I don't know how you can say that!' She struggled to contain her hurt and anger.

'Why do you think I asked you to Whitewaters? Why do you think I keep coming back to you, even though much of the time you can't seem to find a spare half-hour for me?'

Her temper snapped. 'Well,' she said coldly, 'I always assumed it was because you wanted to go to bed with me.'

She saw him whiten. Then he jabbed his foot hard on the accelerator and they drove for the remainder of the journey in silence and at heart-stopping speed.

At the hotel Patrick unloaded her luggage from the car and made a cold, formal farewell. Romy went upstairs to her flat. The memory of her quarrel with Patrick lingered throughout the afternoon. She knew that she had been too touchy, too quick to take offence. She should pick up the phone, she thought, call Patrick's number, apologize and explain.

Yet if she called Patrick, then what would she say? Would she explain to him why Jem hadn't the self-belief to bring up his own child? Would she then go on to explain to him why she herself had left home? Would she say: *My stepfather tried to rape me and my father shot himself*?

She should give Patrick the benefit of the doubt, she told herself; she should trust him. If she explained to Patrick Jem's background, and how hard he was trying to better himself, then he might offer comfort and support.

Or he might turn away from her, his shock and disgust written on his face. Romy stilled, the telephone receiver in her hand. Patrick might see beneath her jewels and fine clothes the old Romy that she still struggled to hide. Phrases from their quarrel echoed. *I always assumed it was because you wanted to go to bed with me ... Sometimes I wonder whether I know you any better than on the day we first met.* And he had been right. Of course she held a part of herself back. And of course she had been unable to explain to Patrick exactly why she had so disliked him talking to Bunny about Danny.

She had lost her temper because she had felt rattled and threatened. The Romy Cole whom Patrick knew was a beautiful, sophisticated, successful young woman. Yet still, somewhere, a young girl cowered in bed, frightened by her stepfather's raised voice. Still, somewhere, a child hid in a cupboard, covering her ears to shut out the report of a shotgun.

She had hated the picture that Patrick had painted of her, of a cold, unfeeling person who compartmentalized her life, whose relationships were characterized by calculation and a lack of spontaneity. She had hated it, she thought with a shiver, because she had seen a grain of truth in it. Secrets isolated you: she had known that for a long time. How many people did she allow to come close to her? Danny, of course, and Jem. But no one else. To her mother she put on a cheerful, confident face; and though she and Carol now rattled along, they had never been close. Busy with the hotel, she saw little of her old friends. She hadn't seen Jake since New Year; though she had sent Psyche flowers to congratulate her on the birth of her daughter, she had not yet visited her.

She found herself remembering New Year and Caleb. The slight thawing of the winter that existed between them. *Happy New Year, Romy*, he had called out to her. And he had smiled.

She sat down at her desk and began to go through

her paperwork. She knew, though, that she had been right about one thing. It wasn't her social unease that had caused her to misinterpret the hard green of Bunny Napier's eyes and the bite of her red, taloned fingernails. Bunny had been warning her off. Of that she had no doubt.

In the New Year James and Elizabeth Harborne had commissioned Caleb to design them a garden. Caleb had telephoned Diana Coulthard to thank her for putting him in touch with the Harbornes, and Diana had suggested a drink to celebrate. Inevitably Caleb had found himself once more in Diana's wide double bed, half of his mind occupied with Diana's broad back and white marble thighs, the other half already mapping out in his imagination paths and terraces and borders.

He worked on the design for the Harbornes' garden during the day and in the evenings began the task of gutting the kitchen in his flat. Really, he thought, as he surveyed the wreckage, it was a good thing that he had an optimistic nature. Plaster dust veiled the rooms, and the gaping apertures around the windows and door frames let in icy air. A carefully placed Oxo tin caught the drips from a cracked joint in a pipe. Ramshackle cupboards hid mouldy wallpaper, which in turn disguised rotting plaster and God knows what horrors beneath. The floor was made up of carelessly applied layers of bitumen, cement, lino and carpet. Hacking it up was like digging through archaeological strata: if you went too far with the pickaxe you might discover Troy.

Alison invited him to lunch one Sunday. 'You can't

cook in here,' she said, peering around the disaster area that was his kitchen. 'You'd catch something dreadful. Weil's disease, or something.'

When he went up to her flat, she was checking the contents of a saucepan, taking care to keep her long red-brown hair out of the gas flame. 'It's almost ready,' she said. 'Could you lay the table, do you think, Caleb?'

Alison's flat was decorated with her pupils' paintings, blobs that might have represented faces or fish or flowers. There was a sofa covered by a brightly coloured blanket and patchwork cushions, and there were scissors, crayons and a sheaf of sugar paper on the table.

'Just dump all that somewhere,' she called out. 'They're for school tomorrow. We're making Chinese lanterns.'

They ate shepherd's pie and drank the cider that Caleb had brought. Alison told him about her family in Lincolnshire: her father, who was an Anglican vicar, her mother and her younger brothers and sisters. Caleb imagined them, tranquil and unargumentative, all large and freckled and red-haired, like Alison.

'Why did you come to London?' he asked her.

For a moment she looked bewildered, as if she could not quite remember. 'I suppose I wanted an adventure.'

'Have you found one?'

'I think so. If I'd stayed at home, I don't think I'd have been able to teach. I was doing the parish's secretarial work and helping my mother with my brothers and sisters. My youngest sister's only five, you see. I could see it going on like that, never being able to make the break. And then someone would have asked me to marry them and that would have been that.'

'Would that be so terrible? Marriage, I mean?'

She looked up. 'It would depend who the someone was, wouldn't it?'

He topped up their glasses. 'You almost make it sound as though people get married by accident.'

'Well, they do, don't they?' She put down her knife and fork. He had noticed that all her gestures were calm and quiet, that she never rushed or fussed. She said, 'My grandfather died when my mother was twenty. My mother didn't know what to do with herself – she hadn't been trained for anything. And then she met my father at a church social and six months later they were married. I don't mean,' she said quickly, 'that my mother doesn't love my dad, just that I don't think there was much choice involved. It all sounded rather ... inevitable. I'd rather remain a spinster than end up marrying someone just because I couldn't think of an alternative. I don't believe in settling for second best, do you? At least I've chosen teaching.'

When they had finished, Alison cleared the plates into the sink. She was washing up, her back to Caleb, when she said hesitantly, 'The head of my school has invited all the teachers to a cheese and wine party at her house. She holds one every year. I'm supposed to bring someone. If you hadn't anything better to do ...'

'Course.' He picked up a tea towel.

'It'll probably be terribly grim. Mrs Metcalf's a bit of a stickler.'

'Then I'll think of it as repayment for the shepherd's pie.'

When he went back down to his flat, the telephone was ringing. Answering it, he heard, to his immense surprise, Romy asking him to call at the Trelawney some time the following week. After he put down the receiver, he went back into the kitchen. Sweeping up fragments of plaster, he remembered Romy at Jake's New Year party. In her close-fitting black top and that peculiar hairy jacket and her hair down round her shoulders, she had seemed much more like the old Romy.

And she had shaken his earlier assumption that life had been easy for her since they had split up, everything going her way. As well as running the hotel, she had taken responsibility for her brother's child. And yet she had passed it off so casually. *Danny's no trouble*, she had told him. Well, he didn't believe that for a moment. He might not have much experience of children, but he knew enough to realize that they were a great deal of worry and responsibility.

Two days later he went to the Trelawney. Romy was in her office at the back of the hotel, looking efficient and businesslike in a grey dress and pearls and her hair pinned up on the back of her head. 'I've been thinking,' she said, 'that I should do something about the hotel garden.'

Caleb glanced out of the French windows. There was a small terrace immediately beyond the window and beyond that a clutter of coal bunkers and outhouses, and scrubby grass and cracked, ugly slabs of cement.

He said, 'There's certainly room for improvement.'

'I want to start up another restaurant, you see. Well, a brasserie. Somewhere for people to eat where they don't have to have starched napkins and waiters hovering over them. Somewhere without any fuss. Rather like

511

the little cafes in Soho, I thought, but more comfortable and spacious.' She came to stand beside him at the window. 'I was thinking of knocking these two rooms together. If I move my office upstairs, this could make quite a good-sized room. But no one's going to want to eat in here if they have to look out at *that*. So *grim*.'

'I've seen grimmer.'

'Really?'

'Much grimmer.' He ran his gaze over the expanse of rough lawn and concrete. 'If you didn't mind losing some of those outbuildings, there'd be quite a lot of space. I could do something with it.'

'Could you, Caleb?'

'Can I have a look round?'

'Of course.'

He went outside. He did what he always did at the beginning of a project, and paced around the perimeter of the garden, getting a feel for it. 'You could pave a fair bit of this,' he called back to Romy. 'Then you could put tables out here in the summer. And you could have vines on a pergola to disguise that ugly wall at the back. It's south facing so it should be a suntrap. And clematis, of course. And box and small conifers for winter colour.'

As he came back into the office, he said, 'How did you get my number?'

'Jake gave it to me.' She was fiddling with one of the buttons on her jacket, had been twisting and turning it, he'd noticed, throughout their entire interview. Then she said, 'I needed a garden and you're the only garden designer I know, Caleb. That's all.'

There was a challenge in her eyes. He guessed that she was half-expecting him to make some excuse, to tell her that he was too busy, that he hadn't the time. And there was the temptation to do just that, to take that small revenge, to give that satisfying little twist of the knife.

But it would have seemed dishonest: a shallow, small-minded victory. Looking at her, all got up in her smart clothes and her jewels, but with the working of her fingers betraying her nervousness, he found that he hadn't the heart.

And, besides, he needed the money. So he said, 'I'll come back tomorrow to take some measurements. Then I'll draw up a design and send you an estimate.' In the doorway he paused. 'I warn you, Romy, I don't come cheap.'

She said demurely, 'I never thought for a moment that you did, Caleb.'

The conservatory at Whitewaters had given her the idea, reminding Romy of the eating places that were springing up in the more stylish parts of London, places where you could have a light lunch without the elaborate ritual of a formal restaurant.

From her new offices on the first floor of the hotel, Romy could see the basement area. As the weeks passed, she watched the slow unfolding of her garden: the clearing of the site, the marking out of path and terrace, the shaping and digging and rebuilding. Once a week or so she would pick her way out through the mud in her high heels at the end of the day, when Caleb and Reggie, the lad who worked for him, were packing up. At first she was brief and to the point, checking on the progress of the garden, discussing any problems that might have arisen. Time passed, though, and, almost without her noticing it, their conversations seemed to digress, to expand, as if of their own volition.

She fell into the habit of offering Caleb and Reggie a beer on a Friday afternoon, before they went home at the end of the day. Reggie would stand in a corner looking embarrassed, his mouth always slightly open because of his adenoids. Romy and Caleb would talk – about the tardiness of the builders, perhaps, or about troublesome guests at the hotel. She would find herself letting off steam to him, confiding in him. There were things she could say to him that she could not say to anyone else. Not important things, not intimate things: she knew they would never be close enough again for *that*. Just small things, things that were too trivial to bother other people with. She could admit her mistakes to him and her fears. She didn't have to put on a front to Caleb, as she did to everyone else in the hotel. She didn't have to pretend to him. He knew her, knew the best and the worst of her.

Sometimes, taking her leave, she was surprised to find that an hour had passed. 'I've had an awful day,' she said one raw February evening when they were standing on the terrace, looking out at the sea of mud that was to be the Trelawney's garden. 'One of the guests got a couple of tarts in last night. The chamber-maid went in to clean the room – he'd forgotten to put the "Do Not Disturb" sign up, I suppose – and she found him in bed with two girls.'

The corners of Caleb's mouth twitched. Reggie went scarlet. 'They were both wearing babydoll nightdresses,'

Romy said, exasperated. 'Black nylon babydoll night-dresses! Well, *honestly*!'

'Good Lord.' Caleb flipped the top off a beer bottle. 'What did you do?'

'I had a quiet word with the guest. I think he was even more embarrassed than me. But I can't have that sort of thing going on. It's so bad for the hotel's reputation.'

'Well, yes. A bit racy for the dear old Trelawney.'

'And that's another thing.'

'What?'

'The whole place needs updating. And I'm going to be hard put to pay for it.' She saw the disbelief in his eyes. 'What are you thinking, Caleb?' she asked smoothly. 'That I look affluent? As though I've never had it so good?'

'Something like that.' His dark eyes settled on her and he said, 'Johnnie Fitzgerald must have been rather . . . rather peeved that you got the hotel.'

'Incandescent, actually.'

'Is he around?'

She shook her head. 'He went to America with Mrs O'Neill. He sold the Marrakesh before he left. Good riddance to him, I say. And you're right, of course, I still can't believe my luck. But the hotel needs so much doing to it – the central heating and the hot water are temperamental, to put it mildly, and a lot of the bedrooms don't have bathrooms. And there's mice and mildew in the kitchens, and all the rooms need redecorating. The other day someone described the Trelawney as having faded glamour. *Faded glamour!*' she repeated indignantly. 'They meant out-dated and old-fashioned, didn't they? And the worst thing is that they're right. Our regulars – our old ladies who come up for the Chelsea Flower Show and our old gentlemen who come to London to talk to their stockbrokers – are dropping like flies. It's almost the Sixties, and I'm not sure the Trelawney's even made it into the Fifties yet. That's why I thought of the brasserie, of course. It'll make us seem more up to date.'

She began to find herself looking foward to Friday afternoons. Because it was the end of the week, she told herself. Because, no matter how busy the coming week-end, there was still that glorious sense of holiday.

One wet Friday she asked Caleb about his gardening business. 'Oh, I do patios and roses mostly,' he said dismissively. 'They're my bread and butter.' Seeing her bewilderment, he explained, 'Everyone who's been on holiday to Spain wants a patio. You know the sort of thing – a small terrace and pelargoniums in pots. And very bright floribunda roses. Harry Wheatcroft roses preferably. They've kept me going. I wouldn't have survived without them.'

They were standing in the shelter of the half-converted rooms. Outside, rain peeled from the slates and gutters. She said, 'It sounds rather ... rather *routine*.'

He shrugged. 'It's OK.'

'I remember you telling me—' She broke off. She was breaking a rule, she thought, an unspoken but closely adhered-to rule: not to mention their past.

But he said, 'Go on. What were you going to say?'

The rain was getting up, battering against the windows. She took a deep breath. 'I remember you telling

me about the garden you were going to make one day.
It would be magical, you said. Entrancing.'

He tipped the dregs of his beer onto the mud, and
said bleakly, 'Well, I always had my head in the clouds
then, didn't I? Always wanted what I couldn't have.'
He took his car keys out of his pocket. 'I'd better go.
Thanks for the drink, Romy.'

When they had gone, she collected the glasses and
empty bottles and went back into the hotel. *Never have
known when to keep quiet, have you, Romy Cole?* she
thought, furious with herself. *Never have known when to
keep your mouth shut.*

Chapter Sixteen

Romy was in the hotel kitchen one morning, checking over the menus with Anton, when Carol came to see her. Sarah, the nanny, was away staying with her sister, who had just had a baby. In Sarah's absence, Carol was helping Romy look after Danny. 'I don't know what's up with him,' said Carol anxiously. She was carrying Danny, who was crying. 'He's not himself at all.'

Romy took Danny from her, joggling him on her hip as she finished talking to Anton. Danny seemed to quieten, burrowing his face into her shoulder and sucking his thumb. She put her hand against his forehead; he felt rather hot.

She put him to bed early that night, but he woke at midnight and would not go back to sleep. Taking him into her own bed, she cradled him against her until he dozed off. He woke frequently, hot and miserable and restless, tears oozing from the corners of his eyes. At four in the morning she took his temperature and found that it was over a hundred. When she sponged him down, she discovered a scattering of small red spots across his plump belly.

In the morning she took him to the doctor. 'Chickenpox,' the doctor said and recommended calamine lotion and plenty of fluids.

Spots blossomed over Danny's entire body. He had spots in his ears, spots on his eyelids, spots on the inside of his mouth. He couldn't eat, couldn't sleep. Romy painted him with calamine lotion and coaxed him to drink diluted rose-hip syrup. His wails echoed through the hotel. The following day his temperature shot up to a hundred and two. She wondered whether to phone Jem, whether she should tell him to catch the next train to London.

She thumbed frantically through her copy of Dr Spock, terrifying herself by reading about the complications that could follow chickenpox. She gave Danny tepid baths and dosed him with junior aspirin and glanced at the telephone every now and then, torn between frightening Jem unnecessarily and not phoning and Danny getting worse and ending up in hospital. She carried Danny while she made urgent phone calls or dictated letters that couldn't wait. She talked to the mother of a bride about wedding reception arrangements while Danny dozed, cocooned in blankets, on an armchair in her office.

He woke every hour or so throughout the night. Putting on her make-up in the mornings, she tried to disguise the circles around her eyes and the pallor of her cheeks. She was stupefied with fatigue, frazzled with trying to do half a dozen things at once. She lost the keys to the safe one morning, unlocked it to take something out, and then couldn't find them again and had to get Carol to come and help her search the office. Eventually they found the keys in a plant pot.

At last the spots crusted over and Danny slept uninterrupted for the first time in a week. Standing at her office window in the evening, Romy drew back the curtains to look outside. It was past eight o'clock and the garden was dark, empty, deserted. There was just the rain, and the paths and terraces growing out of the mud. She couldn't remember what day it was. When she looked at the calendar and saw that it was a Friday, she felt a cold wash of disappointment. She had imagined talking to Caleb, telling him about her awful week, telling him about Danny, how worried she had been, how tired she was.

She let the curtain fall from her hand. She wondered whether he had noticed her absence. Or whether he had been relieved to get away from work promptly. She sat down at her desk, her thumbs pressed against her aching temples. She wondered whether Caleb ever did as she did, whether he went over their conversations with a fine-tooth comb, whether he became exhausted with picking over the phrases, examining carefully every word and expression.

What was she looking for, she wondered, in those solitary moments when she mentally reran everything they had said to each other? She was trying to decide, she supposed, what he thought of her now. Whether they were just business acquaintances; whether, after the garden was finished, she would ever see him again. Or whether, in spite of all that had happened, they were friends again. She knew that he could never be anything more than a friend, knew that she had forfeited any right to Caleb Hesketh's love the day she had spoken to Evelyn Daubeny in the rose garden at Swanton Lacy. But friends . . . surely she might hope for that?

There was a tower of correspondence in her letters tray. She picked up the topmost and began to read it.

But her concentration slipped and slid. She had hardly been out of the hotel during the entire week. Her head ached and she longed to stretch her legs. Suddenly she began to search frantically through the in tray. Unable to find what she was looking for, she upended the entire tray onto her desk. And there it was, the leaflet with Caleb's address on it.

She ran upstairs, stuck her head into the nursery and had a quick word with Carol, then she grabbed her raincoat and bag and left the hotel.

Romy's comment had sown a seed that had taken root. Caleb was dividing his time between the Trelawney's garden and the Harbornes'. Neither, he thought grimly, could exactly be described as magical. Or with only just a very little magic, perhaps. Both were square, confined urban gardens; in both he battled against the problems of pollution and lack of light. Both were to serve a purpose, the Trelawney's to act as a backdrop to the brasserie, the Belgravia garden a setting for the Harbornes' gracious lifestyle. Though he had done what he could, it did not seem to him that either garden offered much in the way of entrancement.

He told himself that it was inevitable that magic should be limited. You had to cut your coat according to your cloth, you had to make the best of what you'd got. Yet something niggled and, walking home with Alison from her headmistress's cheese and wine party that evening, Caleb was aware of a dissatisfaction, a growing impatience with himself.

Huddled beneath his umbrella because of the rain, Alison was apologetic. 'Oh dear, I am sorry. It was rather awful, wasn't it?'

'It was fine,' Caleb said, rather dishonestly. 'I enjoyed myself.'

'You don't have to say that. Sweaty Cheddar and warm Liebfraumilch—'

'Nothing wrong with sweaty Cheddar and warm Liebfraumilch.'

'*Caleb.*'

'Half the time I don't really notice what I eat.'

'So the suppers I've cooked for you—'

He had supper in Alison's flat once a week or so. They just seemed to run into each other, collecting their post from the hall table or walking back from the shops.

'That's different,' he said. 'Your shepherd's pie is different. Fanny Craddock, eat your heart out.'

She said, 'Jenny Hodge told me that she thought you were very handsome.'

'Did she?' They were heading down Highbury Grove. 'Good old Jenny Hodge. Which one was she?'

'Ponytail and freckles. Pink jumper. Tells me her troubles.'

'What sort of troubles?'

'Boyfriend troubles mostly. They all do. Jenny and Nina and Karen.'

'That's because you have a sympathetic nature. Does Mrs Metcalf tell you her boyfriend troubles?'

She giggled. 'No, thank goodness.'

'She told *me* her troubles. Apparently her camellia

hasn't flowered this year. She was quite severe – I almost felt it was my fault.'

'She has a knack of doing that,' said Alison ruefully. 'Whether or not you've done anything wrong, she always manages to make you feel guilty.'

She tucked her hand around his arm as they waited at the roadside for a gap in the traffic. She said hesitantly, 'If you really enjoyed yourself tonight, Caleb . . . well, perhaps we could do something else. I don't mean another cheese and wine party, don't worry. I thought maybe the cinema or a pub or something. It's just . . . *winter* . . . It does get quite miserable, doesn't it?'

The phrases had become rather incoherent. He felt rather a heel, suddenly, for not thinking of it himself. Poor Alison, stuck up there in her little flat. Plenty of girls didn't like going out on their own. He said, 'Yes, why not?' and she flashed him a radiant smile.

They walked for a while in silence. Eventually she said, 'Penny for them.'

'Sorry,' he said. 'Something on my mind.'

'Tell me.'

'It's just something someone said to me.' The rain was bouncing off the pavement. He moved the umbrella over so that she didn't get wet.

'About anything in particular?'

'Oh—' He grimaced. 'Lost ambitions, I suppose.'

She squeezed his arm. 'Cheer up.'

'It's just that . . . you think you're doing all right . . . that you're, you know, surviving . . . and then you realize that you've completely forgotten what you meant to do in the first place. And she reminded me.'

'She . . . ?'

'The woman I'm working for at the hotel.' He glanced at Alison. 'I knew her before, you see, years ago. When I was a good deal younger and a great deal more innocent.'

'You're hardly *ancient* now,' she teased him.

'What have I done? A dozen or so uninspiring little city plots.'

'*Caleb*,' she said softly.

Recently he had found himself thinking of the Rolands' garden, with its terraces and fountain. 'I'd meant to do something ... something *wonderful*. Still, my gardens bring in the money, don't they, Alison? They pay the mortgage.' He hadn't intended to sound so bitter.

'Caleb,' she said again. 'You have to give yourself time, that's all.' They had reached the house; pausing outside, she put her arms around him and hugged him.

Romy got lost, of course, walking from Canonbury Tube Station to the street in which Caleb lived. She should have taken a taxi, she thought. Here she was, Miss Cole of the Trelawney Hotel, and she was still taking the Tube. Old habits of economy died hard.

But she found it at last, Canonbury Park Road, and set off, checking the house numbers as she walked. She was halfway along the street when she saw them standing outside the house. Caleb and a woman. They were embracing. An umbrella lay discarded on the pavement beside them. The streetlamp caught the woman's long, reddish hair, which coiled in whorls and snakes on her shoulders because of the rain. Caleb's hand, as it touched that long, wet hair, appeared greenish-white.

Romy crushed her knuckles against her mouth. How stupid she had been, she thought, how very, very stupid, to think that their conversations might have mattered as much to him as they had to her. And how doubly stupid not to have guessed that he would have found someone else long ago. She turned on her heel and walked back to the Tube station.

Back at the Trelawney, she had poured herself a drink when the telephone rang. Blurred with fatigue, she picked up the receiver.

'Romy?'

A split second before she recognized his voice. 'Patrick?'

'How are you?'

'I'm fine.' She twisted the flex of the phone around her fingers. 'And you?'

'I'm phoning from the bar across the road. I wondered whether you'd let me buy you a drink.'

Seeing Patrick again might end in another scene, another undignified tussle between the sexes. She was too tired for that, far too burnt out to cope with the long-drawn-out game of her relationship with Patrick.

'I'm not sure . . .'

'Romy, please.'

'I'm a bit of a fright, at the moment, to be honest, Patrick. I was just about to wash my hair and I'm not really dressed for—'

'I don't care what you're wearing,' he interrupted rather vehemently. 'I don't care about your *hair*. I just want to see you. There's something I need to say to you. Please come, Romy.'

He was standing at the bar, his back to her, his shoulders hunched, a glass in front of him. He turned as she came into the pub.

'Romy. How lovely to see you.' He kissed her cheek. 'What would you like?'

She asked for a Scotch and sat down at a table. He brought over the drinks.

'You look tired,' he said.

'Danny's been ill. It's been a bit fraught.'

'That's bad luck. He's better now, though?'

'On the mend.'

He frowned. 'Romy—'

'Patrick—'

'You first.'

She took a deep breath. 'I wanted to apologize for what I said to you. When we were driving back from Whitewaters.'

'It doesn't matter.'

'Oh, it does. It was unkind and untrue and I'm sorry.'

The corners of his mouth curled. 'It may not have been particularly kind, Romy, but it wasn't untrue. I do want to go to bed with you. I spend a great deal of time thinking about it, actually.'

'Oh,' she said. She shouldn't have come, she thought. Patrick still wanted what Patrick had always wanted.

He had been right about one thing, of course. She would fend him off because that was what she did, fend people off. Either that or circle round those she couldn't have, trying to decide whether she dared risk liking them again.

But he was still speaking. 'That isn't the only reason I keep bothering you, though, Romy.' He took out his cigarette case, but did not yet open it. 'I have tried to forget you. These last couple of months I've tried very hard. I saw some old friends – I even went to Switzerland for a fortnight. I thought a few mountains and a bit of ski-ing might stop me thinking about you.'

She looked up at him. 'Did they?'

'I'm afraid not.' He frowned. 'And it seems to me that there's only one cure for this particular disease.' He took her hand in his and ran the ball of his thumb across her palm. 'I came here tonight to ask you to marry me, Romy. Could you, do you think?'

She stared at him, shocked, her mind blank. Then, when she opened her mouth to speak, he put up a hand, silencing her. 'I don't want you to answer me now. I know things have been difficult between us. But I want you to think about what I've said. Will you do that, for me?'

Caleb spoke to Romy about the garden. 'I bought some nice stone urns from a house sale,' he explained. 'They weren't cheap, but they'd be perfect for the terrace. I'll bring them in next week so you can have a look at them.'

They were in the rooms that were being converted

into the brasserie. The builders had gone home for the day, leaving the hollow shell they had knocked through and the wet-dog smell of damp plaster.

'I'm sure they'll be fine,' she said.

There was a silence. She looked, he thought, rather distracted. He said, 'Do you want to see how the garden's getting on? I'll show you round, if you like.'

'I don't think that'll be necessary, thank you, Caleb.'

Her voice was clipped and efficient. If there had still been a desk in the room, then she would have been sitting behind it. He had thought that in the past few weeks the distance between them had lessened. Now, talking to her, he began to wonder whether he had been mistaken.

All the while, she was tapping a pen impatiently against the palm of her hand. 'The builders have told me they should be finished in about six weeks,' she said suddenly. 'Can you estimate a completion date for the garden? I'd like to think about opening the brasserie in July.'

'Most of the work should be done by the end of May ... mid-June at the latest. Obviously a bout of bad weather could hold us up, but not too much, I hope.'

'I just need a definite date, Caleb.'

She might have been talking to one of her staff, or to a tradesman. Which he was, in a way, he supposed.

There was a knock at the door and a young woman looked in. 'Dr Napier's on the phone for you, Romy.'

Romy flushed. 'Tell him I'll phone back later.'

When they were alone again, Caleb tried to explain. 'I meant if there was a late frost, for instance. But that's not all that likely in London. And plants take time to grow. I can fill in the gaps with pots to begin with, but—'

'I don't need a lecture on gardening.' The pen was still tapping impatiently. 'I just need you to do your job.'

He had to bite back an angry retort. He said, 'I missed you on Friday,' and her head jerked up.

'I was busy.' The pen was still tapping. 'If that's all, Caleb . . .'

He was at the door when he remembered. The Harbornes' party. And Patrick Napier: smooth, yellow-haired, expensive-looking.

'Dr Napier—' he said slowly.

'He's a friend of mine.' She glared at him. 'Not that it's any of your business.'

'Romy—'

'More than a friend, actually.' Her chin jutted out. 'Patrick has asked me to marry him.'

It was as though she had slapped him. He said without thinking, 'Marry him? You won't, will you?'

'I might do.' She sounded defensive. 'Why shouldn't I?'

'Because he's not right for you.'

Her brows lifted. 'And you know what's right for me, do you, Caleb?'

He said, 'You don't love him,' and she seemed to falter.

'I *like* Patrick.'

'That's not the same.'

She shrugged. 'Maybe not. But maybe it doesn't matter. Maybe liking's good enough. Maybe it's better. Maybe love's not all it's cracked up to be.'

'Maybe you haven't given it enough of a chance.'

'Well,' she said sharply, 'I suppose you're the expert on *that*.'

'What's that supposed to mean?'

'Only –' the pen slipped out of her hands to the floor; she gave an impatient hiss – 'only that you've more experience in these matters.'

He said heatedly, 'I can't see what my ... my *experience*, as you call it, has got to do with you marrying Patrick Napier.'

'Can't you?' She moved away from him. As if, he thought, she could not bear to be near him. 'But then it's different for men, isn't it? That's what Mrs Plummer always said. One rule for men and another for women.'

He didn't know what the hell she was talking about. But he heard her add, as if it settled things, 'Patrick's kind and generous and intelligent and interesting. I'll marry him if I want to marry him.'

Pots of money, Diana Coulthard had said, describing Patrick Napier. And to Romy money mattered. Caleb said slowly, 'I don't doubt Patrick Napier's all those things. Intelligent and interesting ... whatever you say. And he's rich, too, isn't he?'

'I don't see what that's got to do with it. Now, if you'll excuse me, I've work to do.'

She had reached the door when he said, 'Oh, come *on*. Surely it's got everything to do with it? Always fancied the good life, haven't you, Romy?'

'What do you mean?' Her eyes had narrowed to gold-brown slits. 'You're suggesting that I'm thinking of marrying Patrick for his money?'

'Aren't you?'

'How dare you?' Now her face was white with fury.

He seemed to see it all quite clearly. It wasn't enough that Romy Cole from the council house in Stratton should own a hotel. She had always been ambitious, she had always wanted things. Things that only someone like Patrick Napier could give her.

He said, 'Tell me I'm wrong, Romy. Tell me honestly that I'm wrong.'

She was trembling. She wrenched open the door. 'You don't deserve that,' she whispered. 'Now get out. Just get *out*.'

As Caleb entered the house, he saw that Alison was coming down the stairs. She called out a hello, and then, glancing at him, said, 'Are you all right?'

'Fine.' He fitted the key into his front door. 'Absolutely fine.'

'We can leave it for another night if you're not in the mood,' she said. 'Our drink—'

He remembered that he had promised to take her out to the pub that night. She added, 'Or I've a bottle of wine in my room, if you don't feel like going out.'

He said without thinking, 'That'd be great. I'll see you soon,' and went into his flat.

Inside, he relieved some of his anger by knocking down another large chunk of larder wall, and then he stripped off his muddy work clothes and had a bath. When he had dressed, he went upstairs to Alison's flat.

The electric lights were switched off and she had lit candles instead. She had put a record – slow jazz music – on the turntable, and she was wearing, instead of her usual skirt and sweater, a voluminous, flowing dress in a pattern of browns and gold. Her long hair was loose and she was, for the first time he could remember, wearing make-up.

She poured out the wine and came to sit beside him on the sofa. Then she told him about her day, and he in turn gave a rather edited version of his. The jazz played and the wine began to dissipate some of his anger.

It was when her fingers tentatively threaded through his own and her head fell against his shoulder that he began to see the point of the candles, the music, the dress and make-up. Alison's lips brushed against the side of his face. All he had to do was to turn towards her, to kiss her properly. It was what she wanted, after all. And there was, at first, the fleeting temptation to let events take their course, the easy option that would, for a while at least, blank out the furious mental repetition of his argument with Romy.

But this was Alison, not Diana. Nice, motherly Alison, who cooked him suppers and brought his post in. Alison the vicar's daughter. Alison, who deserved better.

He said gently, 'Alison,' and withdrew his hand.

She looked up at him. Her eyes were rather blurred. 'What?'

'I think I should go,' he said.

'Go?'

'I think so.'

'I don't want you to go.'

Disentangling himself, he stood up. 'Sorry.'

Now there was hurt in her eyes. 'Don't you like me?'

'Of course I do.'

She frowned. 'But only *like*.'

'Alison,' he said, 'I think you're one of the nicest people I've met in years.'

She looked down at herself. '*Nice*,' she repeated viciously. 'Fat old, virginal old, *nice* old Alison.' Standing up, she scrabbled in her bag for cigarettes. She lit one and went to stand at the window, her back to him.

'Alison,' he said, 'I didn't realize—'

'Didn't you? Then how *stupid* of you.' After a few moments she said more quietly, 'I'm sorry. That's not fair. But, oh Caleb, you *must* have realized.'

He couldn't think of anything to say. Couldn't think of a single thing that wouldn't be cheap or insulting.

She had tilted back her head, exhaling smoke through her nostrils. After a while, she turned back to him and said wearily, 'Perhaps you're right, Caleb. Perhaps you should go.' The expression in her eyes as she watched him leave the room seemed to follow him downstairs.

The passing years, thought Romy, had not altered Caleb Hesketh's low opinion of her one jot. She kept men at arms' length because she could not bear to feel like this, this hollowness around her heart, her world turned upside-down.

She would put him out of her mind, she resolved. Perhaps she would marry Patrick Napier. If she married Patrick, then she would have a comfortable, ordered life. She wouldn't be tired any more and she would never have to worry about money. As Patrick's wife, she would become part of a wide and glamorous social circle. She would want for nothing. She would live in a lovely house; she could holiday in the south of France and she could learn to ski. Most important of all, if she married Patrick, she wouldn't be lonely any more.

On Monday she had a visitor. Bunny Napier was elegant in a black skirt and coat. A small black feathered hat perched to one side of her head, like a wounded bird, and around her neck she wore an onyx necklace the colour of her eyes. Trying to disguise both her astonishment at Bunny's unannounced appearance, and her wariness, Romy offered Bunny lunch.

In the Trelawney's restaurant Bunny's fork remained poised over her prawn cocktail as she launched her attack. 'This liaison of yours and Patrick's . . . one can hardly call it an engagement—'

'Patrick spoke to you?'

'I told you, Miss Cole. Patrick always tells me everything.'

Romy had woken that morning with a headache and a grittiness in her eyes. Now the prawns in their glass dish looked pallid and uninviting, and her stomach churned. She said, 'Then Patrick was rather premature. He proposed to me. I haven't yet given him my answer.'

Bunny's fork stabbed at a prawn. 'I suppose I should feel a measure of relief. You won't accept him, will you?'

'It's none of your business, of course.' She had to struggle to keep her voice level. 'But if you must know, I haven't made up my mind.'

'Then let me try to help you.' Bunny put down her knife and fork and folded her hands together. She had taken off her gloves, and the red nails gleamed. 'Patrick needs a particular type of wife—'

'Yes. You said.'

'If you would please let me finish, Miss Cole. A particular type of wife. I don't think you qualify as that type of wife.'

Romy shifted prawns and lettuce around the dish, trying to make them appear less. 'Patrick may feel differently about that.'

'He may. But I shall do my best to point out certain ... *realities* to him.' Bunny dabbed her mouth with her napkin. 'There is this place, for instance.' A disdainful wave of the hand.

'The hotel?'

'Yes. If you were to marry Patrick, he would not want you to continue working here.'

'That's up to Patrick and me, surely.'

'It is a fact.' The grey-green eyes were coldly self-satisfied. 'He would not. Believe me.'

Romy signalled to the waiter to clear away the plates. Bunny said, 'And then there is your background.'

'My background?' She made sure not to betray her sudden sense of alarm.

A small smile. 'You are obviously not, shall we say, out of the top drawer, Miss Cole. Oh, you try hard, you put on a good show – were it not for your interest in my son, I would almost admire you. But you betray yourself in a great many little ways. Of course, standards have slackened so since the war. But the woman Patrick marries will need to be an asset to him. She will need to be a good hostess and she will need to know how to behave in society. She will need to be a helpmeet – an ornament to him.'

'A china doll? To be taken out of the cupboard and dusted off as required?'

'Don't be ridiculous.' Bunny's long, slim fingers pulled irritably at the onyx necklace. 'You would not be an asset to my son, Miss Cole. And I will not let you drag him down.'

'I've no intention of dragging Patrick down.' In spite of herself, she heard her voice rise.

'You promise that you will not marry him, then?'

She shook her head. 'I promise no such thing.'

Bunny's lips tightened to a thin, hard line. There was a silence as the waiter served the main course. Beneath the tablecloth, where no one could see, Romy knotted her hands together.

When they were alone again, Bunny said, 'And then, of course, there is the child.'

Romy's head jerked up. 'Danny?'

Bunny said softly, 'We all make mistakes. But there are mistakes that one can recover from, my dear, and mistakes that are, by their very nature, rather *permanent*.'

It took a moment for Romy to understand Bunny's implication. Then she felt herself flush. 'You think that Danny's mine?'

'Well, yes. Isn't he?'

It was hard to speak. She shook her head. 'Danny is my brother's son.'

A patronizing smile. 'I quite understand why you would choose to maintain such a fiction. As I understand that Patrick has accepted it. Men can be so naive, can't they? However, *I* am not so easily fooled. And I will have no compunction in telling Patrick the truth if you persist with this charade.'

It was on the tip of her tongue to say: *Tell Patrick the truth, then. I've nothing to hide.* But that was not, she thought, quite true.

Bunny rose to her feet. 'I think that we understand each other.' She put on her gloves and picked up her handbag. As she turned to go, she said, 'Oh, and the steak was overcooked, Miss Cole. You should have a word with your chef.'

Caleb was about to leave for work on Monday morning when the phone rang. The voice at the other end of the line told him that his mother had been injured and was in hospital. He asked for details, and then he drove to Reggie's house and gave him a list of tasks to get on with during his absence. Then he headed for Southampton.

The hospital ward was one of a series of prefabs, spread out like ribs from a central spine. There were a couple of dozen beds neatly lined up along the walls; Caleb caught sight of Betty's powder puff of blonde hair.

Her face was turned away; he said her name softly. She turned to him. 'Caleb.'

Dark bruises blotched her pale skin. Her left eye had swollen up to twice its normal size.

'Mum,' he whispered, shocked.

'I'm fine, really, lovie. It's not as bad as it looks.'

A couple of broken ribs and a broken collarbone, the

nurse had said, showing him into the ward, her stout black lace-up shoes slapping on the polished lino. 'Mum,' he said, 'what happened?'

'Didn't they tell you?'

'Just that you'd been hurt. An accident—'

'It wasn't an accident.' He only just caught the whispered words.

It wasn't an accident. It took a few moments for her meaning to sink in. Then he said, 'Someone did this to you deliberately?' She did not reply. 'Who, Mum?'

'It doesn't matter.'

'Of course it *matters*.' He could have closed his thumb and forefinger around her bird-boned wrist. Hitting her – hurting her – would be as easy as hurting a child. He said, 'You've told the police, haven't you?'

'No. And I'm not going to.' Her eyes had opened: the one grotesque, the other sharply blue.

'You have to, Mum.'

'*No*, I said.'

Something in her tone silenced him. He ran his hands through his hair. He felt slightly sick. He said, bewildered, 'Why not?'

'Because . . .' With difficulty, she hauled herself up on the pillows so that she could look at him properly. 'Because it wouldn't do me any good, Caleb. Because I picked him up in a pub. And because I'd had a few drinks and because I know what they would say. They'd say I was asking for it.'

He stared at her. Her voice faltered, her fleeting defiance evaporating. 'I didn't want them to phone you,' she muttered. 'I didn't want you to know.'

She had turned away again, but not before he saw

the shame in her eyes. He said slowly, 'Because you thought I'd ... disapprove? Because you thought I'd judge you?'

She looked up at the ceiling. She whispered, 'I was lonely, you see. It's been hard to make friends here. The girls at the shop are nice enough, but they're half my age, most of them. And the neighbours keep themselves to themselves.'

On the undamaged side of her face, which was without its usual covering of powder and paint, he noticed for the first time the mesh of tiny lines around her eye, and the slackness of her skin. His heart ached. He whispered, 'You should have phoned me, Mum. If you were lonely, you should have phoned me.'

'I didn't want to worry you, lovie. And anyway –' the one good eye met his gaze – 'things haven't been the same between us, have they? Not since you found out about Daubeny.' She was silent for a moment, and then she said, 'I was lonely then, too, Caleb. All those years ago. Archie was away, he'd been away for months, looking for work. And I never really fitted into the village. I was a townie, wasn't I? I didn't dress right, speak right. I was different. They used to look down on me.' Her voice lowered again. 'And Daubeny ... he was a handsome man, in his way.' She paused and said sadly, 'I was just lonely.'

He had nursed his grievances too long, he thought. There had been something self-indulgent, vindictive even, in his neglect of her. And while he had failed to forgive, both of them had failed to live well.

He took her hand in his, holding it very carefully because of her bruised knuckles. She gave a little laugh and said, 'This was my own bloody fault. Went off with the wrong bloke, didn't I? Serves me right. And so was Daubeny my fault, but I don't regret that, because it gave me you, Caleb. Archie and me – there was never a whisper of a baby for us. I sometimes thought he wondered about that – I don't know. He never said anything. But he loved you. You were the apple of his eye. And *he* was your father, lovie, not Daubeny. Archie was the one who rocked you at night to get you to sleep. He was the one who taught you your letters and to ride a bike. He was the one who looked after you when you were sick. And in my eyes that makes him your dad.'

The swing doors at the end of the ward opened. A nurse came in, pushing a trolley. Betty muttered, 'Tea's bloody weak and the cocoa's made with water. What I wouldn't do for a gin. And they've taken away my cigs.'

He said, 'When you're out of here I'll buy you a bottle of gin, Mum. And I'll make you a decent cup of tea.'

'Thank you, lovie.' Reaching up, she stroked his face.

Towards the end of the week, Patrick called. As he entered Romy's flat, his expression was expectant, confident.

Romy said, 'Your mother came to see me a few days ago.'

'Bunny?' He looked surprised.

'She listed all the reasons why I wouldn't make you a good wife.'

He kissed the back of her neck. 'Bunny's very

protective. Only chick in the nest and all that. She'll come round.'

She poured him a drink. 'Do you think so?'

'When she gets to know you properly then she'll adore you as much as I do. You're just ... *different* from some of the other girls I've dated, Romy. Bunny needs time, that's all.'

'I think she thinks I'm a bit too different.'

'Nonsense,' he said indulgently.

She swung round to face him. 'Did you know, Patrick, that your mother thinks that Danny is my child? My *illegitimate* child, I mean.' She saw his eyes widen. 'He isn't, of course. But he *is* illegitimate. Jem and Liz, Danny's mother, were never married.'

Patrick frowned. 'I hadn't realized.'

'As Danny will be living with me for the foreseeable future, I thought you should know.'

'I thought your brother—'

'Whoever marries me will be taking on Danny as well. You have to understand that, Patrick. We're a package, Danny and I. You don't get one without the other.'

'I see.' He looked down at his glass. His silence, she thought miserably, lasted just a few moments too long. Eventually he said, 'It's not that I don't like children, Romy. But I'd imagined *our* children.'

'Legitimate children?'

He shot her a glance. 'I prefer to have everything above board, yes. Is that wrong of me? It makes things easier. And I've always disliked untidiness ... squalor.'

She said angrily, 'Danny isn't squalid.'

'Of course not,' he said. 'I meant that I dislike ...

laxity. I prefer everything to be just so.' He smiled. 'It's a characteristic I've inherited from my mother, I suppose.' He took her hand. 'Don't be cross, darling. I do understand that you and I have differences. Bunny's quite right about that. But it's what I love about you. You are original ... unique. And we don't have to let our differences come between us, do we?'

She drew away from him. She said, 'And then, of course, there's the hotel.'

'The hotel?'

'What did you imagine would happen to the hotel if you and I were to marry, Patrick?'

'I assumed you'd get in some sort of a manager.'

'And if I didn't? If I wanted to continue to work here?'

'Romy.' He gave a little laugh. 'You know that wouldn't be possible.'

Her heart sank. But she said obstinately, 'Why not?'

'Because –' he spread out his hands, palms up – 'because you can't be in three places at once. Because if you continued to work here, then you wouldn't be able to run a home, and in time, I hope, care for our children. And besides...' He took out his cigarette case and offered it to her; she shook her head. 'And besides, it just wouldn't do.'

'Why not? Why wouldn't it do?'

'Well, for one thing, it would look as though I wasn't able to support you.'

She stared at him. 'Would that matter? We would know that wasn't true. Does what other people think matter?'

Patrick tapped a cigarette against the case. 'I think so, yes.'

'And if I told you I felt differently? If I told you that I didn't care?'

Another, longer, silence. He flicked his lighter and said bluntly, '*I* care.'

'What other people think is more important to you than what I feel?'

He flushed. 'I didn't say that.'

'You implied it.'

'For heaven's sake, Romy.' He looked annoyed.

'If I told you that I would marry you if we agreed that I could go on working at the hotel, what would you say, Patrick?'

'I would say that you were not being reasonable. I don't know how much money you make out of the Trelawney, but however much it is we wouldn't need it.'

Yet she saw for the first time that it wasn't about money. Money was important, yes, but the hotel had given her so much more than that. It had given her an identity and a place in the world.

Patrick was still talking. 'My job is a demanding one, as you know. And I can see how much this place takes out of you, Romy – think how often we haven't been able to be together because you were too busy. You can't expect me to be happy with that. You can't expect me to want an exhausted, preoccupied wife.'

Romy sat down on the arm of the sofa. 'So for me marriage must be my full-time occupation,' she said slowly. 'Yet it needn't be for you.' There was a heaviness about her heart. 'It's different for men and women, is it, Patrick? Is that what you're saying?'

'Well, it is, isn't it?' Then he said more gently, 'Romy, you know that I would do anything for you. But there are some things which can't be changed. Women give birth to children, after all. And they must care for them. There's a great deal of new research coming out at the moment showing the importance of the mother and child bond. I wouldn't want my children to have something –' he frowned – 'something *second-rate*. I would want them to be cared for by their mother, not by some stranger – a nanny or whatever.'

'Like Danny, you mean?'

He looked away. Her headache had come back. 'This hotel is the first thing that has truly been mine,' she said quietly. 'I had nothing before and I have had nothing since. Even Danny is only borrowed.'

'You would have me.'

'Yes.' She felt exhausted. She sat down. Suddenly she wanted him to go. 'I'm sorry, Patrick.'

'Sorry?' He glanced at her sharply. 'For what?'

'I don't think I can marry you.' She tried to smile. 'It would have been nice, in many ways.'

'You're turning me down?' She thought he looked more surprised than hurt.

'I think so.'

'Romy – for God's sake – we could sort something out about the child ... Even the hotel, if you really insist.'

She shook her head. 'I don't think so.'

'*Why?* I don't understand why.'

'Oh ...' The old reason, she thought. Because she

didn't love him enough. And because, in spite of all that had happened to her, she still believed that out there was something different, something better.

But she said instead, 'If we married, I should have to share you, Patrick, shouldn't I?'

'Share me?'

'With your mother.' She gave a little smile. 'And I don't think either Bunny or I could bear that.'

After Betty had been discharged from hospital, Caleb stayed with her for a few days, doing the shopping and the cooking, sleeping on the two-seater sofa in her flat. The sofa was uncomfortable, but nowhere near as uncomfortable as his thoughts.

His mother had protected him for years, had put his needs before her own throughout his entire life. She had worked hard to give him the best: now, when he thought of how she must have scrimped and saved to buy his school uniforms and his books and toys, and when he remembered how, these past few years, he had judged her, he felt ashamed. As for her relationships with men, it seemed to Caleb that they weren't so unalike, he and his mother. He wondered whether, more than a quarter of a century ago, Betty, too, had needed to escape. Unlike him, she hadn't had the option of packing a knapsack and crossing the Channel. Trapped by the times and her gender, caught in the unforgiving confines of a small English village, she had fled narrowness and convention through a series of lovers.

When he thought of his quarrel with Romy, he knew that again he had been unjust. Knocked off balance, unable to accept the thought of her marrying Patrick Napier, he had set out to hurt her. If she did marry Patrick, then it would be in part his own fault. He had been too stuck on his high horse, too slow to forgive. He could hardly blame Romy for wanting to marry Patrick Napier – after all, he himself had walked out on her when she had needed him most. He had left her to endure Mrs Plummer's death and Jem's imprisonment on her own. That she had not only survived, but had run the hotel successfully and had brought up Jem's child as well was hugely to her credit. And he, of all people, had no claim to moral superiority. He had used Diana to satisfy himself sexually and he had used Alison for company and friendship. He had hurt Alison; that he had not hurt Diana was due more to her thick-skinned character than to any thoughtfulness on his part. He hadn't loved either woman. He was beginning to wonder whether he might live his entire life only loving one woman.

At the end of the week he went back to London. In the evening he went to the hotel. Romy was in her flat on the second floor. She opened the door to him.

'Caleb,' she said.

'I wasn't sure whether you'd see me.'

She showed him into the room. 'I seem to have had quite a number of unpleasant conversations recently. I thought I might as well get the next over and done with.'

'I haven't come here to be unpleasant.' She had been drinking; he noticed the bottle, the glass.

'I thought you were avoiding me.'

'Avoiding you?'

Her fingers pulled at the long cuffs of her cardigan. 'The garden ... You haven't been working on the garden.'

'Didn't Reggie tell you?'

'Tell me what?'

'I asked him to give you a message.'

'Caleb, you must have noticed that Reggie is incapable of speaking to me. Whenever he looks at me he goes scarlet and trips over something.'

'*Hell*,' he said. He realized how it would have looked to her: that he had picked a quarrel and then spent the next week sulking. He explained, 'My mother's been in hospital. I've been in Southampton.'

'Oh,' she said. 'I'm sorry. Is she ill?'

'Some bastard beat her up.'

'*Caleb*.' Her eyes had widened.

'Three broken bones, Romy. And you should see what he did to her face. I'd like to kill him.'

'Caleb, I'm so sorry.'

'She won't tell me who he is, or I would kill him.' He looked away. 'When I saw her, I felt so bloody guilty. She looked so small. As if a puff of wind would blow her away.'

She picked up the bottle. 'Would you like a drink?'

'No thanks.' He saw how white she was. 'Do you think you should have any more of that?'

She seemed to pale even further. 'I think that's my business, don't you?'

'I meant – it doesn't always work, that's all.'

'*Caleb*.' Her voice was low, warning him off.

'OK. But whatever it is that you're trying not to think about, Romy, getting plastered won't necessarily help.'

She said huffily, 'If you've said all you came to say, then perhaps you should go. It's late.'

He watched her pour the remainder of the brandy rather messily into a tumbler. He seemed to see again the girl he had first met, all those years ago. *You stole my house and you killed my father.* She was still small, angry and fighting for survival. He had been so wrong: she hadn't really changed at all.

He said, 'I haven't said all I came here to say. I also came here to apologize. What I said to you the other day – I had no right. It was out of order. Actually it was pretty unforgivable.'

She gave a fleeting smile. 'At least it makes a change. You speaking out of turn rather than me.'

'I wish you well, Romy. Honestly. I'll always wish you well. I hope you and Patrick will be very happy.'

As he turned to go, he heard her say:

'I'm not going to marry Patrick.'

He swung round. 'Why not?'

'Because . . .'

'You don't have to tell me, of course.'

'I'm not going to marry Patrick because we're too different. We have nothing in common.' She seemed to droop, her shoulders falling and her head tilting forward. 'And, besides, we both have too many other claims on us.'

She looked, he thought, very tired. There were dark shadows around her eyes and her face looked drawn. She sat down on the window sill, and said slowly,

'There was so much Patrick didn't know – and so much I couldn't bear to tell him. Perhaps there's a limit to how much you can remake yourself. Perhaps you can't really wipe the slate clean.' Her voice was low and flat. 'There's Jem, of course. I don't think that either Patrick or his wretched mother would ever understand about Jem. I don't think they'd even understand about Middlemere. They would just think it was all rather ... *disreputable*. And as though I were somehow to blame. And, anyway, you were right, Caleb, I don't love Patrick. I'm not very good at loving people, am I? All my life, I've only loved a handful of people.'

'Romy,' he said gently.

She turned to him, a warning in her eyes. 'That girl—'

'Which girl?'

'The one I saw you with outside your flat.'

He stared at her blankly. She said, 'It was a Friday night ...'

Confusion persisted a moment longer and then he remembered. *Friday*. The cheese and wine party. 'Oh, *Alison*,' he said. 'She lives in the flat above me. She's a teacher.'

'And she's your girlfriend?'

'No.' He thought of the candles, the wine, the expression in Alison's eyes when he had left her room. And it took a few moments to work out the implications of what Romy had just told him.

'You were in Canonbury?'

'I wanted to talk to you about the garden,' she said quickly.

'But I didn't see you—'

'I went home.'

Pennies dropped with a deafening clunk. 'You thought—'

'I didn't want to interrupt.' She looked flustered.

She went to the sideboard and took out a new bottle of brandy. Her fingers wrestled clumsily with the stopper. He said, 'Romy, you don't always have to manage on your own, you know.'

She gave a little gasp and pressed her lips together. He took a step towards her, intending to open the bottle for her, but she moved away, holding up a hand to ward him off.

'You have to go, Caleb.'

He looked at her closely, realized that she meant it, and picked up his coat from where he had flung it on the sofa. He had reached the door when she said, 'But my garden? You will finish my garden?'

'Of course,' he said shortly. 'It's my job. Then I won't trouble you again.'

She closed her eyes tightly. 'You have to go because I've got chickenpox. That's all. It's so embarrassing at my age. I thought I'd had it, but I can't have. Anyway, I have all these dreadful spots.'

'*Chickenpox* . . .'

'You mustn't laugh.'

'I wouldn't dream of it. Poor Romy. Anyway, I've had it.'

'Are you sure?'

'Positive.' He crossed the room to her. 'Is there anything I can do?'

She gave a gasp of laughter and held out the bottle to him. 'Well, you could open this bloody brandy.'

Chapter Seventeen

The brasserie was a success. A month after opening every table was full. A minor film star dined there one evening, and the Trelawney's brasserie was mentioned in the *Tatler* and in the gossip column of the *Daily Mail*. They rolled a baby grand into a corner of the room and engaged a pianist to play. The fine weather held: at lunchtimes they put out half a dozen tables on the terrace. Working in her office, Romy could hear laughter and music and the chink of glasses.

The success of the brasserie encouraged her to make a start on the renovation of the hotel. Interior designers drew up colour schemes and decoration plans; builders began the task of ripping out the heavy, cast-iron radiators and removing paper and paint that had been put up in the Thirties. Romy could see in her mind's eye how it would look when it was finished. She thought of Bunny's house, with its floating, cream-coloured curtains and its pools of light on pale floors.

Yet sometimes that summer she found it hard to concentrate on her work. There was the warmth and the blue sky and the piano playing. Sometimes she found herself longing to leave the office for the garden that Caleb had made for her, to sit among the flowers and let the sun wash over her. Or, sitting at her desk, she would close her eyes and dream that she was beside the sea. She could almost smell the salt in the air and hear the hush of the waves. She would open her eyes and, focusing on the typewriter and the pile of letters and bills, feel oddly jarred, disorientated, as though she had suddenly realized that she was in the wrong place.

For the past year Jem had been living in a small stone cottage near Grassington in Yorkshire. The cottage stood on its own at the end of a wooded track. There was a kitchen and a living room downstairs and two bedrooms upstairs. Jem grew vegetables in the back garden and, in the outhouses behind the cottage, kept a pig and hens.

Romy visited in September. Danny had been staying with Jem for several weeks. On Sunday afternoon they had a picnic, and Jem showed Danny how to catch fish in the river. Further upstream half a dozen children played on the stepping stones. Jem's three dogs – Sandy, the lurcher, now rather old and slow, Tess, the sheepdog, and a three-legged mongrel puppy that Jem had adopted to save it from being put down – darted in and out of the water or dozed on the bank.

Jem was crouching down beside Danny, helping him to trail the net in the river. Romy said, 'You've enjoyed having Danny to stay, haven't you, Jem?'

'Dan and me have had some good times.'

'Maybe you should think about letting him live with you all the time.'

Danny paddled into the shallows. Jem watched him. 'I don't know, Romy.'

'He'll be three next month. It would be best if he were settled with you before he goes to school. And you get on so well. He loves it here, you can see that he does. And you've always said you thought the countryside was better for kids.' She poured herself a drink of Tizer. 'And you're settled now, aren't you?'

He came to sit on the bank beside her. 'That's the thing. What if something goes wrong?'

'Why should anything go wrong?'

'It has before, hasn't it? After I came out of the army – after Brighton. I thought I had everything worked out then. I had a job, somewhere to live. And I had Liz.'

She looked at him closely. 'You still miss her, don't you?'

'I'll always miss her. If Liz came round that hill right now and asked me to take her back, I would, Romy. Like a shot. I know I'll never find anyone like her again.'

'Maybe not *like* her. But there are other girls.'

'Not for me.' He took an apple out of the bag and glanced at her. 'Here we are, both of us, middle of our twenties, and not a husband or wife between us. No sign of one, neither. Loners the pair of us.'

The thought made her uncomfortable. 'Anyway, Danny's not a baby any more, Jem. He's a little boy now. Needs his dad.'

'It's not that I don't want him, you know that. But I keep myself to myself. It's better that way. And with a kid, you can't do that. It wouldn't be fair. They need friends, don't they?'

'But you're getting on all right, aren't you?'

'I love it here, Romy.' He stood up and hurled the apple core into the river. 'But no one *knows*, do they? They don't know what I did. Mike doesn't know what I did.' Mike Green was the farmer Jem worked for. 'They don't know I've been in prison. You remember how it was in Stratton. Once people knew we were from Hill View – once they knew we were Dennis Parry's kids – they'd look at us differently. If Mike found out I'd been in prison – well, he might not want me any more. He might give me the push.'

'There's no reason why he ever should know, Jem.'

'But if he did. I might have to leave, start over again somewhere else. I've had to often enough before. And that wouldn't be fair on Danny, would it?'

He went to the water's edge and, crouching down, held out his arms to Danny. Romy tried again. 'But you'll think about it, won't you, Jem?'

She saw that there was in Jem's eyes a mixture of fear and longing. 'Course I will,' he said. He swung his son up into his arms.

On the far side of Parfitt Gardens an entire row of tall Georgian houses had been bought up, converted and sold off as flats. Most of the houses now had a car or two parked outside. Nowadays, when Romy walked through the gardens, she heard not the birdsong she had listened to that first day she had arrived at the hotel, but the clamour of horns and the gunning of engines.

The hotel was changing too. The work of renovation was under way. It was a slow, stuttering, piecemeal business, and each job begun seemed to necessitate

another. The builders would lift off a rusting radiator
and find damp underneath. Or they would peel away
lining paper and an entire bedroom ceiling would come
down in great chunks of crumbling horsehair plaster,
showering rooms and corridors with a fine white dust.
Romy began to wonder whether she should have left
the Trelawney as she was: an elegant, dignified old lady,
attractive enough at a quick glance, but going at the
seams if you inspected her too closely.

She was sitting in the bar one lunchtime when
Terry, the head waiter, came in. She looked up at him.

'Trouble, Terry?'

'Could be, Miss Cole.' He kept his voice lowered.
'We've got a visitor.'

'Who?'

'Mr Fitzgerald.'

She stared at him. '*Johnnie?*'

Terry nodded. 'The new doorman didn't know who
he was. He let him into the hotel, I'm afraid.'

Romy rose from her seat. 'I didn't know he was
back ... Where is he now?'

'In the brasserie, Miss Cole. He's asking to speak to
you. I seated him at a corner table. I thought it best.'
Terry looked at her hopefully. 'I can have him thrown
out, if you like.'

She shook her head. 'I'll have a word with him.'

'He's had a few too many—'

'I shouldn't think I've ever spoken to Johnnie Fitzgerald when he was sober,' she said sharply. 'I probably
wouldn't recognize him.'

She left the bar. She felt a fleeting glow of pleasure as she saw the crowded tables in the brasserie, a

pleasure that died as her gaze alighted on Johnnie Fitzgerald, sitting in a corner of the room. She paused for a moment, taking in the expensive, slovenly clothes and the dark, hungry gaze.

Johnnie shuffled to his feet as Romy approached him. 'Well, well,' he drawled. 'What an honour. Miss Cole has found time to talk to me.'

'Sit down, Johnnie.'

He fell back into the seat. He had aged, she noticed. His face had become fuller around the chin and neck, and there were pouches of flesh beneath his eyes. Though he was still a startlingly handsome man, something in him was dying, killed by drink and self-pity and the passing of time.

She sat down. 'What did you want to say to me?'

'Haven't got a drink,' he mumbled. 'That ape of yours wouldn't give me a drink. Can't talk without a drink.'

'You should leave, Johnnie. If you're thinking of throwing a tantrum, no one wants to know.'

'Don't they?' His gaze settled on her. Behind the blurring of alcohol, she glimpsed intelligence. 'In my experience people are always interested in scandal.' He scowled. 'A drink,' he said obstinately. 'I need a drink.'

If he had another drink, she thought, then he might fall into a stupor and they could dump him outside in the gutter where he belonged. She signalled to the waiter and ordered two gins and tonics. When they were alone again, she said, 'What are you here for, Johnnie? Come to talk about old times?'

'Hardly.' His gaze trailed unsteadily around the

room. 'You've done this place up nicely. Got an eye for this business, haven't you, Romy? Mirabel was always too conservative. A bit dull.' He offered a packet of Player's to Romy; she shook her head.

She noticed how his fingers trembled as he lit his cigarette. 'How's Norah?' she asked.

'Norah stayed in America.' He gave a sour grin. 'Wouldn't come back with me. No loyalty, women.'

'Not like you, eh, Johnnie? You were always faithful, weren't you?'

His eyes narrowed. He took a slug of gin. 'I only ever *loved* one woman. I only ever *loved* Mirabel.'

'Love,' she said scornfully. 'You don't know the meaning of the word.'

'And you do?' A cynical smile. 'I don't think so. You're no different from me, Romy.'

'That's not true.' The expression in his eyes – that familiar mixture of greed and dislike – unnerved her. She found herself tugging down the hem of her skirt, checking that the top button of her blouse had not come undone.

'Never met a woman to match Mirabel. Best of the bunch.'

'It's taken you rather a long time to work that one out, hasn't it, Johnnie?'

'She was damned good to me. Never messed me around. Not like some,' he added self-pityingly. 'She had class, Mirabel. Didn't matter that her people were labourers, or whatever. She had class.' His gaze slid to Romy. Then he said, 'Of course, I'll be honest with you, sweetheart. In your position, I'd have done much the same.'

She blinked. 'Pardon?'

'I mean, I'd have done what you did. I'd have made damned certain Mirabel left me the hotel.'

She stared at him. 'I didn't know that Mrs Plummer was going to leave me the hotel – I didn't *plan*—' She had to struggle to regain control of herself, to absorb the shock of his words. 'It wasn't like that.'

'Oh, come on, Romy.' His eyes narrowed as he drew on his cigarette. 'You got what you always wanted, didn't you? I underestimated you. You're cleverer than I thought you were.'

She wanted to throw the drink in his face, as she had done once before. But she was older now and wiser and, besides, to make an exhibition of herself in her own restaurant would harm her far more than it harmed him. Getting him out of here without a scene, that was all that mattered.

She took a deep breath. 'Was that what you came to say to me?'

'Who said I came here to speak to *you*?' His dark eyes fixed on her. 'Though there is just one thing . . .'

'Go on,' she whispered.

'Only that, if you think I'm just letting this place go, then you're not as clever as I thought.' He leaned forward, his expression malevolent. 'If I can't have the Trelawney, then I'll damned well make sure that you don't keep it either.'

She had to make a conscious effort not to shiver. She heard him go on, 'There's always been gossip. Everyone knew that Mirabel was going to leave the Trelawney to me. I think I might jolt people's memories

... stir things up a bit.' He shambled to his feet. 'I've come here to speak to *them*, you see.' He gestured widely around the room. 'As for *you* – you're just my audience, Romy.'

As he spoke, his voice rose. The people on the adjacent tables turned to look at him. Johnnie's grin widened. 'You see, Romy, they *do* want to know. They *are* interested. Aren't you?' he called out. 'I'm going to make sure that everyone knows what you did, Romy Cole. I'm going to make sure that all London knows what you are.'

Now he had the attention of everyone in the room. Diners paused, curiosity in their eyes, their forks halfway to their mouths. Romy, too, watched, mesmerized. Johnnie thumped his fist on the table. 'I'm going to tell them how you stole the Trelawney from me. And I'm going to tell them how you kept me from the woman I loved – the woman who loved me!'

Get him out of here, she thought. As she signalled to Terry to fetch help, Johnnie called out, 'Shall I tell them how you kept Mirabel under your thumb? Shall I tell them how you forced her to change her will when she was dying?'

They hauled him from the room, struggling every inch of the way. His accusing voice echoed as they dragged him down the corridor. 'Shall I tell them how you took advantage of a sick old woman? Shall I tell them that, Romy?'

Fifty pairs of eyes followed her as she rose from the table and walked out of the room. And she had just enough time to reach the privacy of the Ladies' Powder

Room before her stomach rose and she was gut-wrenchingly, resoundingly sick.

Caleb had been approached by some friends of the Harbornes, the Delafields, about the possibility of being commissioned to design a garden for their house in Norfolk. Jack Delafield was a sculptor; Louise, his wife, a potter. The plot was large but awkwardly shaped, the soil sandy, friable, difficult. *We don't want herbaceous borders and lily ponds*, Louise Delafield said as she showed him around the garden. *We want something different. Something special.*

The day Caleb received the news that the Delafields were to give him the commission, he drove to the Trelawney. He had to tell someone and Romy, he discovered, was the person he most wanted to tell.

It was late afternoon, fiveish, and Romy was in her office, sitting at her desk, a heap of papers in front of her. She didn't seem to register much surprise at his appearance. He began to tell her about the Delafields' garden, but realized after a while that though she was nodding her head and murmuring approval, she wasn't really listening. The words trailed away; he felt rather crass.

'I'm sorry,' he said. 'I've interrupted your work.'

She looked down at the desk. There was a bewildered expression in her eyes, as if she had forgotten what she was doing there. 'It doesn't matter.'

'I'll go. Let you get on.'

She gave a crooked little smile. He went to the door.

Then he heard her say, 'Johnnie came to the hotel today.'

He swung round. 'Johnnie . . . ?'

'He's back, Caleb.'

'And? This wasn't a social call, I take it.'

A quick shake of the head. 'He said . . . terrible things. About me. In front of everyone.'

'What sort of things?'

She stood up clumsily. Papers and pens cascaded to the floor, but she did not pick them up. 'I have to go outside,' she muttered. 'I can't think here.'

They went into the garden. In the brasserie waiters moved around the room, setting tables, putting out menus. Outside, there was still a warmth in the air, and a white butterfly flitted among the crimson leaves of an ornamental vine.

A wrought-iron bench at the far end of the garden made a small oasis. Caleb said again, 'What sort of things?'

'He said that I'd made Mrs Plummer leave me the hotel.' Romy sat down on the bench, eyes focused ahead. From behind the windows of the brasserie, the movements of those inside appeared silent and dreamlike. 'He said that I'd forced her to leave me the hotel.'

He stared at her. '*Christ.*'

She was hunched up, her arms wrapped around herself. 'Everyone heard him. The guests . . . my staff . . . everyone.' Her voice had dropped and Caleb had to strain to hear. 'It wasn't like that,' she muttered. 'It wasn't like that at all. She didn't want to see him. She was too ill, far too ill. And it was awful. Watching her die like that . . .'

'Where's Johnnie living now?'

'At the cottage, I suppose. Mrs Plummer's cottage in Henley. I don't know where he stays when he's in London. At his club, perhaps.' She gave him a sharp glance. 'Why do you want to know, Caleb? You're not thinking of putting a brick through his window, are you?'

'Wouldn't be a bad idea.'

'I don't want that,' she said vehemently. 'You're not to pick a fight with him. Promise me.'

To please her, he promised. And thought privately that, if the opportunity arose, then he'd make sure Johnnie picked the fight first.

Her hands twisted together. 'I didn't know Mrs Plummer had left me the Trelawney until after she died. I honestly had no idea until Mr Gilfoyle told me.'

'Yes,' he said. 'Of course. You mustn't worry, Romy. Everyone will know he's lying.'

'Johnnie has friends. He *knows* people.'

'He has enemies too,' he reminded her.

'He seduces people. Not just women. If he makes the effort, turns on the charm, people fall for him. They believe him. *I* almost did, that time in the pub. Just for a moment, but I did. He might have offended half London, but the other half is in love with him. And why should people believe me and not Johnnie? After all, he's one of them.' She was frowning, looking down at her white-knuckled hands. 'I've been thinking about it, you see. There's Johnnie, Mrs Plummer's well-connected lover of more than a decade. Everyone knows she adored him. And there's me, a nobody from nowhere, who hadn't a penny to her name until the

Trelawney falls into her hands like a ripe plum. Can't you see how it must look?'

And, unnervingly, he could. Johnnie Fitzgerald might be a self-centred, avaricious scoundrel, but, as Romy had pointed out, he fitted in, knew the ropes. Whereas, however hard she tried, there remained, in spite of the expensive hairstyles and elegant dresses, a touch of the urchin about Romy and more than a hint of the outsider.

When she looked up at him, he saw the fear in her eyes. 'What if people believe him, Caleb?'

'Then they're fools.'

'Do you believe me?' Her voice faltered.

'Of course I do.'

'Why? How can you know?'

'Because I know *you*,' he said gently. 'I know what you would do and what you wouldn't do. And I know you wouldn't do that.'

'That's very ... very generous of you.' Her voice shook slightly. 'So you don't still hate me?'

'Hate you? Oh, I don't think so.'

She stood up. 'Danny,' she said. 'It's time for Danny's tea.' Heading back to the hotel, she paused and looked back at him. 'I keep remembering,' she said. 'I keep remembering what I said to Johnnie, that time in the pub. Just before you had the fight with him. I told him that if it was up to me I'd make sure he never saw Mrs Plummer again.' Her eyes were anguished. 'Fifty, maybe a hundred people must have heard me say that, Caleb.'

Caleb watched her go back into the hotel. *So you don't still hate me?* she had asked him. Well, no. He watched the swing of her hair, the grace of her walk. And acknowledged what he had known for months now: that he still loved her, had never really stopped loving her, and would probably always love her.

Romy began to notice that there were parties she had not been invited to, and that the invitations to dinners and receptions were drying up. Several people whom she had thought to be her friends now cold-shouldered her. In Fortnum & Mason's, she caught sight of an acquaintance and waved. The woman turned away without acknowledging her and began to talk, very pointedly, to her neighbour.

She would fight back, she resolved. She wouldn't hide away, wouldn't skulk in her office, waiting until the rumours died down, waiting until Johnnie Fitzgerald had tired of spreading poison. She called in favours, looked up old friends. Some stammered excuses to her – so busy, booked up till Christmas, quite ridiculous, so sorry. It was all she could do not to slam down the phone.

She ran into Nicholas Thirkettle in the Chanterelle. Parting from her, he murmured a vague invitation to a party at his flat in Portobello Road. *Half London will be there*, he told her. *Darling Romy, you must come.* She bought a new dress for the occasion, of jade satin, decorated around the bodice with tiny black beads. She had her hair swept up in a chignon and she applied her make-up with care. She studied her reflection in the mirror: a last flick of lipstick, a curl twisted into place. She mustn't look as though she minded.

In Nicholas Thirkettle's flat guests spilled from the reception rooms into the hall and corridor. Jewels sparkled at the women's throats, and the men lounged against door jamb and piano, smoking, their eyes following Romy as she moved around the room. A drink or two to shore up her confidence and she, too, glittered as she passed from guest to guest. Buoyed up by the cocktails, the compliments, the music, she chattered and laughed and flirted.

She was on her way to the bathroom to powder her nose when she paused, hearing her name mentioned. Standing in the corridor outside the bedroom in which Nicholas had put the guests' coats, women's voices drifted to her.

'. . . how she has the nerve. Poor Nick only invited her out of politeness. He assumed she wouldn't turn up.'

'Frightful for him.'

'He met her at Bunny Napier's, you know.'

'Lend me your lipstick, Kathy, I seem to have forgotten mine.' A pause. Then, curiously, 'Do you think it's true, then? That she's a gold-digger?'

'She had her claws into poor Patrick Napier. He had a lucky escape. She used to be a chambermaid in a hotel, but apparently she did something dreadful – Nina Marshall told me, I can't remember what exactly – and now she owns the hotel. Queens it around, thinks a lot of herself. *And* –' the voice lowered – 'did you know that she has an illegitimate child?'

'*No!*'

'It's perfectly true. Bunny Napier said. A little boy. Nina saw them once in Selfridges.'

'No wonder she's on the prowl for a husband.'

'Ciggie, darling?' Romy heard the rustle of a packet, the flick of a lighter. Then, slyly, 'Your Leslie certainly seemed rather taken with her.'

'Leslie wouldn't look at a woman like that twice!'

'Of course not, darling.'

A sniff. 'He told me he thought she looked like a tart.'

'Well, my dear, that *dress*! So garish. Sallow women should never wear green.'

It seemed to Romy that it took much the same amount of courage to walk into that bedroom as it had taken her, years ago, to run away from Stratton. But her coat was on the bed – her favourite coat, the pale blue Paquin that Mrs Plummer had given her – so she really had no alternative. There was a sudden silence as she went into the room and put her coat on. One of the women was suddenly very busy dabbing powder on her face, while the other – plump and fair-skinned – went the same shade as her Schiaparelli-pink dress.

At the door, Romy paused and looked back. And made sure that her voice was perfectly level as she said, 'Perhaps you're right about the green. But then over-weight women shouldn't wear shocking pink. It really doesn't do anything for you at all.' Then she walked out of the house.

Outside her bravado crumbled and she leaned against the wall, her fists pressed against her mouth. Above her, in Nicholas Thirkettle's flat, someone was playing the piano. Music, sweet and plangent, seeped out of an upstairs window. Across the street half a dozen men spilled out of a pub, football scarves knotted round their necks.

She began to walk. She couldn't think where to go, at first, couldn't – anticipating the curious glances that she would receive as she returned, far too early, from the party – face going back to the hotel. Nor could she bear to be alone in her flat.

It had begun to drizzle. She put up the collar of her coat and, when a taxi drove past, she hailed it and asked to be taken to Canonbury.

Caleb showed her around his house. As she moved from room to room, running her finger along a row of books, a pile of bricks, she sensed that he waited for an explanation – her dress, her jewellery, so obviously unsuitable for this dilapidated house – but felt unable to offer him one.

In the kitchen he said, 'It's in need of some attention, as the estate agents say . . .'

'It's lovely.'

'You're very polite, Romy.'

'It'll be wonderful when you've finished.'

He threw back his head and laughed. 'That's what everyone says. Except Freddie, who can't think why anyone would want to live in Canonbury in the first place.' He held up a glass. 'Beer?'

She shook her head. She felt restless, fired by a furious, prickling energy, unable to sit still.

He was watching her. There was a sledgehammer propped against the wall. He picked it up and held it out to her. 'Go on,' he said. 'It's very therapeutic. You can let off steam knocking down walls after a difficult day.'

'I'm fine,' she said sharply.

'No, you're not,' he said. 'You are very, very upset about something, but whatever it is you don't want to tell me about it. So rather than me spending ages trying to worm it out of you, why don't you just give my wall a few good thumps?'

'Caleb—'

'And if you're worried about your dress, I'll lend you a pair of jeans and a jumper.'

She looked down at the green satin dress. 'I'm not worried about my dress. I'd like to burn this bloody dress.' She sat down at the table, suddenly exhausted, and put her head in her hands.

She heard him say softly, 'It's a nice dress.'

'You don't think it looks . . . *tarty?*'

He was stroking her neck. 'Not in the least. Seductive. Sexy.'

'Oh,' she whispered.

His forefinger ran down her spine. 'Of course,' he said, 'if you hate it that much you could always take it off.'

'*Caleb!*' As rapidly as it had appeared, her exhaustion had gone. Though the restlessness had returned, it now had a different, hungrier feel to it.

He kissed her shoulder. 'Just a thought.'

Her mouth was dry. After a second or two, she said, 'Well, it is boned.'

'Boned?'

568

'In the bodice. So it keeps its shape.'

'How extraordinary.'

'How uncomfortable. You don't know how lucky you are, Caleb, being a man and not having to wear this sort of thing.'

He ran the zip down the back of her dress. Then his hands slid beneath the two halves of satin. He kissed the small, knobbly bones of her spine, one by one, and she felt desire uncurl inside her. When she stood up, the dress fell to the floor in a shimmering jade-green pool.

'It's not *that* easy being a man,' he said, 'having to fight your way through all this.'

She was wearing a slip, a strapless corselette, stockings and suspenders. His mouth was at her breast; she dug her fingers into his thick black hair. 'Would you like me to help?' she said mockingly.

When he looked up at her, his eyes were dark and intense. 'Oh, I think I can manage,' he said.

Later, when she lay in his bed wearing only her pearl necklace, she said, 'The last time we did this—'

'You mean, in the kitchen?'

'*Silly*. No, at Stratton.' Her head was on his chest; the palm of his hand ran along the curve of her thigh and waist. She looked up at him. 'Do you remember?'

He shook his head. 'Not a thing. I've completely forgotten.'

'Silly,' she said again fondly. 'Only you said—'

'The Savoy. I said I'd meant our first time to be in the Savoy.'

'Yes.'

He glanced around the room. 'Well, it's not quite the Savoy.'

'At least we've a bed this time. Better than leaves.'

'D'you think so? I rather liked the leaves.'

'And we've a roof and four walls—'

'We'll just have to keep trying,' he said. 'And perhaps one day we'll find ourselves in the Savoy.'

He was stroking her stomach. There it was again: that ache of desire. But there was something she had to know. 'Caleb,' she said.

'Yes?'

'You remember that you said you don't hate me any more—'

'Uh-huh.' He had moved down the bed; now his mouth brushed against her belly.

'Does that mean that you like me again?'

'Like you?' He shook his head. 'Romy, I adore you, I worship you, I love you. Don't you know?'

He shifted down the bed a little further. She closed her eyes and did not talk any more.

When she wasn't with him, she couldn't concentrate. She was late for appointments, had to read each letter or bill three times. When they were together, she wanted to know every bit of him. The little things that they had in common delighted her: that they had read the same books, seen the same films. That he, like her, preferred coffee to tea, whisky to gin. Being with him made her feel in the centre of things, not on the periphery any more. Often the hotel seemed to retreat, to become less important. Sometimes she played hookey, took the train down to Norfolk, where Caleb was working during the week, and wandered with him around the strange, beautiful garden that he was making out of the sandy soil. Once they went away for the weekend. 'But the *hotel*, Caleb,' she said feebly and then bundled her clothes into a bag anyway.

They headed south-west. By the time they reached the narrow, high-banked lanes of Dorset, dusk was falling. 'There should be a church,' Romy said, glaring at the map, 'and then a *wood*. The stupid map's wrong.' She flung it into the footwell.

'It doesn't matter.'

'But we're lost.'

'How can we be lost when we haven't decided where we're going?'

They booked into the first hotel they found. The Alma Hotel perched on top of a cliff, and its shabby sign, fending off travelling salesmen and hawkers, should have warned them. A smell of Jeyes Fluid and boiled cabbage pervaded the reception area. A woman in her fifties, with rigidly permed hair and a fox-fur stole wrapped tightly round her shoulders, eyed them suspiciously as Caleb asked for a room for the night. Caleb introduced himself and Romy; she dug her left hand into her pocket. Yet it had a nice ring to it, she thought: *Mrs Romy Hesketh*.

The woman with the fox fur took a bundle of keys from a peg. 'I shall require a deposit, of course.' The fox's glassy eyes glared, too, fleetingly reminding Romy of Bunny Napier. 'Breakfast at eight o'clock sharp, no food or wellington boots in the bedrooms, rooms to be

vacated by ten o'clock in the morning. There is a
bathroom at the end of the corridor. The geyser is not
to be used after half-past ten, and you must provide
your own soap.'

They managed not to laugh until they were out of
earshot. Then, reaching the landing, they collapsed
against each other, helpless. '*I shall require a deposit, of
course,*' gasped Romy, pressing her fingers against her
mouth. Caleb leant his shaking shoulders against the
wall, tears in his eyes. 'No soap. No bloody soap.'

Their bedroom was painted brown up to the dado
rail and a faded cream above. The floor was covered with
brown- and grey-streaked lino; on the bed there was a
maroon eiderdown. Prominently placed on the dressing
table, a typed list reiterated the rules of the hotel.

Romy touched the radiator. 'It's cold—'

'Probably costs extra—'

'And dinner ... do you think we'll be allowed to
have dinner?'

'Dinner at seven o'clock sharp. It's twenty past. We'll
have to eat whatever's left in the van.'

'*Caleb.* No food in the bedrooms—'

'I was thinking of the bed. I haven't found a rule
about eating in bed.' His arms circled her waist and his
lips brushed against her neck.

She turned to face him. 'I'm not all that hungry.'

'Well,' he said, '*I* am. Damned hungry.'

His eyes glittered. There was a pulse of excitement
in the pit of her stomach. As he unbuttoned her cardigan and blouse, as he drew her slip over her head and
kissed the small swell of her belly, as each garment fell

to the floor, all other preoccupations fell away. There were only his hands, touching her skin, and his mouth on her mouth, and the chill slither of the maroon eiderdown beneath them. There was only his body, which fitted so neatly, so pleasurably, into hers. And there was that sudden expectation of delight, a delight of such overwhelming intensity that she, Romy Cole, who always schemed and planned, who always liked to be sure of her way, let herself go, toppled, fell, lost herself.

Much, much later, he pulled on jeans and a jersey and crept out of the hotel to the van and then smuggled back indoors the remains of their picnic. He fed her pieces of Kit Kat and segments of orange. Then they made love again, slowly, taking their time, getting to know once more the planes and hollows of each other's bodies, and the touch that pleased, that set on fire.

The bed was empty when Romy woke in the morning. She dressed and went outside. The Alma stood on a clifftop, in the curve of a bay. A rickety sign pointed out a footpath down to the beach; several acres of garden surrounded the hotel. Thickets of rhododendron battled against the breeze; wherever you were, you could hear the rush and the hiss of the sea. Like the hotel, the garden had the look of having been given up on years ago. Flowers, their petals browned and withered, drooped in beds. Weeds forced their heads through concrete paths, and the scattered trees had been bent and distorted by the wind.

Yet the situation and the view were glorious. It

might not be the Savoy, but she knew, suddenly, that she had never felt happier. Knew also how glad she was to be away from the Trelawney and how relieved she was to escape all her growing problems and anxieties.

Catching sight of Caleb, walking along the cliff, she called out his name. Then she ran to meet him.

Returning to the hotel, she found herself in the eye of a storm.

It was her accountant, Mr Ingram, who pointed out to her the extent of the Trelawney's problems. He put the books in front of her on Monday morning and showed her the steep decline in the hotel's income. August was never a good month for the hotel, but this year it had been worse than usual, and neither September nor October had brought any improvement so far. Though the brasserie was still doing well, the restaurant was struggling, and the cost of the renovation work had begun to look as though it would far exceed the original estimate. As she went through the figures, Romy began for the first time to feel alarmed.

She stayed up till midnight going through the books. Checking the register at reception, she realized that some of the hotel's regular guests – provincial ladies who stayed at the Trelawney once a month to shop, and couples who booked in for a weekend to visit the theatre – had not returned to the hotel for the last few months. She checked the staff records, too. Once more she noticed a small but relentless desertion. Of the staff who had recently left the hotel, some had been with the Trelawney since Mrs Plummer's time. Now, when she thought back, Romy remembered their mumbled excuses as they gave in their notice, and their refusal to meet her eyes.

She remembered, too, what Johnnie Fitzgerald had said to her. *If I can't have the Trelawney, then I'll make damned sure that you don't keep it either.* At midnight, sitting at her desk, she felt chilled and frightened. She poured herself a drink, swallowing it quickly, but the fear lingered, dark and enveloping. Rumours were shapeless and clinging. To fight them would be like fighting her way through a spider's web.

Perhaps, she thought, she should talk to her solicitor. Spreading malicious gossip was slander, wasn't it? Yet she rejected the idea almost immediately. How could she possibly go to court when the memory of Jem's trial was still so recent, so raw? She had no faith in the legal system's ability to give justice. The law hadn't helped Jem, and it hadn't helped her father. And, besides, going to court would only give further publicity to Johnnie Fitzgerald's accusations. Mud, however unfairly hurled, stuck.

In public she was charming, assured, amusing. In private it seemed to her that something inside her was struggling to survive. When she had inherited the Trelawney, she had believed that she had put her Hill View years behind her for ever. Now she could feel her self-confidence slipping away. It had taken her years to claw her way up the ladder, yet it had taken Johnnie Fitzgerald only a few short months to kick away the rungs.

One of the guests confirmed her worst fears. George Everett, a wealthy property developer, sixtyish and silver-haired, was a regular visitor to the Trelawney. In the bar one evening, over a drink, he said gently, 'You have to do something about these rumours, Romy, my dear. You have to put a stop to them.'

'Rumours?' The word jolted her.

'About how you came by this place.'

She said dismissively, 'Anyone with any sense knows that sort of gossip is nonsense.'

She saw him glance around the bar. It was half-empty. 'A great many people haven't a great deal of sense, I'm afraid,' he said sadly.

She thought of advertising the hotel – Mrs Plummer had never approved of advertising, had believed it vulgar. But advertising cost money, and suddenly she didn't seem to have any money. She went through the bills, searching for opportunities to make savings. She found a cheaper laundry and, when a couple of the cleaning staff left, did not replace them. To reduce staff costs she cut down on overtime and did more of the paperwork herself. Some of the little luxuries that had always made the Trelawney distinctive – the French soap in the bathrooms, the elegant, deckle-edged writing paper – she replaced with cheaper alternatives. She hated doing so, felt that she was betraying something, saw clearly in her mind's eye Mrs Plummer's disapproving lift of the eyebrows.

It wasn't enough, though. The Trelawney's monthly outgoings now exceeded its takings. She went to see the bank manager, to ask whether the loan she had taken out to cover the renovations could be extended. Leaving his office half an hour later, having met with a politely worded refusal, she was aware of a mixture of fury and humiliation. Just a few short months ago he had been only too pleased to lend her money. Now there was a warning in the delicately couched phrases, a reminder of the penalties of defaulting on the loan. It was hard to take in how close she had come to the edge in so short a time. The interest accruing on the loan and the losses incurred because of the fall in guests had mounted up with frightening speed.

She remembered, as a child, rolling a snowball down the hills beyond Middlemere. How the snowball had been small to start off with and how it had gathered layers, swelling in size until it became too heavy to push. She seemed to be struggling against something immovable and weighty. Her mind darted frantically round, looking for a solution. She slept badly, and the broken nights cast a shadow over her days so that now, when she most needed to think clearly, she was unable to do so.

She spoke to George Everett once more. Over a drink in her private sitting room, she gave a careful gloss to her predicament. 'It's only a temporary cash-flow problem,' she said. 'The Trelawney will be back on its feet in a couple of months. Dear George – if I could just borrow a couple of thousand pounds to get me through this difficult time . . .'

Another refusal, this one more kindly worded. Most of his money was tied up, he explained, in property or equities; he had few liquid assets. Then he said, 'You're not thinking of selling, then?'

'Selling?' She stared at him.

He clipped his cigar. 'Valuable property, this. Nice part of London. You wouldn't believe what places in Bloomsbury go for these days, Romy.' He glanced at her. 'No? Pity. Still, if you change your mind...' Then he said, 'I'll ask around, see if I can come up with anything.' He patted her hand. 'Don't worry, my dear. Business always has its ups and downs. You'll pull through. You're a stayer.'

She realized, working late each night, that she must face up to the inevitable. She must put a halt to the renovation of the Trelawney, must put up with crimson brocade curtains and Regency striped wallpaper for a few more years. It took her by surprise how disappointed she felt, how greatly she had wanted to mould the Trelawney to her vision.

Yet the following morning Mr Potter, the decorators' foreman, came to see her.

'If you've a moment, Miss Cole. We may have a problem.'

In the bedrooms on the second floor of the hotel, paper had been stripped from the walls and layers of sticky brown distemper scraped from doors and windows.

Mr Potter pointed to a corner of the room. 'If you'd have a look here, Miss.'

A growth, yellow-ochre in colour and greyish at the edges, blossomed on the skirting board. Romy gave it a poke. There was something repellent, even sinister about it. She heard Mr Potter say, 'Could be dry rot, I'm afraid. There was a wardrobe in that corner – must have been there for years, so no one noticed.' He slapped a broad, chalky palm against the wall. 'Bit of a state, this room. Plaster's a mess and the brickwork was bomb-damaged in the war. They didn't do the repairs right and it's let in damp.'

Romy straightened. 'But it can be put right, can't it?'

'Depends how far it's spread. It can eat through walls, that stuff. It's the devil, if you'll pardon me, Miss Cole. I've seen buildings fall down because of dry rot.'

Going back to her office, she told herself that he must have been exaggerating. It seemed inconceivable that a blob of yellow fungus, however repulsive, could destroy an entire building. That sort of thing only happened in science fiction. *The Thing from Another World. Quatermass.* And the yellow fungus in the Trelawney's second worst bedroom.

It seemed to her that there was now a raggedness about the Trelawney and an air of decline. Even the bookings for the brasserie had fallen. You couldn't blame them, she thought. Who would want to visit a hotel that was being eaten away by a horrible yellow fungus? Who would want to visit a hotel owned by a manipulative, greedy woman, the sort of woman who would impose her will on the dying?

She spoke to her accountant again. She would put a halt to the renovation work as soon as the dry rot was sorted out, she told him. Then they could use the remainder of the bank loan to make good the hotel's losses.

Mr Ingram looked up sharply. 'Dry rot?'

'We're not certain yet. A wood treatment expert is coming to have a look.' She added, with a confidence she no longer felt, 'I'm sure it's nothing serious.'

'I hope you're right, Miss Cole. The business would be hard put to absorb any significant expenditure just now.'

'How hard put?'

He looked grim. 'Extremely hard put.'

She made herself ask, 'If the worst happened ... if I couldn't keep up the payments on the loan ... or if I couldn't afford to pay for the repairs—'

'Then you would have to declare the business bankrupt, Miss Cole,' Mr Ingram said crisply. 'You would have no alternative.'

Bankrupt. The word had a hollow, frightening ring. She struggled to absorb the fact that what had so recently seemed unthinkable – that she might lose the Trelawney – had now become a possibility. It couldn't be true, surely. She couldn't be about to endure dispossession, exile, for the second time in her life, could she?

A Mr Nelson from the timber-treatment firm visited the hotel. A tall man, he folded his long, thin body in half to examine the damaged skirting board. Romy watched him poke and prod and make little sniffing sounds. Eventually he uncoiled himself. When he straightened, the bones in his spine clicked audibly.

Dry rot was a fungus, he explained to her. It was caused by damp and was usually found in timber that had been in contact with wet masonary. Allowed to spread, it soaked up moisture from the timbers, drying them out until they turned to dust. When it had finished feeding off a window sill or a skirting board, it grew long filaments that went in search of other timbers – floorboards or roofing rafters. The filaments could travel through bricks and plaster. They could thread themselves around an entire building, strangling it.

He would carry out a full survey of the hotel the

following week, Mr Nelson told her. Then he would be able to tell the extent of the infection.

When he had gone, Romy stooped and pressed her knuckles against the damaged skirting board. The wood fragmented at her touch, and she seemed to see the Trelawney wrapped in ochre fronds, its timbers crumbling, its brickwork splitting, tumbling, to lie in dusty little heaps in Parfitt Gardens. Her home taken from her, destroyed. There was that sick, hollow, disbelieving feeling inside her again. Her world turned upside-down. And she thought of how she had battled against poverty and loneliness, and how she had believed that she had won, only to discover that she might be beaten by Johnnie Fitzgerald and a scrap of yellow fungus.

That night, in her dreams, she found herself in a familiar place. She was in a small, dark room, and there was a notch of light in front of her. She was afraid to put her eye to the notch, afraid of what she might see. Enclosed in the darkness, it was hard to breathe and yet, against her will, she found herself leaning forward, pressing her eye to the light.

When she awoke, she was crying. She was alone and, with the nightmare still vivid, she could almost smell the stale, enclosed air. If she closed her eyes, she would see around her the broken things they had kept in the cupboard. The jigsaw pieces and the boots without soles or laces and the jugs without spouts. And feathers: she thought there had been feathers.

She scrubbed her eyes with her sleeve and put on the lights and went into the kitchen. There was the rasp of the match and the hiss of gas as she put the kettle on.

She knew where the small, dark room was, of course, knew that in her dreams she returned time and again to the cupboard at Middlemere, the landing cupboard, where she had hidden on the day of the eviction. When she looked down, it surprised her that she was wearing her silk negligee. As though she had half-expected to see her school clothes, the hand-knitted jersey and box-pleated skirt that she had worn each day to the shabby little school in Swanton St Michael.

Yet there was so much that she could not remember, had never been able to remember. She had little memory of the months that had preceded the eviction. Though she recalled clearly the sense of bewilderment and rootlessness that had accompanied the years between leaving Middlemere and living at Stratton, she had no memory at all of the immediate aftermath of her father's suicide. She had been only eight years old. And it had been a long time ago. And perhaps time had been kind, blacking out the worst memories.

Yet the dream still haunted her. There, memories existed, almost within her grasp. There was the certainty that beyond, just out of her vision, something terrible was happening. Had she put her eye to the notch, she would have known everything.

The sense of dread lingered as the days passed. It was there when she looked into the half-empty restaurant, or saw the fall in the hotel's advance bookings. It was there when she read through Mr Nelson's report and knew that she would have to close all the rooms on the first and second floors of the hotel while the dry rot treatment was carried out.

It was there, when, waking one morning, the solution came to her. She brushed it away at first, refusing even to contemplate it. *I won't do it*, she whispered to herself. *I won't go cap in hand to Johnnie Fitzgerald.*

Jake told her that Johnnie now owned a garage in Warren Street and had part-ownership of a West End club. Then he eyed her suspiciously. 'What do you mean to do?' he asked. 'Set fire to the club? Smash a few windscreens at the showroom?'

'Certainly not,' said Romy. 'I was just wondering.'

Jake looked disbelieving. 'I should tell you that, whatever you do, I won't be around to put up bail for you. I'm going away, Romy.'

'To paint?' she said. 'Or for a holiday?'

'For ever. I'm moving to Majorca.' He heaved himself out of the chair and refilled her wine glass. 'Can't face another winter here, to be honest.' He shivered and gave the one-bar electric fire a kick. 'I always seem to be so bloody cold. And it doesn't seem to be so much fun here any more. So many of the old crowd gone. And my doctor's fussing about my heart. Tells me I shouldn't smoke, shouldn't drink.' Jake snorted. 'Perfectly ridiculous. I'd rather be dead.'

She stared at him, dismayed. 'You can't go, Jake! What about me?'

He lit another cigarette and waved his hand dismissively. 'Oh, you've got your smart friends now, Romy. You'll hardly notice I'm gone.'

'*Jake*. You can't just go.'

'Don't blub, girl.' He gave her a handkerchief and she blew her nose loudly. 'You know I can't stand weeping women.'

Patting her back, he said, 'You can come and visit me in Majorca. You look like you could do with a holiday.'

'But the hotel—'

'Oh, let the bloody hotel go hang.'

'I can't do that. Everything's difficult enough as it is. If I weren't there to keep an eye on things—'

'And would it really matter if the wretched little place went to pot?' Jake threw up his hands, exasperated. 'Would it really, really matter, Romy, if there was one less hotel in London? No one would give a damn!'

'*I* would. It's my *home*—'

'You have to live, Romy! Have some fun! Middle age will catch up with you soon enough. No point getting old and creaking like me, and then thinking about all the things you wish you'd done.' He hugged her. Then he said, 'I'll miss you, you know. You're one of the most bloody-minded women I've ever met, but I'll miss you. And you're to come and visit me in Majorca. That's an order.'

Johnnie's club, the Manhattan, didn't open until eleven in the evening. Sitting in a bar on the opposite side of the road, Romy had a drink to steady her nerves. From where she sat, she could see the men going into the club. Heavy coats flapped open over evening suits, and white silk scarves showed beneath black umbrellas. The bright lights of the West End were reflected in the puddles and in the sheen of rain on the pavements.

She finished her drink, left the bar and crossed the road. When she gave her name to the doorman and asked to see Johnnie, she was shown into a small vestibule, where narrow steps curled away into darkness and she could hear distant laughter and music. After a while a young girl wearing a cocktail dress appeared and escorted her downstairs. There were two more doormen – bullet-headed, thickset men – lounging beside the swing doors. Their eyes raked her up and down as she passed.

The swing doors opened and the music and bright lights hit her. A girl wearing an elaborate costume of ostrich feathers and sequins was dancing on a small stage. The band played a samba; the girl writhed and pouted. At the tables men smoked and drank and flicked a glance every now and then at the stage.

The hostess threaded between the tables in the auditorium; Romy followed her. Johnnie was sitting alone at a corner table. There was a cigarette between his fingers, and a glass and a whisky bottle stood on the table in front of him.

'Romy,' he said. And, 'Run along, Tina.' The hostess scuttled away. Johnnie smiled. 'How very gratifying to see you, Romy. Have you come about the job?'

'Job?'

'One of the girls has got herself up the duff, the silly little cow.' His long lashes flickered; beneath them, his eyes glittered, enjoying her humiliation. 'So there's a job going. Serving drinks, maybe doing a turn on stage. I heard you weren't doing too well at the Trelawney. Thought you might need a bit of extra cash.'

She had to swallow down the retort that rose to her lips. 'Oh, I wouldn't believe everything you hear, Johnnie,' she said lightly. 'Things aren't quite that desperate.'

He waved a hand at a seat, inviting her to sit down. 'Well, if you change your mind ... I think you'd be quite good at it. Bring in the customers. And I'd enjoy seeing you in sequins and ostrich feathers.' He picked up the whisky bottle. 'Drink?' She shook her head. 'If you prefer champagne—'

'No thanks.'

He poured an inch of whisky into the glass. 'What do you think of my little club?'

She looked around. 'You've done well for yourself, Johnnie.'

'It's high class. Not some cheap pick-up place. One of the best membership lists in the West End. We've got politicians ... medical men ... royalty – tin-pot Eastern European princelings who were thrown out of their rotten little kingdoms in the war, all of them, but still ...' He sat back in the seat, smoking, his eyes narrowed. 'What can I do for you, Romy? I'd like to think you were here for pleasure, but I rather suspect that it's business.'

Her mouth was dry. She wished she had accepted the drink. There was a flicker of applause as the samba ended and the girl in the ostrich feathers left the stage. She said, 'I wanted to talk to you.'

'About anything in particular?'

'About the Trelawney.'

'Ah,' he said. 'Hard times, eh, Romy?'

'Not the best.'

'So how can I help you?'

'I've come here to ask you to leave me alone,' she said calmly. 'To stop spreading lies about me. To say you were mistaken – anything.'

'Now why on earth should I do that?'

'You've made me suffer, Johnnie. If that was what you wanted to do, then you've achieved your aim. And what would be the point of closing the Trelawney down?'

He shrugged. 'I might enjoy it.'

'If you really loved Mrs Plummer like you said you did, then you'd know that closing down the hotel would have been the last thing she wanted.'

He seemed to consider that. 'True. She was devoted to the wretched place.'

'And it's not as though you want to manage it yourself, is it?'

'Certainly not. Dull as ditchwater. I leave that sort of thing to busy little bees like you, Romy.'

'Will you, then? Will you take back the things you're saying about me?'

He pursed his lips. 'No. Sorry. No, I don't think so.'

Hope died, and she said slowly, 'Then I have a proposal to put to you.'

'Fire away, then.'

She shot a glance around the crowded room. 'Here?'

'Why not?'

She pleated her fingers together. 'You want the Trelawney, don't you, Johnnie?'

'It was mine. It was meant to be mine.' Behind the lizard-like stillness of his eyes, she caught a flash of anger. 'Mirabel *promised* me.'

He was like a spoilt child, she thought, squabbling over a toy. 'Mrs Plummer gave the hotel to me,' she said levelly, 'because she knew that I loved it. And because she knew that you would squander it.'

His eyes flashed. '*Bitch*,' he said softly.

'Maybe. But better, perhaps, than being a spendthrift and a drunkard like you.' She took a deep breath. 'I've come here to offer to sell you a forty per cent share in the hotel. I would continue to manage the Trelawney, but you would have a financial interest. That would suit us both, don't you think?'

He crushed the cigarette end in the ashtray. 'No. It's not enough. Not when I think of all the trouble you've put me to.'

She swallowed. 'Forty-five per cent, then. That's my best offer.'

He shook his head. 'I don't think so. In fact, I think I've changed my mind. I don't want the hotel any more. I mean – ' he shrugged – 'why would I? I didn't want it when Mirabel was alive and I don't want it now.'

She said desperately, 'Then why won't you leave me alone?'

He frowned. 'Oh – pique. Look upon it as pique. I don't like to be beaten. And anyway, there is something I want from you. It just isn't the Trelawney.' His eyes gleamed. 'Oh, Romy, don't be so slow,' he said silkily. 'I want you, of course.'

She heard her own rapid intake of breath. She rose, almost knocking over the chair. He said, 'Don't go yet.

I was enjoying our conversation. And, anyway, you haven't heard all I have to say.'

'It wouldn't make any difference, Johnnie. Nothing you say would make me even consider—'

'Really? Are you sure about that?'

Something in his voice warned her. She looked back at him. He was swirling the whisky around his glass. 'I've been making a few enquiries,' he said. 'Murky little past, haven't you, Romy?'

She became very still. 'What do you mean?'

'Well,' he said, 'there's the suicide father. And the jailbird brother. Does the worthy son of the soil who employs your darling brother know about his prison sentence? And does the little boy?' He paused, smiling at her. 'Private detective. Wasn't difficult.'

'You bastard—' She raised her hand to slap his face, but he caught her arm.

'Naughty girl.' His fingers dug hard into her wrist. Then, letting her go, he said, 'Think about it, Romy. Think about whether you'd prefer to keep your secrets to yourself. Think about what *that's* worth.'

Chapter Eighteen

'What are you thinking?' Caleb said, and Romy answered, 'Nothing. I'm not thinking of anything at all.'

They were in bed in his flat. Her head nestled in the hollow of his shoulder.

'It's just the hotel,' she said, after a while. 'I'm worried about the hotel.'

'You're worried about money?'

'Yes.'

'How bad is it?'

'Oh –' she gave a little laugh – 'pretty bad.'

He wondered whether it really was the hotel, or whether there was something else. He said, 'Johnnie—' and she said quickly, 'Johnnie doesn't matter. I can deal with Johnnie. It's just that the bank's being difficult and the timber treatment is going to be so expensive and . . .'

It was odd, he thought, how, when you could not see someone's face, when you could only touch them and listen to the timbre of their voice, you could sense things you might not have otherwise been able to. He could tell, for instance, that, if she was not exactly lying to him, then she was only telling him part of the truth.

He kissed the top of her head. 'I told you before, you don't always have to manage on your own.'

'What are you suggesting, Caleb? You could lend me a thousand pounds, could you?'

'Sorry, no. Though we could always merge our overdrafts. It might not help the Trelawney much, but there could be other advantages. Someone to talk to over breakfast, for instance. No more having to creep around, pretending we're not sharing a bed. Someone to listen when things go wrong.'

'Caleb,' she whispered.

'Will you marry me, Romy?'

He felt her become still. When the silence had gone on too long, he said, 'Well, it was probably rather optimistic of me to think that you might leap at the offer, but—'

'It's not that.' She gave a little gasp. 'But I can't marry you just *now*.'

He tried to disguise his disappointment. He, too, had his pride. 'I wasn't thinking of tomorrow,' he said. 'But after a decent interval – however long it takes to call the banns – or a bit longer, if you insist—'

'It's just ... the hotel. It's all so difficult – I can't seem to think what to do any more—'

'Then I'll wait.' In the dark he smiled. 'Just you watch. I'll wear you down.'

He had seen, these last few months, how Johnnie Fitzgerald's gossip mongering had eaten away at her. He could see also that she had reached a point where she was too exhausted to think clearly.

'I thought,' he said carefully, 'that if we were married, it might give you an alternative to the hotel. If it was all getting – well, so that you weren't enjoying it any more – then perhaps you might want to think of doing something else.'

'I could be a housewife, I suppose,' she said sarcastically. 'Stay at home and wash the dishes.'

'You know I didn't mean that. But you could do anything you wanted, Romy. It might be exciting to make a fresh start.'

'I don't want to make a fresh start. I can't think of anything else I want to do.' She sounded defensive. 'The Trelawney's mine. No one's going to take it away from me.'

There was another silence. After a while she reached up and stroked his face. 'Caleb? Don't be cross with me. I just need some time.'

'Of course,' he said. 'Tell me what I can do.'

'Nothing. There's nothing. Only—'

'What?'

'Put up with me.' Her voice was harsh. 'Whatever happens. Will you, Caleb?'

'You know I will.'

'Whatever I do – *whatever* – I love you. Promise me you'll always remember that.' She had knelt up in bed. In the darkness her eyes were black and burning.

'I promise,' he said. He knew that she was crying. He took her in his arms and began to kiss her again.

There had been heavy rain for the last two days, and the river was swollen. Following the footpath up the hillside with Sandy and the sheepdog, Tess, at his heels, Jem looked down to where the thick, brown water churned and writhed through the valley. Only half a dozen or so of the twenty-odd stepping stones were now visible. Along the banks of the river the weight of the fast-running water had crushed grass and reeds to a pulpy mat.

It was November, a time of year Jem always disliked. The chill grey skies and the wind whipping the last of the leaves from the trees brought to mind all the bad things, the things he tried not to think about. They had left Middlemere on a cold November day, and several years later Mum had married Dennis in late autumn. Two days afterwards, no longer needing to be on his best behaviour, Dennis had hit Jem for the first time.

Years had passed and it had been during the autumn of 1956 that he'd had the letter from Liz telling him that she had married Ray Babbs. He'd been in prison then, a few months into his sentence, and the walls had closed in on him, crushing him. He'd made the mistake of howling out his pain and one of the screws had thumped him and told him to shut up. Worse, that was when Riggs had seemed to notice him for the first time. Riggs – heavyset and brutish, with a liking for boys – still came to Jem in his nightmares.

Jem shook his head and walked on. He tried to think of better things. His vegetable garden, and the dogs, and Danny. The garden had done well this year; in the summer he'd lived off the carrots and beans and potatoes that he'd grown himself. Danny had enjoyed helping him pick the peas. Jem smiled to himself, remembering the weeks he and Danny had spent together. He'd shown Danny how to shell peas. Danny had eaten most of them raw. Jem had been worried that he might get a stomach ache, but he'd been right as rain. He was a tough little kid, who always had a smile on his face. It troubled Jem that Danny lived in London; Jem didn't want Danny growing up to be one of those kids who thought milk was made in bottles and peas in tins.

Romy was always on at him, trying to persuade him to have Danny come and live with him all the time. She never gave up, Romy, which was why, Jem thought, she'd done so well for herself. Jem sometimes thought that he himself had given up long ago. He wouldn't tell her that, of course, because it would upset her. He'd upset her often enough through the years, with the mess he'd made of things, and he didn't mean to do so again. And, anyway, most of the time he was OK, he managed. It was only some days, days like this, that he felt bad.

Just now the dark thoughts weighed on him, bowing his shoulders, making tears sting behind his eyes. He wouldn't cry, of course. He hadn't cried since he was a little kid – well, only that one time, when Liz had sent the letter and he'd seen doors closing, shutting him out for ever. Now Jem sat down on the slope, his elbows on his knees, pushing his fingers through his hair. Sandy nuzzled up to him and Jem kneaded the lurcher's neck. 'Poor old thing, you're getting on a bit, aren't you?' he whispered. There were grey hairs amongst the pale gold, and Sandy had got rather thin lately. Best dog he'd ever had.

Looking down the hillside to the river valley, he saw that two boys were now playing on the bank. One was fair-haired and one had brown curls, and they had with them fishing nets and jam-jars. They must be about seven or eight, he guessed. Much the same age as he had been when they'd left Middlemere. Jem often thought that if he could just turn back the clock and get back to that point and start again, how differently things might work out. But he knew that you couldn't start again, not really. Romy believed you could, but he knew that she was wrong. She was right about most things, but not about that.

Most of the time he didn't think about Middlemere, but today he didn't seem able to get it out of his head. He didn't feel angry about it, like Romy did. He just missed it. Well, he missed his dad; he didn't miss the house because he could hardly remember it. Just bits, like a jigsaw. All the bits he did remember had his dad in them. His dad letting him ride in the hay cart, or sitting him on top of the huge carthorse, or waving to him as he ran down the short cut by the field, coming home from school. His dad had been tall, strong, certain. Jem knew that though he might have inherited his dad's height and strength, he hadn't an ounce of his certainty. Romy had got all that. Jem hardly ever felt sure about anything. Just Liz, and he'd messed that up good and proper, hadn't he?

Glancing down to the river again, he saw that the smaller boy, the yellow-haired one, was standing on a stepping stone. He had a jam-jar in one hand, the fishing net in the other. Jem kept an eye on him. After such heavy rainfall, the river flowed fast and was deep in the middle. If the boy went onto the next stone, he'd go down to them, he decided, have a word, tell them to play somewhere safer.

Meanwhile, he got his tobacco and papers out of his pocket and rolled himself a cigarette. He didn't drink any more, but he still liked a smoke. He'd stopped drinking after the fight with Ray Babbs, when he'd realized what drink did to him. People like him shouldn't drink, people who lost their temper too easy. Once his temper had gone, he couldn't seem to hold himself back. In drink, he had seen Dennis in himself, and it had sickened him. He'd wanted to hurt, wanted to yell out all the things that Dennis used to yell at him. Jem shut his eyes tightly, but the words still echoed, still seeped their poison. *You worthless little bastard . . . Why do you think your old man blew his brains out? Because he couldn't face a lifetime of staring at your ugly little mug.*

When he opened his eyes, he saw that the child was heading towards the centre of the river, leaping from stone to stone. Jem opened his mouth to call out a warning, but then, realizing the danger of startling the boy, began to scramble fast down the hillside instead. He was within twenty yards of the river bank when the lad, jumping onto the next stepping stone, lost his footing. There was a split second when Jem thought the boy might be able to right himself, but the wet stone was slippery, and the worn rubber sole of the child's plimsoll could get no grip, and he slid into the water with hardly a sound.

On the bank the other boy cried out. Jem yelled at him to go and fetch help, and at the same time pulled off his jacket and kicked off his shoes as he ran. Leaping from stone to stone, he tried to keep track of the small, blond head bobbing downstream. Then he was in the river, hitting the water with a hard, cold, smack, and he was fighting against the current, struggling to go where he wanted to and not where the river wanted to take him. Though he was a strong swimmer, it took every ounce of his strength to reach the boy. Boulders scraped his skin and icy water filled his nostrils and eyes. He was within a few feet of the child when his muscles threatened to seize up on him. Yet he forced himself to keep going: he wouldn't have some poor bugger know that his son had drowned because a useless jerk hadn't made that extra effort. He knew how he'd feel if it were Danny. And he knew how treacherous the river was, how it dragged you down, trapping you beneath boulders or in deep, underwater caves until it was tired of you and spat you out, days later sometimes, downstream.

Reaching out, he grabbed at a handful of jersey. Though the current tried to tug the child away, Jem held on, clawing his fingers into the sodden wool, dragging the small body towards him, making for the bank. *Let him be alive*, he prayed. *Please God, if you're anywhere, anywhere at all, let him be alive.*

Then he was on the river bank, on his hands and knees, all his muscles shaking, staring at the kid lying on the grass. And the boy was screwing up his eyes and giving out a thin, high wail, and Jem sat back on his haunches, weak with relief.

When he was sure the boy was all right, he looked around for the dogs. Tess was on the other bank, waiting for him – good old Tess, such a sensible dog. He couldn't see Sandy. Shakily Jem stood up. He glimpsed something in the river. He thought it was a bit of flotsam, at first – an old sack, a bit of wood. Then, recognizing Sandy, realizing that he had followed him into the water, trying to help, he began to run along the bank. He could see that the dog was too weak, too old, to battle against the force of the river.

He didn't hesitate. Sandy had always been faithful to him, and he'd always preferred dogs to people anyway. They were straight with you, they didn't try to trip you up. He could see Sandy and thought that the dog had seen him. Jem struck out into the water, away from the bank. He felt the force of the current fighting against him, sapping his strength. He knew that he was exhausted, that he had reached the limit of his endurance. It didn't bother him at first: sometimes he'd thought he'd had enough anyway, but then he thought of Danny, and how a kid should have a father, and what losing his father had done to him, and he pushed on, not letting himself give up.

Romy sat in the bar opposite the Manhattan Club. She wore the pale blue Paquin coat and a black hat with a little veil pulled down over her eyes and she was drinking a whisky and soda. It was just before eleven. Across the road, the black-coated, white-scarved men had begun to disappear through the doors of Johnnie Fitzgerald's club.

She thought of the last time she had seen Jem. She remembered the mixture of fear and longing in his eyes. She knew that he was inching, slowly and tentatively, towards believing that he might be a good enough father for Danny. Towards believing in himself. She knew also that his self-belief was fragile, hard-earned and easily broken. So many times in the past she had begun to hope that he might at last become settled, rooted; so many times her hopes had been destroyed. Her greatest fear remained with her: that he might never settle, that he might one day drift away from her, so far that she never saw him again.

She had kept the gifts that Jem had given her over the years. Earlier that evening she had taken them out. The pink rabbit, the swan brooch made of pearls, the bottle of perfume. She had unstoppered the perfume bottle, which, though now empty, still retained an evocative, lingering scent. *Think about whether you'd prefer to keep your secrets to yourself. Think about what* that's *worth to you.* As she had breathed in the perfume, Johnnie Fitzgerald's voice had tormented her, spelling out the choice she had to make.

It was, after all, just another transaction, another piece of business. Start to finish, how long would it take, to sell herself to Johnnie Fitzgerald? An hour? Less? An hour of her life to guarantee Jem's safety and her own privacy wasn't much of a price to pay, was it? And she could close her eyes while he touched her. She could think of something else while he kissed her.

The men had the money and I had something they wanted, Mrs Plummer had told her. Decades ago Mrs Plummer had saved herself with much the same bargain. And it wasn't as though she herself was a virgin. It wasn't even as though she had only gone to bed with men she loved. In the first two years of her ownership of the Trelawney she had slept with one man because she had been lonely and with another because she had believed it might erase the memory of Caleb.

And that was the trouble. Caleb. He had asked her

to marry him. Every part of her had longed to say yes. Yet how could she accept his proposal of marriage, knowing that she meant to give herself to Johnnie Fitzgerald?

She would keep it a secret, she thought desperately. Yet she knew immediately that would not do. Secrets had a way of coming out just when you least wanted them to; secrets had a habit of growing in magnitude over the years. She could not found her marriage on a secret. Betty Hesketh's secret had come back to haunt her. So had Osborne Daubeny's.

In bed with him the other night, she had not told Caleb the truth. She had been afraid of the consequences were she to do so. What would Caleb do if he knew what Johnnie Fitzgerald had demanded of her? He would fight for her. Perhaps he would kill for her. She imagined Caleb arraigned for murder. In her mind's eye, she saw the dock at the Old Bailey, saw the gibbet on Inkpen Hill. How her life ran round in circles, she thought wearily. In tight, concentric, ever-repeating circles.

Her glass was empty. She should go now, seek out Johnnie Fitzgerald and tell him that she agreed to the terms of his bargain. Yet she remembered how, as she had offered Johnnie a financial interest in the hotel, she had hated herself. It had been as though she were inviting herself to be violated. She had felt self-loathing too, all those years ago in Stratton, when Dennis had kissed her. However tightly she closed her eyes, however hard she tried to think of other things, she would not be able to shut Johnnie out. He would become a part of her, ingrained in her. It wouldn't only be for an hour, it would remain with her for the rest of her life. It would claw at her, belittling her. Mrs Plummer had changed her name to escape her past, yet her past had stayed with her, an ever-present threat to what had always been most important to her: her reputation.

A voice said, 'Can I get you another drink, love?' and she jumped.

He was pleasant-looking, thirtyish, wearing an overcoat that had worn through at the cuffs. He said, 'Only I've seen you here the last few nights. Wondered whether you wanted some company. Nothing funny – just a drink, and then we could go some place.'

She realized that he thought she was a tart. What other sort of woman would sit alone in a bar, drinking? How men judged, she thought. How they watched and estimated and calculated a woman's worth.

She murmured a polite refusal and left the bar. *Jem*, she thought, *Jem*, and she paused momentarily, looking across the road.

Then she turned and walked away, her head held high. 'I am Romy Cole,' she whispered aloud. She had always been proud of being a Cole, and she meant to go on being proud. And they would manage, she and Jem: they would find a way. Just as they had always done.

She went back to the hotel. And found that Carol was waiting for her in reception and was telling her, in a jumble of fast, excited phrases, something about a phone call, and Jem, and a boy and a dog.

*

601

It was in the papers. *Hero rescues child from river.* Yet she shouted down the phone to him: 'You could have *died*, Jem! You could have *died*! And for a *dog*!'

Then she burst into tears and she heard his voice, made thin by the phone line, saying, 'I'm sorry, Romy, I didn't mean to. But I couldn't just leave him, could I?'

She didn't know whether he meant the dog or the boy. But she blew her nose and said, 'You don't have to apologize, you idiot. I'm not cross with you. I'm *proud* of you.'

People were making such a fuss, Jem told her. He sounded bewildered. People he had never met before would come up to him in the street and shake his hand. The mother of the boy he had rescued had come to his cottage and had stood in his front room, weeping. Jem hadn't known what to do. In the end he'd made her a cup of tea and then told her that he had to get back to work. It was much worse than going into the river, he said to Romy, all these women crying over him.

The parish council had wanted to make him some sort of award, but he couldn't have borne that. He'd asked Mike Green, his boss, to have a word with them. He'd told Mike it was ridiculous, all this pretending he was a hero when he wasn't, anything but. To explain things properly, he'd had to tell Mike the truth. About the schools he'd been chucked out of, the jobs he'd been fired from, and his two miserable years in the army. Then he'd found himself telling Mike about Ray Babbs and about going to prison. As he had spoken, something strange had happened. He had seemed to feel a weight falling from his shoulders and he had seemed actually to grow taller. As though something heavy had been crushing him, making him keep his eyes on the ground.

And the even stranger thing, he added, was that Mike hadn't seemed bothered at all. He'd just clapped Jem on the shoulder, and said, 'Aye, we all do daft things when we're young, don't we?' and had offered Jem a beer. Jem had opted for Tizer and they'd sat at the Greens' kitchen table, drinking and smoking, hardly exchanging a word, but perfectly content.

'And the little boy?' Romy asked. 'And Sandy?'

'The kid's fine,' Jem said. Hundreds of miles away, his voice seemed to contract. Poor old Sandy hadn't survived his swim more than a couple of days. The vet had told Jem that the exertion and the shock of the cold water had been too much for the old dog's heart. Jem had buried him in a corner of the field.

'Oh, *Jem*,' she said.

'It's OK. He was getting on a bit.'

There was a silence. 'Danny,' she said eventually. 'There's no reason why you shouldn't have Danny to live with you now, is there, Jem?'

She could almost hear him gathering up his courage, taking the huge step of beginning to believe in himself. Harder than diving into an ice-cold river.

Then he said, 'Maybe I should give it a go. Me and Danny. See how it works out.'

She packed up Danny's belongings and helped Jem load them into the car. The clothes, the toys, the books, and the tall stool she had bought when Danny had grown out of his high chair, so that he could sit at the table. Hugging Danny goodbye, she closed her eyes tightly so that she would remember him better. The smell of him, the touch of him, the weight of him in her arms.

When they had gone, she went back upstairs to her flat. She could hear the drip of a tap, the tick of the clock. In Danny's room the drawers and shelves were empty, the bed stripped down to the mattress. She should be feeling triumphant, she told herself. This was what she had always wanted.

Yet she felt only emptiness. She remembered the day she had brought Danny back to the Trelawney. How frightened she had been and how, suddenly, alarmingly, aware of the responsibility she had taken on. How they had come to terms, she and Danny; he disregarding her clumsiness, she learning to recognize his needs. She remembered his first smile, his first step, his first word. How he had changed from a baby into a little boy. The things that made him cross, the things that made him happy. How, when they had walked along the Embankment together, he had bounced up and down in his pram and hooted, like the boats.

She hadn't needed to close her eyes to make herself remember. He was there, and he would always be there, and his absence now was almost too dreadful to bear.

She went to see Johnnie. He was sitting at the corner table in the Manhattan Club. The harsh stage lights showed up the puffiness around his eyes and the extra weight around his jawline. Nicotine yellowed his fingers and the first broken veins blossomed on his cheekbones.

In five years' time, she thought, he would be an ageing, unattractive drunk.

She pitched her voice loud enough to be heard above the orchestra and, using the sort of words she had rarely employed since leaving Hill View, told him what she thought of his proposition. The complacency fell from his eyes; the colour drained from his face. When she had finished, she said, 'Do your worst, Johnnie – I really don't care. But there's something you ought to know. You said that I was like you, but you were quite wrong about that. I've learned how to love people, but you've never loved anyone but yourself. You say that you loved Mrs Plummer, but you've never known what love is. Love is putting someone else's needs before your own. Love is knowing when to let go. Those last few months of Mrs Plummer's life, she didn't want you. She loved you, Johnnie, she would have given you anything you wanted, but you broke her heart over and over again. In the end, you broke it once too often. Remember that, Johnnie, and remember that *you* were the person who killed her love for you – *you*, not *me*.'

As she walked out of the room, there was a ripple of applause and the crash of a glass being hurled with great force on the floor. She ran up the narrow stairs and out into the cold, fresh air.

George Everett phoned her. He had spoken to a friend of his, a financier, who had offered to make her a short-term loan. 'The interest rate will be a bit over the odds, I'm afraid,' he said 'but it should help you pull through.'

Guests had begun to return to the hotel and diners

to the brasserie and restaurant. She supposed that people had forgotten, that the appetite for scandal was easily jaded and forever in search of something new. In the upstairs rooms all the timber damaged by the dry rot had been removed and replaced. The workmen had begun to plaster over the raw brick, to paint the new sills and skirting boards.

It seemed to her that it was possible that she might be able to save the hotel. If she were careful, if she met with no more disasters. She continued to make economies, continued to fill in herself when they were short-staffed. She was careful with money, counting every penny. She knew how close they had come to the edge and how easily they might threaten to slip over it again.

Though she should have been relieved at the Trelawney's survival, instead she felt exhausted and ill. However long she slept, she could not seem to stop feeling tired, and she was sick two mornings running: a stomach bug, she supposed. And the Trelawney, as always, cast up an endless series of minor problems, problems that had once fascinated her, yet now wearied her. Though she continued to work long hours with a dogged conscientiousness, she found herself lacking patience with the failings of others. Complaining guests and inefficient staff made her grit her teeth with irritation. She couldn't seem to care any more whether the restaurant served turbot or skate, or whether the decorators painted the skirting boards white or cream.

She missed Danny, now happily settled in Yorkshire. She spoke to him once a week on the phone and wrote frequent letters for Jem to read out to him. She sensed that he was growing away from her, and knew that soon he would no longer remember his early years in London. She missed Caleb, whom she had seen only occasionally during the past few weeks. She had put him off, she thought miserably, and he had become fed up with her. She couldn't blame him, really: she knew that she was snappy and short-tempered and not much fun.

She was checking the next week's menus one afternoon, when her eyelids grew heavy. Her thoughts began to shift and shimmer, and the menus, which until a moment ago had listed sensible things like roast pork and beef tournedos, now included dishes she had eaten as a child in the war: Woolton Pie and cabbage fritters, and the pheasant and rabbit that her father had shot. A twist of the kaleidoscope and she was fighting with Annie Paynter. One sharp push and Annie was in the horse trough, screaming like a stuck pig, dirty water streaming from her yellow curls.

Another twist and Romy was walking up the track that led to Middlemere. It was a clear blue summer's day and she was pushing a pram. The pram was navy blue, big and battered and old-fashioned, and it bounced on the ruts. Though the baby in the pram slept uncomplainingly, every now and then Romy would stop and check that she was comfortable, raising the hood when the sun was too bright, and adjusting the baby's bonnet, with its narrow pink ribbons. She ran her fingertip along the curve of the baby's cheek, delighting in the velvety softness. She had never loved anyone as much as she loved this baby. Her heart ached with the weight of her love.

But the pram was heavy and hard to push. She

wasn't much taller than the height of the handle, and her arms had begun to ache. As the track went on, her progress became slower. Puddles spread across the impacted mud and the incline became steeper. Though she knew that she must reach the top of the hill soon, her way was now impeded by tall trees. Peering through the dense thicket, she could not see Middlemere. The sky had darkened so that the valley now lay in shadow. It was possible, she realized, that she had taken the wrong way, that she had become lost, that she would never find her way home again. And when she looked back inside the pram, she saw that it was empty. She had been careless, she supposed, and the infant had tumbled out somewhere in the hard, bumpy push along the rutted track.

The telephone rang, jolting her awake. After she had answered the call, she asked Carol to bring her tea. Tears still ached behind her eyes, and her panic and grief at the loss of the baby lingered. The infant had been Danny, she supposed, though the child in the pram had been smaller and more fragile than Danny had ever been. She was dreaming of babies, she told herself, because she was missing Danny.

Yet something niggled. *Babies.* Recently she had found herself peering in prams, cooing over the guests' small infants. So unlike her. Visiting Psyche earlier in the week, she had cuddled Pysche's eleven-month-old daughter. Psyche thought she was pregnant again: she had missed her last period and was sick in the mornings.

Sick in the mornings . . . Romy froze, the cup clutched in her hand. There were things a girl was supposed to keep track of which she had let slip, swamped by all the anxieties of the last few months. She found her diary and began to leaf frantically through it, thumbing the pages back: four, five, six – oh, dear God – *seven* weeks – *seven* – since she had last had her period.

She sat down at the desk and ran her forefinger down the calendar once more. She couldn't be pregnant. It was impossible. Only not so impossible, really, when you thought of how she and Caleb had spent a great deal of their time together.

But not *now*. Not when she was just getting back on her feet. Not when she was just beginning to get straight again. She, Romy Cole, couldn't possibly have made such an old, old mistake, and have fallen pregnant like some stupid shopgirl.

The letter arrived first post on Saturday morning. It was from Evelyn Daubeny. It told Caleb that Osborne Daubeny was dying and had asked to see him.

There was the impulse to crumple up the letter and throw it in the bin. But he couldn't quite bring himself to do that. *He has only a very short time to live*, Evelyn had written. Death was so final, so absolute. It allowed you no time for a change of heart. And besides, it seemed to Caleb that the tangled story of the Daubenys, Heskeths and Coles was peppered by an inability to forgive.

As he drove west out of London, he thought of Romy. *I can't marry you just now*, she had said, when he had proposed to her. *I can't seem to think what to do any more.* So he had put his energies into thinking for her. He had made phone calls, paid visits. He intended to show Romy that she had choices and possibilities. That she didn't have to keep to the one path fate had set her on. That there were other roads, roads that branched off into unknown lands, roads that could take her to all sorts of marvellous and unexpected places.

On Saturday morning two of the waitresses called in sick. Romy made a note to dock their pay. Then the accountant telephoned; she went through box files, searching for the answers to his questions. It was hard to concentrate; she couldn't keep her mind on the job any more. How would she manage all this and a baby? Though she had run a thirty-bedroom hotel for the last three years; though she had propped up her family throughout her adult life; though she had dealt with Johnnie Fitzgerald, and had endured and survived rejection and exclusion, the thought of pregnancy and childbirth made her feel panicked, flustered, all at sea.

Mid-morning one of the porters managed to lose a guest's case between the reception area and her suite. Soothing the guest, a demanding, hysterical woman, dissuading her from calling the police, she thought, And *Caleb*. What would Caleb say when she told him about the baby? She didn't doubt for a minute that Caleb would do the honourable thing. But, telling him, would she sense that he felt trapped? Would she detect in his voice, in his eyes, shock or, worse, reluctance? Several times that morning she dialled his flat, but the phone rang out, unanswered.

The vanity case turned up after ten minutes. Then Terry stuck his head around the door to ask her whether she had found any temporary waitresses. One of the chambermaids came to her office to complain about another chambermaid. *She never does the windows. You can't see through her windows and then I get in trouble because Mrs Motte thinks its my fault.* A *baby*, Romy thought, as the girl chattered on. A *baby*, next summer.

Terry came back into the room. 'Linda's gone and cut her hand — that's three waitresses we're short of now.' Carol rushed in, in a panic. 'Romy, I think Mandy's double-booked the honeymoon suite.' The chambermaid was still talking. 'And if I've told her once you have to use Silvo on the taps I've told her a thousand times.'

Their voices seemed to fill Romy's head. They seemed to increase in volume, clamouring, wanting every bit of her. *Miss Cole, I have to know about the waitresses ... Romy, shall I tell Mandy to give the Scotts the blue room and the Marriotts the honeymoon suite? Or the other way round? ... Can't possibly run two restaurants with only four waitresses ... And the baths, Miss Cole! I can't tell you what a state she leaves the baths in!*

Romy stood up. As she walked out of the room, the voices tailed off into shocked silence. She imagined them, motionless, wide-eyed, open-mouthed at her desertion.

She swept up her bag and coat en route and headed down the stairs, through the reception area and outside. Sitting on the bench in the gardens, she took in lungfuls of cold air. She remembered the first time she had seen the Trelawney. She had had bruises on her face and a few pence in her pocket. Mrs Plummer had picked her up out of the gutter, had rescued her, had given her a chance. What would Mrs Plummer say if she could speak to her now? What would Mrs Plummer say if she could explain to her that she was tired of the hotel, tired of the demands it imposed on her, tired of the fair-weather friends who had deserted her when she had needed them most, tired of the struggle to climb up the social ladder and the fight for acceptance, a fight that she had once cared so much for, but which no longer seemed important. What would Mrs Plummer say if she were to tell her that she wasn't enjoying the hotel any more, hadn't been enjoying it, in fact, for rather a long time? Would Mrs Plummer, who had reinvented herself over and over again, condemn her for choosing to make a new start?

She rose from the bench and, without a backward look at the Trelawney, walked to Soho. She remembered her first visit there. She had been nineteen years old and she hadn't even known what most of the items in the delicatessens were. She had never drunk espresso coffee, had never been to a nightclub or a bar. She had been a poor little thing, as narrow and insubstantial as the environment in which she had grown up, her horizons limited, her vision confined to the small world she knew.

Without Mrs Plummer, without Jake and his friends, she would have been nothing. With Jake she had come to know the raffish, unconventional London that had flourished in Soho. She had discovered different ways of thinking, different ways of living. With Mrs Plummer, she had travelled to France, and had seen the Mediterranean Sea and palm trees fringing a bay.

Between them Mrs Plummer and Jake had allowed her to cast off her provincialism, had allowed her to grow and to discover who she was. They — and Caleb, of course — had made her a different, better person. They had taught her to love.

Yet the early years of her life had taught her valuable lessons too. The expulsion from Middlemere and the years in Stratton had taught her to survive. They — her father, her mother, even Dennis — had given her strength and a determination to succeed. She no longer felt ashamed of her background; she had learned to be proud of what she was. She had travelled a long, long way, and she was beginning to see what direction she must take next.

She went into a cafe and bought a coffee. Half a dozen girls drooped over the jukebox, whispering and giggling. They were wearing black polo necks and bright, circular skirts. They wore their hair chopped short in a bob or shorn in an urchin cut. Their feet, in flat-heeled shoes, tapped to the beat of the rock and roll. Their hips swayed, their kohl-lined eyes narrowed, and they exuded youth, sensuality, *liberty*. She might have been their mother, Romy thought, in her sober grey two-piece, her tweed coat, and her pearls and chignon and old-fashioned red lipstick. She had let herself fall behind, excluded from the excitement and the sense of freedom that, as the end of the decade approached, had begun to pulse through London.

She couldn't drink the coffee; she pushed it away. She took out her compact and scrubbed off the red lipstick. Then she let down her hair. It fell to her shoulders, smooth and shining, the colour of falling leaves.

Swanton Lacy had altered since Caleb had last seen it. Rust pitted the great wrought-iron gates and puddles pocked the narrow path. In the flower beds, the summer's perennials had gone to seed.

Evelyn Daubeny answered the door. Caleb had steeled himself for this moment, anticipating resentment, hatred even. But she said only, 'Caleb, how good of you to come,' and showed him inside.

Like the house, Mrs Daubeny had changed. Her hair was shorter, greyer. She was wearing a thick jumper and trousers. A sensible choice: the house was freezing. At the top of the stairs, she turned to him. 'Just ten minutes, Caleb. He's very sick. Dying, actually. He has days at most, Dr Lockhart says.' She paused, and seemed to be searching for words. Then she said, 'Be kind to him, if you can.'

Along a corridor, she opened a door. This room was stuffy and overheated, with the hospital smell of disinfectant. Osborne Daubeny lay in bed, propped up on pillows. Caleb heard the rattle of his breath.

Evelyn touched her husband's shoulder. 'Osborne, Caleb is here.'

Daubeny's breathing seemed to alter in timbre. As he approached the bedside, Caleb saw what disease had done to Osborne Daubeny. The once-imposing frame had been eaten away to skin and bone. The ruddy skin was now yellow and waxy. The smallest movement seemed to require of him a dreadful effort. Though he must be only about sixty years old, Caleb estimated, sickness had made him an old man.

'Caleb,' Daubeny whispered.

Evelyn left the room. Daubeny's breath wheezed and rattled. Then he said, 'Wasn't sure whether you'd come.'

Caleb's mouth was dry. 'Neither was I at first.'

'Glad you did. Not asking for anything from you. Wanted to give you something.' He paused. 'I'm dying. This place – Swanton Lacy – will die with me. But I've put something by for you. Evelyn will give it to you.'

'There's no need—'

'I *wanted* to.'

In the dying man's voice, there was an echo of the old obstinacy and pride. Looking up, Caleb saw that the heat in the room had made the window panes blur with condensation, blotting out Swanton Lacy's gardens.

Daubeny muttered, 'The estate will be sold up when I die. They'll knock the house down, I daresay – it's all it's good for now, anyway. Falling about my ears. Then they'll sell off the land to pay off the death duties. Put up dozens of little shoeboxes. Make their millions.' He made a curious sound; it took Caleb a moment or two to recognize it as laughter. 'What do you think they'll call the nasty, mean little streets that they'll build? Swanton Street? Daubeny Close? Some such nonsense? Is that how my name will live on, do you think, in a row of tin-pot red-brick bungalows?'

He began to cough, a choking, terrible sound, as if the fluid in his lungs was drowning him. 'Water,' he hissed.

There was a carafe on the bedside table. Caleb

poured water into a glass and helped him sit up. After he had drunk, Daubeny slumped back on the pillows, his eyes closed.

He said softly, 'I never meant it. What happened to the Coles. Always felt bad about it. Especially the little girl.'

Caleb felt a surge of anger. It was on the tip of his tongue to say: You might not have meant it, but you did it. But he bit back the words and said instead, 'I'm going to marry her. I'm going to marry Romy Cole.' Because he was. However long it took to persuade her.

Daubeny's eyes had closed again. When Caleb was sure the old man was asleep, he touched Daubeny's hand. The bones seemed to be forcing their way through the paper-thin skin. If he squeezed that hand, it would crumble to dust. Whatever Daubeny had done, he thought, whatever his pride and arrogance had led him to, he didn't deserve *this*.

He went to the window and ran his palm across the pane. The mist on the glass blurred the garden, smudging the lawns, trees and lakes into a wash of blue and silver and green.

He left the room. Evelyn was waiting for him at the foot of the stairs. 'How was he?' she asked.

'He didn't say much. He fell asleep.'

'He sleeps most of the time now.' She glanced at him. 'You'll have a cup of tea, won't you, Caleb?'

It would have seemed churlish to refuse. He followed her into the kitchen. She said, 'I saw the piece about you in *Homes and Gardens*. That was how I found you.'

There had been a paragraph in the magazine about

the garden he had designed for the Harbornes. He watched Evelyn Daubeny make tea, cut bread and ham.

He said, 'Mum told me you'd left Mr Daubeny.'

She put plates on the table. 'I went to live with my mother in Bournemouth. I've been there for over three years now. My mother died eighteen months ago.'

'I'm sorry.'

'It was quick, mercifully. Not like this.'

'So are you—' His voice trailed away; he couldn't think of the right words.

'All right?' She smiled. 'Is that what you'd like to ask me, Caleb? Well, yes, I am, actually. No more wandering around in rainstorms accosting innocent bystanders, you'll be pleased to hear. I am sorry about that. It must have been so embarrassing and painful for you.'

He muttered, 'I don't know about innocent.'

'Of course you were,' she said briskly. 'None of us can help the circumstances of our birth. My babies have taught me that, at least.' Catching his glance, she said, 'They are only borrowed, but they are my babies, for a while. I run a hostel for unmarried mothers, you see.'

'*Oh*,' he said.

'It's a nice hostel. No rules and regulations. I try to make it a home for the girls, a proper home. The sort of home I should have liked to have myself when I was younger.' She took a cake tin down from the shelf. 'The vicar at our parish church gives my address to any girls he hears of who are in trouble and have nowhere to go. I take them in if I possibly can. They stay with me for as long as they like. Some of them just stay until they have their baby, and then they have the child adopted and go back to their families. Others choose to keep the baby. One of the mothers has been with me for almost four years. We are great friends. She helps with the hostel.'

She opened her handbag and showed him a photograph. 'This is Coral. She was our first baby. She was born when my mother was still alive. Four generations of women in one household – you would think it would be a disaster, wouldn't you? But it wasn't. It was a very happy time.'

He looked down at the round, laughing face, framed with dark curls. 'She's beautiful,' he said.

'Isn't she?' Evelyn said proudly. 'And I've done all sorts of things these last few years,' she went on. 'I've been abroad – I've even flown in an aeroplane. And I have a friend, a dear man who teaches the piano, and we go to concerts together. I've learned a great deal about music – I never knew anything about it before.' Her blue-grey eyes focused on him. 'And I've learned to stand up for myself. I help out my girls. I make sure that no one takes their babies from them. I protect them. Sometimes, when I look back, I can hardly remember the person I used to be.'

He said, 'Yet you came back here.'

'For Osborne? Yes. We are still married, you know. We never divorced. He is still my husband.' She frowned. 'Since I left him, I have remembered that, when we first married, we were very happy. When I was living with him I had forgotten that. Isn't that odd, Caleb?'

*

Osborne Daubeny heard the boy leave the house. There was a murmur of voices and then doors opened and closed. The pain was seeping back, but he put off the moment of asking for the next dose of morphine. He needed to think clearly.

Lacking money to pay labourers, he had begun, soon after Evelyn had left him, to try to repair the bridge himself. In the summer, when the lake had dried up, he had waded into the water and lashed ropes to the blocks of marble. He had used the old carthorse to drag them to the bank. Over the years he had hauled more than a dozen stones out of the lake. They remained on the bank, green lichen staining their porous surfaces. In the evenings, he had studied old engravings in the library, trying to work out how the bridge had been constructed. He had needed something to keep him busy; time had hung heavily on his hands and the house had seemed too big, too echoing, without Evelyn.

Each summer the lake had shrunk to half its winter size. The dried mud that surrounded the water cracked, and the veils of pondweed solidified into brackish shrouds. A smell of decay had lingered in the air, drifting, on hot evenings, into the house. The house itself had acquired, in Evelyn's absence, a sullen, dusty air, and the myriad small domestic tasks that he had once thought so easy, so unworthy of his notice, had seemed to defeat him.

One day he had stooped and prised something glittering out of the fudgy grip of the mud. It was a cap badge; rubbing it clean, he saw that it belonged to the regiment which had been stationed at Swanton Lacy during the war. He had slid the badge into his pocket.

The arrival of the army at Swanton Lacy, so soon after Samuel Cole's death, had seemed to him a punishment sent by God. He had never really succeeded in thinking of it in any other way. Now, lying on his deathbed, he remembered Betty Hesketh, remembered her as she had been more than a quarter of a century ago. Never a passionate man, her effect on him during the few weeks of their love affair had been both disturbing and exhilarating. He recalled her small, voluptuous body and her greed for life. She had not hid from him her enjoyment of sex. Married to a woman who regarded sex as a duty rather than a pleasure, it had at first shocked him that a woman could be so unashamed, so openly demanding. But shock had quickly turned to pride. He had felt powerful and, yes, manly, when Betty Hesketh had cried out with ecstasy in his arms. They had copulated in fields, in haystacks and (Evelyn's accusing voice still echoed) in the back of his car. Once he had made love to her standing up in the small room where they made tea at the village hall.

She had been a rule-breaker, Betty Hesketh. He had been in thrall to her. Whatever she had asked of him, he had done. Part of the attraction for her, he had later suspected, had been in seeing the self-important, proud Osborne Daubeny with straw in his hair, or with his trousers at half-mast, gasping out his worship of her to the hiss of the kettle and the echo of disputatious voices from the adjacent room.

It had been Betty who had broken off the relationship. 'I'm pregnant,' she had told him one afternoon, 'and I think it's yours, Osborne.' He had offered to set her up somewhere, to buy her a little flat in London, imagining heady visits to some secluded love nest. She had refused, telling him that she would not see him again and that she would bring up the child as her husband's. He had protested; he adored her, he told her. No, you don't, she had said, with a cool look in her eye. You desire me. And that's different. And besides, the only man I've ever loved is Archie, and I've no intention of leaving him.

Afterwards, his affair with Betty had slid into the past, to be recalled occasionally with a mixture of shame and disbelief at his own recklessness. He had at first taken little interest in his son. A mild curiosity had prompted him to peep into the pram when he encountered the Heskeths in the street. But then, as the child had grown older, as he had become able to see himself in the boy's features, and as none of Evelyn's babies had survived, he had begun to feel an unexpected affinity, even a longing, as well as a pride in knowing that he was capable of siring a healthy son. He had hated to think of his only child growing up in a squalid little cottage in the back lanes of Swanton le Marsh. He had not dared to offer to improve the cottage: it might have provoked suspicion, and anyway by the end of the Thirties the estate had already been in severe financial difficulties.

His opportunity had come after Archie Hesketh's death. It had seemed decent and even compassionate to rent Middlemere to the surviving Heskeths and, not long afterwards, to help Betty find a school for the boy. Decent and compassionate. Caleb Hesketh hadn't seen it like that. Even now he remembered the contempt in the boy's eyes. I did it for you, he had said, on the day

Caleb had discovered his parentage. I wanted you to have a good home. That wasn't wrong, was it, to give you a good home? It wasn't wrong to give you Middlemere?

Middlemere ... Daubeny remembered the horror he had felt on the day he had learned that Sam Cole had turned the gun on himself. Guilt had clung to him ever since, becoming ingrained in him, like lichen on marble. Why had he evicted the Coles? Now, when he had so little time left, he could at last acknowledge the truth. It might have been preferable, he thought, to have done as Evelyn had believed and as he had told Caleb: to have evicted Cole so that his one-time mistress and his only child should have a decent home. To have been motivated by passion, rather than pride. But renting Middlemere to Betty and Caleb had been an afterthought, a way, perhaps, of trying to make good come out of bad. A sort of atonement.

He had evicted Cole because Cole had become intolerable to him. He had evicted Cole because Samuel Cole had been the only man in the Swantons not to touch his cap to him. And because he had been the only farmer not to give him at least the appearance of respect. He had evicted Cole because Cole's disdain had been written in his sharp brown eyes and in the scorn in his voice. Cole had believed himself better than Osborne Daubeny. Cole's contempt had been that of the self-made man for those born with silver spoons in their mouths. Every gesture, every challenge to his authority, had been underwritten by Cole's unshakeable belief in his own worth.

Cole's estimation of him had touched a raw nerve.

Osborne had rarely had the opportunity to prove himself. It had been his elder brother who had fought and died in the First World War, not he. He had still been at school when the war had broken out and then, when he had finally been shipped to the Front in 1918, he had contracted measles. Measles, of all things – such a humiliating, childish disease. The illness had left him partially deaf in one ear, and by the time he had recovered, the war had almost been over.

The death of his father in 1912 and his elder brother in 1915 had left the estate severely burdened by death duties. Throughout the Twenties and Thirties he had been preoccupied with the futile struggle to make Swanton Lacy profitable once more. Though he had volunteered for active service in 1939, he had been turned down because of his age and poor hearing. He had glimpsed his destiny in the formation of the County War Agricultural Executive Committees. He had understood straight away the importance of efficient food production to Britain's war effort. He had thrown himself into his duties with a crusading zeal: fallow fields were ploughed up and planted with seed potatoes, land which for centuries had grazed only sheep was turned over to arable. Marshland was drained, thickets of thorn and bramble uprooted. Thistles and ragwort were pulled out in their thousands.

Then Cole had crossed him. Cole always believed he knew best. You couldn't grow root crops in the fields on the north slope of the hill, Cole told him, because they were too stony. You couldn't plant grain in the fields in the valley because you couldn't drain the land. Once he had come out of church after morning service and Cole had been waiting for him. Cole had harangued him in front of everyone, his weather-beaten face red with fury, his words intemperate, accusing. Cole's wife had eventually dragged him away, but not before he, Osborne Daubeny, had been humiliated in front of the entire village.

Paynter, too, had clashed with Cole. Daubeny had suspected at the time that Paynter's damning survey on the state of Middlemere Farm had been motivated by spite. And he, Daubeny, who had by that time hated Cole, had left things to Paynter, had refrained from reining him in. *Could you have prevented it?* Evelyn had asked him three and a half years ago. Of course he could. There had been a time when he could have intervened, could have stopped events getting out of hand. But he had not done so. His pride, his inability to admit that he might be in the wrong, had not let him, and the vendetta had gathered a life of its own, crushing and unstoppable.

A year after Cole's death he had gone to check on the farm. He had rented out the Middlemere lands to the man who farmed the adjacent fields, an amiable giant by the name of Abbott. The valley was still undrained; sheep still grazed on the north meadows. No point in ploughing, explained Mr Abbott cheerfully. Root crops would never grow in those fields. Too stony, too boggy. Daubeny had thought he heard the crack of a gun, echoing against the hills.

Evelyn came into the room. She gave him morphine and the pain retreated. He knew it was only at bay, though, that it was waiting for him. Just as, since Cole's death, guilt had always waited for him, had been there in the wings, watching to take its cue. Guilt, and the remorse that had accompanied it, had stunted the remainder of his life. It had trapped him in the past. Now, remembering the touch of the boy's hand, he felt a little of that burden slip away. His only son was to marry Sam Cole's daughter ... Well, he thought, you won in the end, didn't you, Sam Cole?

The morphine conquered him and his mind drifted. He was walking through the garden. It was summer – June, always the best month in the garden. The air was sweet with the scent of roses and honeysuckle. Delphiniums cast up their tall, blue spikes, and the copper beech and cedar threw dark, mysterious shadows. Beneath his feet, the lawn was smooth green velvet. In the distance, the lake shimmered. In its glassy surface he could see the sky, scattered with a few puffy white clouds. Spanning the lake, the bridge was a pale and graceful arch, doubled by its reflection.

He walked across the lawn. He looked back, just once, at the house. Then he set foot on the bridge.

Caleb didn't open the parcel that Evelyn Daubeny had given him until he was back in Canonbury. The parcel was large and oblong in shape. He set it on the kitchen table and peeled away the brown paper wrappings.

He saw that Osborne Daubeny had given him a book. As he turned the pages, phrases written in faded brown ink caught his eye. *Wind SE, fine in morning, coming over cloudy after dinner, then rain fell in torrents*

... fruit trees in orchard disbudded ... pineapples fruiting in glasshouses ... the engineer from London arrived to oversee the construction of the weir.

Within the book were a set of plans. Unfolding them, laying them out on the table, Caleb saw terraces, flower beds, and an arboretum. Osborne Daubeny had given him the original plans for the great garden at Swanton Lacy, as well as the diary of its creator. Reverently he touched the thick, yellowing paper and seemed to see a garden unfolding before him, an earthly paradise.

Romy went to Stratton to see her mother. Wiping her hands on her apron, Martha opened one kitchen cupboard after another. 'If you'd let me know you were coming ... there's not a thing in the house. And the shop's shut, or I'd send Ronnie. It'll just have to be bread and jam.' She plonked a loaf on the bread board.

'I'm not hungry, actually, Mum.'

'You have to eat.' Martha looked disapproving. 'You're as thin as a rake.'

'Later, maybe.'

'Tea, then. Or coffee.' Martha brandished a jar of Nescafé.

'Not coffee. I don't seem to fancy it any more.'

Martha looked at her suspiciously. 'Romy? What's up?'

'I'm pregnant, Mum.'

'*Pregnant*—' Martha stopped cutting the bread and leaned against the kitchen table, staring at Romy. She looked winded. She said sharply, 'Does that young man of yours know?'

'Caleb? Not yet. He isn't at home. I expect he's in Norfolk.'

Martha looked worried. 'He will do the decent thing, won't he, Romy?'

'Course he will.' If Caleb had changed his mind, then she'd damn well change it back again. She wanted him, she was sure of that now. And what she most wanted, she always got.

'I could send Dennis round, have a word with him—' Martha was fingering the breadknife.

'No, Mum,' she said hastily. 'That won't be necessary.'

Martha put a tentative hand on her shoulder. 'Are you sure, Romy? About the baby?'

'Pretty sure. I keep being sick in the mornings, and I've been dreaming about babies.' She rested her palms on her belly, thinking of the tiny heart that beat there. 'It's always the same dream,' she said slowly. 'I'm at Middlemere and I'm pushing a pram up the track. A big, heavy, navy-blue pram. I thought it was Danny in the pram at first, but I don't think it can be. The baby's a girl – she's smaller than Danny ever was and she's got pink ribbons in her bonnet.'

Martha said, 'I expect you were dreaming about Maisie.'

'Maisie?' At the back of her mind, memory stirred.

'I thought you'd forgotten her. You never talked about her. Mind you, you never talked about any of it, did you, not once we left Middlemere. You only ever talked about what you were *going* to do, how you were going to buy us a house, make us all rich, all that. And Jem, of course, Jem never talked about anything at all.' Martha looked at Romy. 'Maisie was your sister,' she said gently. She sat down beside Romy. 'She only lived a few months, poor little thing. She died the summer before we left Middlemere. She was always sickly. She didn't grow proper. You doted on her, used to take her out for walks in her pram. And she was the apple of your dad's eye.' Martha looked sad. 'He thought it was the water that had made her ill. The well always dried up in the summer and we were forever getting stomach aches. Sam blamed Daubeny for not giving us piped water, said he made us live like beasts.' Martha's face seemed to crumple. 'But I *knew*,' she whispered. 'I knew she wasn't right the day she was born. I could see it in her eyes.'

She rose, and began to search through the cupboards again. 'Water biscuits,' she said briskly. 'They were the only thing I could keep down when I was expecting.' She took out a packet and shook a few onto a plate. 'Eat some of those. You have to keep your strength up.' She paused. Then she said, 'That's why they fell out, Sam and Daubeny. Because of Maisie. After she died, Sam said he was going to tell Daubeny what he thought of him. I tried to stop him, but he wouldn't listen. He went to the church, waited till Daubeny came out. Told him that it was his fault that Maisie had died.' Martha frowned. 'Daubeny didn't like that, being made to look a fool in front of everyone. I don't think he ever forgave Sam that. And Sam never really got over losing Maisie. I think it turned his mind. The baby ... and then the house ... it was all too much for him.'

Martha made the tea. Then she shook her head. 'Clever girl like you, Romy, and you've gone and got yourself caught out.' She tutted.

Later she walked to the phone box at the top of the hill. When Caleb answered, she said, 'There's something I have to tell you.'

'And me you. Fire away then.'

She was suddenly shy. 'No. You first.'

'I've been thinking about what you said the other week. About not knowing what to do next.'

'Go on.'

'Well, I've come up with a few things. But it depends.'

'On what?'

'On you, Romy. On whether you'd like to marry me, for instance.'

'Oh,' she said. She was twisting the flex of the telephone around her fingers. 'I think that I'm going to have to marry you, actually, Caleb. And another thing – I've been thinking that I might sell the hotel. A friend of mine has offered to buy it. I seem to have had enough, somehow. I'd like to make a new start. I'd like to do something different.'

From the other end of the line, she heard him say, 'Darling Romy. We could travel, if you like. I can work anywhere, remember.'

She remembered her dream of a house by the sea. 'Or I could buy another hotel. A different hotel. On the coast, perhaps.'

'Perhaps they'd sell you the Alma.'

She thought of how it had perched on top of the cliff, surrounded by acres of garden. 'That wallpaper,' she said. 'That awful lino.'

Then he said, '*Have* to marry me . . .?'

On New Year's Day, the first day of the new decade, Romy asked Caleb to drive her to Middlemere.

The house was empty. Shadows pooled in the court-yard, and the previous night's rain clung to the roof and walls. Caleb waited in the van while she circled the house. She thought of the dispossessions that echoed through the century. She saw the great rivers of people who had made their way from one country to another, pursued by war or hatred, pushing their belongings before them in a pram or a wheelbarrow. She saw them slowed by their children and their aged.

She and her family had been a small part of that great exodus, their lives overtaken by the times they had lived through. Now they had roofs over their heads and food in their bellies. They had survived, to have children of their own and to grow old.

The men in the forest, they once asked of me, How many wild strawberries grow in the salt sea? She dashed away the tears with her sleeve. *That was then and this is now*, she whispered, and knew that she would not come here again.